C.O.L.A.

A novel

William Stuart Gould, M.D.

WMG LTD.
New York

WMG
WMG Ltd. Publishers
288 Lexington Avenue
Suite 6-F
New York, New York
10016
wmg.ltd.publishing@gmail.com

This book is a work of fiction. Names, characters, places, and incidents are either products of the author's imagination or are used fictitiously. Any resemblance to actual events, locales, or persons, living or dead, is entirely coincidental.

For information about WMG Ltd.'s Speakers Bureau or discounts for bulk purchases, please email: wmg.ltd.publishing@gmail.com

ISBN: 0997980419
ISBN: 9780997980417 (pbk)
ISBN: 9780991223732 (ebook)

To my patients:
It was a privilege to serve you.

*A physician's highest calling is to relieve pain and suffering,
not to prolong life or to cure illness*

PART ONE

CHAPTER ONE

North Stadium Hotel
The City of Galena Hills
6th September 2001

It was to be his night. The wait was finally over. Dr. Solomon Forte was to be cleansed of the dread that had infected his heart for nearly a year. He would emerge unspoiled, for he had prepared harder for the inquisition than he had for his medical board examinations. The endless hours of research he'd invested to absorb every detail of drug addiction and narcotic abuse, the sleepless nights culling data from the National Institutes of Health and the most esteemed medical libraries in the world, all of it, worth the price. Every word, every sentence he'd deliver to the Commission had been scripted and rehearsed.

Despite his meticulous planning, the evening clouded before it began. SMAC, the State Medical Abuse Commission, had engaged North Stadium Hotel's Grand Ballroom for their semi-annual meeting. Though Sol had arrived early, there wasn't a single parking space in the hotel's tower. On his third fruitless revolution through the lot, he began to fidget, for the authorities would convene in just minutes.

He had forgotten, or been too busy to realize, that the Silver Heels were playing their best baseball in franchise history. Headed for the World Series, they were drawing unprecedented crowds, and that night were hosting their archrival Yankees. The hotel and pay parking lots abeam the stadium's main entrance were packed with cars and revelers. The Silver Heels' faithful sang and danced, hoisting bottles of Red Hook Ale, shaking them merrily at Sol as he crept around and around the lot. Although an unusual late summer chill and rain battered the streets surrounding the stadium, a shirtless fan dashed out from under a broad umbrella and pranced around Sol's car, a beer in each fist. When Sol honked testily, the frightened drunk tripped and lost his grip on both bottles. Shards of glass crunched under Sol's tires as he sped off toward the downtown parking lots.

Forte was soaked after the half-mile trek back to the hotel lobby. In minutes, he would stand before the dozen or twenty of the chosen who had been mustered to listen to his side of the story and pronounce judgment.

He was so late, he did not have time to duck into the men's room and unsnarl his jet-black hair, though he caught his reflection in a lobby mirror and realized the barber had clipped him so short that afternoon, there was nothing left to comb. For a moment, he felt better, but that comfort faded when he noticed the deep blue and burgundy of his tie had bled into his soggy white shirt. He wrapped his suit jacket tightly about himself.

At the Silver Miners' Bar, his attorneys, Eugene Fluellen and Michael Matsukawa, looked up and smiled mechanically. Though Sol fancied a cold Samuel Adams, or two, his lawyers' dour expressions dictated club soda. They sat and talked strategy for a few minutes, and as they rose to leave for the hearing room, Fluellen cleared his throat, mentioning in passing that he had spoken with Commission Chairman Jergesson on the phone that afternoon. "I wasn't impressed with the man's warmth," Gene muttered. "He's a DA wanna be, Solly, like so many of them, so we're going to be careful, but we're not going to allow him to get away with anything, are we?"

Sol smiled thinly and muttered, "No way."

Gene laughed and put his arm around Sol's shoulders. "Good. I'll take care of this guy. I've handled much better in my day. Don't you fret, not for a second." Sol nodded distantly.

Mike Matsukawa paid the bill, and the three took the escalator to the Grand Ballroom, where Sol and his lawyers remained standing, ignoring the folding chairs outside the hearing room. A minute after they arrived, at precisely 7 P.M., the doors were thrown open, the trio beckoned by the court reporter. Matsukawa took a seat in the gallery; Fluellen and Forte marched to the witness table. Sol's waterlogged shoes squeaked as he approached his station.

The commission members sat poker-faced as Sol took a seat directly in front of a tall, thin, gray-haired man who peered down at Sol solemnly over half-glasses. Radiating from the man's flanks at the dais were ten other evaluators, all behind stacks of files and rule books. Sol could barely make out their faces.

The man at the center tapped his water glass with a fork. The members of the Commission straightened their backs and necks and further hardened their façades. The speaker read from a prepared text. "Dr. Forte, good evening. Let me introduce myself. I am Jens Jergesson, Chairman of the State Medical Abuse Commission."

Sol recognized the face from the Commission's website, and his voice from the frantic call he'd made to the Chairman nearly a year before. Sol answered with a deep, "Good evening, Dr. Jergesson," but his voice cracked halfway through the man's name.

Jergesson went on. "Thank you for appearing here tonight. It is our sincere hope that we will be able to work together in the spirit of collegiality to obviate further disruption for you. This process is designed to be a give and take of information so that we may arrive at a reasonable solution. We are aware of the pressures this process engenders, but I hope that you will understand our mission is to protect the patients of our state, for they put their trust in us. Sometimes, feelings get run over in the process. It is not done purposefully, I can assure you.

"Let me introduce the members of the Commission. They are from my far left," and he spoke their names, specialties, and cities of practice. By the time he turned and began naming the right-sided members, Sol felt as though his hour had vaporized. As the last of the commissioners nodded in reserved introduction, the door at the rear of the meeting room opened and a lissome, raven-haired, elegantly dressed woman tiptoed in and took a seat at the back of the ballroom. A moment later, the door opened again. Another woman, in modern nun's habit, entered and approached the first woman, who rose gently. The two hugged and spoke in whispers, their eyes reddening. When they again took their seats, they held hands. The commissioners stared.

Jergesson paused for a moment, allowing the visitors to settle, then continued. "Dr. Forte, a complaint has been filed against you by the State Medical Abuse Commission because a fundamental question was raised in regard to your prescribing habits, particularly in regard to the manner in which you provided narcotic medications to a specific patient. Are you aware of the charges lodged against you?"

"I am aware of what the charges say, all of one sentence, but not of their substance or by whom they were filed, and I find that disturbing and unjust."

Fluellen grasped his arm tightly. "No," Sol continued, pulling his arm away angrily. "You asked me if I was aware of what laws I supposedly violated, and I've waited patiently for nearly eight months to come before you people and find out, but to this day, I have no idea what I did wrong. No one has sent me a list of charges or even had the courtesy to give my attorney a call to inform him of what crime I have committed. All I know is that I treated a dying patient's suffering, and I did so with the only tool our lofty profession has at its disposal—pain medication."

Jergesson's back and neck further tensed. "Dr. Forte, I have to explain that this board was not convened to probe the shortcomings of modern medicine. We are all acutely aware of the limits of our profession. We've convened to adjudicate the charges filed by a concerned observer…"

Sol interrupted, "And who the hell is that observer?"

"Doctor, we needn't get off on that path, with profanity and…"

Sol sprang to his feet, his deep blue eyes on fire. "That is not profanity, sir. What is profane is that charges can be leveled by a nameless, faceless entity who obviously made statements to harm me based on a personal agenda. But you were right about one thing: these charges have already caused me profound harm. I have put in years of work and study and deprivation to become a physician, and, apparently, I'm about to see that sweat evaporate in milliseconds on the basis of the utterances of a mysterious being. I am asking you to tell me, sir, before we go on any further in this process, just who filed the charges. I have a right to know."

"Dr. Forte, we cannot do that. That's not the way we operate here. This is not a court of law in the usual sense."

Though Attorney Fluellen had been gently tugging at Sol's sodden jacket, trying to restrain him, he loosened his grip, stood, and growled, "Sir, my client has a point. We will gladly comply with the Commission's desire to engage in a professional discussion between colleagues, but Dr. Forte should and will be afforded the basic entitlement to know who leveled the complaint, as we feel it was done in retribution for my client's willingness to see injured workers, and the financial and, shall we say, class considerations that commitment raised at the Galena Hills Medical Center. We must be apprised of the source of these allegations so that we can mount a cogent defense. You see, if there was a personal agenda involved, that would serve to impeach the quantity and quality of the evidence against my client."

"I've already made it clear that we are not empowered to provide that information, nor is it necessary."

Fluellen scoffed, "May I remind you of another recent case that came before this body?" The Chairman's hand rose to stop him, but Fluellen went on. "The state just paid six-hundred-thousand dollars because you hounded an innocent doctor. Ruined his career, in fact. You accused him of alcohol and drug abuse. Surely you remember." Gene waited a fraction of a second, his glare burning into Jergesson's eyes. "I'll remind you. It was the wife he was divorcing who leveled the charges, and you failed to investigate sufficiently to determine that small fact. His reputation was shattered. How did that happen?"

"Sir, what is germane is that certain prescribing guidelines have been violated, not who brought that to our attention. And, anyway, this is a completely different case. Here we have undisputable evidence that your client abused his prescribing parameters. Counselor, we need to move along here. The Commission has several cases to adjudicate tonight, and a full schedule starting in the morning. We'd like to get to bed at a reasonable hour."

Fluellen bristled. "Well, Mr. Chairman, we firmly believe it *is* necessary, and if you don't provide us with that information, that is, the input we need to construct a solid defense, I will personally, and without remuneration, file a suit against every one of you in federal court on the basis of denying my client his civil rights. Your track record ain't all that good."

The members looked up and glowered at Fluellen. The slight attorney waved his finger at the commissioners. "It will cost each of you fifty to a hundred thousand dollars to defend yourselves. And, be assured, I can, and will, structure the complaint to insure it comes out of *your* pockets and not the state's coffers."

Jergesson's face became scarlet. "Counselor, we are getting way off track here, and you might be interested to know that maneuver was tried years ago. The courts ruled unanimously in our favor."

"*Our* favor?" Fluellen shook his head angrily. "So, it *is* a case of us against them."

Jergesson spat, "We represent the citizens of this state against quackery and loose cannon doctors."

Fluellen went on passionately. "If you did your homework, you'd know the case to which you refer was filed by some twenty-six-year-old ACLU hack back in '93. He was suspended for incompetence on that case. Times have changed. You're playing in a whole different league now, my friend. Dr. Forte did nothing to warrant this investigation. If you want to try and discipline him for soothing the final months of a tormented patient's life because you don't have the spine or mercy to treat the terminally ill, fine. Level the punishment. We'll fight that, too. But before he answers your questions, he wants to know who said what. Tell him."

Jergesson's color deepened to a reddish purple. "Don't threaten me!"

"You've threatened my client for the past year. What's good for the goose is good for the gander. Nobody here is any better than anyone else."

"I *am* the Chairman, and this committee has important work to do. This hearing will go forward with or without your cooperation."

Sol stood and took a step to the front of Fluellen. "Go ahead and ask your questions. I'm ready to answer. But I assure you, I will find out who did this, and I'll take the steps necessary to ensure this never ever happens to another innocent doctor."

Jergesson calmed a bit. "And you will have the opportunity to prove yourself innocent, Dr. Forte. I will add, however, that after a very long time on this commission, I have come to believe that where there's smoke, there's fire."

Fluellen jumped forward as if he and Sol were playing leap-frog, and Sol worried that if the quarrel went on much longer, he and Fluellen would be wrestling in Jergesson's lap.

Fluellen snapped, "There you go again. He doesn't have to prove himself innocent: *you*, sir, have to prove him guilty, even in this non-judicial court setting. And you certainly won't do that on the basis of a meaningless aphorism. I object strenuously to that statement, and I want my objection noted in the record."

Jergesson nodded and apologized. "You're absolutely right, Counselor. In the heat of the moment, I misspoke. The burden is on the Commission, not your client, to establish a breach of professional standards. Now, may we proceed?"

Fluellen nodded his accent. Jergesson went on. "Dr. Forte, and please do be seated, both of you. Let's all take a deep breath. As I said at the outset, we aren't here to torture you."

"You've already done that."

"May I continue?"

"Proceed."

Jergesson pulled a paper from the pile to his front and began. "Are you aware, Dr. Forte, of the medication named hydrocodone APAP, also known as Vicodin?

"Yes, I am."

"Are you aware that it is a strong narcotic?"

"Well, it's a narcotic. It's not particularly strong when compared to many of the medications we use in treating those with moderate pain, and especially those who are terminally ill. As a matter of fact, it is fairly benign when you consider the pain suffered by those dying of widespread cancer, which my patient was."

Jergesson's voice rose. "Are you aware, Doctor, that Vicodin is a Schedule III controlled substance characterized by an abuse potential, and the possibility of causing psychological or physical dependence?"

"Of course, I am, and had I been a better physician, I would have provided my patient with Percocet, oxycodone, a Schedule II medication, a stronger and more effective pain killer. Better yet, had I the nuts, he would have been pickled in OxyContin. Then, perhaps, you might have a case." He hesitated for a moment, "No, you wouldn't."

"Are you aware," Jergesson asked crossly, "how many hydrocodone tablets you provided the patient in question?"

"In fact, I am." Without referring to his notes, Sol continued. "Over the months the patient in question was under my care, I wrote prescriptions for..." Sol hesitated. He considered adding that some of the medication had been called in to pharmacies under his name, but without his knowledge. Perhaps he should tell them that his nurse, Roxanne, had taken it upon herself to prescribe Vicodin just to get this patient off her back, but he judged making that public would only lead to questions about how he controlled his practice. He swallowed his anger over Roxanne's conduct and continued, informing the committee of the number of tablets of hydrocodone he had prescribed. He waited for a chorus of oo's and ah's, but of course, the commissioners had long since been apprised of all the statistics that had brought Dr. Forte in front of them. A few grunted in mock surprise, though Sol didn't see them, for his eyes had closed as the beginning flashed before him.

CHAPTER TWO

The Galena Hills Hospital and Medical Center
August, 2000

Dr. Solomon Forte's first hint that all was not going to be copasetic with Ralph Tarkington came from Roxanne. Her ear had been glued to the door of his office as Sol spoke on the phone in hushed tones. Roxanne was confident a woman was on the other end, and that her doctor was talking about spending the night. Without specific proof, though, the conversation was one that would have to be enhanced before it could be pounded into grist for the Center's rumor mill, over which she had presided since her second day on the job.

Roxanne finally opened the door, stuck her head into the office, and nipped, "Chop chop Doc, got a new COLA in Room Two. Guy's weird. Talks like a baby. Can't get a history out of him. Something about he got electrocuted on the job twenty years ago."

"Well, if he was electrocuted twenty years ago," Sol smiled, "he's been dead for two decades, and if that's the case, I'm probably not going to be able to help him. Let's send him to our illustrious department chief. Maybe there's some charge left in the patient's pancreas or gall bladder, and Dr. Rosebac. can use him to power up his new fluoroscopy machine."

"Great idea, I'll get maintenance to wire him up when you're done talking to him, if you can talk to him," Roxanne grinned, "and in the meantime, Room Two. Let's go. We're getting behind already, and we haven't even started the morning."

Sol walked toward the exam room nonchalantly, not a second thought given to his right to throw open a door unannounced, saunter into a private room, engage yet another perfect stranger in the most intimate of details, and then touch any part of that soul's body he wished. Sol had knocked on exam room doors far over thirty thousand times in his fifteen years in medicine: four in medical school, three in residency, and now eight on the job at the Center. The entry process, long-practiced, had become knee jerk—the gentle rap of his knuckles two times, the slow opening of the door, and the friendly expression.

The "smiling doctor" he'd been dubbed, a compliment he supposed, but he often wondered if being happy was such a good thing. Perhaps a doctor should scowl to establish his hubris. Few of his colleagues were happy— how could you be, roller skating from room to room, nine and ten hours a day, five and six days a week? They were all so pale; few ever laughed. Sol wondered if there was something wrong with him, but, on the other hand, he thought of his pop, a cement truck driver in Little Italy, in New York City, a tough guy, but always with a smile. And he had done just fine, never any trouble with the union, or the bosses, or the protection guys. So how bad could it be to walk into an exam room happy, even if all the healers around him weren't?

Outside Room Two, he lifted the thin chart from the holder, relieved that it had no girth, no notes to read, no letters to send to other doctors, just a plain old patient with a sore back or achy shoulder. In reflex, he tapped on the door and rolled the handle slowly, smiling to himself that he was still smiling.

"Good morning, Mr. Tarkington." The body odor and spoor of stale urine stopped Sol in mid-stride, but he continued in, and he left the door open halfway. "I'm Dr. Forte. How can I help ya, sir?"

"Don't know."

"Well, sir, why are you here?"

"My daughter brought me. She wrote you a letter." With that, Mr. Tarkington nodded at the desk in the corner of the exam room. Beside the sink sat a one-foot stack of medical charts. Sol took a pace toward the sink. On the top of the pile was a scrawled note:

Dr. Forte,
 Our lawyer told me to have you read this chart before you treat my father.

J. Famot

The "L" word flattened the arch of Sol's smile even more than the mountain of paper and the cryptic message. He asked, "Well, sir, why did he, ah, your lawyer, send you?"

"Don't know. Ask him."

Roxanne stuck her head into the room. "Dr. F., I'm gonna close the door, if you don't mind."

Sol turned back to Tarkington. "Well, are you in pain?"

"Yep."

"Where?"

"Everywhere."

"Well, then, where is it the worst?"

"Whole body."

"Yeah, I see you're really bent forward. Have you had back or neck surgery?"

"Yep."

That response ground the camber of Sol's lips a bit more toward the floor. "What for?"

"Pain."

Sol picked up the Galena Hills Hospital and Medical Center's intake sheet and perused Roxanne's notes. "It says here on your chart you're COLA, and the date of your on-the-job injury was November, 1982. That's nearly twenty years ago, sir."

While Mr. Tarkington was apparently considering the question, Forte thought back to 1982. He was just starting grad school in biology at Columbia, a year before his father's first heart attack. How he wished he could wrest back the time.

"Yes," Tarkington mumbled, tugging Forte's attention back to Room Two.

"What happened?"

"I don't remember."

"Tired of telling the story, sounds like."

"Don't remember what happened. Just the flash and the fall, and that was the end of me."

"A flash, I see. Well, is there someone who can help us get to the bottom of this thing? Who was your last doctor?"

"Don't remember."

"Guess we'll need to call COLA and find out what's going on. Then maybe I can help you. By the way, what's your lawyer's name? I'll give him a call, too."

"Damned if I know. Some Chinaman."

"Do you have family here?"

"Yep."

"Is that the J. Famot who signed this note?"

"Yep."

"Does she know?"

"Know what?"

"The lawyer's name."

"Yep. Drives me to his office."

"Well, sir, you wait here for a minute. I'll get my nurse to look into this for us. Is that okay with you?"

"You're the doctor."

Solomon Forte left Mr. Tarkington, considered propping the door open a bit to allow the man egress if he became disoriented and panicked, but closed it to mollify Roxanne. He searched the hallway for her, cursed under his breath, and started for his office to call one of the numbers on Tarkington's chart.

Sol was not, however, surprised when Roxanne flew around the corner from the waiting room where she was chattering with a cluster of receptionists. She cackled, "Not so fast. You got a new back in Three. It's a hot one. You're gonna love 'im. Great day to be alive and at work at the Galena Hills Hospital."

"And Medical Center. Fine, I'll see my patients if you wouldn't mind hanging around here in the back by your workstation. And while you're sitting here, please find out something about our Mr. Tarkington. Like who's his lawyer. See if you can get the guy on the phone. His information sheet's in a woman's handwriting. Maybe someone came with him, and she's sitting out there in the waiting room. Take a look, would you?"

Gathering that Tarkington was surely going to cost more than the fifteen minutes the Center allotted to see new patients, Sol turned quickly to the door of Room Three, hoping to make up some time with the next patient. He snapped the chart out of the rack and noted Roxanne's scribbled: COLA LBP!!! "Good, Commission on Labor Affairs, on-the-job, low back pain," he muttered, "another opportunity to excel." He sucked in a cleansing breath, like he'd seen his OB patients take just as the baby's head delivered, and tapped gently on the door.

Solomon Forte was not the first doctor in history to enter an exam room and discover a patient who did not acknowledge the arrival of the healer. This was, however, the first time he had slipped into a room to find a muscular, tanned, twenty-six-year-old ignoring him, *and* bouncing in and out of his chair, legs churning like the counter-rotating rotors of a Chinook helicopter.

Sol reminded himself that people with genuine pain sat quietly, inertly. He suppressed a smile and muttered to himself, "Well, Mother Theresa, you're the one who chose to treat the ill." Aloud he asked, "Mr. McAlister, what's going on, sir."

"I was just doing my damn job and ruined my back."

"Well, tell me the story so I can understand."

"It was right after lunch, and there's this pipe that sticks out of the ground. I told 'em, 'Move the goddamn thing,' but they don't listen." McAlister paused and stared, shaking his head angrily.

Sol asked seriously, "So you tripped on the pipe?"

"No. I'm tryin' to tell ya. I was carrying this ladder down the stairs to the paint shop, and I knew the pipe was there, so I walked around it."

"Well, good. That was very observant. But how did you hurt your back?"

He tsooked impatiently, "I walked around the pipe. It shouldn't be there."

"No, I'm sure it shouldn't. But I still don't understand how you injured yourself."

"That's what I'm tryin' to tell ya. I was walking toward the paint shop, so I had to swing left and the ladder swings too, and I try to stop it before it hits somebody, and they blame me, and the next thing I know, I feel this pain in my back, and I fall down on the ground, and I can't get up, so my supervisor sends me down here. You're the COLA doctor, ain't ya?"

"Mister Commission on Labor Affairs. That's me."

"Doc, I think there was oil on the ground. They never clean up over there. They don't care. They figure if a guy gets hurt, the state pays for it. What's it for them to care unless it's comin' outta their pockets?"

"So, Mr. McAlister, where exactly do you hurt?"

"*My back*. I told ya. It's killing me."

"Any pain down your legs?"

"Yeah."

"Which one?"

"Both."

"Both. How far down?"

"Like I was telling your nurse, Roxanne, wasn't it?"

"Yep."

"All the way down."

"All the way. You have any numbness and tingling in your legs?"

"Yeah."

"Which one?"

"Both."

"Both. And all the way down, I imagine."

"Yeah. How did know that, Doc? You seen this before?"

"Once or twice."

"Then what's wrong with me, Doc."

"Well, first, let me ask a few more questions. Any problem holding your bowels or your bladder?"

"Huh?"

"You know. Having trouble with number one and number two?"

"Oh, you mean did I piss my pants or shit my drawers?"

"Yep, that's what I mean."

"Not since the last time I tied one on."

"I mean since you hurt your back?"

"You mean this time?"

"Ah, so, you've hurt your back before?"

"Never bad like this."

"Tell me about the last time."

"You know, the usual. Some shitty boss makes you lift too much and the next thing you know, you can't stand up."

"Ever lost work because of back pain?"

"Nothing to speak of."

"Yeah, well, just for the fun of it, why don't you speak of how much time, if you don't mind. *Only*, of course, so I can better understand your injury."

"A month or two, maybe three. I don't remember."

"Mr. McAlister, I'm curious. How long have you been working at Sunset Aircraft?"

"Ah, let's see." He scratched his head and gazed up at the ceiling. "Gimme a minute. Lemme me try to figure it out here. I think it's two-and-a-half weeks. Maybe only two. I donno know. A while anyway."

"Where'd you work before that?"

"California."

"Well, let me extend a hearty welcome. So, let's take a look at you, then we'll get you fixed, on light duty for a few days, and then back to your usual work at Sunset. How does that sound?"

"I don't know about that. There ain't no light duty at that place. Either I lift a hundred pounds, or they don't want me around. And ain't you gonna take an x-ray?"

"Usually we don't on the first visit. But we'll see."

"I want you to know I don't like too many of them x-rays. No good for ya."

"Lot less bad for you than the two packs of smokes you got going. Each one of 'em's the same as a chest x-ray."

"Each pack?" McAlister asked, concerned.

"Nope, each cigarette. Same amount of cancer-causing effect in each cigarette as the radiation in one chest x-ray."

"Hey, I'm gonna quit, just can't when I'm hurtin' this bad. You know how it is, Doc."

"Well, first let's define the problem, see what's going on in your back, then we'll talk about what you can and can't do."

McAlister could not sit still long enough for an examination, and there was no way to know if his patient had suffered significant trauma. He excused himself and went to his office to think.

Forte fretted over ordering the standard set of x-rays—five films, five exposures—of the lower back in a young patient on a first visit, unless there had been forceful trauma, as in a car accident or a fall from a roof. If the patient was under eighteen, or over fifty, there was a chance of cancer or an unusual, serious disease, but statistics had shown, over and over, it was near zero in a guy like McAlister. He thought about the recent admonitions in the orthopedic journals that the prudent physician waited until the patient had six weeks of unremitting low back pain before taking a picture. Sol knew that a third of back pain disappeared within three weeks, two-thirds of patients were better after six weeks, and nearly all were pain free after three months, regardless of what the doctor did or didn't do. Since the chance of finding a treatable problem on an x-ray were less than winning the lottery, Sol had made a New Year's resolution at the millennium to break his x-ray addiction and leave the taking of unnecessary x-ray to his medical brothers and sisters, who spent over a billion dollars a year, just in the U.S., on needless back films.

On the other hand, though, as soon as Sol settled on his decision, his stomach began to churn. Kevin McAlister was COLA, and he already had a history of time loss for his lower back. The man was simply not going to vanish in three or four weeks. A patient of this pedigree presaged Sol would someday be obliged to justify to the Commission on Labor Affairs everything he'd done or not done to McAlister. It would not be that week, or even that month, but some year, perhaps even a decade later, that case managers, employers, attorneys, judges, and juries would parse what Sol would do in next the ten minutes.

With his perpetual smile drooping, he pondered the matter further. McAlister wasn't highly educated, or so it seemed at first blush; he was a heavy smoker, already hated his boss, hated his work, and was a transient who'd only been working at Sunset Aviation for a few days. This was the classic recipe for misadventure, for endless litigation, the warning signs, flapping red flags. The omens had been identified and published in medical journals from lands as far flung as China, Sweden, and Mozambique. The studies revealed that a large percentage of injured workers headed for permanent disability demonstrated an identical set of predictable behaviors.

An intern could puzzle out that McAlister's industrial injury was a textbook case of "NEWCS," the Never-Ending Worker's Claim Syndrome. So, Sol really had no choice. He gave in to the monkey on his back and grunted, "Roxanne, why don't you send our new friend over to radiology for a complete lumbo-sacral series."

"Wait a minute, Dr. F, I thought you said we weren't going to be doing them on new patients anymore."

In the meantime, he checked on Mr. Tarkington. Roxanne was still working on finding the man's daughter, and Sol stuck his head in the door. "Hang on, sir. Staff's on top of everything."

Mr. Tarkington barely looked up as he mumbled, "Huh?"

Sol walked over to Radiology and perused McAlister's spinal films with the radiologist—normal, in fact, pristine. When Sol came back around the corner, he spied Kevin jabbering happily with Roxanne, the excruciating back pain having ebbed, effectively treated by the curing vapors of the x-ray machine. Nonetheless, Forte whispered to himself the mantra he'd learned from the blind psychiatrist in medical school a decade before, "You will believe a patient until he gives you a reason, and a damn good one, not to believe him. Pain is a subjective experience. Pain is a subjective experience. Pain is a subjective experience." Chanting the refrain nearly audibly, he granted Kevin McAlister a week off work; wrote prescriptions for Soma, a muscle relaxer; a paltry sixteen Vicodin, the everyday narcotic of choice for acute back and most other moderate pain; and a note for physical therapy, which Sol instructed his patient to attend three times before he returned for a recheck in a week.

Sol's jaw dropped when McAlister nodded, the man failing to mount a vociferous plea for more, and stronger, pain meds, a few weeks of time loss, and less physical therapy. Sol signed the prescriptions and started off toward his office to dictate a few charts, nodding to himself comfortably, acknowledging his experience, his medical wisdom, and the fifteen years of seasoning that guided him to provide Kevin McAlister with just enough Vicodin to keep him from grousing, enough to treat his pain without addicting him to the medication, and few enough to keep the pharmacists happy with a decent sale, but not enough to raise their eyebrows and report him to SMAC.

He took his seat at the desk and began chattering into the little recorder, but Roxanne cleared her throat loudly, yanking Sol from his reverie. "Lupe Sánchez. Room Two. She's sitting on the floor curled up in the corner babbling like a baby."

"I thought Mr. Tarkington was in Two."

"Moved him back to the waiting room."

Forte shook his head. He asked, "Who's who? Who's where? Never mind. Is Mrs. Sánchez doing better?"

"How do I know? She doesn't speak English."

"Is her interpreter here?"

"Yep. But he's too scared to talk."

"He? What happened to that little old lady she used to bring?"

"Died last week. Lupe's got her son here today."

"He speak English?"

Roxanne shrugged. "I don't know. He's just sitting there staring at his mother."

"How old is he?"

"I don't know, maybe eight. I think I heard her call him Carlos."

The first thing Forte sensed as the door opened slowly was Mr. Tarkington's lingering scent. That weakened what was left of his smile. The next perception was visual: Lupe Sánchez was hunkered in a corner, an upright, fetal ball chanting unintelligibly in a high, squeaky whimper. The edges of Sol's lips flatlined. He walked over and touched her shoulder gently. "Mrs. Sánchez. *Buenos dias. Esta bien?*"

"Carlos," she sang in English, "tell doctor my sick pain berry berry bad today."

Carlos, still staring at his mother, whispered, "My mother, say he pain berry berry bad today."

"Yeah, I got that. Thank you, Carlos." Sol stepped over to the boy and placed an arm around his shoulder. "Hey, Partner, is your mother taking the medicine the psychiatrist gave her?"

"I donno know."

"Well, let's go ahead and ask her."

Mrs. Sánchez stared into a corner of the ceiling, giggled, then wailed, "*Dile al Doctor que tu eres mi padre.*"

"She say I am his father."

"Carlos, how long has she been like this?"

"Now."

"No, I mean, was she like this yesterday?"

"No."

Mrs. Sánchez yowled again. Carlos' eyes opened wider. "She say she no crazy."

"I know that, Carlos. Tell you what. You wait here. I'm going to get some other doctors to help us. Tell your mother everything's going to be okay. Just sit here with Mom. Don't go anywhere, okay?" Forte kneeled to touch Lupe's shoulder again, but she cringed so violently, her body toppled.

Carlos wailed, "Mama, Mama!"

Once she ceased rocking on the floor, Lupe lay in a rigid, now lateral, fetal position, whimpering in English, "Carlos, you are *mia* papa."

Forte jogged into his office and lifted the phone to call 911, but as he glanced out his window, he saw the City of Whitaker's freshly painted red and white medic van gleaming in the emergency room parking lot, two floors below. The crew of paramedic firemen sped up to his office. Forte smiled. Lupe would soon be loaded aboard a gurney and transported to Whitaker General, to the psych ward of the most respected hospital in the region. He brightened with the thought his morning might still be salvaged.

Sol met the medical team in the waiting room, directing his comments toward a dark-skinned man whose embroidered nametag read Aquino. Forte led the three blue-uniformed firemen toward the exam room. "Firefighter Aquino, I think the most important thing to determine is if she has been taking her medicine."

Aquino took the point and opened the door without knocking. He asked the crumpled figure on the floor, "Ma'am, what's wrong?"

Forte stepped forward and barked, "No, no, you have to speak to her in Spanish. Like I said, she hardly speaks English."

Aquino turned to his crew and asked, "Any of you guys talk Spanish?"

They shrugged, and Forte squinted. "You mean you don't speak Spanish? I thought you spoke Spanish."

"No, man, I'm Filipino."

Forte threw his arms into the air as if in prayer and asked, "What good is that?"

Aquino turned away but whirled back angrily, "It's good if your heart stops or if..."

He was unable to finish for Mrs. Sánchez wailed, "*Cuenta lo que no estoy loca.*"

Carlos, his eyes still bonded to his mother's vibrating fetal form, whispered, "She say she no is *loca*."

A large, gray-haired man, the medic still outside the door, wove his way through to Mrs. Sánchez. He spoke softly, and in a few seconds, with her hand in his, she rose to her feet and sat in a chair. When the medic smiled gently, her lips curled up almost imperceptibly.

The man spoke to her for a few seconds then turned to Forte. "She says, you think she's crazy."

"No, I don't. You speak Spanish?"

"Took it in high school, but we'll get along."

Forte relaxed a bit and spoke quietly. "Look, I understand the pressure she's under. Let me give you a little history. She fell at work, I don't know, maybe eight months ago. She was a housekeeper at the Martine Hotel, cleaning a bathroom, standing on the edge of a bathtub. From what I understand, she fell backwards, hit her head on the toilet, and wrenched her back. She really doesn't remember what happened, but ever since, she's been complaining bitterly about her whole left side. Says she hurts so much, she can't walk up the stairs on the bus to get to work. The hotel manager calls me, and I tell her we can't say for sure what's going on, so she refuses to let Lupe go back to work unless *I* say she's able to wash mirrors and fold towels."

One of the medics croaked, "What's so hard about folding towels?"

"Nothing, unless you can't spend two hours riding busses from South Whitaker to the hotel because you can't hold your head up."

The man growled, "Tell her to move out here."

"Look, my friend, her water bill in this neighborhood would be more than the monthly rent she's paying down on Central

Avenue. And anyway, I can't force a person to work. She's not a slave. She says she can't work, I have to believe her until I learn otherwise.

"COLA puts her on time loss payments, two-thirds of her regular pay, two-thirds of nothing. That's not enough to pay rent *and* feed her kids, so she's stressed out and falling apart. She's seeing a shrink at Whitaker General for depression, but she's getting worse, and the way I see it, all of a sudden, she's a danger to herself and needs to be transported downtown."

There was a rap at the door. Roxanne stuck her head into the room and blurted before Sol could stop her, "Dr. Forte, sorry to bother you, but that McAlister's back. Says you didn't give him enough pain meds to get through the week."

"Damn, I knew it. Too good to be true. Look, I gave him enough."

Roxanne spoke quietly. "Good, I'll tell him that."

Sol snorted angrily, "Okay, give him ten more, but that's it, forever. Period. You tell him *that.*"

"That's what you told him half-an-hour ago."

"Roxanne, please. And, in case you didn't notice, I'm a little busy at the moment."

Sol turned back into the room. Mrs. Sánchez was speaking quietly with the medic. He nodded to Forte. "She's doing much better. Says she was just trying to make you understand that she really did hurt herself last year at the hotel. She says she doesn't want to live if she has to have this pain, and worse, nobody believes her, especially you."

"I believe her. I believe her. I've spent what, forty-thousand bucks on lab tests, three MRIs, a CT scan, let's see, two EMGs, a bone scan, a three-month stint in the most expensive pain clinic in Whitaker, and God knows how much on psychiatric care. So, you can be sure I believe her. I just haven't found the cause, and I probably won't. Look, she's hurting. I don't think there's any question about that. She's feeling pain, and I've been treating her for it with some Vicodin, and it's helped. At least she can take care of her kids, now. But I haven't been able to find anything objectively provable, at least, not on an x-ray. And all of it's complicated by the depression. Who knows? That may be the root of her problems. Certainly got my attention today."

The third medic, Sims, snipped, "So, it's all in her head, chronic pain syndrome. We see it all the time in these people that won't go back to work. Someone ought to tell her to get off her butt and get a job. Look, we need to get back on the road. There's actually sick people out there who could use a hand."

Forte shook his head. "Nope, not that easy. This may be chronic pain syndrome and, or, depression, whatever you want to call it, and I'm sure you can find a hundred hard-nosed docs who'll label it factitious syndrome." The medics' eyes were drifting. "You know, the patient's doing it all on purpose to get money or something. Like malingering. And maybe they've got a point, but at this moment, I don't care whether they're right or wrong. All I know for sure is that what's she's got is lethal. If she had cancer, would you transport her?"

"Of course."

"And if she commits suicide, she's just as dead as if she had inoperable cancer. You gents need to get her to the psych ward at Whitaker General before she, her kids, or someone else gets hurt. I'll have Roxanne call 'em and tell 'em you're on the way."

As Sol turned to leave the room, Ramirez shook his head. "No, Doc, we're not a taxi service. We come to treat people who're really in a jam. Lupe's already under the care of her personal doctor. What more could you want? She's fine. Just confused, and like you just got through telling us, she doesn't have any physical ailments."

"Wait a minute," Forte hissed, taken aback. "I didn't say she wasn't sick; I just can't *see* what's causing her pain. It's not her fault;

it's yours and mine. Our tests suck for the average patient. I mean, you got a honkin' tumor on your brain, I'll find it. And who cares, you're already as good as dead? But I'm talking about the rest of us, the ninety-nine percent who come to the doctor, *and* you guys, for help. Back pain, neck pain? You got damn near no chance of finding it on a test. Maybe one in nine or ten times you see something on the x-ray or MRI, and that usually isn't the cause of the pain anyway. Look, you, me, all of us in the trenches deal in what we can see. I understand that. That means I spend my life guessing. It is what it is. And right now, I don't care. I can see she's dangerously depressed. And that's good enough. I've already explained that to you."

Ramirez grumbled, "Look, Doc, we all get depressed. You just put your boots on and go to work."

Sol shook his head. "I'm not talking about having the blues for a couple of days." Sol stared at the three EMTs. "I'm telling you, gentlemen, this is serious."

"Well, she looks fine now," Sims chuckled.

Sol implored, "Listen, normal folks don't sit on the floor in the corner of a doctor's office shrieking that her son is really her father. If she commits suicide, it's going to be *our* responsibility, and I'm going to make sure the judge and jury understand that 'our' doesn't include me. This ain't gonna be my executive decision when it gets to court. It's gonna be yours. Are we clear?"

"Doc," Aquino spoke quietly, "we're not trying to bust your hump, but look at her. She's better. I'm not saying she doesn't need care. It's just that we can't take the unit out of service for two hours for a non-emergency. You seen the traffic tryin' to get into Whitaker? Look man, I'll be happy to give her cab fare to make the trip, if that's what it'll take, but I have a responsibility to the Fire Department."

Roxanne knocked on the door and stuck her head in. "Dr. Forte, excuse me, but the natives are getting restless, especially that Tarkington."

Sol surrendered. "Have a great day, gentlemen. I'm not screwing some cabbie. I'll call a private ambulance. I'm not letting her out of here on her own. Thanks for your help, and be sure to call me for a donation when the next referendum for the medic program rolls around."

The firemen turned to leave the room, grumbling about not being a chauffeur service, and Forte walked out grumbling about the American work ethic. Lupe Sánchez also grumbled, though in Spanish, and about nothing Forte could fathom. Only Carlos was quiet as he sat on the floor, his eyes terrified saucers.

Lupe rested docilely in Room Two as the medics rolled their gurney toward the elevator and the ER. With their exit, an agreeable calm came over the Department of Orthopedics, and Sol took the tranquility to query Roxanne about Tarkington.

"His daughter's sitting in the…" Lupe Sánchez sprang out of the exam room, knocking into Roxanne as she ran past the receptionist, out the door, and past the firemen. At the elevators, she banged at the buttons with both fists, waited for less than three seconds, keeled around, and doubled back past the medics. She screeched to a halt at the glass doors that opened onto the tiny terrace next to Sol's office. She screamed and blasted onto the patio, took three giant, loping steps, and halted, her torso teetering over the waist-high railing. She was directly over, and two stories above, the medic van.

Lupe snapped her head toward the window of Forte's waiting room and screamed, "I no *loca*."

The older medic was the first of the sprinting firemen, doctors, nurses, receptionists, and security to lunge onto the patio. Lupe stared into the distance quietly until the man took a step forward. As he placed his hand on her shoulder, she burst into a flood of sobbing tears and leaned further over the rail.

The fireman spoke gently, and she took a step away from the bar. She turned to him, her head and shoulders sagging lifelessly.

There was absolute silence on the patio for several seconds, broken finally by the pant of a collective sigh. As the air was being returned to the atmosphere, though, she spun back to the edge and shouted, "I no *loca*."

The medic had not loosened his grip. He tugged aggressively at Lupe's arm and spoke kindly. When her body slackened again, he led her back into the building.

Fire Fighter Aquino, eyes fused to a wall, mumbled, "Okay, new situation. We'll transport her to Oak Grove. They have a psych ward, sort of. They'll have to take her. They can stabilize her and transport if she needs it. We just can't tie the unit up to drive all the way to General. Is that going to work for you, Doc?"

Sol considered the compromise and nodded. He knew that Oak Grove wouldn't keep her. When the psychiatric staff discovered she had been admitted to Whitaker General's psych unit a dozen times over the past few months, and worse, had no means, they would turf her before the sun set. At the outside she would languish at Oak Grove for a day, maybe even two, but in any case, Sol was safe for the moment.

He grumbled a condescending, "Thank you," and returned to his office as the medics lifted Lupe onto the gurney and secured her hands and feet. He stood at his office window, watching numbly as she was rolled into the medic van, and he continued to stare as the truck crept away to enter the stockade-like traffic inching along the interstate.

Roxanne poked her head in. "You got a patient in Three. Nice lady. Leukemia, so be polite."

"And Mr. Tarkington?"

"Nothing yet, but I'm waiting for a call back. I'll take care of it. Don't you worry."

Forte glanced at his watch. Tarkington had been in the Center for over an hour. Sol wasn't any closer to understanding what the man was doing there than when he had first opened the door to the exam room.

Sol tapped on Room Three's door and pasted on the smile. Sitting before him was a thin, elderly woman in a faded housecoat, tufts of yellow-gray hair barely covered by a cheap wig skewed twenty degrees off-center. Sol's jaw tightened as he offered, "Good morning, ma'am. I'm Dr. Forte. How can I help you?"

"Well, Doctor, like I told the nurse, I have that leukemia, and I'm doing chemo now."

"I see, Mrs. Berry. I'm not sure we can help you with the leukemia. This is an orthopedic office. Says here you're COLA. I guess I don't understand."

"No, I'm not here for the leukemia, I just wanted you to know about that so you had all the information."

"Good." Sol smiled. "You're happen to be absolutely right. I need to know everything. So, how *can* I help you?"

"I twisted my ankle at work when I got out of my chair."

"Did you fall out of the chair?

"Nope, just got up to go to the lady's room. Gotta go a lot with that chemo. And it's hard as hell to get going. I'm like some old man. Sometimes can't go at all, and I just sit there. I can tell you that because you're a doctor."

"I'm so sorry. I bet that's a real pain. I'm not quite old enough yet, but I'm gettin' there fast. Okay, so tell me about the ankle."

"Like I said, I got up to go to the lady's room. I go every fifteen minutes. It's terrible. My boss don't like it."

"Well, he just has to understand. So, Mrs. Berry, what happened?"

"Like I said, I just stood up from the chair, and I hurt my ankle. But the problem is, it's not a good chair. It don't swivel right."

"Ah, so you *are* here for your ankle. Now, I understand. We can handle ankles. And when was that? That you fell?"

"I didn't fall. I just got up, but like I said, he don't have good chairs. It's his fault."

"And, again, when was that?"

"Couple a weeks ago," Mrs. Berry nodded.

"And you're still hurting?"

"No, not really, but I told my daughter this morning that it was still swollen, and she told me to come in to have it checked, just to make sure. You know, you can never be too careful when you have that leukemia."

Forte smiled inwardly. He had seen well in excess of a thousand ankle injuries over the years, and he knew that the swelling lasted long after the injury had healed. He wouldn't even have to second-guess himself on this one, a-cut-and-dried problem, a slam dunk. He'd examine her ankle, lay hands on, skip the x-ray, reassure her, and ask about her leukemia, about the latest treatments, for after all, she already knew more about it than did he. He'd learn something from Edna Berry, just as he insisted upon learning something from every patient he saw, even the teens.

"Well, I certainly agree. One must be very careful. Anyway, you look as healthy as a kid. You're beating that leukemia, aren't you? Good for you. Now, let's take a look at that ankle. Slip off your shoe and let me just move the ankle around."

Mrs. Berry leaned forward and tugged at her shoe but was out of breath before she could undo Velcro. She gave up, straightened, and gasped, "I guess I can't get it off by myself."

As Sol knelt to help her, his eyes opened as wide as the ankle was round. It wasn't just distended—it was enormous and deeply discolored with regions of black and blue surrounding areas of bright scarlet. "Sure the thing doesn't hurt?" he asked incredulously.

"I don't feel anything, but, then again, I'm a tough old bird."

Sol bent forward again and pushed on the ankle over the most swollen area as he watched her eyes carefully. When the pupils remained unchanged, and she did not flinch, he pushed a bit harder. Her eyes remained sad but calm. He asked, "Can you feel me touching you?"

"Of course I can feel you," she added curtly. "There's nothing wrong with me."

"Of course not. I can see that, but just let me try this, my dear." Forte rolled his chair backwards toward the cabinets surrounding the sink. He took a wooden Q-tip from the drawer, snapped it into two sharp halves, and moved back to Mrs. Berry. "Let me touch your toes very gently with the tip of this stick." He held it up to make sure she saw it. "Tell me when you feel it."

He moved his hand toward her foot, and she jumped. "Ouch! Hey, that's sharp."

Sol was suddenly very uncomfortable. "Mrs. Berry, I didn't touch you yet. You can't feel your feet, can you?"

"Of course I can."

"Well, maybe all those medicines you're taking are affecting your nerves. It's not your fault. That happens a lot. Let's get a quick x-ray of this ankle and make sure everything's where it's supposed to be. Hang on a minute. The tech'll come and get you. Meanwhile, let's have you ride in a wheelchair until we get things sorted out."

"Is that really necessary? I'm fine. I'm not an invalid, you know. I just twisted my ankle. Doctors are always making such a big deal outta nothing."

"Yeah, guilty as charged. I'm just an overly cautious doctor. I wish someone would wheel me around. It'll just take a minute."

At the door, he called out blandly, pretending to be unconcerned, "Roxy, how 'bout a quick x-ray of Mrs. Berry's left ankle, and let's have her ride in a wheelchair."

"Why?" Roxanne snapped. "She was fine when she walked in here. What'd you do to her?"

"Roxanne. Wheelchair."

⊷ ⊶

Forte took the interlude to walk down the three flights to the cafeteria and sit facing the wall, drinking green tea, hoping not to be recognized. A second after he took his seat, though, he heard shuffling and looked up to see his patient, Ralph Tarkington, obediently following a lithe, petite blond in tight jeans. As they approached the table, Sol rose. The woman said softly, "Dr. Forte, I'm Judy Famot. I'm his daughter." She flicked her head toward Mr. Tarkington. "Did you read his file like I asked?"

Forte glanced at her face. It was a bit hard, but very pretty. He took a quick look at her left hand. There was no ring. "Ms. Famot, yes, I looked through the notes. Quite a pile. Probably take me a couple of hours on my own time to really understand what's going on with your dad."

She did not bother to face Sol when she grumbled, suddenly impatient, "Well, we just called the lawyer, and he says you're going to be the doctor, so we need to have you write a few letters. The case is going to court next week."

Sol raised his palms defensively. "Whoa, let's slow down for a second here, ma'am. This has been going on for nearly twenty years, according to your father. No need to act that fast. All you have to do is get your lawyer to file for a continuance. It's easy. These guys do it all the time. I'm not sure I can do a good job without studying the chart, and to be honest, I'm not sure I can help your fath..."

Forte's pager beeped, and he stared wide-eyed at the number—Roxanne. "Oh, my gosh, it's an emergency. Gotta run. Look, I'll call in a day when I've had a bit more time to look things over."

34

Sol started toward the door, leaving his unfinished tea on the table. Judy Famot took a stride toward him, grasped his arm, and enjoined, "I'll expect your call."

He turned and met her piercing eyes ever so briefly. Halfway out of the cafeteria, Forte turned again and nodded, "I'll call."

On the ortho floor, Mrs. Berry was back in her room; a three-view ankle x-ray was hanging on the light box next to her. As Forte walked through the door, he saw the fracture. "Ma'am, you broke one of the bones in your ankle."

"I didn't know you had more than one."

"Yep, this skinny bone right here." He turned to the wall-mounted view box and pointed at the bone on the outside of the leg, just above the ankle.

"You ever eat a chicken leg?"

She rolled her eyes and clucked, "Yes, of course."

"Well, this is that little bone you can pick your teeth with."

She harrumphed. It was cracked through, though not terribly angulated. As he had been taught in medical school, he scanned the rest of the x-ray, because the obvious answer wasn't always the answer. There was the tale about a young radiologist sitting for her boards. The examiner flipped a chest x-ray onto the light box and asked the examinee to point out the major problem faced by the patient. In a split second, she haughtily pointed to a subtle broken rib.

The examiner puffed, "Nope. Look to the tops and the sides." The patient's left arm had been amputated at the shoulder.

Sol looked harder and saw the quality of Mrs. Berry's bone was no sturdier than that of an eggshell. The break was not serious, and the average person could have gotten around in a walking boot, but Edna Berry was going to be in a wheelchair for a while to keep her from keeling over and snapping the tibia, or worse, her hip. And if that happened, she would be hospitalized, undergo surgery, and because of the post-op pain, would lie in a bed motionless, refusing to jolt her body with a cough. And because she couldn't cough them out, any stray, potent bacteria floating around the hospital would get a foothold in her lungs, and with the underlying leukemia, and especially because of the cancer medications, she would not be able to fight off an infection, and she'd be dead ten days later from a hospital-acquired pneumonia.

Sol had seen it a dozen times—an older woman with osteoporosis drops the teapot on her foot and breaks the pinky toe. She limps around carefully during the day behind a walker, but gets up in the middle of the night to go to the bathroom, forgets about the toe, stands, the pain shoots up her leg, she collapses to the floor, and breaks her hip. He remembered the gerontologist in medical school and the first slide in his lecture, "WOMAN KILLED BY TEAPOT."

Mrs. Berry squinted at the films from across the room. "That's impossible. I think you're wrong. I can't see any broken bones, and I've been walking on it for all this time. Are you sure?"

"Yes, ma'am. The chemo's messed up your ability to feel things."

"That Sullivan should have sent me here sooner."

"Who is that, ma'am?"

"Sullivan? He's my boss," she seethed.

"Mrs. Berry, did you report the fall to him? There's a special form for that."

"I must have been limping if I had a broken leg. That's just common sense."

Forte started to answer but took a breath and smiled. "Well, we'll need to put you in a wheelchair, and you're going to be fine in a few weeks. I'll fill out your COLA paperwork, and we'll get the claim filed."

"Oh, Doctor, I'm not going into a wheelchair, and I certainly can't put this on COLA. Sullivan'll fire me, for sure. He's not a very nice man, you know. He has an awful temper. She lowered her voice into a whisper and raised the back of her hand to her mouth. "Especially when he's been drinking, you know."

"I understand, Mrs. Berry, but it happened on the job, so we don't have any choice. It would be insurance fraud if I doctored the records to say this happened at home. I know you wouldn't want me to do that." Before she could protest, he added, "Now, about work, I'd really like to have you rest with your leg up above your heart for the next couple of weeks to let some of that swelling go down. Then we can get you back to your office."

"Oh, gracious me, I can't go back to work with a broken bone. How long will I be out?"

"Well, that depends on how you feel. Let's try a week now, and then we'll play it by ear. In the meantime, who's your cancer doctor? I need to give him a call."

Mrs. Berry gasped. "My God, I don't have cancer. I've got leukemia. Why would you say such a thing?"

"That's right, Mrs. Berry, you're going to be just fine. I'll talk to my nurse, Roxanne. She'll fix you up with a wheelchair. We'll see you back in a week."

Mrs. Berry's head shook. She muttered, "The insolence!"

Forte opened the door. "Roxanne."

"Yes, boss."

"Put Mrs. Berry in a wheelchair, and get the name of her *leukemia* doctor."

Roxanne chirped, "Okay, and by the way, Mr. McAlister called again. He says if he takes his pills every four hours, like it says on the bottle, he'll be out by tomorrow. What's he supposed to do?"

"That's the maximum he can take them. Tell him to take half-a-Vicodin and one extra strength Tylenol every eight hours. That'll fix 'im up, or, at least, tell him it will."

"I'll do that. And, before I forget, a Whitaker General psych nurse is on hold. Wants to talk to you."

Sol exhaled, and his head drooped. "What about?"

"He says they're sending Mrs. Sánchez home."

"Who's *he*? And how did she get down to Whitaker General so fast?"

"*He* is the psych technician over there. He says they're not going to admit Lupe.

"Why?"

"He said COLA won't pay, and she doesn't have insurance, so he recommends you write to COLA and tell them to stop hassling her about her claim. Then she won't need to go to the hospital because she won't be stressed out anymore, and she won't act out."

"Act out. And what's a psych technician? What's he do, balance your marbles?"

"I don't know. Ask him."

"I'll take it in my office."

Galena Hills Hospital and Medical Center's policy regarding telephone communications had been overhauled. As of the first of the month, all employees were to smile into the phone when they offered their initial greeting, and maintain a level of cheer throughout the conversation. That was the verdict of the marketing firm CEO Hayes Anacota had hired, and Sol admitted grudgingly it did lower tensions. He pasted on his best grin, lifted the receiver, and pushed the hold button.

"Good morning. This is Dr. Forte. How may I help you?" Sol listened, though the smile slowly languished. "Yes," Sol conceded, "I don't understand why the Commission on Labor Affairs has refused to pay for her admission. They accepted her claim that she hurt herself on the job. I know they're disputing falling just eighteen inches can hurt you so bad you can't work for a year, but they had no right to stop the pittance they were giving her in time loss. She's destitute trying to raise kids. And she's psychotic, as I am sure you diagnosed. I would be, too."

There was a protracted answer, Sol's smile flattening with each syllable. He spoke quietly. "Look, we're all health professionals here. Let's think about this rationally. I mean, she was never nuts until this happened. I have no reason to disbelieve her. You know, you should always believe a patient until they give you a good reason not to."

Roxanne came to the door and tapped a pencil impatiently against the sill as she whispered, "We're two days behind," tap, tap, tap. "Let's wind it up, Doc."

Sol interrupted the man on the phone. "You know, I don't really care who's going to pay for it. Right now, she needs hospitalization. She's suicidal, she's sitting in your hospital, and you people need to take care of her. She's your patient."

Sol growled, "No, you're not going to make the unilateral decision to discharge her. You don't have that authority. You're not a shrink. You're not even a nurse." Sol pulled the receiver away from his ear. "Technician, whatever. If you turn her out onto the street, I'll get her to file an abandonment claim against you, your superiors, and the hospital. And I'll get my staff here and the medics to testify that she was a danger to herself and the community. So, admit her and get off my case."

Forte slammed the phone down so hard, a fragment of plastic broke off and skidded across the floor, stopping at Roxanne's feet. She asked, "You okay? You should let me handle dealing with the public. You're not so good with people. And Mrs. Berry's daughter's out here. Wants to talk to you. Says her mother can't ever go back to work in her condition. She wants you to start the paperwork for a permanent COLA pension."

By the time Sol compromised with Mrs. Berry's daughter, bestowing three weeks' time loss and agreeing to allow more if the swelling wasn't gone, Roxanne was rapping on the exam door, to rescue him, he believed, but she clipped her words nervously. "Dr. Rosebac needs to see you. He says it's urgent." In the hall she continued, "I think it's about that call you made to Whitaker General."

"I didn't make the call; they did."

"Be sure to tell him that. He's waiting for you, and he's looks more sourpuss than usual."

"Dave, what's up?"

"Sol, got a call from Four West over at Whitaker General. Actually, I didn't get the call, Anacota, our delightful CEO, did. He shared with me."

"How PC. You're really coming along. Look, I smiled into the phone. Did Anacota smile when he just called you?"

"Now, Sol, he's not very happy at the moment. Half the doctors in this Center are on the staff at General, including me. So, we're not going to be suing anybody, are we?"

"No, sir. Let's just tell 'em to dump ole Lupe back on the street, and when she blows her brains out, or even better, someone else's, the Sánchez clan'll sue me. Fair exchange, eh what?"

"Who's Lupe?"

"She's the one all this is about. COLA, fruitcake."

"Nucking futs, huh?"

"You can't even begin to imagine, Dave."

"You know, Sol, a man might begin to wonder why so many of your patients are, how shall I say, *challenged*? What's the attraction?"

"Dave, you know damn well what's going on here. Anacota's looking for a chink in my armor to carp about the practice. You know his next move: convene the Board of Directors, who'll follow his sage business advice like puppies and declare that, despite the best efforts of the Galena Hills Hospital and Medical Center, things are not working out; i.e., Forte's grand social experiment has failed. Then I'm going to get stuck at the Walk-In Clinic again, headin' 'em up, movin' 'em out—drivin' cattle, pushin' beef, treat 'em and street 'em, make another buck for the shareholders. I can't stand that life, twelve hours without a break, no time to take a leak, no patient follow-up. Lotta legal risk, too. I did it here for four years. I ain't goin' back to prison."

Rosebac interrupted, raising his hands sharply in Sol's face. "It was your idea to come to the Orthopedic Department and see COLA patients exclusively. If you're in our house, you gotta play by our rules." Rosebac's expression hardened. "This isn't Manhattan, my friend. It's not some cement company. You're not going to use the Center or this department as a venue to avenge how your father was treated when he got sick on the job. You want to make a commitment to care for injured workers, great, but you have to take the bad with the good. And there's more bad in that system than good, and by a long shot. Your call."

Forte sat frozen for a moment but growled abruptly, "I'll apologize to the nurse, or whatever he is, but you need to back me on getting Mrs. Sánchez admitted over there. I'll argue with COLA later. Deal?"

"Okay. I'll talk to Anacota and have him contact the nut floor over there, but make sure you mend some fences with our psychiatric colleagues."

Sol considered taking a moment to have the cup of tea out of which he had been cheated nearly an hour before, but Roxanne was on him before he could reach into his pocket to see if had a dollar. "Dr. F., Whitaker General just called. They want you to dictate a note outlining Mrs. Sánchez's present medical and psychiatric status before they'll admit her. They said like they want it right now."

"So, now they're going to admit her? And you say we're a dysfunctional practice. They know her history better than I do. She lives up there! What is wrong with these people?" Forte considered Roxanne's scowl, nodded obsequiously, and went on, "Okay, I'll call them, grovel at their feet, and tell them right from the horse's mouth what's going on. Kill two birds with one stone. And then everything will be cool with the Board of Directors, and I'll live happily ever after." He put his index finger on the top of his head, did a pirouette, and bowed.

"Dr. Forte, what are you talking about? You're scaring me more than usual. It's making me afraid to call them. Doesn't sound like I can trust you. Can I?"

"Just get 'em on the phone. I can be charming when I have to."

Roxanne's eyes rolled further up into her head than had Mrs. Berry's. But when she got the psych ward on the line, her eyes popped open as large as pizzas. She covered the receiver and whispered, "You're not going to believe this. Lupe Sánchez just signed out AMA, against medical advice."

"Ah, for God's sake. How could they let her sign out? She was a suicide risk. What is wrong with them? They could have held her for thirty-six hours against her will."

Roxanne set her jaw. "Yeah, well, they still want a dictated letter for their records, and that nursey boy wants to talk to you." She put the phone on hold and handed it to him with an extended pinky.

He handed it back. "You listen in, as if I had to ask. I'll take it in my office."

Roxanne whispered back, "I have a feeling you're going to be taking it somewhere else." She laughed and flicked her eyes twice.

"Technician Dilworth, this is Dr. Forte, and I'm really sorry for what happened before. I just hope you understand how tough it is to be hung out to dry." Sol paused for a cleansing breath. "I know you were just doing your job. Anyway, she's signed out of your life, not your problem anymore. Mine again..."

Dilworth interrupted. Sol listened and answered, "I know she thinks I don't believe her, but what's there to believe? Chronic pain syndrome with psychiatric overlay…"

The technician barged in again., and Sol mimicked in reply, "Borderline personality, schizophrenia, whatever you say, you're apparently better informed than the resident psychiatrist over there."

The click in Forte's ear was deafening. So was the discussion with Dr. Rosebac fifteen minutes later. Forte listened for a while and shook his head musing, "Dave, you've been a doctor for a long time. When did you start taking crap from a nurse, a psych nurse, and a boy nurse at that?"

Rosebac thought for a moment. "You've got a point. When I was a brand, spanking new doctor, before the flood, when a doctor walked into a room, the nurses, females all of them, thank you very much, stood up and stayed that way until we nodded for them to sit. They even wore those little hats. I really liked those hats, so crisp and white, the way they were folded, like it was Freudian or something. But times have changed, my friend, and all of us have had to adjust to survive. Not saying it's right, but it's the way it is. And, anyway, he's not a nurse, but a psychiatric technician, whatever that is."

"Look," Forte spoke, his shoulders drooping, "I spent nearly thirteen years in college to get here. I don't need to take that kind of crap from a glorified medical assistant with six months of training after graduating from high school, if he even did."

"Not arguing with the concept, only the execution. Call the guy's boss, talk to him, and be nice, because, obviously, you're not having a smooth ride with your new pal."

CHAPTER THREE

At 6 P.M., Solomon Forte took a call from Mr. Tarkington's attorney. Forte told Roxanne to listen in. With the edges of his lips barely and painfully curled upward, Sol picked up the phone on his desk. "This is Dr. Forte. How may I help you?"

"Doctor, I am Anwar El Haq. I represent Mr. Ralph Tarkington in his legal situation with Argent Public Utilities. Thank you for seeing him today. I need for you to fax me a report on Mr. Tarkington's case by ten tomorrow morning. We have a sudden hearing date at one. In order for the case to go forward, I'm going to have to show the judge that your patient was permanently injured by the gross negligence of Argent Public Utilities over the past eighteen years."

"Waaaaaaait a minute, Mr. Anwar El Haq. I just saw your client today for the first time. He's not my patient yet. Anyway, I haven't had time to look at his chart…it's thousands of pages. Like you said, this thing is nearly twenty years in the making. And let me ask you, how long have you represented Ralph Tarkington?"

Al Haq answered impatiently, "Eleven months. Why is it you ask?"

"Eleven months. So, we don't have to get all of this done overnight if it's been that long."

"Doctor, you don't understand the legal profession..."

Sol interrupted. "That is true."

"May I go on?"

"By all means."

"We work on one or two cases at a time. And when one of those cases gets close to trial, we work on it twenty-four-hours-a-day. Our professions are very different. You see, we are at the beck and call of the judges. When they say jump, we jump. And the judge, he said, 'Jump'."

"I understand that the legal profession is very different from medicine, sir, like when the Clinic doctors play the yearly softball game against the town's lawyers—stealers versus the healers. But, my friend, I have other plans for the next twelve hours, and it's going to take me about that long to go through his records and dictate a report. Then there's a couple of hours to get it typed up. Also, I need to ask you, who's paying the Center for my time?"

El Haq spoke as if a Supreme Court Justice rendering a decision. "You are entitled to bill the Commission on Labor Affairs for seeing Mr. Tarkington today. Part of the fee they pay you is intended to cover the expense of dictating a chart note and having it transcribed. I am a private attorney, and we are in the process of litigation against them. They certainly aren't going to pay for my legal services or for the papers I need to represent my client. I'm sure you understand that."

The weak smile with which Sol had begun the conversation deteriorated into an ugly tumor. "Is this some kinda joke, sir?" he spat. "My nurse put you up to it, didn't she?"

"I can assure you, this is a very serious matter."

"Look, it costs my office eighty-five or ninety bucks just to get the dictation typed up on something this complicated. What COLA pays doesn't even cover the paper. I lose money on the deal."

"Doctor, that's the cost of doing business. You took Mr. Tarkington on as a patient, and it is your responsibility to familiarize yourself with his situation. It's all there in the records. You also have a legal obligation to write a comprehensive note regarding your visit with Mr. Tarkington. On the other hand, he tells me you only spent a few seconds examining him."

"What's there to examine? He didn't come to me for treatment. He told me you wanted me to look at his chart. I had no idea what he wanted."

"Exactly my point, Doctor. Mr. Tarkington is incompetent. You should have understood that from talking to him for thirty seconds. After all, you had his entire record. Everything you needed to piece together his heart-rending history was right before you."

"Mr. Anwar El Haq…"

"It's just El Haq," he interrupted.

"Sorry. El Haq, I know you can subpoena me as a witness and not pay anything for my time. I lose a day or two of work every time a patient decides to go to court. That's already happened to me several times with some of your colleagues. But I've learned a lesson or two over the years. When you get me on the stand, I might not be all that helpful to your case. I might just testify to make it sound like your client is a malingerer, a master at committing insurance fraud, and has been for the past twenty years."

El Haq answered tartly, though he measured his words carefully. "And we will be forced to sue you for medical malpractice for not examining him, for not treating him, for ignoring his records, and for giving false testimony. Cost you a hundred thousand dollars to defend yourself. And you might win; in fact, you probably will, but if you can ever find malpractice insurance again, it'll be pricey."

Sol was seething. "Let me get this straight. If you don't care for my testimony, you'll sue me for medical malpractice and use the transcript of my testimony in a COLA case to prove to a jury that I refused to care for this man, just like Argent Public Utilities has refused. Is that what you have in mind?"

"You are spot on, Doctor."

"No problem. I'll write to your professional society within the next thirty seconds and tell them about our conversation. See you in court." Sol was about to drop the receiver into the cradle, but his chest gripped as he realized he was speaking to an attorney. The word *tsuris* from his medical school days at Albert Einstein popped into his head. He listened for another second.

El Haq, sensing the opening, added quickly, "Doctor, give me just one more minute of your valuable time. I can hear a female breathing on the extension line. You feel very confident because you have a witness. But all I did was quote the law. I must inform you that there is no statute in this country that prevents an attorney from suing anyone who harms his client. That is one of the reasons I love it so much here. The little man has protection.

"You see, my client was harmed by the negligence of Argent Public Utilities, who went on to treat him like a dog for eighteen years. Sadly, so have many of the doctors who have seen him. Since no one else will advocate for him, it falls upon me to do so. That is what lawyers do. We represent those who don't have the wherewithal to do so on their own.

"Now, with all due respect, I believe you were lax in your care of Mr. Tarkington this morning. According to Mr. Tarkington, you didn't do a physical exam, and you didn't come up with a treatment plan. So, feel free to make a transcript of everything I said. I'll be happy to sign it, and we'll send it to the Trial Lawyers Association together."

"Good. I think I will. And you're guilty of predatory litigation. I don't think your Trial Lawyers Association will tolerate that."

"No, Doctor, I am not guilty of anything untoward. And there is no such thing. I am representing a beaten man. And even if I were guilty, did I fail to mention that I don't belong to the local Trial Lawyers Association?"

It was within a millisecond after Forte dropped the phone that Roxanne appeared at his desk. For the first time in the years he'd known her, there was an edge of concern in her voice. "I know doctors can't stand lawyers and vice versa; only problem is, they make the rules. What are you going to do, Dr. F.?"

"Talk to Dr. Rosebac. Better get the administration involved. It's going to cost me a bite out of my ass, but it'll be worse if they think I blindsided them."

Sol sat in Dave Rosebac's office and spun the yarn of Tarkington and El Haq. The older man shook his head and smiled sarcastically. "Forte, I've talked to you, and about you, more today than in the four years you've been in this department. On the other hand, the tenor of this conversation is essentially identical to every conversation we've ever had. My advice is, get out of trouble. Start by not antagonizing Anwar Sadat."

"Anwar El Haq."

"Whatever. Anwar has you over a barrel. Take the hit and just forget it. Let it go. Anyway, he was just posturing. He may be a skunk, but he's not going to take the time to sue you. He needs a letter to help a patient, but you don't want to do the letter, probably because you had a particularly unpleasant day, which you did, so you snapped at him, and the two of you got into it. You left him no choice but to use his only trick, a threat to sue, and you fall for the bait.

"Look, dictate a quick note and be sure to mention that this is a chronic problem, that the patient did not appear acutely ill, and you felt changing the present treatment plan was inappropriate, and likely, dangerous. Add something about your plan to examine the records meticulously over the weekend on your own time, and without compensation. That'll take the wind out of Anwar Sadat's sails."

"*El Haq's* sails. Now, planning ahead with COLA patients, like you always advise, and expecting the worst, like you always guarantee, do I avoid problems by just stating on the report that Tarkington was screwed by APU? There's no time for me to make that decision by morning, but it looks like that's what it will boil down to, and I might as well cover my rear for later."

Rosebac answered without hesitating. "Skim through it and find a letter from the employer where they deny responsibility. Then make up something like, 'On my initial review of the records, questions arise regarding the employer's commitment to pay for Mr. Wilmington's accepted industrial claim of date, blah, blah, blah, though a thorough evaluation of the voluminous chart notes would be required before this examiner would feel comfortable making any binding statements.' Something like that. There's no liability for you if you don't say anything."

"It's Tarking…And by the way, how do I get this typed by morning?"

"You do it. Actually, when you think about it, you don't even really need to look at his records now. Just sit down at the typewriter. It'll take you fifteen minutes. Just make sure you put in the disclaimer about planning to spend your entire weekend working on the case and that, 'Considering the exceeding chronicity and complexity of Mr. Parker's problem, it would be inappropriate to draw immediate conclusions regarding this patient's care, blah, blah, blah.'"

Sol brightened. "Yeah, good. Sounds like you've been over this ground once or twice. Thought you didn't see COLA patients."

Rosebac's lips curled down. "Hey, I've had dozens of lawyers hound me over the years with all sorts of demands about all sorts of patients. I've been to court many a time, spent two days away from the office, maybe four, and not a red cent to show for it. You think you're the only one they pester? The difference is, I learned a long time ago how to appraise a patient for the lawsuit virus. If they have the early symptoms, I stand up straight, say how sorry I am that I can't help, and I'm out of the room in a flash. I leave the door wide open. And I never turn back. Takes about thirty seconds for them to realize they're done, and they leave the room head down, grumbling about arrogant doctors. By the time they reach the front desk, they're really worked up. But I let the receptionist handle it. That's why they get paid. Now, the key principle here, Doctor, is what?"

"That they leave."

"Precisely. There *is* hope for you. You need to work on that skill—detaching yourself in fifteen seconds. Doctoring is a lot more than prescribing pills. Half the time it's about getting them before they get you."

Sol nodded, though he sensed an uncomfortable heat rising within him. He tried to smile as he asked, "Should I put something in the statement about having had to go to the cafeteria to hunt down the family member who wasn't in the room with her father like she was supposed to be, but was outside smoking in the parking lot when she should have been in the exam room, if she really cared so much, and he was so debilitated?"

"I don't know about that. It's too late for you on this one. You're stuck, so now you have to make a plan for what you're going to do in front of a jury, because that's sure as hell where you're going to wind up. If you put in a statement like that, you're making value judgments about the patient's social class. And the lawyer'll just argue that poor Mr. Parkinson's daughter was stressed out from taking care of her father for twenty years. She'd gotten to the point that she couldn't bear to hear how hopeless he was, so she stopped sitting in the doctor's office, but always went outside to calm her nerves. After all, she was leaving her dad in the hands of a supposedly caring physician.

"But what kind of caring physician doesn't even bother to do a physical exam? That shoots your credibility in the foot at trial. Plan ahead. I wouldn't get into that territory. Think about who's on a jury. Never forget, every word, every sentence you dictate, is going to be parsed...and several times. Our attorney friends can turn the *Lord's Prayer* into a contract with the devil. I've seen 'em do it. Be careful; that's what they do for a living, day and night. They're good at it—as good as I am at doing nose jobs. Plan ahead." Rosebac leaned back. He stretched, adding, "It's been a long day. Now, you're wasting time. Have a great evening."

CHAPTER FOUR

S olomon Forte drove south toward his studio apartment on
Whitaker's Sterling Hill, glancing sideways the whole trip at the
bulging briefcase on the front seat. He had nearly written the entire
note on Mr. Tarkington in his head when his car phone chirped to life.

"Hey, Dana, how are you?" And by the end of her reply, he
was turning off the interstate, heading west the few miles to her
condo. He awoke at four-thirty and asked if he could use her
computer, where he fashioned a short letter addressed to Mr.
El Haq. Laughing over coffee, he admitted that Rosebac was
right—Sol hadn't had to open his briefcase. In fact, he hadn't
even bothered to carry it into Dana's apartment the night before.

The missive read:

Re: Tarkington, Ralph

To Whom It May Concern:

This is a preliminary report regarding the above-captioned pa-
tient, who presented in my office this morning for the first time,

but for unclear reasons. He was accompanied by thousands of pages of records and a note from his family ordering I evaluate the chart in preparation for litigation within the next twenty-four hours.

As Mr. Tarkington's condition is chronic, and in that it has been present and apparently unchanged for the past eighteen years, and further, because he voiced no new physical complaints today, it was my professional opinion that it would be imprudent and inappropriate to establish a new treatment regimen in this complicated patient after only one contact.

I will be able to evaluate Mr. Tarkington's medical situation only after I spend many hours of my own time reviewing his voluminous chart. When I have carefully studied that data, I will be better able to make the professional determination as to whether I have any effective medical treatment to offer Mr. Tarkington, or if his industrial claim is justified.

Respectfully submitted,
Solomon Forte, M.D.

He dropped the report off in Whitaker, on the steps of a tiny clapboard house on Morgan Street. The mailbox was behind a large, weathered, plastic sign stuck in the front yard reading,

ANWAR EL HAQ
TRIAL ATTORNEY

⇒⇐

At the Center, Roxanne greeted him with a playing-card-deck-sized pile of the morning's telephone messages. On top was a note from Mrs. Berry's employer complaining that Forte had had no right to accept her COLA claim. "He wants to talk to you ASAP," Roxanne muttered. "Says if you don't call him, he's going to get in touch with the insurance commissioner. Said Mrs. Berry's claim is bullshit."

"Did he use those words, 'Bullshit'?"

"Yep."

"Well, screw 'em. He can't talk to you that way. Only I'm allowed to. Good work. Now we have an excuse to ignore him."

"Okay, but he sounded mad as hell. Next one is from Mr. McAlister. Says the pain is getting worse, and he needs something stronger than Vicodin."

"Good. Give him twenty Ultram. Tell him it's new and much stronger than Vicodin."

"He's already on to you. His very words, '…and tell that doctor, I'm deathly allergic to codeine, and I have a history of seizures, so I can't take Tylenol #3, or Ultram.'"

Sol clucked, "Nope, not giving him anything more. If he doesn't like it, tell him to find a new doctor, which is what I wish I had told him twenty-four hours and thirty messages ago."

"I'll tell him, but you know he'll be up here in ten minutes demanding an emergency visit. And we also have a call from Whitaker General. Sheeeee's back. Mrs. Sánchez was admitted last night. Something like she took ten aspirins. Cops brought her in and told the loony bin at the hospital to hold her for seventy-two hours."

"So the cops are making medical decisions, but I can't."

"When the hospital called COLA to get the insurance thing straightened out, the claims manager refused to accept her mental problems as part of her fall. They want you to fax a letter to COLA immediately to get the thing straightened out."

"Who's they, the cops?"

"No, the hospital. Also, they want to know who's going to pay for a live-in interpreter at the hospital, so you need to contact COLA and get that approved also, unless you want to foot the bill. And now, I saved the best for last: Mr. Tarkington was admitted to the hospital early this morning with a seizure."

"Great. Maybe he was taking Ultram."

"Very funny, but guess what? He was. It was right on his records."

"How do you know?"

"Swami El Haq called and told me. Says he wants to talk to you the moment you set foot in this office."

"Young lady, did you call him, 'Swami'?"

"I may have whispered it. Why?"

"Great. A swami is from India. Mr. El Haq is from the Middle East. Tarkington thinks he's Chinese; you think he's from South Asia. The two of you need to brush up on your geography. Maybe you could attend night classes together."

"What's the difference? India, Iran, China?"

"Huh. Very tolerant of you, Florence Nightingale. And he's not from Iran. He has an Arabic name. Iran is not an Arabic country." Sol took a breath to continue, but Roxanne yawned, and her eyelids drooped. "Okay, you win. Let's just phone El Haq first. That way, the rest of the day can't get worse. You place the call. Makes it look like this is a professional office."

"I think he already knows better. Can't even understand him, but I think he was talking sweet to me, or trying to. Can you believe that?"

"Here's your big chance, Rox. Rich lawyer. You could be set for life."

She walked back to her desk mumbling but stopped to call over her shoulder, "By the way, that friend of yours, what is it, Dana? She phoned. Said you'd know what it was about."

As Roxanne searched her desk for El Haq's number, the receptionist rounded the corner and groaned, "Hey, Roxanne. That John Sullivan guy, Edna Berry's employer, he's on the line again. Sounds angry. Wants to talk to Dr. Forte. Says he won't stop calling until he talks with him."

Sol heard her. He nodded and wiggled his index finger toward the phone on Roxanne's desk then at his ear.

"Morning, Mr. Sullivan This is Dr. Forte. How may I help you, sir?"

"Dr. Forte, I'm Edna Berry's employer. I noticed you placed her on COLA. With all due respect, Doctor, I'm not responsible for her breaking a bone by standing up off a normal chair. It's a good quality chair. I take care of my employees."

"I'm sure you do, and I understand your concern. But, sir, my hands are tied. The rules say I have to listen to my patient's statement and fill out the paperwork based on what she tells me, not what I think happened. And if she got hurt at work, even getting out of a chair, it's COLA, simple as that. I have no control over it."

"That's bullshit."

"Now see, sir, we can't have you talking like that to my staff."

"I'm not talking to your staff, I'm talking to you. Do you understand that if this injury gets charged to my company, my rates go up—damn near forever?"

"And if I make up a story and don't charge it to COLA," Forte snapped, "it's a $40,000 fine on my back for insurance fraud."

"Now, wait a minute. This isn't fraud. She has that leukemia. She can't remember a damn thing. Stares off into space most of the day. I'm not Jesus Christ, you know. I can't heal the sick. That's your job. I'm sorry she's got a disease. She used to be a good employee, but now she's not worth a damn. I should've fired her, but then the goddamn lawyers would sue me for violating the ADA, and also, I wanted to help her out. But what the hell's goin' on here?"

"I understand, sir, but my charge is to facilitate my patient's medical care. That's the rules."

The man was snorting like a bull. "What is this crap? You get a little education under your belt, and then you go out and screw the little guy?"

"Now, sir, I'm not the one who made the rules. If you want to deny that she got hurt on the job, please do so. There'll be a court case, and you can present your side of the story, but I can tell you that if she broke her leg on your premises, in the course of her normal duties, she has the right to file a COLA claim. I'm sorry. I have to follow the law, and I also took an oath to support my patient."

"You sound like one of these goddamn lawyers. I'm going to fight this one to the Supreme Court. You're a rip-off doctor. All you're worried about is making money because she has state industrial insurance that I had to pay for with my sweat." The employer's final sentiment was followed by a piercing click.

Roxanne stuck her head into Sol's office. "Well, Dr. F., what'cha gonna do?"

"Call Ghost Busters. Nah, I'm going to make sure my chart notes are perfect; I'll put down every word he said. And you need to make a statement and put down every word he said, and what you say he said, and what I say he said, better be the same. Then I get to hope like hell Mrs. Berry finds another doctor. But for right now, I need a snack. You'll find me in the cafeteria."

"Are you stressed out about this thing?"

"Nope. I'm tough. New York City, Manhattan, remember. I can handle anything they throw my way."

"Then why are you going downstairs to eat? You just ate breakfast a few minutes ago. Plus, you must have forgotten that you need to call Swami El Haq."

"Later."

"No, not later, now. Get it over with. I'll listen in."

"Okay, okay. Get 'im on the line. And you be nice while you're doing it. Pretend you work for the United Nations." Forte shook his head and grumbled, "Swami El Haq. She's going to get me sued, that one."

Roxanne came back to the door of Sol's office and smiled, "No, you'll manage that on your own. And the Swami's a waitin' for ya. Be nice. Where's that Galena Hills Medical Center smile? Come on now, let's see it."

"Mr. El Haq. Good morning. How may I help you?"

"Doctor, have you checked on your patient this morning?"

"I'm sorry, I don't know what you mean, sir."

"Your patient. Mr. Ralph Tarkington."

"What's wrong with him?"

"He's in the hospital. Serious illness. He almost died last night, and they didn't call you? Come now, Doctor. You should know what's going on with your patients. Is your answering service a sieve?"

"Mr. El Haq, let's cut to the quick. This man's not my patient. He's a prop for a frivolous lawsuit. Just raw meat for your third of a wad of cash. There isn't a jury on the face of this Earth that's going to convict me of a damn thing. This is a set up, and you know it."

"It may be, but it's still going to cost you half-a-million dollars to defend yourself."

"That's up from last night." He relaxed, having sensed El Haq's first fumble. He plastered the compulsory smile on his lips and popped, "And tomorrow it'll be a million. Who cares? That's why I have malpractice insurance. Let my lawyers handle it. Let you gentle folk cut each other's balls off. I look forward to watching it happen. Win, lose, or settle, I sit back and laugh. I've already called my insurance carrier. They told me to ignore your threats. No matter what you do, it's no skin off my back, so don't try to intimidate me."

"Oh, I think you have misjudged. You'll be very deeply involved. I can assure you. There is no escape."

His bravado building, Sol laughed pompously. "I simply won't participate. Nothing you can do about it."

El Haq replied soberly. "Well, let us examine what you just said. Your insurance company has in-house lawyers, I presume."

"I have no idea. I don't know, or want to know, the inner workings of my insurance company, or even the name of my insurance company. To be frank, I don't even know what an in-house lawyer is."

"Doctor, those are attorneys who work only for the insurance company, in little offices in the insurance company's building. They are paid a salary. They accept less income than entrepreneurs like me because they are willing to settle for the security of a steady job."

"Sounds like a good life. What's your point?"

"Doctor, there are pitfalls associated with that career path. For instance, there is little impetus for those lawyers to settle claims immediately. If they resolve lawsuits quickly, the insurance company CEO isn't going to have niggling little problems like Tarkington v. Forte to worry about. Then the CEO is going to sit those lawyers down and say, 'Good job, ladies and gentlemen. Now work your magic again, and let's see if we can get a whole bunch of these cases settled early. Let's get them off the table.' Suddenly, your malpractice company's board of directors sees how much they can conserve by settling early. They instruct the CEO to let two or three of the in-house lawyers go, and the corporation saves nearly half a million dollars per year just in office space, salary, and benefits, to say nothing of administrative costs, Lexus Nexus, etcetera, etcetera. No, we can't have early settlements or early summary judgments. In-house lawyers would become extinct. Judges would be happy, though—clean dockets, more time for golf."

Sol was lost before the end of the first sentence. He blustered, "That's truly disgusting. You would hurt someone, even your client, to make a buck? You call yourself a professional?"

The register of El Haq's voice rose. "Doctor, I didn't call you to discuss ethics, but I assure you, I have not hurt anyone. I am trying to the best of my humble ability to represent a man who has been crushed by a huge, uncaring corporation. It is interesting, however, to note just how caring and ethical you doctors can be. Never a single fiduciary concern, no, not a physician, not the nation's royalty."

"What is your point, Mr. El Haq?"

"My point is, Dr. Forte, that when a patient comes to you for, let's say, a lump in her breast, and she's worried sick, you do your job dispassionately and instruct your secretary to call the surgeon's secretary and schedule a biopsy in a few days, or more likely, a week later. Then, after the surgery, the family has to wait how long for the pathology report? Another week? In the meantime, her children are frightened to death, and how about her husband? He's watching the family vaporize right before his eyes." El Haq's voice became harsh. "I ask you, Doctor, how long do you make them wait for those test results? Another week, maybe more?"

"Mr. El Haq, I'm really busy, sir."

El Haq's voice became piercing. "Just one more minute of your time, Doctor. Why not hire a person to make sure the biopsy gets done that day, and that the results come back by the next morning? Or maybe you could find a general surgeon willing to do a quick biopsy. There are many caring surgeons out there; maybe some have ample mortgages that need to be met. If you don't want to hire someone to make scheduling calls for you, you could get on the phone and do it yourself; cajole a surgeon-friend into getting the biopsy done that day.

"But you see, Doctor, that is an imposition, isn't it? Middle of a busy day at the office, you have to take time out to make a couple of calls? And then, of course, demanding immediate biopsy results costs too much, doesn't it? Medical insurance won't pay for it, so you'd wind up paying out of your capitation, or however that works. But in the long run, it would come right out of your own pocket, wouldn't it? But you care so deeply, so much more than I do, I'm sure you would go ahead and pay for the test yourself, wouldn't you?"

Sol was nearly breathless. "That's absurd, and you know it. A doctor has a right to make a living, too. We don't control the insurance companys' payment policies, not by a long shot. We can't pay out of our own pockets for the care that insurance companies refuse to cover. Be reasonable."

"Pardon me, Doctor, but I have to make a living as well, though all I do is *meaningless* lawsuits. But there is a crucial difference—you have someone's life in your fist. A family mourns for, what is it, only two weeks, if they're lucky, before they find out the result of mom's breast biopsy? They're dying as they wait to hear if mom is going to suffer a painful death from cancer, and all the time, the information to soothe their worst fears has been in your hands, if only you had taken a moment to make a call to the pathology lab."

Sol hissed, "The system doesn't work that way. I don't control all the pieces of the puzzle; just like you don't control the judges."

El Haq paused and answered more gently. "You have a point, Doctor, but if I may, all you'd have to do is ask the surgeon to do the biopsy quickly, maybe even that evening. The procedure only takes twenty minutes, if that. It's not as if it was a trial that takes weeks and dozens of people to get done. You see, sir, if the biopsy got done late that afternoon, you could call the lab and have them pick up the specimen before dark, or maybe you could send it over by cab and split the cost with the lab and the surgeon, or how about dropping it off yourself on your way home? Bet you would do it if it was your own wife. Then you could ask the lab to do the pathology before dawn. It only takes a few minutes to prepare the tissue and look at under the microscope. They have pathologists on duty at night. Then you could make a call in the morning and let the patient know the results. And nine times out of ten, the biopsy report says no cancer. So you call your patient and you've changed a whole family's life. They'd never forget you, would they? It's not as though this happens every day in a medical practice. What, perhaps once a year, if that?

"And if it *is* cancer, you could have them come right in, couldn't you, and you could outline the problem and sit with them and create a plan to treat the disease. You could be the general of the army, gathering the forces to meet the enemy. In one day, you would have diagnosed the disease and given these innocent patients hope. Isn't that what we're here for? Both of us? To intervene in the lives of those who come to us for help? To show our concern and offer them something they can't get or do on their own? Hope. We deal in hope, those of us who call ourselves professionals.

"But doctors don't do that so often, do they? You take the biopsy and tell your patient, '…just go about your business, Mrs. Smith, and don't worry.' That's nonsense. It's cruel, and it's uncaring. So, please, don't talk to me about professionalism. I was easy on you with that example. I've got a hundred more. I will dispense them three times a day for ten days, because for the next couple of weeks, we are going to be working together closely.

"Please remember, Doctor, Mr. Tarkington was clearly mistreated by his former employer, a huge, powerful corporation. If I don't represent him, this little man, will you?"

Sol's replied, his voice tremulous. "What do you want, sir?"

El Haq answered sternly. "I want you to read the file on Mr. Tarkington. Really read it. Read between the lines. You dislike lawyers so much, see what the in-house attorneys at Argent Public Utilities did to this man. Then tell me if he can fight this one on his own."

"Okay, I'll read it."

"Good. Now, about Mr. Tarkington's medical condition. Frequent seizures, an unfortunate, but plausible, result of the trauma he suffered twenty years ago. Everyone is afraid to take him on as a patient—too risky, no compensation, an unlikely prescription for a happy ending. On the other hand, he needs you now. He won't go back to that other doctor. That one had him on Dilantin for five years, ever since his first seizure. Hasn't checked a Dilantin blood level in two years because he doesn't get paid to see the guy. That doctor did a wallet biopsy on Mr. Tarkington a few years ago when COLA stopped paying. You can be sure *that* biopsy didn't take a week to come back."

"Mr. El Haq, I'll look in on Mr. Tarkington, but I am an orthopedist, not a neurologist. I will also be calling my malpractice insurance carrier again about this, and the State Medical Society. You are forcing me to practice medicine for which I am not trained. And I'm calling the State Bar Association as well. I am not God."

"Feel free to call anyone you choose. I just ask that you read the case, as you have agreed, and look in on Mr. Tarkington. All you need do is draw a Dilantin level, get a curbside consult from a neurologist or an internist on how to get his level high enough to prevent further seizures, then discharge him. Call me when you're done."

Sol thought for a moment. He spoke softly. "I have one question to ask you."

"Go ahead."

"Why did you choose me for this thing?"

"This 'thing.' Very interesting perspective. I had my reasons."

Roxanne shuffled into Forte's office as slowly as he had ever seen her move. Her face was ashen, and she spoke quietly. "Dr. Forte, do you know what he was saying?"

"I'm afraid I did. He's not a dope. Hell of a lot smarter than me."

"I couldn't understand anything except that he was threatening you. And, I'm sorry, but you've got three patients stacked up. Really, I'm sorry. Can I help you with the Tarkington thing?"

"Tarkington *thing*. Interesting perspective. Nah, I'm okay. Let's go see a patient and save a life. Who's here?"

"Well, there's good news and bad news."

Sol's head drooped and he sighed. "Gimme the good first. I know, I know, state's cancelled the COLA program."

"Hey, close. Actually, your first sacrifice of the morning is none other than Mr. California, Kevin McAlister."

"What the hell does he want?"

"Says he gave his pain pills to his girlfriend to carry in her purse, and they were in an accident last night, and she left her purse in the car when it was towed away, and she had to go to work this morning, and she went by the junkyard, and the purse was gone. He says his back is killing him."

"Yeah, well, my back's killing me, and the dog ate my homework. And what's the bad news?"

"You have a new patient before him."

"Great." Sol touched the side of his head with his index finger and closed his eyes. "I predict myocardial infarction, heart attack, that happened on a golf outing in Scotland."

"Nope, back pain, happened on the job. And then you have another new patient." The color was returning to Roxanne's face. "I forget what he has. No, no, wait a minute, I got it, gimme one more second. It's coming, here it is, ah, COLA back pain. Then you need to look in on Mr. Tarkington. If you want, I can have the hospital draw a Dilantin level, send it out stat, and it'll be ready when you get there. Also, I'll call Ed Rosenberg, the neurologist. He's my pal. He can tell you what to do, because you're just an orthopedist."

"Thank you, Dr. El Haq."

"Do you also want me to get the numbers for the doctor society and the lawyer society?"

"Nah, let's just wait and see how things go with Mr. Tarkington at the hospital."

Roxanne pointed left, but Sol sucked in a deep breath and headed toward McAlister's room. She called in a loud whisper, "Wrong direction. That room houses our connoisseur of narcotic pain medication. He's a walk-in, last on the list."

"I know. I'm gonna disobey your direct order. Let's do this first and get it over with." He picked up the chart and searched for his note of the day before to remind himself how many narcotic capsules he had finally agreed to. The pages were blank. He called loudly to Roxanne. "Nurse, find out where the notes are from Mr. McAlister's visit yesterday."

Roxanne dialed transcription and spoke for a moment. Her eyes widened as she turned to Forte. "They say the chart notes were sent to Dr. Rosebac for review. Something about the number of pain pills you gave him." Sol began to raise his voice, but Roxanne raised her index finger straight up then pointed it at him. "Don't get on my case. I didn't send the notes to Rosebac."

Forte nodded grimly. "Tell me, please, how many pills he's gotten. There were the fifteen I first gave him, and there were the ten more during the Lupe Sánchez debacle. What else? That's not enough for the dictation ladies to have a cow and turn me in. And isn't there some law about reading a man's mail?"

Roxanne's voice sighed nervously. "I gave him a few more at four-fifty-eight last night. The front desk was bugging me to get off the phone so they could turn the lines over to the answering service."

"So, you *did* have something to do with it. And?"

"And that was supposed to be the end of the day. I couldn't find you. You were in with Dr. Rosebac, *again*, and anyway, Dr. F., why do I have to argue with that trash? Why should I have to go down to the record room, wait for them to pull his chart, find out who the on-call doctor is, page him, wait for him to call me back, then take his crap because I'm just a nurse, and he's a doctor, and I'm bothering him, and then he tells me to call the prescription in myself. And when I call the pharmacy, they tell me I have to fax them a formal prescription to prove it's really me calling, '…and it better have the doctor's signature on it, and I better be able to read it, and don't let it be a signature stamp…' And then I have to write a note in the patient's chart, and then take it back down to central records. 'And blah, blah, blah,' as Dr. Rosebac says. Be ten o'clock before I get home. I got kids, you know. It's not like this happens once a year. It's every night with these drug seekers. Wait until the last minute. They're smarter than the both of us put together. You think the Center pays me overtime for that extra hour? No way. When I bitch, they just say, 'Roxanne, you need to learn how to get your work done in the allotted hours.' Assholes. And what's a few dozen Vicodin between friends, anyway?"

"A few dozen, Roxanne?"

Kevin's legs churned like GE turbofans. "Mr. McAlister, what's this about a car accident? If you're hurting so bad, how can you be driving, my man? It's not safe for you to be behind the wheel. You know, the pain and the narcotics."

He looked up slowly, his arms twitching as he flashed the 'hang-loose' sign. "Thanks for seeing me, Doc. Guess you heard, huh? It was terrible. Hurt my back worse, and couldn't get no sleep at all. And I ain't got none of them pills."

"You just got a shitload from this office."

"And it was my girlfriend driving, her rig. She left her purse in the car when it got towed. She was like in shock. You know how it is. Then someone stole it from the car. We went down there this morning to get it back, and the whole car was bashed in, windshield full of holes. Fuckers took her purse. Probably just wanted the drugs—scumbags. Now I'm stuck. I know you can you help me out, Doc. Something's got to be done about this pain."

"Well, Mr. McAlister, like I told you yesterday, COLA's watching. This isn't California. I can't be writing prescriptions for pain medication every third hour. We're going to have to make a move to get you back to work. I don't want to see you become dependent on the state. It'll make you crazy. Give you depression."

"Shit, I don't want that, Doc, no way, but what am I supposed to do? Live in pain? Answer that for me."

Sol shook his head. "Well, you're going to have to learn to live with some pain, my friend. It's not like it's forever. Your back'll get better with time. I don't want to add a problem with addiction to your back troubles." Forte eyed the half-smoked, extinguished cigarette butt behind McAlister's ear. "And, one of the things you need to do is stop smoking. It's ruining your back, my friend."

McAlister rolled his eyes. "You telling me smoking causes back pain? Make you short-winded, okay, but hurt your back? Come on Doc, cut me a break with that shit."

"I'm serious. Smoking makes the blood vessels going to the lower back shrink. Also, blocks the amount of oxygen that can get into the blood through the lungs. You need oxygen to heal. You're a bright guy; you know that. Bottom line is, a lot less blood with a lot less oxygen and nutrients getting to the lower back to repair the damage. Look, I'm not here to hassle you. I want to see you get better."

"I know that, Doc. Okay. I'll quit today, but for right now, man, I'm hurtin', and I need some help."

"I'll give you a few more pills to get you through the next couple of days, but we're going to be taking a new approach. I want you back here in a week, and you need to get into physical therapy as soon as possible, as in like today. I'll call them and have 'em find an opening for this afternoon." Forte jumped up and made for the door, a sour feeling pouring over him as McAlister renewed his moaning. Sol recognized he had taken the first wobbly steps down a dark path.

In the hall, Forte whispered to Roxanne, "Give him six Vicodins and six Somas. Go ahead and stamp it with my signature. I'll be in Room Two with the next victim."

"Good. Make it snappy. We're behind."

Forte had just finished asking the new COLA back patient how it had all happened when Roxanne knocked. "Dr. Forte, can I see you for a minute?"

Sol followed and turned toward her desk. McAlister had lifted himself into Roxanne's chair and was slouching, staring into her computer. She drew Sol by the elbow down the hall in the opposite direction. McAlister popped out of the chair and followed them.

Roxanne whispered, "He said six wasn't enough, and he wasn't going to leave until you took care of his pain."

"Doc," Kevin groaned "I got to have something. We'll never get my girlfriend's purse back. Six ain't gonna do nothin'. What am I supposed to do? Just suffer?"

Sol, loathe to disbelieve a patient until proven beyond the shadow of a doubt that he was a liar, and also wary of the million-dollar malpractice suits that had recently been won by patients whose doctors had not given them sufficient medication to ease their pain, nodded quickly, raised both hands to the heavens, and blurted, "Tell you what we're going to do. Where's the car? I'll call the boneyard and ask if they know where the purse is. If they say yes, you're on your own. Deal?"

McAlister's face deepened two shades of vermilion. "I told ya, it was stole. It ain't there, Doc."

"Well, let's call anyway and see what's what." Sol laughed as he told Roxanne to get the towing company on the phone.

Thirty seconds later she covered the phone and whispered, "The car's there, and if it's really a doctor's office calling, they say they'll have someone bring the purse over here."

Sol took the phone. "Sir, this is Dr. Forte. Are you saying the car *was* in an accident last night?"

A voice over the phone brightened. "Hey, is this Dr. Forte at the Medical Center? Man, you treated my broken arm when it got crushed. You remember? The night I forgot to put the cable around the tires and the car rolled off the tow truck and pinned me against the telephone pole? Doin' great. You were the best."

"Oh, yeah, I remember that—telephone pole and all. Glad to hear you're better. I was worried about you. Hell of an injury. Took a tough guy to get through that. Hey, how 'bout the accident last night?"

"Pretty bad one, Doc. Vehicle's totaled. Surprised there weren't worse injuries."

Sol asked, slack-jawed, "Is there a purse in the car?"

"Well, no, Doc. We take personal stuff outta the wreck before we lock up for the night. The purse is all sealed up in plastic. I got it in the safe. If the owner says okay, we'll bring it on over. No problem."

Fifteen minutes later, Kevin McAlister removed the three bottles of Vicodin from his girlfriend's handbag with a flourish. He turned the labels forward, nearly sticking them in Sol's face. "Here ya go, Doc. You wanna see how many are left?"

Sol did want to count them, but he smiled vacantly, "No, Mr. McAlister, we're cool. Just use them prudently. But promise me you're going to start physical therapy, right?"

At 10 A.M., Sol ran into the hospital wing to look in on Mr. Tarkington. As he approached the man's room, he smiled, calming himself, reasoning that Tarkington obviously had a private physician, for if he didn't, Sol would have been called several

times during the morning to write admission orders, orders for lab tests, orders for medications, and diet orders. On the other hand, he felt for the internist already seeing Tarkington, a doctor who couldn't refuse the man care for fear of being tagged with an abandonment lawsuit. So, Mr. Tarkington did have an attending physician, and Sol raged at himself for having lost sleep over Anwar El Haq's toothless threats.

But Mr. Tarkington was not in the neurology unit, where seizures were treated, but on the internal medicine floor, under the care of Ivan Rascalovitch, M.D., Board Certified Doctor of Psychiatry. Ralph Tarkington, the chart note read, had not suffered a grand mal seizure at all, but an anxiety attack, only the latest of the six or so dozen such episodes for which he had been hospitalized over the past twenty years, since the explosion that had been the end of him. In fact, there was no record of a single witnessed seizure anywhere in Tarkington's hospital chart, only of psychiatric admissions, all for uncontrollable shaking and shortness of breath. The verdict had been anxiety attack for all but one admission, the time an intern had diagnosed malaria on the grounds of the mad shaking and the fact that the patient had served in Viet Nam. Each episode had resolved after he had been given two aspirins, though told the pills were double-strength Valium. Forte's grin broadened.

Mr. Tarkington's daughter, Judy Famot, was sitting by the bedside. She looked up and challenged brusquely, "I'm glad you're finally here. Did you read the file?"

"I went through as much as I could last night. It's going to take me quite a while to understand it fully." Sol wondered just how much time he would ever put into Mr. Tarkington now that found himself drifting toward the periphery of the man's care. "I thought I'd spend the weekend studying it," he added, glancing briefly at Ms. Famot's eyes.

She looked up at him and smiled sarcastically, "That all you have to do over a weekend?"

Forte's chest tightened. "Work, work, work. No rest for the weary, and the wicked don't need it."

"You don't look very wicked."

"Oh, I'm a bad boy. I just hide it well."

"Doctor," she spoke earnestly, the first time he had seen emotion in her face, "the lawyer said we need a good man to take my father's case. Otherwise, Argent's going to win, and they're going to take his house and savings."

"Ma'am, I'm not sure I understand. Your father did mention something about Argent suing *him*, but, to tell you the truth, I've never heard of such a thing, and I thought, well, maybe, he was a little confused."

"No, unfortunately, it's the truth. He hurt his neck in the original injury. Then, three years ago, it became so painful, some neurosurgeon operated on it, and COLA paid the bills, at first. That's because the surgeon told COLA that if there wasn't immediate surgery, my father might be paralyzed. He said something as simple as a fender-bender, or even if he hit a curb while parking, it could cut his spine. The COLA case manager was scared, and so were we, so he approved the surgery. Came to a hundred thousand dollars.

"A month later, Argent said they did an investigation and decided he hurt his neck *after* the accident, and they sued *us* to get the medical bills reimbursed. The neurosurgeon got on the stand and agreed with Argent, then that damn Rascalovitch, my father's so-called psychiatrist, did, too. Guy's a real fink, said my father was showing signs of malingering.

"The judge was mad at our lawyer for not doing a good job defending us, but he couldn't do anything about it, and we couldn't find anyone to file an appeal. Our lawyer screwed the whole thing up so bad. Argent tasted blood, so they sued us for their legal fees: two hundred thousand more. They won again."

Sol's jaw dropped. "That's three hundred thousand dollars. How can they collect? Your father was a lineman. He doesn't have that kind of money."

"Of course not, but they put a lien on the house, so the day we sell it, every penny goes to Argent. They're charging interest, too, so even if the house sold for three hundred thousand, and they got every penny, we would still owe them thousands of dollars. And that grows every day. It's a nightmare."

Sol asked, "If the case has already been determined, and you didn't do an appeal in like thirty days, it's too late, the way I understand it. Why do you have a lawyer now?"

"Our new lawyer said that if we can reopen my father's COLA case, that is, if we can show they made a mistake in denying the neck pain, the Commission on Labor Affairs will pay his bills. I don't understand all of it, but El Haq told me you have seven years from the day the claim is closed to reopen it. That's what our lawyer is trying to do. If we could find a good doctor who was on our side, someone who would study his records—that's why I asked you to—and find that he complained of neck problems starting on the day of the accident, and the pain kept on getting worse, we can reopen the claim. Then we can go to COLA court and force the state to accept the claim as legitimate. If we could do that, the findings of the civil court won't stand. Something like that. It's all there. It just needs to be told to the court. We can't do that. It has to be a doctor."

"Wow, you sound like you're on top of things. I'm impressed, but what about Rascalovitch, I mean Dr. Rascalovitch?"

"Like I said, he screwed us in court. He lied."

"What did he lie about?"

"He agreed with the surgeon that my father didn't hurt his neck in the accident, and that my father was crazy. Dr. Forte, it's all there in the chart. I've seen it. I can show you, but Rascalovitch didn't bother to look."

"Well, first, Rascalovitch has no right to comment on neck pain. He claims he's a shrink. And next, if there wasn't something very wrong with your father's neck, the surgeon wouldn't have operated on him, so we have to assume that there was actually a neck problem. If he complained of pain from the date of the injury, whether your father has psychiatric problems or not has nothing to do with the fact that he injured his neck. I am curious, though. Why do you still use Rascalovitch?"

"What else are we going to do? No other psychiatrist will see my father. At least he has to. If he quits, then he gets sued for abandoning his patient. Our lawyer told us that."

"Well, yes and no. He can send you a divorce letter that'll give you thirty days to find other care. Can't sue him then. And I've got to be honest with you. It may not be pleasant to keep using his services, but that may be the only way to protect your father medically."

"Another divorce letter. That'll be three in the last few months."

Mr. Tarkington, who had been drooling and staring out the window into the parking lot, apparently oblivious to the conversation, slowly and stiffly turned his head toward his daughter. "I don't want that Rascal-bitch. I want this one."

His head turned back toward the window, and Judy Famot smiled wanly at Forte, who patted Mr. Tarkington on the leg and stood. Sol took a doctorly deep breath, set his jaw, and said, "As much as I personally want to help you, I just don't feel qualified to take over your dad's care. I'm sorry."

⊶⊷

After lunching on a Mars Bar slipped off the tray of a deceased patient, Sol returned to his office at the Center to find a note taped to his door. Roxanne had scribbled, "See Dr. Rosebac re: McAlister drugs ASAP."

The older man was resting on the couch in his office, reading *Angela's Ashes*. "Come in, Sol. We need to quit meeting like this."

"A problem with one of my patients and pain meds?"

"You know how the transcriptionists downstairs are trained to alert us when something doesn't smell quite kosher?"

"Let *us* know, huh? Yes, I am aware of *Füher* Anacota's diktat.

"Good. Well, this McAlister of yours, he's been getting a lot of pain medication. What's your thinking on the matter?"

"Couldn't agree with you more, Dave, but I told him he's cut off as of today."

"You gave him more today?"

"Not really, but he had a story about his girlfriend who lost the prescription and…"

"What was his girlfriend doing with his prescription?"

"Well, there was this car accident, and it was in her purse, and the car was towed…"

"And the purse disappeared along with his pain meds. Sol, the guy's a drug seeker. Oldest fairy tale in the book. Get rid of him."

"Well, in fact, his story was true, Dave, though I want to get rid of him a lot more than you want me to get rid of him. I just don't know how. He may have a legitimate injury."

Rosebac folded his hands and offered calmly, "Simple. Just don't give him any more pain medication, not a single pill. If all he's after is narcotics, you'll never see him again. Just say no. Works every time."

"Okay, I'll give it a try, but you know how these drug-heads act. There's going to be a scene when I tell him he's cut off. Can't you just picture it? He'll be flipping everyone off in the hallway, and then he'll throw in a couple 'a 'fuck yous' just for emphasis as he flies through the full waiting room. I was trying to avoid that."

"You avoid that with prior planning, i.e., not letting these guys get into the system in the first place. I'm not chastising you. You just need a little more suspicion. Remember, I know I've said this before, most, maybe all COLA patients, certainly the ones who keep showing up wanting something from you, usually want *something* from you. Not saying they're bad people, but it's never only treatment for the medical problem. Sometimes it's drugs, sometimes it's pay for time loss, or it can be as simple as one letter after another to insurance companies so they can collect on disability policies or miss their next car payment. There's always something. I hate to be so cynical about my fellow man, but there is no such thing as a benign COLA, I mean a guy floats in, takes his two aspirins, and floats out. No such thing my friend, so be alert. Save you a lot of agony in the future."

"The whole thing makes no sense, Dave. It's beyond me how a man can live on what the state gives 'em for time loss. First few days aren't even reimbursed; it takes weeks and weeks before the first check gets mailed out, and then they only get two-thirds of their normal pay. These guys are usually close to minimum wage to start with, most of them. They don't have sufficient savings to live on waiting for that first check.

"It's hard to argue that workers don't deserve that insurance. Lot of 'em lost their lives fighting to make the workplace safer. My father was a union man. You know that, but you should see the way he was treated right after his union got a new contract and they were years away from the next strike. Bosses rode free for a while. Safety went out the window. You could plan on hearing once a month about one of my uncles' or my pop's friends losing a hand or an eye.

"The way my father saw it," Sol went on stiffly, "the only way to protect the worker was to have the employer pay when someone got hurt, and then raise the employer's rates each time it happened until the message got across. Sad but true. Nothing else works like a bite out of the wallet."

Rosebac shook his head. "I know your take on the world, Solly, but I'm afraid you're in the grand minority when it comes to how your colleagues see things. And, in answer to how a man can live on what he gets from COLA time loss, think about if you go out and get another job in the meantime for five or six bucks an hour. Add that to the time loss pay from the state, and that's ten or twelve bucks total an hour for as long as you can get away with it. Not terrible for flipping burgers," Rosebac shrugged.

Sol smiled. "Well, not to worry about McAlister. That clown is officially cut off, and we'll see if he takes the hint. Also, going to send him back to work. His employer said they'll find something for him to do—sweep floors or sort nuts and bolts."

"Good. The longer a guy like that duns you for time loss, the less chance he'll ever go back to work. By the way, how are we doing with that lawyer and his electrocuted guy? What was it, Pilkington?"

"Tarkington, and his family wants me to take over as his primary care provider, his PCP."

"Do you think that's wise?"

"I didn't do it. Just telling you that's what they asked. I may be dull normal, but that's still a few points above schmuck."

"Good thinking. You can't save the world, Solly. The secret to getting along as a doctor is knowing your limitations. Why would you want to be his doctor anyway? I thought I heard your Roxanne say something about Rascalovitch seeing him for a lot of years. Rascalovitch isn't a primary care provider, so he's had to get a million consults on the guy. Looks like the patient's already got a bunch of people who know him well. System's in place. He's cared for just fine. Keep your nose out of it. Let Rascalovitch handle it."

"Tarkington and his family hate him."

"So does everyone else in town. Everything about this guy sounds like a pile of quicksand, and that's being polite."

"You mean Rascalovitch?"

"No, your patient. You want some free medical advice?"

"Shoot."

"Get out of it as soon as you can. Just don't make any mistakes on the way."

CHAPTER FIVE

Forte brooded over Rosebac's admonition as he headed toward Room Three to start the afternoon. He tried to ignore the growling in his bowels that deepened as he pulled the chart from the rack outside the room and stood reading the nurse's note. Roxanne's scribbling spoke of a thirty-two-year-old man who had slipped on oil at work and landed on his outstretched right hand. Roxanne had already taken x-rays of the man's wrist, and the films were sitting in the rack as well. Sol flipped them onto the hallway light box and made a very brief perusal, satisfying himself that there was no bony damage. He hissed to himself, "Let's see what this one wants." He opened the door without knocking.

A large black man sat quietly on the exam table holding his right wrist defensively. Sol spoke first. "Mr. Porcher, how did you hurt yourself?"

"It's 'Porchayyy'. And I already told your nurse."

"Sorry. I just need to hear it for the record."

"I slipped on oil," he spat angrily.

"Well, sir," Forte tightened, Rosebac's words jabbing sharply at both his mind and his heart, "I've looked at your x-rays, and I don't see any broken bones."

"Then how come it hurts so bad? Answer me that."

"Soft tissue damage. A contusion can be very uncomfortable."

"A what?"

"We'll put you in a brace, have you ice it, and get you back to work."

"I can't work like this. Damn thing hurts too much."

"Well, I'm sorry. Nothing's broken. I'll put you on light duty for a couple of days."

Porcher snapped, "Ain't got no light duty on my job. You work, or you stay home."

Forte whispered to himself as he stood to leave the room to get a brace, "You work at Sunset Aviation with a guy named McAlister?"

As the door opened, Porcher called after him, "Ain't you even gonna look at the damn thing?"

"Soon as I come back."

"Man, where the hell you goin'? This thing's killing me. What'cha gonna give me for pain?"

"Ah ha," Forte whispered, "That didn't take long," and then aloud, "When I come back, Mr. Porcher."

Sol was facing away from his patient, and felt safe in letting his eyes roll like he had seen Rosebac's teenaged daughter's flutter days before at the Center picnic. And Sol's eyes were still gyrating when he bumped into Rosebac, who was standing in the hall looking at Porcher's x-ray on the wall box.

Rosebac glanced at Forte and laughed. "You look like my daughter. Nice pick-up. That's a subtle scaphoid fracture. They're hard to see. Lot of doctors miss them. We'll make a real doctor out of you yet."

Forte peered at the film and noticed a grease pencil circle casually, sloppily, drawn around the scaphoid bone right under the thumb. Before he could comment, Roxanne strutted to the light box, twirling a grease pencil in her hand. She hovered around the two doctors, though behind Rosebac, her chin resting between her thumb and index finger mocking him. Forte turned and noticed her arrogant grin and up-rolling eyes. He snorted, "You look like Dr. Rosebac's daughter."

"I do? Thank you, Dr. Forte, that's a compliment."

Sol's smile degenerated into an embarrassed grin as he marched back into Room Three. "Mr. Porcher, let me examine you. You know, you were hurting so bad, I took another look at your films, and there may be something wrong on the x-ray."

"May be?"

Sol pushed on the little indentation south of the thumb, on the back of the hand, where the wrist ends and the hand begins. It was exquisitely tender, and Porcher howled in pain, pulled his wrist back, and doubled over, nearly in tears.

"Sorry, didn't mean to hurt you, but it's the only way we have of really finding out what's going on."

"It's okay, man."

"You do have a broken bone there. I'm afraid you're going to have to be in a cast for twelve weeks. This is a bad fracture."

"Fracture, I thought you said it was just broke."

"Fracture is what doctors call a break. They're the same thing. This is a bad one though; six weeks in a long arm cast from your shoulder to your fingers, then six in a short arm cast, from your elbow to your fingers. Then, we just hope the thing heals."

"What if it don't?"

"Surgery, and twelve more weeks in casts."

"How am I supposed to work like this?"

"You can't. You're probably off for four or five months."

"What the hell you talkin' 'bout? One minute you tell me to go back to work today, and now you say six months? Look man,

I can't afford that. I got kids and a wife. What the hell am I supposed to do?"

"Some employers make up the difference between what COLA gives you and your full salary."

"No way, man. My boss hates me. He ain't givin' me shit."

"You can ask."

"No, I can't. Told ya, he hates my guts."

"Why?"

"Man, you ever been black? Construction company? They gotta hire you, or they don't get no government contracts. But they make it ugly. You quit, no sweat off their ass. Be a month or more before the government take another look at you. I'm the only black face in a sea of white."

"I'll give him a call. See what I can do."

"No! Don't be doin' that shit. I'll lose my job. And I ain't no gotdamn child. Won't never get rehired you stick your nose in my business. Just put on the cast and gimme the papers. I can take care of my own ass."

"Okay, but the offer stands. We only put on a splint today to give room for the wrist to swell, supply you with enough pain medicine to keep you comfortable, then see you back in five days for a full cast. Any questions?"

The patient shook his head slowly and angrily as he turned away from Forte, who had moved quickly through the door to summon Roxanne. "Long arm splint for Mr. Porcher, and let's give him twenty-four Vicodins, Dr. El Haq."

She answered quickly, "Not so fast, hospital's calling. They want amended orders on Mr. Tarkington."

"Tell 'em to ask Rascalovitch."

"I did. They said Rascalovitch said you were his doctor now, and that he was no longer involved."

Forte looked at his watch. "That's a record. I never agreed to take over his care." He was about to order Roxanne to tell the hospital that, but from the look on her face, he knew better than to put her in the middle of the war between the Hospital and the Clinic, the two arms of the Galena Hills Medical Corporation that had spent the past eighty years at each other's throats. "Okay, let me take a quick look at Tarkington's chart notes. I'll discharge him on the same orders Rascalovitch did last time. Give me three minutes. We'll get it all straightened out later."

"Three minutes only. You've got a bunch of new patients to see. One's from Rosebac. He says he won't see the guy 'cause he got hurt on the job, and that's why they keep you around here. Dr. F., we're already behind, so make it quick."

Lagging or not, Sol felt an uncomfortable stirring in his chest. He stopped in mid-stride and concentrated very hard, seeking to ferret out the source of his restlessness. Was it that Rosebac felt he could simply dump undesirables on Sol's schedule at his whim? Was Sol that insignificant, considered that vacuous, that subordinate? Maybe that was part of it, but there was more, and it struck him abruptly—Solomon Forte had fallen victim to the roller skate model of medical care. He had just failed a patient miserably. All he had done was order three dollars of plaster and a few pain pills for a man who was about to descend from solid working class into a flirt with homelessness. Sol's legs weakened and became shaky as he questioned if that was how he would have wanted his pop treated. Was this the fruit of twenty years of schooling?

He ducked back into Porcher's room, closed the door, and sat down, crossing his legs, though leaning forward. "Mr. Porcher, look. I'm sorry you hurt yourself. But, sir, shit happens to every one of us sometime in our lives. *Everybody* goes through it. It's just part of the ride. I'm sorry, sir."

Sol perceived Porcher's face relaxing a bit and took the opportunity to go on. "But I can tell you one thing I've learned after fifteen years of this work. And I'm serious. Every time something like this happens, something better comes along. *Every time.* I can tell you're a hardworking, no nonsense, family man. But somehow, you'll make it for the next few weeks, and then, if your arm is still a problem, we'll get you retrained. I'll see to it. Your life'll be better for what happened today. I've seen it a thousand times."

Porcher looked up. "Doc, you read my mind. But screw COLA. I still got my GI Bill from the Marines. I was a A&P on choppers in Desert Storm."

Sol appeared confused, and Porcher explained. "That's aircraft and power plant mechanic. I miss it. I was good, Doc; made E-6 in four years. Nobody does that. Not in the Marines. But when I got back, I got married, had a kid, then another. No time for school. So, now I'm stuck."

"No, you're not stuck. You're a good man. We can get started on the retraining paperwork right away. I've never done that on the first visit before, but why not? Like I said, Mr. Porcher, you need other letters, anything, you let me know. Work with me on this one. I'll make sure you don't get screwed. See ya in five days."

Sol started toward the next exam room, but Roxanne coughed, "Ah, Tarkington."

Forte nodded and went to his office. He rifled through the nearly three thousand pages of doctor visits and court proceedings that chronicled the twenty-year saga of Ralph Tarkington. Sensing the pall of angry patients hovering over him, Sol did not sit. He stood bent over his desk, searching the pile quickly for the most recent hospital discharge note. The papers, though, were not in any particular order; some were backwards, many upsides down; others were stained with coffee, and some with what he hoped was dried ketchup. His eye caught several particularly faded sheets dated from the early eighties gummed between pages of the most recent file. It was an emergency room intake note describing the accident as provided by a witness. He pulled the papers apart as well as he could and perused the first. Though the handwriting on the witness's account was barely legible, Forte was able to piece together the events of that day.

Mr. Tarkington had been a long-time employee at Argent Public Utilities, working up from oil changer in the motor pool to lineman on the trucks that repaired cables toppled by trees and wind. The episode on the day of injury began when a teenager racing in a Chevy pickup slammed into a utility pole. The kid died at the scene, and the police cordoned off the road. When they removed the barriers, Argent Public Utilities set up to restore a fair swathe of the county that had been without power for hours. Tarkington was first up the cherry picker to inspect the damaged wires on the badly leaning pole. A drunk rubbernecker nicked the bumper on the utility truck. Tarkington's cage shot backward, and he was thrown over the cherry picker's railing into the air. As he grabbed wildly to hold on, his hand closed around a cable on the dead side of the transmission line. It wasn't dead, though. There were home generators working, feeding power into the line in reverse. As he fell, he reached frantically for a wire, and though his hand was gloved, it wrapped around his unprotected wrist and forearm. There were sparks, according to the witness, and it wasn't clear if Tarkington had lost consciousness due to the electrical shock, or when his head slammed onto the road.

On the ground, it appeared he was dead, and little was done to help him other than dousing his smoking body with a bucket of water. Mr. Tarkington, however, suddenly regained consciousness when some of the water splashed on his face. He stood and babbled that he was deaf. He smelled so of burned flesh, most of the workers refused to go near him, and it fell to the supervisor to drive him back to APU's headquarters. He was taken to the in-house nursing station, where all injured employees were required to report before the decision was made to let them open an industrial accident claim and see a real doctor.

The next note was in the hand of an emergency room intake nurse at Whitaker General who recorded the arrival of Mr. Tarkington, not by ambulance, she noted in bold letters, but in the back seat of his own car, driven from the Argent main office by a coworker. She noted that the patient sat by himself in the waiting room. His supervisor, the plant nurse, and the co-worker who had witnessed the accident sat across the room. She also wrote in stout letters that the nurse and supervisor had arrived at the ER in a separate vehicle.

Farther down the chart note, the emergency room nurse mentioned that she was directed to speak first with the Argent supervisor and the Argent nurse, both of whom assured her the injury was trivial, and that there was no need to check Mr. Tarkington into the emergency room and initiate a messy COLA claim. They asked only that a quick test of the patient's vital signs be accomplished, just to confirm that the worker had been seen at the hospital. The supervisor half-winked, "You know, for legal purposes. Everybody with a hangnail wants to sue these days. Just makes your electric rates go up. You don't want that. Nobody does."

The ER nurse agreed to take Mr. Tarkington's vital signs in the waiting room as a courtesy to the nurse and one of the county's largest employers. But with a blood pressure of 192/132, a pulse rate of 116, a respiration rate of 40 per minute, electrical burns of the wrist and forearm, and facial burns capped by singed eyebrows, she had the orderlies place her new patient on a gurney, which she personally wheeled into the treatment room. When she started an IV, the corporate grousing escalated, and soon became so scathing, she put in a stat call for the emergency room doctor. There was a memo in large, printed letters on the top of her nursing note that it took over fifteen minutes for the man to arrive as he was at lunch in the hospital cafeteria with his pager turned off.

Forte, having dropped unwittingly into the desk chair, shuffled through the utterly disheveled record, choosing the oldest notes, based on the extent of browning of the paper. He relaxed, drawing out of the pile several sheets as deeply sepia as the emergency room records. He started to read a chart note from the next doctor to see Mr. Tarkington, but there was a sharp rapping at his door.

"You said three minutes. It's been fifteen. You know, if 'cause of this I don't get my break, I'm going to take it anyway." She banged twice on the door as if one of El Haq's hostile judges and stormed back to her station. By the time Forte jumped from his desk, Roxanne was holding the phone out toward him. "Hospital again—nursing supervisor. Probably made her call because you weren't responding to their request for orders. And don't get too cozy on the phone. You've got two new COLA back pains and a COLA groin pain: some guy says he got a hernia playing basketball on lunch break."

Forte backed into his office, but dared not take a seat. He picked up the phone and, before the nurse on the other end could speak, Sol barked, "Good afternoon. This is Dr. Forte. Okay, let's give him a normal diet, a sleeper only if he needs it, and continue his present meds. Okay? By the way, is his daughter, I think it's Judy Famot, there?"

"No, doctor."

"Well, I need to talk to the family. Tell Mr. Tarkington I'll be over after clinic hours. Try to keep him oriented. Keep asking him what year it is, where he is, tell him he's in a hospital not a hotel, ask him who's the president, stuff like that. If the family thinks he's not oriented, they'll refuse to take him home…and we don't want that, now, do we? And…"

As Forte took a breath, the nurse offered calmly, "Doctor, may I please say something?" Without waiting for an answer, she added, "Your patient just signed out AMA."

"Why didn't you tell me?" The nurse gasped. "Never mind, my fault," he beamed into the phone. "Glory be to God, all my patients sign out AMA."

The nursing supervisor snorted, "So I've heard."

Forte's shoulders relaxed with the weight of Tarkington lifted. He created a divorce letter in his mind, one he would dictate within the hour and send down to transcription as a priority. No jury, especially one being ministered to by the likes of El Haq, would have grounds to hold him responsible for refusing to take over the care of a man who had walked out of the hospital while legions of medical professionals begged him to stay. Sol could picture the platoon of nurses, doctors, and administrators pleading, seeking to reason with the unreasonable patient, cajoling, and finally warning he would probably die if he walked out. Of course, the full court press was not because the players believed in impending mortal danger; it was because the players believed the hospital's malpractice insurance carrier, who had beaten into them the legal theory of safety in numbers. Eight reasonable health professionals sign a document that they begged a wayward patient to stay, and he leaves? And his caring daughter drives him away in a fancy new four by four. No jury is going to hold the hospital responsible. It was a homerun for the team.

The "hernia" from a basketball game at work, during lunch, turned out to be swollen glands in the groin from herpes genitalia. Sol sent him to a urologist for treatment and referred the first of the afternoon's new COLA low back pain patients to a general surgeon for a hernia repair. Both had come and gone so quickly, Sol had a moment to slip into his office and catch up on charts. He snuck around the back hallway to avoid Roxanne, but as soon as he stepped into the office, the pile of papers, the disheveled remnants of Ralph Tarkington's soul, set his innards roiling. He froze. In seconds, Roxanne was at the door tapping her pencil.

"Hey, Dr. F, you don't have time to be standing around with your thumb up…"

"Hang on just a sec, Roxy. Let me jam all this stuff back in the box. Let's get the mailroom to ship the whole thing back to the El Haq. Glory be to God."

"I'll take care of it. Meanwhile, you've got two calls. One from our new friend Dana. She sounds a little put out, kinda *really* wants to talk to you."

"Roxanne, tell her I'm with patients."

"Yeah, well, she said you left something at her place."

"She did not say that!"

"Well, she asked if you needed your dictating machine. I told her you had a spare."

As the crimson flowed into his face, Roxanne shook her head as if a miffed mother then droned, "And the other call is from a Judy Famahttt or something; says she's Mr. Tarkington's daughter."

"It's not Famahttt, it's Famohhhh. I'll take that one. Tell Dana I'll get right back to her. Work first. And I won't need any listening in on this one. She's honest."

"Uh huh."

"Ms. Famot, good afternoon. How can I help you?"

Forte listened before speaking gently. "I know that Dr. Rascalovitch resigned from your father's care but, apparently, he got the mistaken word from someone that I had taken over. You and I both know that I did not agree to become your father's primary care doctor. I think there's been a simple misunderstanding."

She spoke again, and Sol answered, but when she added a final comment, Forte was quiet for a moment. He thought some more and, finally, took a deep breath and nodded his head. "I guess your dad has a new doctor. Why don't you come in tomorrow morning at nine. We can get started then."

Roxanne appeared at his door. Forte asked over his shoulder, "Are you here to torment me?"

"Only if you don't get going and start seeing patients. Were behind, duh."

"Okay, okay. And put Mr. Tarkington on for tomorrow at nine. Let's give him twenty minutes."

"Are you serious? He *is* going to be our patient?"

"Yep. You got a problem with that?"

"No, but you will. How did this happen? I thought you refused to take on his care."

"Something happened."

"What?"

"She said something."

"What'd she say?"

"She asked me if my father was alive. I told her he died ten years ago. Then she asked if I was happy with the way he was treated at the end. No, I was pissed, but what could I do? Those doctors didn't give a rip about him, just some tired, old, blue-collar fart with dirt and concrete caked under his nails. Easier for them once he died—just a pain in their collective asses. He was nothing in this world to them. They were only getting Medicare payments. Not worth the effort. My pop, a pain in some doctor's ass. Yeah, I was pissed. Then she asked me, 'So what would you do if it was your father?'"

Roxanne nodded and added softly, "Dr. Forte, you're an okay guy. I'll put him on for tomorrow morning, but we need to get moving."

It was not until nearly seven that evening that Forte finished dictating his charts. He called Dana. "Hey, I'm sorry. Been a tough day.

I really enjoyed last night. It was great, but I gotta work tonight." Before she could answer, he added, "Remember I told you about that guy who was electrocuted on the job? Turns out, he really was. In the hospital with seizures last night. His family's a real pain. I won't get out of here for a million hours. Hey, I'll call you in a day or so."

At home, Sol unstuffed reams of Tarkington's records from the cardboard box, dropping several pounds of notes on the little round table in his kitchen-living room-bedroom, and the rest on the floor. He was only half-done sorting the chart by date when Jay Leno finished his monologue. Sol took three steps from the table and lay back on his bed, promising to let his eyes close for only ten minutes, but his next conscious thought was the blare of the phone at three- thirty. It was an emergency room nurse from the Galena Hills Hospital. She announced nervously that she was brand new, but had been assigned to care for Kevin McAlister.

Forte listened quietly as the nurse encapsulated McAlister's chief complaint: low back pain that had deepened to the point that he needed narcotic medication stronger than Vicodin. "And he says he's not leaving the hospital until his pain is gone."

Forte shook his head. "Man, is that guy FOS or what?"

"I'm sorry, doctor. He didn't say anything about fos."

"No, that means full of shit, nurse. He's one of the best I've ever seen. Tell him no pain meds. If he's hurting that bad, have him come in to see me at nine."

"Doctor, we've been trying to get him to leave for the past two hours. He refuses to leave. What do you want us to do?"

"Okay. Give him a shot of Torodol and tell him it's Demerol. Send him on his way. I'll take care of it in the morning. And, by the way, this is a good learning experience. As you go on in nursing, you'll be able to spot the drug seekers much more easily. Give me a call if there's a problem."

Sol was unable to fall back to sleep, unable to rid his mind of the vision of Messrs. Tarkington and Mr. McAlister arriving in tandem at nine, and soon thereafter the ingress of the usual potpourri of the ill and maimed. He made a cup of coffee, cursed its bitterness, and then himself for having forgotten to buy milk and even sugar. He thought that just twenty-four hours before, he had been at Dana's, and that she had draped her arms around him as she served freshly ground coffee lightened with sweetened condensed milk. His hand reached out to call her but stopped short, scolding himself for getting too close.

He crept to his desk and began shuffling through the rest of Tarkington's papers. The last sheet was slipped into his now-chronological pile as a first few rays of sun lit the mountains. With the orange glow in his tiny living room, Sol sat back and started reading. The third note in the mound was dated four days after the explosion. It was a letter from an ophthalmologist, a retinal specialist, in Whitaker to whom Mr. Tarkington had been sent by a general ophthalmologist. It was for another opinion regarding his continuing claim of blindness in the left eye. The specialist from Whitaker was brief, concluding that Mr. Tarkington was malingering, faking, cheating the system, or at best hypochondriacal, for there was no evidence, other than the patient's claims, that a loss of vision had occurred.

Upon physical exam, the consultant chronicled, "I see no evidence of trauma—mechanical, chemical, or thermal—to the head, neck, or any other exposed structure of the claimant's body. In conclusion, there are simply no signs of injury to account for

Mr. Tarkington's assertion of electric shock and ensuing blindness." The specialist recommended a psychiatric evaluation.

Forte was confused. The first real health care worker to see Mr. Tarkington on the day of the explosion was the emergency room intake nurse. She had no dog in the fight, and clearly recorded the presence of flash burns about her patient's face, as well as a complete absence of eyebrows due to singing. The ER nurse also chronicled second and third degree burns of the left arm directly above the wrist. There was no medical possibility that those facial and arm lesions could have resolved in four days. Sol reread the Whitaker ophthalmologist's notes, and began to wonder if the consultant had even examined Mr. Tarkington, or perhaps just made his diagnosis from afar, not wishing to sully his hands on so rumpled a mendicant.

Forte shuffled through the next dozen sheets. He went back to day one, but could not find notes from the emergency room doctor. He dug further. Where were the hospital records from physicians and floor nurses where Tarkington had surely been admitted for observation? The early '80s were long before medical insurance companies refused hospital admission for sick patients, before the ill were sent straight home to be cared for by untrained family members. Where was the record of the original ophthalmologist who saw him and requested the consult from the sub-specialist in Whitaker? Sol shook his head to clear the cobwebs. In his exhaustion the night before, he guessed he had misfiled those records, but after an hour of digging, he exhumed not one sheet of missing evidence.

Stymied, he rested his eyes for a few moments, brewed another cup of awful coffee, and another. He went back to the monumental stack of memoranda, dredging up a single, hand-scrawled note from the family doctor to whom Mr. Tarkington had presented the day after the accident. It was illegible.

The next record was dated nearly two months after the accident. It was from a psychiatrist, another consultant, who was writing to yet another doctor, a local family physician, Brian Lippard. Though Sol dug through the pile again, he found no letter from Lippard requesting help from a shrink.

The psychiatrist described the patient as walking stooped forward, complaining of pain from his head to his toes, and grousing bitterly about his inability to see through the left eye. The psychiatrist concluded his observations by noting that Mr. Tarkington spoke in a disconnected, infantile speech pattern.

Though he did not offer an erudite diagnosis, he did treat Mr. Tarkington with Haldol, a powerful anti-psychotic often used to calm schizophrenics, and Sinequan, another potent medicine used in former days for psychotic, neurotic patients, particularly those suffering from severe depression. A strong sleeping pill was thrown in, though the dose was one hundred milligrams QHS, at the hours of sleep, a good ten times greater than the proper dose. Sol grimaced—just your garden-variety, potentially lethal, hastily miswritten prescription.

Forte took from the psychiatrist's remarks that the diagnosis was an undefined psychosis, though the doctor did not opine on how the original injury might have medically produced that state of mind. To make things more problematic for Mr. Tarkington, the psychiatrist stated in his notes that there was no evidence of physical injury.

"Interesting," Sol quipped to himself, "since when do psychiatrists do physical examinations?" And the man failed to mention he was seeing the patient a good two months after the incident, easily enough time for the obvious, second degree burns on his face and hands to have healed, and even for the man to have grown new eyebrows.

The bottom line was that a mental health specialist had labeled Ralph Tarkington psychotic. Forte reviewed in his mind the implications of such a diagnosis. He knew well that the instant there was a trace of mental ailment, even the slightest reference to lunacy, particularly back in the early 1980s, the red flags were hoisted at the Commission on Labor Affairs. With that diagnosis, the case manager simply cited the state legal code that mental illness could not be the *basis* of an industrial claim, and started the process to dismiss the matter. While the Commission might accept *depression* as a result of the loss of one's job and the resulting financial pressures, and they might even cover a short period of counseling and medication, they were not going to pay to treat a worker who had never been injured in the first place.

It followed that if the Commission ruled the accident a fabrication, Argent was off the hook, and the COLA claims manager could terminate the matter forthwith. She would no longer have to deal with the relentless, threatening calls from Argent's legal department, ones far more intimidating than the occasional message from Dr. Brian Lippard's medical assistant. The way the claims manager spun it, it was a win-win-win proposition: everyone was a victor, even the patient, who could now, with the diagnosis of severe mental disease, be inscribed on the social security rolls.

At nine that morning, Judy Famot arrived at Forte's office. Her father was not with her. She sat across from the doctor, staring down at the desk. A hand slid across her face to rid her eyes of still-moist mascara. Sol asked uneasily, "Ms. Famot, are you okay?"

"Just another great day trying to care for my father. I'm fine. Thank you for seeing me, and please, call me Judy."

Sol paused for a moment. "Did you know there are numerous missing chart notes and referral letters? I've been through everything you gave me, and I can't find half of what I need to make sense of what happened to your father. I have to ask, where did you get his file?"

"From the lawyers for Argent, when they sued my father."

"Why would *they* give *you* the chart? They're the enemy."

"I know, but when we went to trial, our lawyer didn't have the file, and COLA didn't have it, either. Our old lawyer had thrown all of it away, then our next lawyer asked Argent to make a copy of their records. At first, they wouldn't do it, but I guess some judge said they had to."

"Are you sure there aren't any other sheets?"

Judy's face hardened, looking again as she had the day Sol first met her. "I don't think so. I gave you everything that lawyer gave us when he quit the case. He charged us a couple of hundred dollars for the records. They better all be there."

"How about this Dr. Lippard? Where is he? He's not in the phone book. I looked."

"He's not a doctor anymore. I think he lied or something; also, something about he was drinking and having an affair with a patient. He got kicked out. We got a card from the doctor society telling us we had to find another doctor."

"Do you know where his charts are?"

"We tried to get them, but the doctor society said you only have to keep medical records for seven years, and that was twelve or thirteen years ago. Everything was lost, at least that's what they told us."

"Maybe COLA has copies."

"We tried them, too; the records are gone. My father's first claims manager committed suicide, and when they looked through his records, they found that he didn't keep any. We wanted to sue them, but the DA said they were a government agency, and we couldn't."

"Then I'll call Mr. El Haq. He can subpoena them from somebody. In the meantime, let me ask you a few questions." He paused and looked her in the eyes. "First, and I don't mean to be rude, but was your dad like this before the accident?"

Judy Famot stiffened and breathed deeply. "My father was a hardworking man before the explosion."

"Yes, but did he do okay, let's say in school?"

"He didn't finish high school, if that's what you mean. My grandmother says he had to work to support her. He wasn't in trouble with the police or nothing like that."

"Was he ever in the army?"

"Navy. He was in Viet Nam."

"They must have medical records. Was he in combat? Was he wounded?"

"Yes, but not in combat. He was on an aircraft carrier. He worked on the airplanes, a crew chief or something. He got hit by a wing on the boat when a plane got out of control on landing. Something about the plane getting shot up over Haney or something, crashing on the ship. He didn't talk about it much, but he was in the hospital for six months after that. Got a Purple Heart, too."

"Crew chief? That's a big job for a man who didn't get a high school degree."

"Oh, he got a diploma from the Navy, GED, just a few months after joining. Then he took college courses. Got a degree from a junior college the Navy paid for. He was promoted to an E-7, whatever that is, but he was very proud of it; he said it was really high. The second time he went there, they put him in charge of the guys that fixed the jets. He had all the pictures with his men aboard ship when he went back to Viet Nam, but they were all lost in a fire on the boat. He was a whiz with his hands. Always inventing a better way to do something. My father was not a stupid man. Not then."

"Not until the explosion that was the end of him." Forte looked quickly at Ms. Famot to see if his verbal liberty had harvested the signs of emotion he wished it had, and also hoped it hadn't.

But a tiny smile curled at the angles of her lips, and she shook her head almost invisibly. She asked gently, "Dr. Forte, what do you think we should do?"

"You're a good lady. Smart, too. Let me be honest. I cannot bring your father back to normal. Please understand that. I'm not a specialist, and even if I was, there is no such thing as a cure for the damage your father has suffered. Obviously, your father had a lot on the ball before the accident. As far as I can see, the only thing that happened in between being on top of things and now was the accident. So, it isn't rocket science to figure that the accident is why he has a problem. Someone needs to help him get the care he needs, not to cure him, but to make his life tolerable. My father was in the Marines in Korea. He would want me to help your dad. If your attorney needs help, I'll do it. That's what I can do for you and your father."

Ms. Famot stirred slightly. Forte knew she wanted to go. He nodded. "Okay, I'll call El Haq. See what records he has. I'll let you know as soon as I hear anything." He stood and tapped her gently on the shoulder with a folder from her father's chart.

She smiled, and as she started out the door, she turned back, letting her eyes rest on his for longer than had to be. She spoke softly. "You are a kind man. Thank you."

Forte nodded, straightened, and turned away, envisioning the State Medical Abuse Commission meeting to suspend his license for unprofessional relations with a patient. But the confusion about just how SMAC defined as a patient approached a roil, just as it had so many times over the years. He walked musingly toward his office, lost in images of the council of doctors disapprovingly glaring down at him as the chairman read the decision to suspend him, but allow him back in three years with the caveat that a chaperone be present when ministering to female patients. Nonetheless, Forte could not help himself, and turned around for a last glimpse. Judy Famot was talking with Roxanne, though the woman's eyes were on Forte until he looked into them. She quickly turned away and hurried around the corner toward the front desk.

Roxanne returned to her desk, grumbling until Forte stepped out of his office. "What's wrong with you?"

"Stay away from that woman, Dr. Forte. She's a painted lady. Wears cheap perfume. You listen to me."

"What are you talking about?"

"You know damn well what I'm talking about. She was telling me that you're going to call her. You're the 'kindest man.' Snot, snot."

"Roxworth, Jeese man, calm down. She's a patient. I don't control her mind."

"And just don't forget it, that she's a patient. In the meantime, our Mr. McAlister is at the ER again. Pain's worse. He says that shot didn't do any good. You told him to come in at eight, but he said he hurt too bad and went back to the emergency room. They're on the line."

"Okay, tell 'em to give 'em Demerol, fifty; Phenergan, fifty; and let's have an MRI done on his back; blood draw for everything—infection, arthritis—cover the bases. And have him come in tomorrow morning. If there's something on his MR or in his blood, good, I'll send him for a consult. But if it's all clean, then it's straight to the pain clinic." He paused for a moment, and when he resumed, his speech was slower, distant. "I don't want to wait on this guy, he's driving me craz…"

Sol became silent, and his eyes drifted to the ceiling. Roxanne poked her head around him and spoke softly. "You okay, Dr. Forte?"

"You know, Rox, all of a sudden, I had a sick thought. This cat's not your usual drug seeker, is he? He's way too persistent.

Most of these guys just wouldn't refuse to leave an ER. No way. They follow the script to the letter. Totally predictable. You don't give 'em what they want, you get the finger, and then there's the explosion of 'Fuck yous.' I don't know. It's almost as if he really *is* in pain, as hard as that is to believe. No, something's going on. I'm beginning to smell a rat." He paused again and smiled, "Nah. I'm nuts, imagining things. Anyway, he's out of our hair for the next twenty-four hours, and that spells relief."

"Yep, you look relieved. But don't be. Guess who's waitin' for ya in Three?"

"Be gentle."

"Just Mrs. Sánchez. Maybe you can send her for an MRI and a consult, and then you can have double relief."

Sol closed his eyes and mumbled, "She's out of the psych ward? That last admission must've been a record. She was barely in the computer before she grabbed her stuff and booked. Maybe she didn't like her psych tech."

Mrs. Sánchez was bundled in an oil-stained, nylon parka zippered to the neck. A middle-aged woman sat quietly with her. Forte introduced himself, walked to Lupe, patted her shoulder, and asked, "Feelin' better? You really look great. Much better than last time."

Lupe blushed and whispered a sentence in Spanish to the older woman, who turned to Forte and smiled, "Lupe is very sorry for the trouble. She thinks you don't believe her, I mean, you doctors don't believe that she is in terrible pain all the time."

"Oh, I believe her. I just can't find out what's wrong, but…and you are? From the state?"

"Yes. I'll be driving Lupe to appointments and taking care of her paperwork, and filling her prescriptions, and…" she handed Forte a pink business card with raised purple letters,

"…and making sure you people are doing everything you're supposed to."

Forte glanced at the card:

RUTH GOLDSTEIN-MIRANDA
PROFESSIONAL HISPANIC INTERPRETIVE,
LEGAL, MEDICAL, FINANCIAL, AND
TRAVEL SERVICES

Forte muttered "Sweet deal, how do I get in on it?" but added quickly, "I've done what I can medically for Mrs. Sánchez. Her situation is called chronic pain syndrome. It's been a year since she hurt herself. If there was really anything seriously wrong, it would have declared itself by now, I mean gotten worse or better. We would have seen *something* on the MRI, the two myelograms, and the electrical studies to explain the weakness on the left side of her body, but nothing's shown up at all."

"Are you saying it's all in her head?"

"No, not really."

"If it is, I have to know, because the state's not going to pay, and I need to look for another client."

"Well, she has a real disease, and it was caused when she fell in the bathroom at work, sort of. Do you want to hear this?"

"Go ahead," she droned.

"Well, I think it's important you understand what's going on with Lupe. After being in pain for a year, the disease is in the nerves; the pain *is* the disease."

The interpreter sat glassy eyed, so Sol took in a deep breath and went on. "I mean, at first, it *was* torn muscles and sprained ligaments causing the pain. But after a few months of pain, the nerves that carry the pain impulses to the brain sort of got in the habit of working overtime. You know, like a muscle grows and gets used to doing things, 'muscle memory,' when you use it all the time. Same thing. And her pain nerves got so used to working around the clock, they can't stop. All they need is the slightest stimulation to turn them on. The system's become so bad-tempered, anything that touches her, even as light as her clothes, can pull the trigger, the nerves fire, and a pain message gets sent up the spinal cord into the brain. Brain can't tell the difference between light touch and painful touch anymore. Once the switch is thrown, all the brain knows is that it's those same nerves firing that for her whole life before the accident signaled pain. The brain doesn't know, or care, that the nerves are firing for no reason at all. See, the pain *is* the disease, like I said. The whole thing stinks."

"Then it *is* in her head. I need to know."

"Calm down Mrs. Goldstein-Miranda."

"That's Ms. Goldstein-Miranda."

"Sorry. State isn't just going to drop her. I won't let it happen. I'm the attending physician. They can't close the claim until I agree, or until the court orders it. And that's a long way off."

"It isn't far off at all, Doctor. You don't seem to be on top of things." She pulled a letter from a thick file and jammed it under Forte's nose. Mrs. Sánchez's employer had brought a suit against her to close the claim, and to recoup the money they had already spent.

Forte rolled his eyes, as if this was just the latest in a string of meaningless COLA documents, but something caught in his belly, and he rethought his knee jerk belief that all things stamped COLA were beneath contempt, not worth the recycled paper upon which they were printed. He realized the disconcerted feeling was the same as when he learned that the state had sued, and won their case against, Mr. Tarkington. The old man was now liable for three-hundred-thousand dollars, plus interest, for nearly twenty years in back COLA expenses.

"Well, I'm going to fight like hell," Forte grumbled toward the interpreter, "so don't quit your day job."

"This is my day job."

"I know. That's what I meant. Now, let's get back to Lupe. What is she taking in the way of medicine for her, ah, what did they give her over at Whitaker General?"

Ms. Goldstein-Miranda spoke hurriedly to Lupe, who whined an answer that even Forte understood. She wasn't taking the medicine. It made her feel funny, "*Loca*," she giggled as she wound her index finger around one side of her head.

"And she falls asleep when she takes the medicine. Then her husband can't have sex with her unless he pulls off her pants, and then he beats her cause of that when she wakes up. So, she better stay awake if she knows what's good for her," the woman nodded seriously.

"Wait a minute. She doesn't have to live that way. Have her call the cops. That's rape. If you don't report it, I will."

Lupe's already huge black eyes opened as large as sombreros, and a stream of rapid, pleading Spanish flowed toward Goldstein-Miranda, whose eyes now also widened broadly. "No! Lupe says if you call the cops, he'll kill her. The police don't do anything but make trouble. Don't call them."

At that, Lupe spat another sentence at her advocate. "Last time, all she did was tell a friend that he had beaten her, and you know what he did? He had one of his drug friends beat her up. She was pregnant at the time. The baby died. Cops came to see her at the hospital, and she told them she didn't know who did it, so at least she didn't get her pregnant sister or her mother smashed, too. Doctor, this isn't your neighborhood out on the hill in Belvedere."

Sol snorted, "Well, I don't live on a hill or in Belvedere, and no matter what you say or Lupe says, she doesn't have to put up with that. This is America. We've got rules."

"Your rules don't reach very far into her world, Doctor. Anyway, Lupe's used to it. Her father was a small drug dealer in Guadalajara. When someone got in his way, someone cheated him, or called the police, he'd take Lupe and the family out for a

Sunday drive in the family car and visit that *amigo*. He'd wait 'till the cheater drove down the street then ride up next to him and shoot him in the head—in the head if the guy was lucky. Whole family in the car, little ones in the back; Lupe, the oldest, she used to sit up front with her mother."

Sol's face reddened. "That's probably more than I need to know about Mrs. Sánchez."

"The reason I'm telling you, Doctor, is that I don't want you interfering in her business. She's got enough trouble, and you don't need to add to it. And now you people are going to take her COLA claim away because you say she's crazy? She has a right to be upset when she gets hurt and can't work. Only thing left for her is to sell drugs, but she won't do it."

"I'm not going to let her down, but she has to do her part. Let's get her started back on the medicine from Whitaker General—quarter pill to begin. We'll move the dose up very slowly; less side effects that way. She won't even know she's taking it if we nudge it just a bit higher each week."

Ms. Goldstein-Miranda hesitated and nodded reassuringly to Lupe. "Doctor, the truth is, she doesn't have the money to buy medicine. Her husband took the old ones away to sell, and he takes all their money when the COLA check comes in, which, because of you, doesn't come anymore." At that, Lupe's eyes reddened, and she stared at her feet. "She doesn't even have money for groceries for her kids. She's been eating rice and fat for weeks."

Forte stood. "Wait a minute. I'll see if we have samples. He came back holding a paper bag stuffed with little cardboard pill-boxes. "Now listen," he urged seriously, "That's for you, not your husband." He stared at her. "I'm not allowed to give out medicine unless it's in the original box. But you need to promise me you'll open it the minute you get outside and hide it in your pocket." He demanded, "You hide it. *¿Entiendes?*"

She doesn't understand English. That's why I need to be here."

"*Si, Doctor.*

CHAPTER SIX

Mrs. Berry's employer had bristled into the Department of Orthopedics announcing, "I ain't leavin' 'till I share a friendly word with that Dr. Forte."

Sol strode into the waiting room, head erect, jaw set, feigning confidence and asking himself what Rosebac would do at that moment. He shook the man's hand hard, invited him back to Room One, and called Roxanne to sit in. The man was huge; seventy years old, a hundred pounds overweight, and discolored with a complexion as ruddy as a bruised, ripe tomato. "Actually, I'm glad you came in. Much better face to face. So how can I help the situation, Mr. Sullivan?"

"Now, you can start by calling me John. Then, let's you and me talk about how to get this thing with Edna over with."

"Edna?"

"Edna Berry, for Christ's sake. Like I said on the phone, she used to be a good worker. Drivers liked her. Now, when someone calls and says there's a problem with their garbage pick-up, Edna gets the wrong name, or the wrong address, and I don't mean skips a number; it's a whole different street, or town, sometimes. And she smells of booze. Always did, but now it's real fresh, not stale like the night before. She fell off the chair because she was loaded, not because of her disease or my furniture."

"Mr. Sullivan, she told me she didn't fall, that she just got up."

"That's bullshit. She fell out of the fuckin' thing."

"Then, sir, you need to protest the claim and put that on your report to COLA."

"Doc, why the hell do you think I came here? To talk to you man to man. I can't put that down on paper. I'll get sued for defamation of character or some goddamn thing, *and* I'll still have to pay for the COLA claim. Gonna cost me a couple hundred thousand I don't have."

"Mr. Sullivan, tell me what you want me to do. I explained that the way this works is you dispute the claim, and let the state worry about it. All I can do is repeat in my notes what the patient told me, and to be honest, now I have to put down that you were here, and what we talked about. You're a bright man, I can tell."

"Yeah, what's coming next?"

Sol paused and thought for a moment. "Let me ask you a business question. What would you do if you knew a client of yours was throwing toxic crap away? Gallons of poison, right there in one of the garbage cans? Would you pick it up and put in your truck?"

"Of course not," Sullivan answered indignantly. "That's different and you goddamn well know it. It's against the law to accept toxic materials."

"Wait a minute. You're going to lose a good customer if you don't take the stuff. Yes, or no?"

"So be it. I'm not going to jail for nobody," Sullivan hissed.

"Wait, wait. The customer comes to you and cries, 'Hey, just this once, John. I don't have time to take the stuff to the Hazmat dump. Help me out one time, please.'

The scarlet of Sullivan's face deepened to an angry purple; his gin blossom glowed red hot. He grumbled angrily, "No way. Cut 'im a break, and that'll be the time they catch your ass at the dump. And even if you get away with it once, you know damn well that's the one customer who'll ask for the favor again. It's the way of the world."

"Just like me committing insurance fraud. I'll get my butt fried, and I'm not doing it."

"What? Telling the truth is not the same as hazardous material. What happened to right and wrong? You know how many years I did a route, emptying garbage cans for hundreds of accounts a day, before I saved enough to buy my first truck? Then I drove the goddamn thing and still did the pick-ups myself. In and out of the truck alone, working like a dog, not in some nice warm office." He let his eyes glance at the calming artwork and the lavender walls. "What for, so I could get screwed by some drunk and a goddamn rich doctor?"

Sullivan jumped up, gasped as if his chest had locked, wagged his index finger at Forte, bowed slightly toward Roxanne, and sailed out of the office door. Seconds later, Cindy, the receptionist, stood at the entrance of Room One, cocking her head in surprise. She was trembling. "That was the oldest drug seeker I ever saw."

"He wasn't a drug seeker," Roxanne whispered, "just an angry man. Had a right, too."

"Well, he acted like a drug seeker, running past the front desk, slamming the door. Just like all the rest of them. Only thing he didn't do was flip me off."

Roxanne turned to Forte and asked respectfully, "Dr. F., isn't there anything we can do?"

"All I can do is report to COLA what he said. Maybe, if he can get some employee to say she comes to work drunk, at least she won't be able to sue him. Then he can fire her, but how's he going to prove she was actually drunk the moment she fell? There's no way. Nobody sent her for a drug and alcohol test. He should 'a done that, to cover his behind. Airlines do it, trucking companies do it. But then that just pisses off the other employees, and it'll cost him a couple a hundred bucks. And no matter what it shows, I mean he can fire her, but he's still stuck for the COLA claim. And let's face it, this lady ain't never going back to work. She's got a great excuse for four or five months—broken leg in a sixty-year-old woman. Then she'll get a lawyer to say the chemo for her cancer, I mean leukemia, prevented full healing, and she'll get another year out of the Americans with Disabilities Act before COLA catches up with her. By then the remission'll be history, she'll have a couple of months to go, and it's to the pension desk. It's a slam-dunk. *I* could be the lawyer on this one, it's so simple."

Roxanne sighed, "You missed your calling, Doc. But in the meantime, we're behind, and can we bill COLA for that pleasant visit with Mr. Sullivan, I mean John?"

"Yep. Counts as a telephone call. We charge COLA five bucks. With my percentage, that's a buck sixty-six *pour moi*."

"Poor what?" Roxanne asked as she came across the room to give him a gentle punch in the arm. He touched her shoulder softly, and they laughed.

⇒⊢ ⊣⇐

When Cindy left, Forte looked up at Roxanne and mumbled, "Okay, let's stop for a second and take stock of the entire situation." He pulled a prescription pad from his white coat, asked Roxanne for a pen, then titled the back sheet of the pad, <u>Our Stars</u>. "Okay, on first we have Tarkington. He's out of the hospital, AMA; should 'a never been admitted in the first place—just your everyday anxiety attack. Hand him a Valium and send him home. Why don't they read a guy's records down there? I'll get something written up for his lawyer tomorrow. Just a quick note. Mr. Tarkington's no biggy for now.

"Next, on second, there's Mrs. Edna Berry. She's in a wheel-chair for the next few weeks, or, mark my words, months, so there's nothing to do for her except chant 'Yes sir, yes sir, three bags full, sir' to her caring boss, Mr. John Sullivan. Not to worry, he'll get over it. They always do. Nope, not losing sleep over the Berry-Sullivan Affair just yet. Couple of years before that one gets serious.

"Then there's loopy Lupe. She's calmed down, but she'll be back—both here and Whitaker General psych ward. But for right now, she's better, well, a little, and I gave her some samples to tide her over. Good.

"And finally, rounding third, is our friend Mr. California, Kevin McAlister. Let's get him into that pain clinic pronto. I can't imagine anything's gonna show up on the MRI or labs. I talked to the ER doc who saw him last night. He thought the guy was acting so bizarre, he sent him for a CT scan of the head. Nothing showed up. *Nada.*

Roxanne sniggered, "Didn't think so."

"No, no funny stuff up there. He also had one of the neurologists take a look at him. They wanted to get a bone scan, but he refused. Said he didn't want any more radiation. He's got a point. Anyway, to the pain clinic with him. That'll get him out of our hair for a few months. That's *if* he keeps showing up over there."

Roxanne frowned. "He'll go once, then he'll swear that they told him to follow up with you."

"Nah, he'll keep going if they give him his pain pills. I need to call them and make sure they dole them out a few at a time. Makes them happy when the attending physician, yours truly, is deeply involved in their patient's care. Also, make them happy that they don't have to write large prescriptions that the regulatory goons down at the State House might get wind of. And if I'm involved, they'll be less likely to toss his butt outta there when he screws up big time, which he no doubt will. I'm telling you, we can be on vacation from him for a bunch of weeks if we treat the pain center folks good.

"Did you know, Roxanne, in Europe, hospitals have blacklists? Inscribe the name 'McAlister' on the lineup of local abusive personalities, and you can turn them away from your doors without an excuse. Just like that. We're heroes here in America."

"Uh huh. Heroes."

CHAPTER SEVEN

Dr. Solomon Forte awoke just before midnight in early September, aware it was only minutes before the clock brought in Labor Day. Having been trapped in school nearly all his life, he considered Labor Day his New Year, a pristine semester, a fresh start, the grade slate wiped clean. He lay in bed formulating his one resolution: I will exercise extreme caution before taking on a single new patient who shows the slightest symptom of the Chronic COLA Pain Behavior Syndrome.

Just two hours later, an emergency room physician's assistant, a hundred-and-fifty miles from Whitaker, called Sol. He asked, "What do you want me to do with Lupe Sánchez? She just bounced into our ER complaining of a total loss of vision. Is she yours?"

"Yep, she sure is. How did you find me so fast?" Sol asked groggily.

"She had your card clutched in her hand. Your home number's on it."

"Did I give her my home number? Whatever. I don't think she's blind, just scared. Try this: wave a twenty-dollar bill in front of her eyes and see what happens. I'll wait on the line."

Seconds later, the doctor took the phone off hold. "That worked. She followed it like it was a vision of God. Thanks for that pearl of wisdom. Okay, she's not blind, but what am I supposed to do with her now?"

"Tell her to come and see me the instant she gets back to Whitaker. And don't give her any Valium. Hops her up instead of the usual sedation. Give her some Tylenol. Tell her it's, let's see, 'Transtryptol' or something."

"It's what?" the ER doctor carped.

"I don't know. I just made it up. Tell her it's strong stuff. Her husband'll take the pills from her, sell 'em, and maybe get his butt blown away by an unhappy customer. Sound like a plan?"

"Sorry, Dr. Forte, they may come back and shoot me instead. I'm turning her loose sans medications. Sound like a plan?"

Two mornings later, as Solomon Forte had predicted, Mrs. Berry's claim was placed on the back burner by the Commission on Labor Affairs. They had decided to hire a panel of doctors to perform an independent medical examination on Mrs. Berry to sort out her claim. The panel's findings were always the same: The claimant is just fine; there is no injury now, nor was there ever any reason to open a claim; the claimant may return to work immediately without any compensation for the loss of time on the job, nor for injury itself, which never existed in the first place; and, finally, even though there is nothing at all wrong with the claimant physically, he or she should not be required to lift more than twenty-five pounds, and do no bending or twisting or rising or sitting in a chair frequently.

The beauty of the IME was that it took months to schedule, receive the report, respond, and wait for the additional months of haggling between COLA and the patient's attorney.

Mr. Sullivan's lawyer had subpoenaed Sol's records on Mrs. Berry, so Sol informed the Center attorney, and for a while, as the lawyers postured, he was out of the loop. Though Mrs. Berry's daughter called several times demanding official letters from Sol stating that her mother was permanently disabled due to the negligence of her employer, Roxanne, following Center policy, grinned rudely into the mouthpiece and directed the daughter to the Center's legal staff.

Anwar El Haq, despite the Center's lawyer's snort that no judge would grant it, managed a continuance on the Tarkington matter, and promptly turned his attention to another case. Mr. Tarkington, on autopilot, found his way, though, to the ER three times. When Sol was called in the middle of the night, he recommended Mr. Tarkington be provided three Valium tablets and a ride home. The ER doctor asked Sol, "Business must be good?"

"What are you talking about?"

"Well, that's the recipe our Dr. Rascalovitch has used for a dozen years: send Tarkington home when business was hopping, admit him when things were slow, and he needed the bucks for seeing patients on rounds."

Armed with a few Valium tablets, there was not a single breath from the Tarkington camp for several weeks. Rosebac nodded professorially, "As I said, Solomon, when you use your head and not your heart, these problems evaporate. Wasn't that hard, was it?"

Kevin McAlister was also not heard from for weeks. He had ignored Sol's dictum to report back to the Center immediately after his MRI, and never showed up at physical therapy. It wasn't until mid-October that McAlister limped through the front doors of the Galena Hills Medical Center groaning, body contorted in paroxysms of agony. The main desk receptionist looked up anxiously from her computer, though when Kevin's eyes locked on her tight sweater, she slid her chair backward toward the wall.

McAlister clutched an eight-and-a-half by sixteen-inch, multi-sheeted blue and red Commission on Labor Affairs form which he plunked insolently onto the desk. When she didn't move, he flicked it toward her. It fluttered to the carpet. As she scooted forward and bent over to retrieve it, McAlister's eyes again dropped to her sweater. When she looked up, her eyes hardened.

McAlister humphed, "I need to see the doctor about my back."

"Do you have an appointment?"

"Well, the doctor told me to come back. I'm just followin' his orders."

"Who did you see?"

"I forget the dude's name, and I forgot to give him this form last time."

She glanced at the papers briefly. "COLA. It must be Dr. Forte. Take the elevator up two levels to Ortho." McAlister paused, straightened for an instant, stole a final glimpse of her chest, and limped away grumbling, "Goddamn hassle."

The Orthopedic Department receptionist directed him toward a chair in the corner, away from the paying customers, then, breathing out through her mouth, slid her rolling chair back toward the wall. Roxanne was paged. She bristled into the waiting area, hissed under her breath, motioned to McAlister and led him to Room Two. She closed the door behind her just as he finished his sentence, "Hey, you're looking great."

Forte, upon learning of McAlister's appearance, sucked in three liters of air and strode toward Room Two, jumping ahead of several scheduled patients. He began the conversation without a smile. "Mr. McAlister, where you been? Missed you."

"Told ya. Got no car. And even if I did, I got no money for gas. Goddamn COLA, they still ain't paid me. They said you need to fill out this form and write them a letter and explain the whole thing. I ain't gettin' nothin' 'till you tell them how bad my back is."

"Mr. McAlister, I don't know how bad your back is unless you come for your appointments. Looks like you didn't go for your MRI; you don't come in for appointments; I'm not Karnack the Magnificent, you know."

"Car what?"

"Karnack, and what form are we talking about?"

"This one here." McAlister shoved the papers forward.

"This is a PIR, a Physician's Initial Report! You were supposed to give us this form the first time you came in. No wonder they haven't paid you. They don't even know you exist."

"Must 'a been different in California."

Sol's chest shuddered. "You have a claim there?"

"Couple."

"Any still open?"

"Two."

"For your back, I suppose."

"Nope. Hands. Carpal tunnel on the right and broken finger on the left. I called them, and they told me to switch the claims to you. They sent me this other stuff for you to fill out." McAlister pulled a dirty pack of folded printed forms from his jeans pocket. He thrust them under Sol's nose.

Forte unfolded the sweaty paper, allowing cotton droppings to flutter onto the rug. He exhaled, "Okay, we'll get these done. But that means we're going to have to look into both those new problems."

"Fine with me, Doc. I want this stuff fixed. I'm tired 'a hurtin' all the time. I just want it all fixed. I want to be like I was before."

"And how was that?"

"I could play softball. Now I can't even drive."

"Why can't you drive?"

"My hands hurt. They get all numb."

"And your back? How's that doing?"

"Much worse."

"Well, we can't do all of it today. I'm squeezing you in as it is."

Forte's head dropped as he rolled his chair forward toward McAlister, who tensed and howled before Sol touched him. "Oh, the pain!"

"Well," Forte mumbled, "in that case, let's take a quick look at your hands. We'll get to your back later."

McAlister held up the left index finger, but when Forte pushed gently on one of the knuckles, McAlister jumped back, yipped, and cocked his right fist. "Jesus, Doc, I told you I was in pain. I didn't mean to almost punch ya, but what the fuck, you tryin' to kill me?"

"Wait a minute, Mr. McAlister. You told me last time you were here that you'd been in state for a few weeks. So, by now it's been months since you broke your finger. Can't still hurt that much."

"Well, it does. The doctor in California didn't give a shit. Thing's never gonna heal."

"He didn't operate on it, did he?"

"No."

"Then whether he gave a shit or not doesn't have anything to do with how fast it heels. Let's get an x-ray of your hand and see where things are, bone-wise."

"You guys like to take x-rays. Get more money from COLA. Told ya, I don't like that radiation shit."

"Still smoking?"

"How can I quit when I hurt so bad?"

"Uh huh. Mr. McAlister, my friend, this clinic gets around fifty bucks for each COLA patient that walks through the door, whether we take an x-ray or not. I get about twenty percent of that in my pocket; that's about ten bucks, and it takes months for the check to get here, if it ever does. Half the time, claims get lost or refused. The rest of the fifty bucks goes to the Center for overhead. So, let me tell you, I'm not getting rich on you or your x-rays. Now, follow me."

Forte brought McAlister into the next room, a closet Rosebac had commandeered for his personal x-ray machine. He placed McAlister's left index finger under the lens of a computer monitor-sized fluoroscopy machine on wheels. Forte hit a pedal, and the x-ray tube crackled to life. "Well, Mr. McAlister, I see a little swelling, and a small chip of bone right here, but it looks like an old fracture, and an insignificant one at that."

"Jesus, they didn't tell me I had a fracture. They said it was just a minor break. And see, it's still there. Told ya it hurts."

"No, no, fracture and break mean the same thing. And finger fractures, ah breaks, show up on x-ray for a long time, even after they heel. Maybe forever. It doesn't matter what's on the x-ray, it's healed."

"So, why'd you take the x-ray then? And you're tellin' me I'm going to have a bone floatin' around in there for my whole life? How can I work like that? I need my hands in my work."

"Mr. McAlister, listen to me. It's healed. Just because you can see the broken bone in your finger on an x-ray doesn't mean it's still broken. And it's not floating around. It's encapsulated in connective tissue…" Sol looked up at McAlister's blank expression and sighed, "It's just…it's just the way it is."

"Well, I don't get it. And all I know is, I can see it, and that's the place that hurts like hell."

"Mr. McAlister, you know what, this is getting complicated. Let's stick with your back today. I'm going to give you…"

Roxanne tapped on the door of the tiny fluoro cubbyhole. "Doctor, we need to get moving. The rooms are full. Natives 're gettin' restless."

"Okay, Mr. McAlister, let's send you back to work, light duty. We'll write a note to your employer. Let's say you can lift twenty-five pounds max. No bending, crawling, climbing. We'll start you off four hours per day—move you up slowly to six hours, four days each week. How does that sound?"

"Doc, there ain't no light duty. I already told you that. They don't want me there if I ain't a hundred percent. And I need more pain pills. I'm getting' worse, not better, and I need some of that Soma, too. I can't sleep without it."

Sol's face hardened. "Mr. McAlister, we're getting to the breaking point here. If you're getting worse, then you're getting an MRI right away. No excuses. I'll give you three more days off. That's enough time to get that done. I'm not giving you any more time loss without the MRI. And, I'm sorry, I cannot write any more prescriptions for pain medication. The state won't let us unless there's something wrong, and right now, as far as I'm concerned, I don't have a single test that proves anything. Their rules, not mine."

"So, what do I do about the pain? I don't like takin' pills any more than the next guy. I like to go natural, but I gotta sleep."

"Take Tylenol. Like I said, not my rules. It's theirs. And the Tylenol works just fine."

Sol left the cubicle like a judge scampering from the bench after an unpopular ruling. He snapped at Roxanne, "Who's next?"

But before she could answer, Rosebac placed himself in front of Sol. "Forte, good to see you're using that fluoro machine. We get that thing paid off, and you'll get a little extra spending cash in your lab coat pocket. Lot of money in that machine."

"Maybe for you and the other surgeons. Not for me."

"You're wrong there, as usual. Help us over the next six months, and we'll reimburse for every time you use it. You're one of us now, the Department of Orthopedics. You're entitled. Everyone else in this place has a trick. The ophthalmologists own the Optical Shop; ear, nose, and throat guys own the Hearing Aid Center, and they're getting rich on their extracurricular activities. We can share in the pie, yes? We're performing a vital service. Nothing illegal or unprofessional about it."

"Not saying there is. But I'm not getting reimbursed for fluoro."

"What are you talking about? We've had the thing for months, and I've made a few bucks already," Rosebac blustered.

"That's because you see private insurance patients. You decided not to see COLA. Too messy, remember? And COLA's not interested in paying for images printed on toilet paper. They've denied every one of my charges. They say they want to see real x-rays, on real film, before they'll cough up any dough."

"Sorry to hear that."

"Me, too."

"Well, then maybe we should send a few regular patients your way."

"Maybe I'll send a few COLAs your way. That would be a novel experience for both camps."

Rosebac laughed sarcastically and turned brusquely, but paused to look back at Forte, his smile erased. "Doctor," he grumbled, "every one of us had to start at the bottom. Don't you forget, this was your social experiment, not the Orthopedic Department's. Like I've said a hundred times, champion the workingman, avenge your father, I've got no problem with that, but there's a price to pay for everything you do in life, and I don't feel like paying for your decisions."

CHAPTER EIGHT

Roxanne walked up to Sol and Rosebac. "Dr. Forte, the phone's for you, your sister." Sol's chest clutched. Michaela was a third-year novice at the Sisters of Ireland in Boston, and though relegated to a life of silent contemplation, she was first a Forte, and would occasionally crawl behind the kitchen, up the fire escape, through the ever-open window, and into Mother Superior's private office. There, she'd call Sol, usually at midnight, sometimes at three or four in the morning, but never during daylight hours.

Though Sol was shaken, he had to smile to himself, thinking about Mother Anastasia and her Achilles heel, the open window, a symptom of the hot flashes and the profuse sweating that had begun months before. It was also a sign of her refusal to open her collar or wear anything but traditional habit. Though Mother Superior dared never mention the problem, it made rich fodder for the novices, who giggled behind her back as the sweat sprayed from the woman's face. The steady decay of Mother Anastasia's mood, however, did not glean as much laughter. In the past, while Novice Michaela had taken a serious risk making midnight calls, a daylight foray into Mother Superior's office was suicidal. Sol was concerned.

"Commando Michaela, you okay?" Sol asked brusquely.

"Solly, I just needed to talk to you right away. I don't know how much longer I can do this. Am I doing the right thing being here? I mean, if I leave, will I roast in Hades? That's what Mother Superior says. I just don't know what to do."

"Sweet Pea, we've been through this. You will never roast in hell, or anywhere else, except maybe Bermuda."

"Big brother, watch your language"

"Sorry. Look, there's a million ways to show your love and respect for God. The Order's only one. I wish I could give you an answer, but all I can say is, I'm so proud of you. It doesn't matter if you stay or go, you're still the best in the world—no matter what you decide."

"Then I should quit?" she brightened.

"Hey, tough guy, I'm not telling you one way or the other, but you remember how Papa prodded me when I wanted to quit medical school. God, I hated it."

"Solly, please! Watch your mouth." She paused for effect, but before he could apologize, she blurted, "I'm just kidding. Yes, I remember how he helped. But being a doctor means something. What you're doing matters. You save lives. People count on you. This is dumb. It's so self-centered. I can't talk because some angry, old, menopausal lady says so. What's the point? And even if we actually become nuns, most of us won't ever do anything important. And there's something else." Her voice became more edgy. "If you ever tell anybody…"

"Hold on. Let me get my tape recorder. I'll never tell, you know that."

"There was a man here yesterday."

He cut her off. "Oh, my God, and don't tell me I'm being blasphemous. You didn't…you're not pregnant!"

"I should hang up on you. No, dopey," she brightened," but I've seen him before, in the brown delivery truck. I forget the name. Oh, it's been so long since I was out of here in the real world. But anyway, he had a package for Mother Superior, and he was wearing brown shorts, and Mother Superior saw some of us looking at him, and if looks could kill, she would have been arrested for a massacre. And then when he turned to leave, *she* was watching him. Not his back, but I saw where her eyes were. This isn't natural. I never kissed a man. I don't know what to do."

"I kiss you every time I see you."

"Sol, don't be a goof. You're just like Papa, always saying things God will punish you for." Her voice cracked. "I miss him so. I wish he were here to tell me what to do."

Sol gasped, "What, I'm chopped liver? I'm not good enough?"

"Sol, I love you, but you know what I mean. Five words out of Papa's mouth, and the problem was solved." She became quiet again though Sol heard her stifle tears. "It hurt so bad how he was at the end. When Mama died. She went so fast, but Papa, he withered away. That tough old guy, and all that there was at the end was a skeleton, but still the huge thick hands and the cement under his nails. I'll never forget his hands."

"No, me neither. I loved him so much. He worked so hard, but the best thing about him was that he could pass on what he'd learned without talking down to you. Pop knew right from wrong without having to think about it. What a gift. You got it, too. Me, I gotta get hit in the head a few times for the lessons to take hold."

Michaela's voice calmed. "My favorite story is how Papa gets shot in Korea, and some Jewish man gets shot himself but pulls Papa out of the battle. Papa's never even seen him before, but he says, 'I'm gonna name my first-born son after you,' and after he crosses his heart, *then* he decides to ask the guy, 'and by the way, Sergeant, what *is* your name?' The guy says, 'Sol Schlamowitz' and Papa says, 'Solomon Forte it is, thank you very much.'"

Sol laughed. "Too bad he didn't name his first-born daughter after the sergeant. Me, he named Sol, so you would have to be Schlamowitz. Nice ring to it. Mother Superior running around the vent screaming, 'If I ever catch that Novice Sister Schlamowitz looking at the UPS man's butt again, she's dead meat. He's *my* man!"

"Okay, kiddo," Michaela laughed, "I gotta go. I love you Solly, my brudder the doctor."

He smiled into the phone as she clicked off but sat quietly, wondering if any of his grand problems, or his sister's, amounted to a hill of beans. There was no one else for him to talk to, not in terms of family; Michaela was the only spark left in him, and he the only one left in her.

He laughed again as he heard the fall of Roxanne's feet padding toward his office, but cringed as he heard her draw a deep breath. "You done for the day? Come on, Doc, there's that Mrs. Perkable you were seeing. She's sitting there waiting. Tomorrow's her ninetieth birthday. I think she wants to spend it at home with her family, not in Room Two.

CHAPTER NINE

S ol sat at his computer that evening checking his e-mail, but his thoughts drifted to his sister and her interest in men. So, they want it, too, even a nun, he whispered, even the menopausal mother superior, and that shook him, as he had been raised to believe, as had every man, that women didn't think about sex, and that if you wound up in bed with a girl, it was because she wanted something from you, was drunk, or maybe a nympho. Then Judy Famot's reflection popped into his head, and his mind vibrated with the image of her alluring eyes. His head turned involuntarily toward his bed and then back to the corner of his desk, where the seven-inch thick chart that documented the saga of Ralph Tarkington sat gathering dust. "Don't even think about it," he admonished aloud, "you're dealing with poison."

Roxanne had, just that morning, crowed in warning, "She's a painted lady", and Sol's stomach soured, remembering all the articles he'd read about a woman's intuition.

But Sol's hand drifted on its own toward the pile, and he picked up the top sheet, the registration data, where he quickly found the woman's home telephone number. He inched toward the phone, though part of his brain, the tiny shard not directly wired to his groin, screamed, "No!" The hand moved back. "Just read the chart and think about Mr. Tarkington drooling on your lips. Still want to see Judy? Be a doctor, not a dog in heat," he mumbled feebly as he brought the whole pile of papers in front of him and opened it to the section where he had left off.

He read that as the months and years had passed, Ralph Tarkington had been shuffled to myriad psychiatrists and psychologists who sent letters back to COLA describing his problem, variously, as reactive depression or depressive neurosis; some said hysteria, others, severe regressive psychology, and a few diagnosed, "…total amnesia and child-like dependency with severe posttraumatic stress syndrome along with obliterated behavior patterns." The consults went on and on for hundreds of pages, a Dostoevsky novel. But whatever they labeled it, just by the weight of the numbers of "experts" who had opined, Tarkington had indeed suffered a mental harm. The rub was that, despite several hundred x-rays, a dozen MRIs and CT scans, four PET scans, arthroscopies, biopsies, and a titanic parade of blood tests, no one had come up with something the claims mangers at COLA could see on paper or x-ray. It wouldn't have mattered what it was—a drop of stray White-Out on a film that mimicked a speckle of abnormal bone, perhaps a misapplied decimal point on the white blood cell count that appeared to mean lymphoma, something— but there was nothing. And by fiat the conservative contingent in the state legislature, a small quorum of whom had voted in an unannounced Saturday evening session, decreed that, "If you can't *see* it, it don't exist. We will, therefore, squander no more state funds treating workers for fictitious ailments." After all, the legislators' dining room was in such need of repair.

Despite the legions of psychiatrists who had testified in appeal before the legislature that analysis of mental disease was the product of an impossible-to-image process in the brain, their input was rejected as tardy. The conservative whip reminded them they'd had a chance to add their clearly constructive input at the Saturday night meeting, but now it was too late. One state senator smiled at the petitioners, "The committee met on a day everyone, even a busy doctor, could attend, a Saturday night, and you weren't here. You snooze, you lose." The die had been cast, and a COLA claims manager was armed, now by law, to slam shut mental claims and remove that smudge from her docket.

In answer to the resulting barrage of letters to the editor from the state's mental health professionals, the conservative politicians joined state budget administrators to fight like cats against reconsidering the decision. They growled that COLA had never been intended as a public assistance organization. The Commission secretary wrote, "We teach our claims managers on their very first day of training that our society already has a welfare system and social security plan, and that is where we want you to direct these workers. We are not the nation's safety net."

The Chairwoman of the State Society of Psychiatrists wrote in rebuttal that when these patients applied for Social Security, they were told they were not eligible because the injury was work-related. A Social Security clerk wrote back that she had been trained to urge these workers to hire a lawyer and sue COLA.

The Secretary of the Commission on Labor Affairs answered that she was sorry to say her commission could not cure all the ills of modern society, and that they also had a responsibility to the employers who were footing the bills for the Commission. And there the chain of protests died.

Sol went back to Tarkington's chart. He discovered letter after letter from the Commission on Labor Affairs, and it was clear that, with the fervor of an IRS agent, the claims manager had parsed every word, weighed every nuance of psychobabble, until she was mired so deeply in the jargon, she enlisted the services of the Commission's own psychiatrists, who she assigned to perform another independent medical examination.

In the next letter to Tarkington's doctor, two COLA shrinks pronounced, after a ten-minute examination, that Mr. Ralph Tarkington was a malingerer of the worst sort, a scammer, a chiseler, and a master at milking the system for all it was worth. They backed their opinions with a short report in which frequent reference was made to the battery of psychological tests that showed Tarkington was a psychological cripple. Their argument was that those diagnostic examinations measured nothing, for they were designed and administered by journeymen, psychologists, not MD psychiatrists, real doctors, and were "…of debatable usefulness."

Tarkington's family doctor, the since-disgraced Brian Lippard, was asked to review that independent medical examination and sign on the bottom line if he agreed, or take several hours and create a full narrative report refuting the findings, for which the Commission paid about twelve dollars. Lippard chose the latter road, setting the scene by explaining that years after the industrial injury, Ralph Tarkington had been discovered nearly unconscious in his bedroom. The medics rushed the dying man to the hospital where a ruptured appendix was discovered. Yes, Ralph Tarkington had complained of an upset stomach for a day or two, but he had made no request to be seen by a doctor, and had actually withdrawn into himself, becoming more isolated as the days passed. Dr. Lippard wanted the case manager to answer how Mr. Tarkington could have ignored the pain for so long unless he was not thinking rationally. Lippard's conclusion: the patient's judgment was distorted to that degree because his brain had been thoroughly cooked, just as the psychological drivel demonstrated.

Sol studied the records. He was struck by Dr. Lippard's logic, that Mr. Tarkington had not rolled around in agony days before the rupture, as the doctor had seen tough guys do countless times during his twenty-eight-year career. "A ruptured appendix isn't the sniffles," Lippard wrote in one report. "Any man who just withdraws into himself in the face of such pain is not acting normally. There is something drastically wrong with Mr. Tarkington's cerebral processes, despite the considered opinion of the state's so-called mental health experts."

Though Judy Famot informed Sol that Dr. Lippard had left medical practice under a cloud, Forte began to wonder if Lippard hadn't simply trod on one too many professional toes over the years, and eventually been kicked in the family jewels by a wrathful medical community. He read on.

Next came to an order from the Commission on Labor Affairs sending Mr. Tarkington to a panel of doctors to determine, once and for all, if the worker had really sustained the injuries he claimed, and if complications were still present. The three examiners, a neurologist, an orthopedic surgeon, and a psychiatrist, ruled word for word with the previous state-hired doctors, affirming that Mr. Tarkington was fixed and stable, and capable of returning to his pre-injury position of utility company lineman. Further, they decreed that, on a more probable than not basis, he had never been injured physically at all in the mishap, for there was no objective evidence to the contrary. They quoted a Whitaker-based ophthalmologist who saw him shortly after the so-called industrial accident, a practitioner, now the President of the State Medical Association, who saw no suggestion of the burns reported by an over-worked nurse in an understaffed emergency room. There was nothing in the record, and certainly nothing on exam that day, indicating the man was incapable of returning to work immediately. They opined he should never have been off work for more than a day or two at the very beginning, and that was based only on open-to-discussion anxiety growing out of the twelve-foot fall from the cherry picker, and the hub-bub at the emergency room.

By this point, the Commission had quietly sent Mr. Tarkington to a total of seven independent medical examinations, manned by fifteen trusted medical doctors, all of whom had been doing these types of evaluations, five and six a day, for several hundred dollars each, and providing the identical conclusion to the Commission in each case. In Mr. Tarkington's instance, the Commission had amassed a sufficient number of the negative opinions to bury the few voices speaking on the patient's behalf.

The family turned again to Dr. Lippard. He recommended they hire a lawyer.

Tarkington's sister called numbers in the Yellow Pages until she happened upon one Douglas Carrier, Esq., who quoted a beefy hourly rate, and the family demurred, but reconsidered a few days later after exhausting the entire panoply of attorneys in the county, all of whom cited their lack of expertise in labor matters. The Tarkingtons dropped to their knees in thanks when Carrier reduced his rate by ten percent, though they had no idea he was fresh out of night law school, and still working as a librarian four days a week to make ends meet.

Carrier had never tackled a COLA case. In fact, the only brush he'd had with workers' comp was when he had personally filed an injury claim against the state. The damage, a kink in the neck, grew out of a dictionary that fell from an upper shelf onto his head. It was not reported, though, that the book was dislodged by the frenzied passion he and a fellow librarian had created when they stole into the stacks during lunch.

Nonetheless, Carrier dove in, chastising the Commission for declaring Mr. Tarkington "fixed and stable," when his client wasn't fixed at all. He was still partially blind, incoherent, given to fits of temper, unable to perform many of the basic activities of daily life, and had not improved a single iota since the day of the accident. He reminded the Commission that Mr. Tarkington had just been readmitted to Whitaker General Hospital for an infection at the surgical wound after the appendectomy, for which the attorney promised to hold the Commission on Labor Affairs liable. "We will never allow this claim to be closed until Mr. Ralph Tarkington is normal again in every sense of the word."

The Commission's case manager's nostrils flared with the scent of blood. She wrote back, forwarding a cc to the family:

Dear Mr. Carrier,

"Fixed and stable" is not like getting your car repaired and arguing with the mechanic until the thing runs perfectly. Perhaps you are not familiar with the legal definition of fixed and stable. As per the State Administrative Code, Chapter 401-849-14-11216, fixed and stable is equivalent to maximum medical improvement, which means simply that the patient is not getting any better or worse, and that his/her condition will not change in the foreseeable future.

It is not the Commission on Labor Affairs's task to bring an injured worker back to his/her preinjury status. Our legal mandate, again I refer you to the SACs, is to provide medical care and time loss payment until such time the injured worker has reached a medical plateau, i.e., fixed and stable.

We are not a welfare agency. This worker is clearly fixed and stable in the opinion of fifteen medical professionals. May I remind you that the preponderance of evidence is the legal standard of proof in civil cases. That is, the weight of evidence presented by one side is more convincing to the trier of facts than the evidence presented by the opposing side. That, Mr. Carrier, is the only yardstick by which we adjudicate cases.

If Mr. Tarkington is unable to engage in activities to support himself, we recommend he apply for social security.

Sincerely,
Tammy Lynn Corridoro
Senior Claims Manager

She concluded her remarks with the decree she extracted word for word from *Claims Managers' Instruction Brief*: "The decision to stop the worker's time loss payments is upheld."

The family, within an hour of receiving their copy of the decision, went back to the Yellow Pages and started at the top of the list of Whitaker's lawyers. The first one eagerly took the case, not to represent the family in its dealings with the Commission on Labor Affairs, but for its potential in a legal malpractice suit against Attorney Carrier. Tarkington's kinfolk met with the new counselor an hour later. He stirred them, conjuring visions of the injustice they had suffered at the hands of Carrier, Argent Public Utilities, and the doctors of Whitaker. He picked up the phone in front of them and made an appointment for the family to see one of his colleagues that afternoon, Whitaker's social security authority.

Later that day, the SS attorney made a few calls and guaranteed Mr. Tarkington would be inscribed on the social security rolls within two weeks. He then referred the family to his colleague, an environmental litigator, who stayed late that evening to file a case against Argent Public Utilities for Tarkington's exposure to a catalogue of toxins as long as the menu at the Waldorf Astoria. The sum of those contaminants, the attorney argued, had so dulled his client's intelligence, the man had been rendered incapable of fathoming the need to test the downed power line before he grabbed it.

Argent's lawyers sought summary relief. The judge demanded from the environmental attorney a formal brief cataloguing where he had obtained the inventory of chemicals to which Mr. Tarkington had been exposed while in the employ of APU.

The man allowed in open court, "From my client, Your Honor."

The case was over three minutes later, dismissed with prejudice by the judge when the attorney could not produce a single document or other shred of evidence proving Argent had ever purchased a single molecule of the toxins, all of which had been banned in the U.S. a dozen years before Tarkington had dropped out of high school.

The judge levied a ten-thousand- dollar fine against the attorney, and Argent sued the man for slander for an advertisement the lawyer published in the local paper to drum up clients for a class action suit against the electric company. The lawyer, desperate to come up with the funds to pay the fine and remain in practice, produced a new theory of the case, and convinced the family to sue the US Navy for exposing Tarkington to asbestos, arguing the fiber caused peripheral neuropathy, that is, a loss of coordination which precluded the dexterity necessary to steer clear of contact with dangerous objects, to wit, the electrical wires it was his job to handle. "But for the Navy's complete disregard for the welfare of its sailors, Mr. Tarkington would be whole today."

The federal court dismissed the case in summary judgment, His Honor grumbling that was what the Veterans' Administration Health Care and compensation program was for. He fined the lawyer five thousand dollars.

But that was fifteen years ago, and, in the interim, Sol realized by the altitude of the pile he had yet to peruse, somehow, Mr. Tarkington's administrative life had been improbably resurrected, much the same as the political careers of Richard Milhous Nixon and Deng Xiao Ping.

Sol had not been so captivated with the printed word since *Pet Semetery*, and he reached for the next few sheets, but the phone shattered his concentration. It was the ER. Kevin McAlister was back, writhing in pain, complaining that the MRI done of his spine that afternoon had left him in agony. Sol explained patiently to the triage nurse that MRIs didn't hurt people. It was non-invasive: all you had to do was lay there for a few minutes, and there wasn't even any ionizing radiation to worry about. It was safer than an afternoon on the beach. There were no injections, no strange positions to assume, no medicine to take beforehand or after to make you sick. The only problem with the MRI was that some patients were claustrophobic. And that didn't hurt six hours later.

"Give him six Vicodins and tell him to come to see me at eight o'clock tomorrow morning. And have him pick up his MRI films beforehand. I want to see them with my own eyes."

Sol gave his receptionist and the woman at the front desk a heads up that Mr. McAlister was due early the next morning, but security had already spotted him lurking about the property before seven. They had him sitting in their little headquarters in the basement, smoking and drinking coffee, before Sol had arrived at the Center. They led McAlister up the back stairs to Orthopedics, but he collapsed, moaning in pain on the first-floor landing, and the security detail had to roll him in a wheelchair to the public elevator.

Roxanne whisked Sol into Room Two, cajoling him to make the visit snappy. Forte found McAlister leaning back in a chair, groaning, his legs whirling mightily, white knuckles grasping his copy of the MRI films.

"Damn, Doc, that goddamn test killed nearly killed me. I can't lay in one place for that long. I'm dyin'. You need to help me out."

Sol muttered, "Glad to. Which way did you come in?" but the movement of air noise from Mr. McAlister's rotating legs was sufficient to drown the sentiment.

Sol patted McAlister's shoulder. "Let's take a look at the MRI. This'll show us if anything's going on. Doesn't miss much. If there's something wrong, we'll find it."

Forte snapped the first two of the twelve sheets of images onto the viewing box and grabbed a plastic model of the back from the shelf above the sink. Each sheet of film was the size of a chest x-ray but contained eighteen miniature images, each one a new picture, several millimeters deeper into the anatomy of Kevin McAlister's spine. "Come on over and look at this with me." McAlister limped to his side.

Forte pointed to each image, showing Kevin all his hidden parts, the bones, the blood vessels, even the wispy nerve fibers that carried instructions to the muscles of his legs, and those that carried pain back, via the spine, to the brain. With each cut, Forte commented, "Wish mine looked that good." By the time they got deep enough to make out the discs and the spinal cord itself, Sol already knew that there wouldn't be anything to show his patient, but he went over picture after picture, studying the spine from left to right, top to bottom, and from front to back, all two-hundred-and-sixteen images.

Sol smiled reassuringly, "A little degenerative disease, par for the course in a man who's worked as hard as you have, but nothing to get excited over. No scary stuff at all. Basically, this is good news."

McAlister gasped. "I have degenerate disease? What does that mean? I want to get rid of it."

"No, no, calm down. You have a tiny bit of wear and tear in your spine just like everybody your age. I have it, you have it, your mother has it. It's normal. It's not what's causing your pain, so relax."

In his heart, Sol was relieved. He felt reassured that there was no organic cause for his patient's interminable complaints of pain. Kevin McAlister's malady was not something that could be diagnosed on an x-ray or reported in an extravagant, new blood test; the menu of options was now far less complex: either he was somaticizing, really feeling the pain because he was depressed or stressed beyond what his brain could tolerate; or he was malingering, purposely deceiving the doctor, the employer, and the claims manager for the sole purpose of obtaining time-loss payments and or narcotics. While the latter seemed the obvious conclusion, much had been written in recent years, and published in respected medical journals that, in truth, while many patients appeared to be malingering, it was rare to find a person who really was.

Despite the gravitas of those findings, they did not address the possibility that Kevin McAlister was simply a drug seeker. He had displayed every element of that behavior on the very first day, thirty seconds into the visit. Save the one break McAlister had copped when Sol discovered he had really been in a car accident, everything his patient did stunk of ruse. He knew it was time to sit Mr. McAlister down and tell him, "I'm sorry that I can't discover what's wrong with your back, but I have done all I can. There's nothing more I have to offer you. You will have to find another doctor."

But a little part of Solomon Forte's brain, and heart, warned against an outright sacking. Though he was about to ignore common sense and Rosebac's advice, a little voice whispered, cautioning, reminding him that he had never been completely sure about anything in his life, particularly since he'd become a doctor. One last nerve fiber in his amygdala cautioned against divorcing Kevin McAlister—just yet.

Sol leaned back and looked Kevin straight in the eye. "I can't tell you what's wrong with your back, my friend. On the other hand, the good news is that you don't have any serious problem. The MRI is very normal. You probably just have soft tissue muscle strain. We call it mechanical lower back pain, and unfortunately, that doesn't show up, even on an MRI. The other good news is, back strain goes away. May even take a year or more, but it almost always fades away, burns itself out, and that's without treatment. So, time's on your side."

McAlister seemed relieved but asked, "Yeah, but what about this pain? Now, it's waking me up every night, not just twice a week like before. And it's different, it's deeper, like the bone's being squeezed or something. I can't take it."

"Mr. McAlister, listen. I know you hurt, but if we use narcotic pain medicine for the next year waiting for this thing to get better on its own, you're going to be hooked and never get off the stuff. I know you don't want that."

"No, Doc, I don't." He paused for a moment and became very serious. "Look, I'm going to be honest with you. I had trouble with drugs when I was a kid, but I got off that shit. I did it then, and I can sure as hell do it now if I need to, but I gotta do something about the pain." McAlister leaned back and closed his eyes. He grimaced, and his legs began to whirl.

"Well, we know from studies that if you miss work for a year because of back pain, or any on-the-job injury for that matter, you're probably never going to return to work, ever. And we also know that the longer you take pain meds, the longer it takes to get back to work. So, my suggestion is that we make plans for light duty, to start immediately. I'm trying to do the best thing for you."

"Back to work, I don't know," he shook his head rapidly, looking more like Nixon and Clinton lying to the whole nation, than a kid with a bad back. Soon his head was spinning as fast as his legs. "There just ain't no light duty at that place. Shit, I can't even sit long enough in the car to get to the job site."

"Mr. McAlister, we have to do something to get you moving again. I just showed you, there isn't anything serious going…"

"Thank God."

"Yeah, we're both happy about that, so let's work together with your employer to get you doing something. You go home, and I'll get back to you later after I call your boss. Deal?"

"Okay, but what about the pain?"

Sol shook his head in disbelief and mumbled to himself, "I'm talking to a wall."

McAlister leaned forward and sat on the edge of his chair, watching Sol's expression intently. "Doc, I'm telling you, I'm dying. I'll go back to work. You want me to crawl across the job-site, fine, I will. I'll do anything you say, but help me with this pain. I need to sleep. It isn't right."

Sol nodded to himself, understanding that McAlister was negotiating with the only chip he had left. Sol could either believe him, or call the man a liar to his face and kick him out of the office once and for all. He sat quietly for a minute, sensing the shadow cast by the Hippocratic Oath, his training, his gut feelings, the warnings of the Orthopedic Commission's director, those of Anacota, those of the hospital's board of directors, and the deep warnings of the State Medical Abuse Commission. Each threat came from a different direction, each obliterating an escape path out of his dilemma.

Was there no way to treat his patient and not harm him at the same time? There had to be a technique, and he dropped deeper into thought, but no matter how hard he pondered, no light emerged from the mire. He sighed and settled upon an ill-advised choice, for there really were no choices other than bad ones. He would believe his patient, sort of, and prescribe a miserly amount of pain medication, and do so perilously, on an ongoing basis. He would keep McAlister relatively comfortable.

"Relatively comfortable," Sol mused aloud, understanding it was a no-win solution for any of the dozen parties concerned. Though Sol would provide a measure of narcotic analgesics that kept him just below both the Center's and the state's regulatory radar, if McAlister really did hurt as badly as he alleged, the few pills would do nothing of substance to help, and McAlister would continue to suffer. So, in the end, Sol was exposing himself to administrative turmoil for nothing more than shooing a sad man out of his office in order to engender the least amount of personal chaos.

Forte set his jaw. "Mr. McAlister, I will prescribe you enough Vicodin for two pills per day. I suggest that if you're that uncomfortable at night, you save them for when you go to bed. That's all we can do. The state's watching."

Kevin McAlister's head drooped, and his face lost its color. "So, I'm just supposed to suffer during the day?"

Sol did not answer and left the room amid his patient's deep breathing and sighing. He announced to Roxanne vigorously, "Fourteen Vicodin only, two each evening for pain, and no refills. We'll see him back in a week."

Forte sought refuge in Room One, but when he popped his head out three minutes later, ready to order Roxanne to call security if McAlister hadn't left, he was astonished to find Roxanne at her desk, alone, quietly playing solitaire on her computer. Sol was so relieved, he walked to Roxanne's desk and whispered, "And next time, we're cutting back to one pain pill before bed." Roxanne did not look up or nod. She was busy pulling an ace to the top of the screen.

It wasn't until the end of the day that Sol had a moment to get back to Mr. Tarkington's records, though sitting on top of the pile was a note that Judy Famot had called. There was nothing about calling her back, just that a hearing had been granted on her father's petition to have his case reopened, and that she hoped Sol would be available to testify. He flinched when he saw a casually scribbled P.S., but it was only a question about his fees.

There was also a message from Dana, and he called her back. She began the conversation with smile. "Hey, got the oven going. You in the mood for lasagna?" His briefcase was packed before the little green charging lights stopped blinking on the cordless phone he kept on his desk for private calls.

Sol had first met Dana Romanov at a medical conference where she was staffing a booth for her employer, Guilliani Pharmaceuticals. The Spanish conglomerate produced Theramar, a powerful new antidepressant that had grown wildly popular for its lack of sexual, blood pressure, or weight-gaining side effects. Sol thought back to the moment he had first seen her. He had been walking toward the Pfizer display and their free donuts. As he passed her corporate exhibition, he stopped in his tracks to stare at her dark, Russian features and blue eyes. Mostly, though, he was taken by the grace she radiated.

He smiled to himself embarrassedly, recalling how he had asked her, "Are you the one who invented Theramar? Great stuff. Miracle drug. Why just one week ago, I'll have you know, I was locked in a psych ward at Bellevue in New York City, two hundred and ten pounds overweight, blood pressure of 235 over 262, and now I'm a happy one-hundred-and-ninety-five-pound orthopedist, BP 116 over 68. It's a bloody miracle."

Dana turned her head to ignore him, but she hesitated for a trice and looked back at the sparkle in Sol's eyes. She giggled, "You're an orthopedist! Oh, I'm really sorry. If you'd only paid a bit more attention in school, who knows, you might have made something out of yourself? You could have become, say, a neurologist or even a psychiatrist. And, Doctor, you missed one of the side effects."

The last fragment of her rejoinder stopped him. They chattered for so long, Pfizer's never-ending donuts had been reduced to a dusting of powdered sugar and rainbow sprinkles.

Dana explained that because Guilliani had already earned uncounted millions from sales in Europe, they had boundless funds for advertising, which translated into spreading dollops of cash to prominent physicians all over America. And sales had soared even higher. Then Guilliani was exposed for having invited hospital CEOs, hospital medical directors, TV doctors, and all manner of healers from around the nation onto lavish private yachts for cruises off the Miami coast, others for weekends at posh hotels in San Francisco, and a few for golf junkets in Scotland. When word spread, plain old doctors, the ones laboring in the trenches, were calling the conglomerate's headquarters in Barcelona, asking how they could get sales reps to come and talk to *them*. Guilliani sent reps out in droves. With their patent only good for seven years in the States, they had to get the product moving at light speed, and at a price that would make up for the hundreds of millions they'd spent in R&D, and the tens of millions securing FDA approval. Another twenty or thirty or fifty million pushing the drug was a drop in bucket.

That was many months before, and to Sol, Dana's life seemed exceptionally romantic, and the corporation paid her well. The downside was that she had no free time. Barcelona phoned in the middle of the night, once or twice a week, with orders to fly to Dallas, Toronto, Cleveland, and, occasionally, back home to Whitaker. Each time she returned, she called Sol.

She hugged him as he walked into her neat condo near the top of Belvedere Hill. He loved the panoramic view of the mountains and the city. He could even see the Clinic off to the north, a tiny, meaningless dot on the horizon. It was if Dana lived high atop a modern, carefree castle.

Sol smiled at the scent of lasagna wafting from the kitchen, and as he passed the kitchen alcove, he could feel the heat from the oven. He was amazed each time Dana opened the door to welcome him. Her eyes shimmered, and her kiss was soft and soothing. He asked himself, as he'd leave her place, how Solomon Forte, son of a cement truck driver, was dating a woman who was, as were the all the things around her, upper crust.

He thought of the cramped apartment in which he'd grown up in Little Italy, the withered furniture and chipped dishes; he and Michaela had shared a bedroom, separated only by an old tablecloth partition, until they were teenagers.

Sol dropped his bag beside the baby grand piano, turned to Dana, smiled warmly, and gave her another hug. He laughed, "You're not going to believe today's players."

"The usual?" she smiled, as she poured from the bottle of Romanov vodka. Sol glanced at the dozens of empty Romanov bottles sitting like a battalion of erect soldiers guarding the mantle above the wood fireplace. Some of the labels had yellowed with the passage of many years.

"Well, Ms. Romanov," Sol nodded, taking a sip of the drink, "let's make a pact to add this one to the collection before the night is through. I must be responsible for half the glass up there."

"No, you silly goose. Not saving them anymore. New bottles aren't near the quality of the ones my father brought from Lithuania. Nothing is, anymore." She became very serious and added, "You know, Solly, I wish you could have met him."

"Me, too. I would have loved to ask him what it was like being a doctor under the communist system. I've just been reading a book about Russia from the 30's to the late 50's. Doctors were paid the same as the street sweepers, but were forced to work around the clock, like me…"

"Poor baby."

"When Stalin's purges came, most of the doctors were arrested for being intellectuals and anti-labor. What a nut house, the Soviet Union. I wonder how your family survived. Just think, if he had taken over the distillery from *his* father, he might have been labeled anti-labor, but at least he would have been a rich misguided soul. His old man must've had a cow when your pop told him he was going to go to medical school." Sol shook his head and laughed. "Wonder what Grandpa would think of his little girl selling crazy pills?"

Before the statement was all the way out of his mouth, and despite Dana's sanguine, yet gentle expression, Sol realized he had struck a sour note. He added apologetically, "Hey, kid, that was pretty dumb. Truth is, Theramar's done more for my practice than all the pain pills I dish out, and by the way, most of the surgery we do. But you know we crack jokes about it. Tell me you guys don't."

"We do, but I don't laugh so hard. Depression is the worst disease there is. You know that."

"I do, Sweet Dana, and I know what your mother's illness did to your family. I wish Theramar had been around then. I'm sorry."

She brightened a bit and nodded with a smile. "Well, never mind. Tell me about your day, or should I say your days? It's been a while, Doctor Forte."

"I'm sorry. I'm getting tired. Only been at this eight years, thirty to go, and I'm already running out of steam. This wasn't what I had in mind when I decided to take on the world."

Dana refilled the glasses and sat back down next to Sol. She folded her legs under her. "Tell me," she spoke softly.

"You know, I'm supposed to be professional at all times. I am required, by the tenets of the Hippocratic Oath, to be enamored of every soul that crosses the threshold into my world. I'm not supposed to harbor doubts in my own mind about the motivation of the patients I treat, to say nothing of actually expressing them. Every sufferer is an emerald; the flicker of God glows in each of their eyes; though, mind you, some only have one eye 'cause of industrial accidents. Sounds great on paper, but you should hear some of these stories. I'll just say that it seems not all the people in this world are so God-like."

Sol took Dana's hand and shook his head. "Then again, most of the patients I see, like ninety percent of them, are just plain people like you and me, slipping-up occasionally, like the rest of us, but not bad folk. No, I'm wrong. They're good people. They make going to work worth it. In fact, I love seeing them. Actually, most of the time, I love my job, but then there's that ten percent. Like everything else in life—always a ten percent—users and bottom feeders."

"You mean COLA?"

"Not all of 'em, no way. But, God forgive me for saying it, more than I thought when I signed on to save the cosmos single handedly. So many people change when they get on COLA. I don't remember the last time I saw an ongoing COLA that didn't want *something* from the system. Rosebac, our cheerful little angel of mercy, told me that, and I looked down my nose at him. But I got to thinking and realized he was right. Maybe it's just a day off, just one more prescription for pain meds, massage therapy, one more week of light duty. I don't mean the simple injury, over and done within a couple of weeks. But that's the exception. There's always some problem, usually with the patient, sometimes with the employer, but nothing ever goes smoothly. Something happens to people when they smell a free lunch."

Sol took a drink and paused for a moment. He pulled his hand away from Dana's. "Damn," he hissed, "alcohol's working in reverse. Does that mean when my father broke his leg falling off the cement mixer he did the same thing? It's easier to think about my parents having sex than picturing my father cheating the stupid system. It's not the way he raised us."

Dana thought for a minute and spoke softly. "Solly, is it really any different with any patient? Your job is to treat illness, not to judge. That's the judges' job, and who would want to do that for a living? I'd rather crawl into a little ball and die than spend my life looking down my nose at creatures in extremis and passing judgment on them when I don't know a darn thing about what's right and wrong myself, as if the judges do. You're lucky. At least you do some good. How many people can say that? And that Mr.

Tarkington you were telling me about last time? You were help-ing him."

"Not medically. Nothing to be done for him; maybe I'll be able to do something in court, but he's way too far gone for these healing hands."

"Well, you said he was getting screwed by the system. So, you're righting an injustice. Who gets to do that?"

"Sure looks like he's getting chewed up. What I read in his chart last night would gag a maggot. That's Marine talk. My fa-ther taught me."

"Tell me."

"Okay. I'm up to the part, oh, this is so good, COLA's saying they're going to cut him off of time loss payments because he's malingering, and they send him for an absolute, complete, no-more-after-this-no-matter-what, final psychiatric assessment. So, they made him take the, let me get it out here." Sol shuffled around excitedly in his brief case, eventually extracting a packet of di-sheveled papers. "Here it is. Listen to this, Sweet Pea. They gave him the *Halstead-Reitan Neuropsychological Battery*, the *Minnesota Multiphasic Personality Inventory*, the *Peabody Picture Vocabulary Test*, the *Wechsler Adult Intelligence Scale, Revised*—wouldn't want to get caught dead using the unrevised version—and the *Memory Scale*."

Dana suppressed a smile but finally interrupted, "I know he scored off the scale: IQ of 166, like yours."

"You're partially right. Well, let's say half right. He scored the same as me: IQ 71, borderline idiot, and he demonstrated a 'pro-found memory deficit.'"

Dana asked, "I know the Navy isn't Harvard, but do they let people with those numbers play with the jet engines?"

"You are a bright one, aren't you? That's the point. This was an acquired problem. The shrinks who gave him the tests even said in their conclusion that there was some, hold on, let me read it, '...some diffuse and moderate brain damage,' and let's see, yeah, here it is, 'original trauma that resulted in some loss of cortical integrity. We cannot, however," Sol made quote marks with his fingers, "'*on a more likely than not basis*, determine if the industrial injury of record was the cause of this damage.'"

Dana shook her head. "Well, if it wasn't the industrial injury, what was it? A mosquito gave him sleeping sickness?"

"So, now you're an etymologist? It happens to be the tsetse fly…"

"It's *ento*mologist, and whatever."

"Look, the system is full of shit. A man's future boils down to a single phrase? If the examiner had a fight with his kid that morning, the one who won't get a job, so the guy's pissed off at a world full of slackers, and he writes the words, 'The patient's condition is *not* a result of the industrial injury on a more likely than not basis.' That's the kiss of death. State ain't responsible anymore. Commission has the legal right, and duty, to close the claim.

"But if the doctor's in a decent mood and decides to give the worker the benefit of the doubt, as they're supposed to according to Title 72, and he scratches out the second not, it becomes, 'The patient's condition is more likely than not a result of the industrial injury,' and the guy's in fat city, well sort of.

"But when it comes to psych tests, there's no way to assign tangible numbers to bizarre answers. Don't forget, the guy who's being evaluated is usually a freaking fruitcake, otherwise he wouldn't have been sent for the test in the first place, and if he's nuts, does he interpret the question the way the shrinks intended? So, the orthopedists and neurologists get the results of the tests, do an orthopedic and neurologic exam, combine all the data, and come up with a decision that will affect the guy for the rest of his life. That assumes the orthopedic surgeon has any idea what the tests show, if they show anything useful in the first place. I mean, maybe they do, and I just haven't been trained how to use them. But generally, bone doctors are the ones passing ultimate judgment on most of these cases, because that's what COLA's interested in—disease that shows up on an x-ray. Why would a bone doctor spend a month studying what the psych tests mean, especially when they don't mean anything? Orthopedists can use a saw pretty good, but I mean, this ain't exactly the Mensa crowd."

Dana shook her head. "So, if you have mental disease or brain damage from an industrial injury, you're out of luck?"

"Well, if a guy gets his gourd squeezed between a dump truck and a bulldozer, suffers a skull fracture, and he's not quite right after that, okay, even the state's shrink's gonna give him something for brain damage. But a schnook like Tarkington, the state foots the bill for the psych tests just to pay lip service to the process. Psychologists don't mind, though. Squeezes a buck or two out of the state, just like Rosebac's new little x-ray fluro machine. Everybody's got a trick, 'cept me. Where did I go wrong?"

"You don't want that, cheap tricks."

"What's wrong with cheap tricks? Anyway, I'm not trained in that psych stuff, and the COLA claims managers, they're not trained in it, either. They didn't know what to do with Tarkington's numbers, so they went out and ordered a few more independent medical exams, and that's as far as I got in the records."

"Don't you think *some* of them care? I mean, they're doctors!"

"Of course. But, Dana, there's such monetary pressure. Hundreds of bucks an hour to sit on the panel. If you rule in favor of the worker a couple of times, the Commission on Labor Affairs doesn't hire you again."

"That's hard to believe."

"Believe it. I did it for a while. One of a panel of three—two 'senior physicians' and me. We snipped for a while over whether one of the workers really got hurt up on Galena Mountain at the ski resort. Guy was driving the groomer. Ski fell from the lift. Hit him in the crotch. Guess one of his tentacles down there got all black and blue. Claimed it was nearly impossible to have an organism. But his employer called one of the panel doctors and told him they had seen his wife, and they were sure she was pregnant. When the report went to COLA, these old fart M.D.s overrode me. They were the tried and true, the seasoned, and when they sent in their report about the panel's 'dynamics,' I didn't get invited back."

She shook her head. "So, they don't care."

"I'm not saying that. When you see the average guy at an independent medical exam, they all act the same way. It's as if there's a pamphlet on how to act at an IME. They moan and groan and twist their faces in pain. It's so obvious they're faking. It's laughable. And most orthopedists are fairly concrete, conservative, and no nonsense. A real blast at parties. It's just who's attracted to the job—and the CIA. So, they don't want to hear about pain levels and mood disorders. 'Just let me see the films.' So, they get all pissed off when they see the obvious pain behavior, and the die is cast.

"But there's another side to the story. I think a lot of these people hurt, really. They can't sleep, they're grouchy all the time, and it affects the family. Makes it worse. But the only way they think they can show it to the examiners is to jump around like they've been snake bit."

Dana shook her head. "Why doesn't their doctor explain all this to them before they meet with the orthopedists?"

"Pretty child, I have tried and tried. Coached some of these people six times before the IME. I tell 'em, 'Don't put on an act. Be honest. No faces, no squirming.' Never works. Report comes back, 'Patient demonstrated pain behavior far in excess of any objective findings.' And they get no impairment rating."

"What a mess."

"Even though I came in here hot as a pistol tonight, I am getting used to it, a little. Doesn't usually bother me so much anymore. It's not like it's the death sentence if a patient thing doesn't go well with the state, and I lose a case. But I gotta tell ya, this Tarkington thing is clinging to me."

Dana crawled along the couch and put her arms around Sol and laughed, "Kinda like I'm clinging to you?"

CHAPTER TEN

Sol was uncharacteristically a few minutes late the next morning. He found Roxanne tapping her pencil impatiently, mumbling to herself as she looked up. "I know. Your car didn't start, or was it you couldn't find your shoes? Poor baby." He didn't answer, though smiled and walked lightly toward his office. "My, my, we're chipper for 8 A.M. I mean eight *ten*. Just drop your bags in the hall, 'cause we're already behind. Hit Room Two first. There's an unhappy man in there complaining of back pain."

He ignored Roxanne and went to his office, though called over his shoulder, "Brand spanking new day. We've been gifted with the opportunity to, once again, do our best to launch Dr. Rosebac's life's plan."

She came to the door. "You mean remain aloof and uncaring, and avoid the BS around here? Good idea. I'll be at my desk doing my nails."

"So, what's new?"

"Dr. F, you don't need to be like Dr. Rosebac, and you also don't need to be carrying that chip on your shoulder. Look what it's got you. Aren't you afraid to come to work? Each day the list grows. All these people taking advantage of you around the clock. Haven't you ever heard the old saying, 'no good deed goes unpunished'? Really, isn't there something in between?"

"May be, but right now it is what it is, and to tell you the truth, Rox, I'm not sure Rosebac and the rest of them are any less stressed than we are, or any happier." He turned away from her and opened his briefcase to fish out a tin of mints. He came first to a thick, creamy, flowered envelope in Dana's hand. He smiled at the words and thought about her for a moment, surprised at the warmth he felt in his chest.

"Don't start falling for her," he grumbled to himself. "There's a lotta ladies out there before your time's up. Go slow, boy." But he also conceded that the only time he was peaceful any more was when he was with her. He loved how she squeezed his arm tighter the deeper he spewed his lunacy, and those blue eyes. Those eyes. She had a great job, and she… He lost himself staring into the hills.

The tapping pencil brought him back. "Come on, Dr. Forte, seriously, we need to get started."

Sol knocked mechanically on Room Two, still thinking about Dana, until the breeze of windmilling legs snatched him from his musings. McAlister's face was gaunt. "Hey, I thought we made a deal to start weaning from the pain meds. Going to the ER in the middle of the night asking for Vicodin's a breach of contract."

McAlister clucked indignantly, "I ain't got no contract with you. All I got is pain that's getting worse. You need to do something."

"I am going to do something. I'm going to have another doctor take a look at you. Get another opinion. If they say you need the pain meds, fine, that's what we'll do. If they can't find anything wrong with you, well, then you know the rest. Deal?"

"Doc, I can't make deals over what I'm feeling. Maybe that other doctor can figure it out. I'm not bullshittin' ya, Doc, I'm dyin', I hurt so bad."

Forte did a brief exam. No change. McAlister still howled in pain with light touch of his back and the other trick tests that had nothing to do with a damaged spine. Forte left the room and called a local back surgeon, who agreed to see McAlister in consultation, but the doctor made Sol promise to take McAlister back no matter the findings, unless, of course, he could find an excuse to do surgery. Forte agreed gratefully.

Roxanne worked on the appointment for half-an-hour, proudly reporting to Sol that she had gotten McAlister into the surgeon that very afternoon. She stared at him eagerly, but Sol growled, "If we had put it off for two weeks, we wouldn't have had to deal with him for a while. Now he'll be back in tomorrow morning, maybe even by midnight. That guy's like a lump of gum stuck to my shoe. I should have the ER call *you* at home."

Roxanne took a breath to answer, but Forte marched to his office, where he swung the door shut noisily.

Late that afternoon, the surgeon called. He had reviewed the MRI and examined McAlister. "Solly, to be frank, I can't tell you what's going on with your boy. He's not a surgical candidate. There was nothing on his plain films or the MRI that I can make better with my scalpel. You need to be thinking about getting him into a pain clinic or something. *I* think he's malingering. Then again, maybe he's just a psych case, or there's always the chance that he's got something nasty somewhere. Who knows? Anyway, good luck. We'll see ya." The phone went dead.

Sol's gut feeling had been buttressed with the gut feeling of a true specialist. McAlister was full of crap, scheming to beat the system. If there was something real going on to make him hurt that badly, the spine guy would've found it. After all, he was a board certified orthopaedic surgeon, or that was the way he spelled it on his business card. And he was Harvard Med, residency at Stanford, a four-year fellowship in spinal surgery at the Mayo, and had been in practice for twenty-five years.

Considering the malpractice defense attorneys' advice that there was never enough proof to place before a jury, Sol considered asking a neurologist to take a look, but he could hear the advice from the specialist: "Look, Sol, he's COLA. If you tell me he doesn't have 'focal findings,' if you can't pick out a particular nerve that's misbehaving, I'm not going to be able to offer you anything. Why don't you send him over here for an EMG. I know that test hurts like hell, but it's not *that* expensive—few hundred bucks. Pennies. COLA usually approves it on the first try. If it shows something, then we'll take a look. Hey, I gotta go. Lemme know."

Maybe Sol could make up a focal finding, like questionable weakness of the EHL, the muscle that makes the big toe go up, or maybe numbness on the top of his patient's foot. That would pique a neurologist's interest, for it would mean that the nerves leading from the lower spine to the foot were trapped, somewhere. But even if Sol put one over on the neurologist, he knew the man would call him back and smile into the phone. "Yep, good pick up; that's a focal finding all right, but we need to verify it, so like I said, send him over for the EMG."

Anyway, if Sol made up a symptom like episodic weakness on the left side of his patient's body, he'd have to coach McAlister to go along with it, and when the neurologist found out, and surely he would, it would be construed that Dr. Forte was turfing undesirable patients, and word would spread. The next time he called any of the Center's consultants, he would be denied access. Even if he got away with a concocted symptom, the neurologist would track that down, and when it turned out to be fictitious, Sol would be back to square one.

Forte considered asking Rosebac to see McAlister, but that would only set the stage for World War III. Maybe one of the Center's rehab doctor would take a peek, but most of them were not taking COLA patients anymore. The Commission on Labor Affairs paid nearly nothing for an office visit, these patients didn't get better, and each doctor who agreed to treat the industrially wounded was hounded by a tsunami of paper work that grew inexorably as the days of time-loss multiplied. Why would a doctor see a COLA patient when Texaco, Toyota, and Bell Helicopter had ignited Whitaker's economy, generating legions of educated, attractive patients whose insurance paid full freight?

How about a psychiatrist? But that's where you sent patients when the work-up was done, complete, and you couldn't find a thing, and you were one hundred percent sure there was no evidence of physical disease. And that also meant a phone call to the psychiatrist, which also meant listening to their personal angst. If you muttered a single sigh of empathy, that cost you a forty-five-minute spiral into their madness. It was like being back in residency, where you *had* to listen.

Nonetheless, Sol accepted he had plunged to the bottom of the diagnostic food chain—a psychiatric consult. McAlister had no palpable malady, nothing objective on x-ray or MRI, and despite the gallons of blood he'd sucked from Kevin, there wasn't a single abnormality on a lab test. He had nothing to present to the claims manager, and soon, with the red flag of so much recent activity on the case, she would be pushing for an answer or claim closure. Sol would demand a psychiatric evaluation, a CYA appraisal, and the Commission, after a week of skirmishing with Sol, would agree to pay for it. But even if the results demonstrated mental disease, they were back to square one—again. Kevin McAlister had not been hit in the head with a wrecking ball, so any psychiatric diagnosis would be deemed a preexisting mental disease, and the end of his claim.

Then would come the flood of letters from COLA, state-hired vocational counselors demanding Dr. Forte complete work capacity forms, a treatment plan, and a contract signed by both McAlister and Forte for the rapid cessation of pain medication. The last line would demand Sol read, agree with, and sign the attached reams of state-created job analyses that offered the patient back his old job, or one more physically demanding.

A week later, after the attending physician had nixed all of the offered positions, a missive from the Career Development Section would land on his desk, a boilerplate paragraph offering a job as, "Clerk at Convenience Store." Invariably, toward the end of these notifications, was the demand he complete a new set of forms, and in addition, provide a written narrative within fourteen days describing in detail why the injured worker wasn't capable of doing the chronicled work. Failure to comply with the Commission's request automatically left the doctor guilty of a violation of the state legal code, and thus subject to countless penalties, not the least of which was to be stricken from the roles of those authorized to see COLA patients.

Sol wondered what the doctor who had taken care of his pop had done. Was it the same in New York? Had *he* been beaten by the paper-work? Did he understand, in his heart, the injunction to care for any man who had come to him for help, or was it easier to bow to the relentless ultimatums of the claims managers at the New York State Commission of Labor? And while the words "claims manager" were as painful to his ears as racial epithets, all the people in the cubical farms at COLA were trying to do was stem the bleeding of the state coffers, the vanishing of his own tax dollars.

What worried Sol, though, was that he was never quite sure if a worker had really been injured, or was conning him, yet again.

He fretted that the other doctors at the Center were so cocksure of themselves and of their diagnoses, which were always the same when it came to COLA patients—malingering. Only if he had not come from a family mired in blue collar poverty, perhaps his parents could have sent him to private schools where he'd have been mentored, taught how to think critically. Only if he had been brighter, studied harder, become a better physician, perhaps he would have mastered the skills to ferret out the truth in the milliseconds it took his colleagues. While a majority of those doctors instantly signed off, agreeing with the Commission's decree that the patient was "fixed and stable," essentially labeling him a panhandler, Sol wondered if his obstinate refusal to allow claims to be closed summarily was simply a kneejerk to protect his father's memory, or perhaps a foolish misunderstanding of the sacred oath he'd sworn on graduation day from medical school. He knew well that the Hippocratic Oath was a two-thousand-five-hundred-year-old anachronism, the vestige of a primitive civilization, one steeped in superstition, not schooled in the rigors of magnetic resonance imaging, nuclear medicine, and brain surgery. While nearly every doctor in the U.S. still swore to some form of the Hippocratic Oath, in truth, with the pressures to pay back the nearly a quarter of million dollars in student loans, those noble words had become muddled. Medicine was a business, not a welfare program.

Rosebac's high-minded public arrogance aside, Sol craved the tranquility of arriving at work each morning sure of his judgment, in possession of a senior physician's wisdom. It would be a gift, armor, a moral wall of righteousness behind which he could stand up to his bureaucratic assailants. Then he could fight the Commission with a clear conscience.

But with his own medical inadequacy, the curse of never, ever being absolutely sure of what was wrong with a patient, even the most obvious COLA case held traps and snares and the potential for fathomless grief. It was a scenario he'd witnessed a hundred times, the simplest injury ripening into a tragic crisis.

Sol thought about the medical and legal perils of a fleck of sawdust, less than a millionth of a pound of wood that blew into a carpenter's eye. Back in training, a fellow resident was tapped to pick the tiny particle off his patient's cornea, a routine, uncomplicated, essentially foolproof procedure. A monkey could put a drop of numbing medicine in the eye, wait three seconds, flip up the eyelid, and wash out the speck. See one, do one, teach one, family practice bread and butter, one of the easier, more instantly gratifying procedures primary care docs get to do.

Gratifying and simple. Sol stood over his colleague's shoulder as the young physician searched the man's cornea, eventually finding the dot of wood dust. The resident appropriately refused to take his eyes off the foreign body, knowing by hard experience that if he looked away and the patient blinked, the particle would disappear, and another half-hour would slip away searching for it. The young doctor stuck out his hand for the tiny bottle of numbing drops he'd ask the nurse to fetch from the lab. A second or two after the first drop splashed into the patient's eye, the cornea blanched, a thick, bubbling, pearly white glob replacing what had been his eye. Next was the howl of pain, and finally the clawing. The doctor-in-training sat frozen for a tick, dropped the bottle, and darted from the room.

While the attending physician and a horde of staff were drawn to the room by the wailing, Sol backed off, picked up the bottle, and read the label: "KOH", and in red letters below it, "Potassium hydroxide"—essentially lye. He also noted the tiny container was the same size and shape as the bottles of ophthalmic numbing drops each of the residents had used a hundred times to remove foreign bodies from eyes. The KOH, used daily to find bacteria under the microscope, had been stored neatly on the lab shelf next to the eye drops. The nurse hadn't bothered to check the label…nor had the doctor. When Sol asked the attending oph-thalmologist how large the settlement was likely to be, the man snorted, "It'll have so many zeros, you'll get arthritis tapping in the numbers into your calculator."

And then there was the plumber who had barely scraped his knuckles on a pipe under a sink. His boss, fearing a ding on his COLA safety record, and the automatic spike in his state in-dustrial insurance rates, sent him to the ER with authorization only to get a tetanus injection. But the rules in every emergency department in the free world were the same: you get the vaccina-tion, but you also get examined by *somebody*. The plumber took his shot from the tech like a man, but became frustrated as two hours passed waiting for the doctor. He rolled down his sleeve, pinched a gauze bandage from the drawer, wrapped his hand, and marched out of the emergency room.

As the minor abrasion began to swell and stiffen that night, the plumber pumped his fist to keep his fingers limber so he could go back to work at dawn and preserve his job. After all, he was already in trouble for having mentioned the injury. He spent the day working with one hand, clinching the worsening fist.

By the next morning, though, with even more swelling, and with the onset of fever and chills, and with a weakness so pro-found he couldn't get out of bed, his wife demanded he stay home. He lay in bed pumping his fist even harder, ramming the wildly multiplying staphylococcus aureus bacteria into his blood stream, the lethal organisms wedging themselves into the far corners of his body.

His wife returned from work that evening to find him toxic, so sick, he looked as if he were going to die. She insisted he go back to the ER, but he was too weak to move, and his wife far too small to move him. By the time his son arrived to transport him to the hospital, he was unconscious. He died in his boy's car of septic shock.

The plaintiff attorney's theory of the case was that the emergency room doctor should have called the man and told him to return to the ER for further evaluation. It did not matter that the man hadn't listed a home or employer's telephone number on his intake sheet.

The doctor's attorney argued that there was no way to contact the man, and, more importantly, by the next day, with the infection spreading, a reasonable man would have sought care. Or at least his wife, who was so angry at the ER, should have intervened and called a doctor, any doctor, even if it was just for advice.

"No matter what he *should* have done," the plaintiff's attorney asserted, "you knew his employer's name, yes? It was on the initial ER intake document, wasn't it?" He waved a long blue form in the air.

"Yes, but…"

The attorney interrupted. "Yes, but call the Commission and find the company and track him down. If you cared, *really cared,* you could have sent the police out to the worksite to get the man."

The doctor leaned forward and spoke acerbically. "Yes, but, *sir,* even if I had seen him the first day, he wouldn't have had any evidence of infection, would he? And the tech had already washed the wound, which is all there was to do. No one with brains can argue with that, even you."

The plaintiff's attorney shot back, "Yes, that is true up to a point, Doctor. But if you had seen him, you would have had the opportunity to instruct him to watch carefully for infection, and you could have told him, face to face, the signs to watch for. You're the doctor. People listen to you."

The defendant screeched from the witness stand, "But the man was so stupid, he didn't have the brains to come in the next morning when his hand was paralyzed! What the *hell* makes you believe he would have listened to me?" The jury winced.

"We don't know that. All we know for a fact is that you never told him what to look for. He was so stupid, Doctor? All the more reason to make sure you followed up. And just think, maybe the bacteria had gone to his brain and he was medically incapable of making rational decisions. All the more reason…"

The lawsuit against the emergency room doctor was settled during the morning break in the proceedings. The $1,300,000 was near the limit of Sol's calculator.

"Nothing," Sol muttered aloud to himself, "is as it seems." So, he fretted for a few minutes that he was missing something on Kevin McAlister, and that an independent medical exam might be just what the doctor ordered—a panel of fresh, non-judgmental, objective physicians taking another look at a colleague's patient, board certified professionals who would take their share the blame if something really was wrong. That's what it was all about, Sol nodded to himself—the *team* working for the common good.

Forte called the claims manger that morning and suggested an IME, promising to concur no matter the findings. The manager was so pleased that a treating doctor was cooperating, she instantly ordered a panel with two orthopedists, a neurologist, and a psychiatrist to convene within a week to see McAlister. She even agreed to look the other way for that week in terms of continuing the pain medication.

Several weeks passed during which Sol waited for the IME to be scheduled. A terse message from the claims manager related the difficulty in arranging the schedules of so many specialists. Days later, a new claims manager was assigned, and then another, and though Sol phoned every three days, an excuse was proffered each time. He finally gave up and put his patient on a regular schedule of medication, which served only to take the edge off the pain.

During that time, however, McAlister would worsen and make periodic visits to emergency rooms throughout Whitaker and the adjoining communities. Most of the regional ER doctors knew Sol's home phone number by heart. Several of those physicians recommended Forte obtain a bone scan on Kevin, but the patient adamantly refused, again citing the dangers of having a radioactive substance injected into his veins. Though Sol explained over and over that the amount of radioactivity of a bone scan was about that of a chest x-ray, and reminded him that that was about the same as one cigarette, and that the imaging study might finally reveal the source of his agony, McAlister would not hear of it.

Sol finally got authorization from the new claims manager for a psychiatric consult, and the shrink put Kevin on an antidepressant, but when McAlister came for a visit in November, he had stopped taking the medication, complaining, "Doc, I can't get it up when I take that shit, if you know what I mean." Sol did, and he asked that a prescription for Viagra be authorized, but the Commission on Labor Affairs did not respond.

CHAPTER ELEVEN

S ol failed to peruse the patient list for the morning, having dashed in two minutes late, the past evening spent with Dana. Already behind by ten, he grabbed the next chart out of the rack outside Room Two for a quick two taps on the door and a dart into the room. Sitting quietly, still stuffed into her over-sized nylon parka despite the unusually warm autumn, sat Lupe Sánchez. A nicely dressed man in a bow tie and rimless glasses sat next to her. Forte couldn't help noticing the long yellow pad in his hands. The corners of Sol's mouth wilted.

The man did not rise, but stuck out his hand. "Doctor, I am Malcolm Beach, AAG. I represent Mrs. Sánchez in her state in-dustrial claim against the Martine Hotel."

"AAG?"

"Assistant Attorney General."

"Oh, good." Sol nodded and asked, "You speak Spanish, right?"

"No, wish I did."

Sol smiled at Lupe. "Mrs. Sánchez, are you going to be able to talk with us today, or should I get an interpreter?"

Though Lupe tried to answer, the attorney cut her off. "That won't be necessary. We don't need to hear from her. I just need a few statements from you. I'd like to get started so we don't take up too much of your valuable time. First, do you believe, on a more probable than not basis, that Lupe Sánchez is permanently impaired as a result of the industrial accident, in which she fell while cleaning a bathroom at the Martine Hotel, on the 10th of September last year?"

Sol sat down on his rolling chair and put his hands up to stop the proceedings. "Sir, excuse me, but I don't know who you are, who you represent, or how you figure in this case. And I haven't seen Mrs. Sánchez in a long time. I have no idea how she's doing."

The attorney spoke curtly. "Okay, briefly, her employer is contesting the claim. They feel Mrs. Sánchez was not hurt when she fell in the bathroom. They forced the claims manager to cut off her time loss payments—she applied for welfare—those people called us. Our office examined the claim and decided there was sufficient evidence that she had, in fact, hurt herself on the job as listed in the records."

Sol started to smile. "Let me get this straight. You work for the Commission on Labor Affairs, and you fight *for* the patient? This is new territory for me."

"Well, I don't work for the Commission; I work for the state. COLA uses the AG's office when they feel a legal injustice has been committed." The lawyer added hastily, "The Commission on Labor Affairs acts as a mediator between the interests of the injured worker and those of the employer. The whole point of COLA is to ensure that a worker injured on the job will be cared for both medically *and* legally. Doctor, I hope that's good enough." He glanced irritably at his watch and added, "I need to be in court in a couple of hours. I'd like to get started."

Lupe sat mute and expressionless until the talk began about whether her pain was real or a function of a pain syndrome. She fidgeted, strained her back, grimaced, tightened her fists, and finally whimpered. The performance was textbook, and to quell his embarrassment, Sol raised his hand to stop the interrogation and stood to examine her.

The moaning and writhing intensified, and when Sol touched her with light, medium, or deep pressure at several random points on the left side of her body, she gasped "Burn, burn hurt." When he took a step back and asked her to show him where the pain was the worst, she pointed to her head, neck, arms, chest, abdomen, legs, ankles, feet, and, with particular passion, touched her left third toe.

When he tested her muscles by having her resist him, they were uniformly weak on the left side of the body and gave way, not smoothly, but as if attached to an internal ratchet. A minute later, when Sol asked her to stand from the exam room chair, she did so slowly, though with fluid movements. When he had her remove her coat, the jerky motions returned, and her face warped in anguish. She walked with a pronounced limp, favoring the left leg at first, but then the right when lifting herself onto the table. Nothing in her exam had changed since the last time he'd seen her, or the time before, or the first time she'd wandered into his office a month after the industrial injury.

His final pronouncement to the attorney was that he still had no answer for what was medically wrong with Mrs. Sánchez, and that since it had been in excess of a year since she had fallen, and she was still alive and unchanged, she was probably legally fixed and stable and wouldn't get better or worse in the foreseeable future.

Though it was clear that Lupe was another of his patients suffering from chronic pain syndrome, Sol was loathe to utter those words. While he was convinced she was truly miserable, as usual, the absence of any obvious trauma he could point to on an x-ray meant COLA would summarily snap its jaws shut on her claim. He sat down and nodded seriously, "I believe it's time to close this claim. Ms. Sánchez should be given an award for permanent partial impairment, and she should move on. That is my best advice."

The attorney promised to make short work of the case, stood, shook hands with Sol, nodded to Lupe, and left. She sat rigidly, waiting for something to happen, for someone to tell her what to do, where next to go, to whom to appeal. But Sol did not know either, so he guided her with his hand on her shoulder into the waiting room. "Do you understand what's going on, who that man is?" When there was no answer, to fill the silence, he blurted, "Lupe, that man is here from the government to help you."

She gasped, "Government?" As Sol put his hand on Lupe's arm, her eyes reddened, and she ran from the waiting room. Sol turned. He saw Rosebac standing in the middle of the hallway staring at him.

CHAPTER TWELVE

The usual pot pourri made their way through the offices of Dr. Solomon Forte, a relatively calm, entertaining day, and by five-thirty, he glanced offhandedly at what appeared to be the completed last page of his schedule. With a smile, he muttered to Roxanne, "Do you think we helped anybody today?"

Her lip curled down corrosively. She handed him an addendum to the day's schedule. As his eyes focused on the lone name, his pupils became tiny, irritated pinpoints. He bellowed, "Ah, for God's sake. Who put him on the docket?"

"Well, he's not exactly on the docket, Dr. F. He just wants to talk to you for a minute. Says the independent medical exam came back on Mrs. Berry, and the panel of doctors found her ready for work, with no residual impairment. And she hasn't shown up, and he wants to know what's going on."

"I never saw that report," Forte growled.

"Well, I've got all the papers right here. You'll probably need them."

Forte snatched the file from Roxanne but got only as far as the cover sheet. "Hey, it says this independent medical exam was done weeks ago. I never saw it. Wait a minute. Who filled out the bottom here where it asks if the attending physician, i.e., me, agrees? I signed this? I didn't sign this. It's stamped that I agree. Did you stamp it?"

"Yes, I did."

"Roxy, you can't do that. I need to read what the panel doctors say. *Then*, I can agree or disagree. I haven't seen her forever. So, is she back to work or not?"

"I don't know. He says she isn't."

"Roxanne, you're going to get me thrown in jail for insurance fraud. And you're going to go free. It's not fair. You can't do that."

"Look, boss, if I had you read and sign every COLA document that sailed across my desk, you'd never see a patient. You don't get paid for this stuff. What's the problem?"

"I do get paid. A buck or two, but now I gotta answer questions about something I don't know a thing about. Maybe she's not ready to go back to work. You don't know if she is or not, do you?"

"Dr. Forte, we both know that Mrs. Berry broke her ankle because she was drunk at work. Why should her boss have to foot the bill for that? Even you said it wasn't fair."

"Fair or not's got nothin' to do with the price of beans." Sol took a deep breath and pasted a smile on his face. "Okay, just bring him back. We'll continue our little talk later."

"Does that mean I don't get to go home until you're done?"

"No, go home. Maybe I'll tell him my nurse was drunk and hit me in the head, but because my employer refused to accept the claim, I didn't go to a doctor. And because I didn't seek medical care, now I have amnesia for all recent events, and I don't know who this Mrs. Berry is he's talking about."

Mr. Sullivan was as red-faced as the last time he'd dropped by. Sol couldn't tell if the man suffered from rosacea, was drunk, or just apoplectic. "Well, have a seat, sir. What can I do for you?" As Sullivan grumbled past, the reek of fresh alcohol nearly knocked Sol to his knees.

"Doctor, you said Edna could come back to work, and that was months ago. Haven't seen or heard from her all this time. I'm hiring temps; that costs a hell of a lot. You people say I have to give her her old job back. That means I can't hire a real worker."

"Excuse me, Mr. Sullivan, but those are not my rules, they're the state's."

"Well, it was your rules that you had to report her so-called broken bone as my fault. I'm sure you remember."

"Sir, I did what the law says I have to do. I know you feel like you're getting screwed, and I can't disagree, but please understand, I have no control over this. You need a lawyer. Told you that last time."

Mr. Sullivan's beet-red complexion deepened into a grisly maroon. "Why did you agree that she could go back to work, and she still isn't there?"

"Mr. Sullivan, I don't control a patient's actions. I'm not her father, nor am I a cop, for that matter."

"Well, then, what's this?" Sullivan half stood and angrily snapped a Commission on Labor Affairs Time Loss Notification form directly in front of Forte's face. "See what it says? See, this box you checked?" he snarled, poking his finger into the paper. 'No change in status. Time loss to continue.' But that was after you agreed with the independent medical exam, which said she had to go back to work immediately. You say one thing on the IME then another on the time loss card. What kind of bullshit are you peddling here?"

"Mr. Sullivan, I told you a long time ago, you can't come into my house and use profanity. And you can't be poking things in my face trying to intimidate me. It isn't going to work. Last chance. Sit down, be quiet, and let me take a look at the form."

"You better damn well look at it. And who the hell do you think you're talking to, you little snot nose?"

Sol rose and took a step backward, but as he absorbed the deepening rubor of the old man's face, Sol's own rage deepened, and he bellowed, "Get out of my office."

Sullivan, though motionless for a moment, jumped to his feet, began to weave toward Sol, then lurched forward, grabbed the COLA form, crumpled it in one hand, and cocked the other. He looked at his fist, drew it back slowly, then banged past Forte. Roxanne had been listening on the other side of the door. When it flew open, she was knocked back several steps and teetered as he bristled down the hall. She regained her balance and struck out toward Sullivan, who had turned right at the end of the hall into the x-ray room instead of left into the waiting room. Roxanne followed him in, lifting and curling her long, deep purple nails. She took a giant step toward him, hands aimed at his eyes.

As Sullivan leaned back and jerked his head away, he lost his balance and his feet slid out from under him. He toppled in reverse. The back of his head hit the edge of the steel x-ray table so hard, there was already a puddle of blood on the floor when his head arrived.

Sol grabbed Roxanne's arms from behind and dragged her into the hall. He asked, "Are you okay?"

"What do you mean?" she answered waveringly.

"I mean is your hand okay? Did he hit you first?"

"No, he shoved me, I think. He didn't really hit me, and I didn't hit him. He slipped."

"Did you shove him?"

"No, I told you. He slipped. Fell backwards. I better call the medics from downstairs. You need to look in on the asshole."

As Forte entered the room, Sullivan was on his knees, his head hanging, as if in prayer. Sol stood over him and said quietly, "The medics are on the way up. You need to lie down and wait for them. And, let me take a look at your head."

But the old man growled as if a mad dog, rose to his feet, and wobbled down the hall. The drunken fighter's face was wet with tears as he shoved Sol aside and zigzagged through the office door. By the time the medics arrived from downstairs, Roxanne had cleaned up the pool of blood, turned off her computer, and snatched her purse from the drawer. She hissed at Sol, "See ya tomorrow, maybe."

Sol recognized two of the medics as those who had escorted Mrs. Sánchez to the psychiatric hospital months before. They wheeled in their gurney, but Sol waved them off with the back of his hand. Sol picked up the crumpled COLA card, the document allowing Edna Berry months of additional paid leave. It was damp and stained red. He held it by the corner, unfolding it gingerly, avoiding contact with Sullivan's life's juices, then perused the signature line. It was, as he had feared, stamped with his name.

Sol sat at his desk for several minutes, aware that he would have to answer for allowing his staff to commit insurance fraud. He recognized that, due to his lack of oversight, he, not Roxanne, was likely to be charged with a felony. He dropped into a seat in a corner of the waiting room. His imagination wandered to the sentence he would draw from the judge, and he leaned back to conjure the weak excuses he would put before the court to justify his failure.

Less than two minutes went by before he was jolted from his musings by an ambitious squealing of tires, a pounding of the air, shattering glass, deep rumbling, and finally, a bang as loud as if a bomb had detonated inside the building. There was a brief pause, but within two seconds, there was another crash, this one closer and even louder. The lights flickered three times, and the office went dark. He felt his way out of the waiting room toward the emergency exit. The crunch of collapsing sheet rock vibrated the floor. Dust and smoke poured from the elevator doors, both of which were sprung a foot apart.

Sol ran down the stairs to the main floor, where powdered sheetrock swirled like the devastating East Coast hurricanes of his youth. The difference that night was not so much the speed of the wind, but its source. Sol was disoriented. The gusts were flowing in through the demolished front door complex of the Galena Hills Hospital and Medical Center. He walked toward the entrance to witness the first of the dozens and dozens of Whitaker's police who would respond to the disaster, excitable young men, their patrol car lights and sirens blaring, many with service revolvers drawn.

The cops pushed past Sol, and he followed them, though stayed a few yards behind as the officers pointed their pistols menacingly around corners as they sprinted willy-nilly about the first floor. There were shouts of "SECURED!" blasting from Internal Medicine, from Pediatrics and, finally, Neurology. Sol choked on the dust as he passed through the crushed entrance to General Surgery, but held his breath and turned left through the blotted-out employees' lunchroom. When he entered the main waiting room through a gaping hole in the wall, the dross was so thick, he could not make out the back of his hand. He drifted toward voices and came to several employees flanking the rear chunk of a relatively new Ford 350. The front half had disappeared into an elevator shaft.

On the floor, a bloodstained white towel pressed to his fore-head, lay prostrate an older man, a huge, ruddy-faced man, who ignored the screaming cops, some of whom were kicking at him. Other peace officers stood half-crouched, surrounding the lump on the floor, their Tasers and pistols aimed at the man's head, barrels trembling in concert with their hands. When the man finally looked up, his face tightened, but not because of the tasers just inches from his temples. His eyes locked on Sol's stunned figure standing outside the perimeter of police. He rolled onto his hands and knees like an elderly orangutan then sprung frantically forward, between the cops' legs, toward Forte. He grabbed Sol's pants then jerked and twisted the material, pulling him closer, his jaws snapping, trying to lock onto Sol's leg. Forte shrieked, "Mr. Sullivan, calm down, damn it."

The cops pulled at Sullivan, but the old man broke free and made a second lunge toward Sol. That was when one of the smaller officers belted Sullivan in the back of the head with his Taser. It reopened the wound, and the old man crumpled back to the floor. When it was safe, the medics rushed forward, loaded him on a gurney, strapped him down, and wheeled him under heavy guard out the far exit of the Center, avoiding the rubble, into the parking lot, onto Mitchie Drive, and around the corner onto Lynton Street. They struggled with the gurney for an eighth of a mile before rolling into the ER.

Sullivan fought to sit up. He screamed, "Now, maybe you bastards'll listen to me."

After a couple of hours of interrogation at the Whitaker Police Department, Sol called Dana and asked to come over for a drink. Though she tried to stifle a smile as Sol unraveled the saga of Edna Berry and John Sullivan, she was quite unsuccessful, and soon Sol was laughing so hard, he slipped off the couch. Dana served the Italian sausages she had rushed out and bought after Sol's call, then poured him a cold Rolling Rock.

Forte arrived early at the clinic the next morning, hoping to get his paperwork out of the way before the call from Anacota. As he approached the remnants of the main entrance, he came upon a crew of laborers who had spent the night scouring the lobby. Though the F-350 had been towed, the elevators remained in shreds. A half-dozen men in untidy, green jumpsuits emblazoned with the logo CAPACITY TEMP SERVICE stood behind a squad of wheelchairs to transport those patients incapable of negotiating stairs. Two of the men wore their sweat-stained baseball caps backwards, strings of greasy hair poking in seven directions.

Sol had taken only three steps through the hanging plastic sheets, where the front doors had been the evening before, when Hayes Anacota and Pierce Dorsett, the medical director, walked brusquely to his side. Anacota took Sol by the arm and pulled him into a dusty corner. He came to the point quickly. "I didn't sleep last night; on the phone until about five minutes ago, so don't expect me to play any PC games with you. First, I want to know, right now, what the hell did you do to that man?"

Sol did not get past the assault on Roxanne before Dorsett rubbed his chin and demanded, "And what about that Hispanic woman's suicide attempt, Doctor?"

"Suicide gesture."

"And the exchange with the nurse at Whitaker General, the young gal on the psych floor?"

"It was an old *he*, and *he* was an emasculated asshole."

"And that malingerer from Oregon? The one with the so-called spinal fracture and all the drugs?"

"I'm working on that," Sol reassured. Got him scheduled for an IME, work hardening, and the pain clinic. Got all the bases covered."

"Well, Dr. Forte," Anacota offered a bit more softly, though shaking his head and tapping his lips nervously with his index finger, "this experiment of yours is drawing some interesting characters into the Center. Now, by itself, the Board of Directors isn't concerned with the concept. Most of the doctors here occasionally see these types of people; it's part of the job, but a steady diet, and the kind of workers being seen in your practice, well, doesn't it make you sit up and, shall we say, take pause?" Anacota stepped back and folded his pudgy fingers.

Forte sighed. "Hayes, look, I'm not going to argue it's perfect. No practice is. Even in Belvedere, they've got tons of problems. Rich kids overdosing, suicides in doctor's offices. Hey, that plastic surgeon gettin' a little while his ladies were asleep. Remember? We see all sorts of patients here, every one of us. Right? And everybody's making a good living—last time I looked."

"So, it's okay to have pissed off employers so bad they blow our buildings apart?"

"Hayes, I know the corporation comes first. And it should. If you and the board think COLA patients aren't positive for the Center, there has to be an adjustment. I'm perfectly willing, in fact, I'd be happy to see more private patients, but I'm not sure my colleagues in Ortho are all that willing to take up the slack. Someone's got to see them. Rosebac and Rooney didn't do so good in the course on sharing back in kindergarten. Please keep in mind, though, if I cut back on COLA, all that means is no *new* COLA patients. I'm stuck with the players I've already got, and that's apparently going to keep us busy for a while. And, by the way, a big clinic can't just stop seeing COLA. Terrible publicity."

Anacota's sausage-like fingers were clasped so tightly, the color had drained out of his knuckles. He thought for a moment. "That's a very good point, but it isn't necessarily COLA patients per se. Let me be frank, it's the way they're being, shall I say, managed. Lot of raised eyebrows around the Center about the number of disruptive episodes."

"We've already talked about that. This didn't happen in a vacuum. When I got here, all the old docs sent me their worst COLA cases and kept the easy ones. All of a sudden, because I had a decent attitude about it, I was the only one seeing COLA patients. No one harped about *that*, did they?"

"New kid on the block has to start at the bottom."

"Yeah, well, word got out that I was available, and now I'm getting patient after patient from around the city."

"You said you wanted that."

"What I said was that because a patient was hurt on the job, he shouldn't be treated as a pariah from the get go. And I probably put too much into acting as an advocate. I guess I'll have to work on being a little less clinically entangled."

Dorsett nodded. "That'd be a start. No one's asking you not to be yourself, but there are ways to do it a little neater. Hayes, let's see how things play out. We can revisit this in a couple of weeks. I got a lot on my plate suddenly." He brooded as he turned and walked off. Anacota left in the opposite direction without another word.

On the way back to his office, Sol was stopped by a dozen staff, all of whom shook their heads in veiled giddiness, the gist of their commentary orbiting around the stupidity of the patient who thought he could drive his Oldsmobile into an elevator. Sol smiled and bothered to correct the first few, "It wasn't a patient, and it was a Ford 350."

Ruminating over Anacota's counsel, Sol sat at his desk scribbling on a pad. The header read: "An Innovative Plan to Care for COLA Patients / Building a Real Practice."

He called Roxanne on the intercom and asked her to come to his office with pen and pad. She arrived empty-handed. He asked her to sit. "Let's review our luminaries once again."

She quipped snidely, "Sorry Dr. F., we ain't got six hours."

"Okay, okay, I'll go talk to Rosebac again and find out how a doctor treats patients like crap, doesn't get sued, or even into trouble with admin, and makes a pile of dough. He knows. He's the master."

Rosebac, however, wasn't in his office. He was down in Anacota's suite, and going to be there "…apparently, for a long time. You know Anacota," Rosebac's nurse snapped as she turned her back to Sol. "We're going to be behind an hour. I'll never get home. Wonder whose fault this could be?"

When Rosebac returned to the floor, he marched into Sol's exam room and tugged him by the white coat into the Orthopedic Department's conference room. The door closed with a bang. Roxanne and Rosebac's nurse turned to each other and glowered, drumming fingers until Sol emerged, pale, shoulders hunched.

Roxanne sprang from her stool and dragged him back to the exam room he had forsaken a quarter-of-an-hour before. She held his arm tightly. "Dr. F., I don't give a shit about Rosebac, and you don't either. You got a job to do, and you're great at it, best in the whole frickin' joint, best I've ever seen. You see thirty-some COLA patients every day. Ninety-nine percent come and go, and when they go, they know they were treated good. Now let's get something straight. I'll never say all that again, so don't wait up. By the way, piss on 'em, all of 'em. Now let's start seein' patients."

Sol walked the abandoned COLA back pain patient to the stairs. "Ms. Saperstein, you call me if your employer makes you go back to lifting a thousand tires a day."

He turned and smiled at Roxanne. "Okay, head 'em up." But there was a sudden paucity of the unwell funneling into the Department of Orthopedics. In fact, there was not a single soul in the waiting area fidgeting, anticipating the call into an exam room. There was nothing to do but watch Rosebac clamber the halls, hissing very audible threats to wring compensation for his lost income from the one responsible for the debacle.

A platoon of elevator technicians had been flown in from half-a-dozen cities. The sleepy-eyed mechanics and engineers assured Anacota there would be at least two lifts going by ten, but at noon, the entire main bank remained a mass of tangled concrete, rebar, and blinking emergency lights. Outside the Center, the men from the temp agency coalesced into a grumbling, milling mass. A tall, cadaverous, stringy-haired soul, shouted, "I ain't dragging no more fat people up and down three flights of stairs for no eight-fifteen an hour. You can kiss my ass."

The balance of the temps held signs scratched on scraps of cardboard: "Pay a living wage, or go to hell." Raising cigarettes and bad coffee over their heads in one hand, they waved their placards in the faces of the Center's waiting patients.

Anacota announced over the PA system: "All nurses, medical assistants, and receptionists are to assemble on the ground floor at the Internal Medicine Department."

Anacota broke them into teams of five, by department. "Ladies and gentlemen, this is a time in which we must join together to save our clinic and your jobs. Please patrol the area outside the Center for your patients. Those over fifty-five will be placed in wheelchairs and brought to the proper department."

"Roxanne snorted, "Even those who can walk, I suppose."

Anacota glared at the Ortho team. He snarled, "Yep, even those who can walk. We cannot afford a lawsuit over a heart attack on the stairs."

In Ortho, Rosebac paced, now growling loudly, spitting orders at his nurse's empty workstation. His fists tightened as he ground to a halt at Sol's half-closed door. "A little sage advice for you today, Doctor. I probably should've given up about seven or eight years ago, but here goes again. This is a business, like IBM or GE. Doing business means service, especially to the people who feed you, like Whitaker's community leaders, Mr. Sullivan for instance. These people deserve deeper consideration than we've extended. Why, just today, one day in the life of the Center, Sol, think how much income we're losing over a meaningless dispute about another baseless COLA claim. A drunk guy falls out of his seat on the garbage truck and breaks an arm. Why the hell would you go to work drunk if you're around machinery? No matter, it's a lot out of my pocket, you realize. And there's also the full day of chaos that'll most likely stretch into a month or two of bedlam. This isn't healthy."

At twelve-ten, Roxanne's team had deposited half-a-dozen patients, what was left of the orthopedically broken who'd had ten o'clock appointments, in the waiting room. Instantly hopelessly behind, Sol smiled at Roxanne. "Not to worry. Word's out, I'm sure. Everyone in the county knows the Center looks and smells like it's been hit by a Saturn Rocket. No one's a comin'."

He marched, head high, into Room Two. "Mr. McAlister, you've lost more weight." And, in fact, the man's cheeks had become hollow, giving him the look of a lean, finely trained athlete. His complexion, though, was wan, and his eyes were bright yellow. Rather than helicopter legs whirling in counter rotating displays of mock pain, he sat hunched forward, crying softly. His girlfriend was standing behind him, her arms wrapped tightly around his shoulders.

She spoke first. "Dr. Forte, you have to do something for Kevin. He got up in the middle of the night screaming, running around the house hitting himself in the head with my son's baseball bat trying to stop the pain. My neighbor had some Vicodins, and I gave him four, and then four more an hour ago. You have to do something."

Sol's chest clenched as if it had been struck by a pile driver. The answer was there, right in front of his eyes. His solar plexus gripped in that miserable smack of dread he had experienced so many times in the past, fearing, and finally accepting, he had made a dreadful medical mistake. He went over to McAlister, put a hand on his shoulder, and whispered, "We're gonna get ya better. Hang in there for a minute."

Sol went to Rosebac and begged. "Dave, I need you to put one of my patients in the hospital for pain control. This is serious. He's got something bad somewhere, I know it, but I can't find it. Please help me."

Rosebac looked up incredulously. "Let me get this straight. I'm already doing yeoman's service, doing penance for your screw up, and now you want me to get farther behind to admit one of your disasters because you don't keep hospital admitting privileges because COLA patients don't need to be admitted, and because of that you don't have to do call every fourth night like I've had to for the past twenty years, and everybody else does. Contact the doctor on call and beg her." With that, Rosebac turned abruptly and stomped into an exam room. The door slammed.

Sol considered his options. It would be better to visit the on-call doctor personally than to just phone down there. He ran the two flights down to what was left of Internal Medicine. At Dr. Kathy Maurane's office, the internist, devoid of make-up, and with clothing that had been slept in, announced, "I'm on call for another thirty minutes, and I'm cutting my day short. I've been awake all night taking calls from frantic patients who had heard the Galena Hills Center had been bombed and reduced to rubble. I'm not happy to see you, Dr. Forte."

Sol stood obsequiously at her door. Considering he had never said "boo" to her, nor she to him in the eight years of his sojourn at the Center, he was surprised at how quickly she refused to take on Mr. McAlister as an inpatient.

"Go and see if the next on-call doctor feels like handling your screw-ups. I need to get some sleep, *and* I'm taking my dog to obedience class tonight, come hell or high water. And why can't you admit him? Oh, I forgot, COLA patients never need hospitalization. So, why should *you* have to pay the four hundred dollars a year for admitting privileges, and let's not forget, live a shitty life on call every fourth night?"

Sol acknowledged quietly with a nod that she had a point. He left and wended his way through the dust and rubble to Dorsett's office in Ophthalmology. As the next scheduled on-call doctor, surely Dorsett would understand Sol's plight, but he, too, refused, suggesting, "Sounds like a neurosurgical problem. Why don't you go talk to them?"

Sol weaved back through the detritus to Dr. Isak Grinberg's office. Sol was reticent to bother him, as he had already imposed upon the old man with a host of interesting patients over the years. But Sol liked Dr. Grinberg a lot, for not only did the neurosurgeon claim an uncommon past, he also greeted Sol and smiled when they passed in the halls.

The wrinkled little man sat with his feet propped on his desk, staring into space, looking more like Albert Einstein in his concentration than a foreign-trained doctor serving out his years at a modest medical clinic in a modest suburb. He smiled when Sol knocked, dropped his feet to the floor, and motioned warmly for him to come in. He nodded toward a chair. Grinberg listened to Sol's plea, thought for a moment, and answered in the thick Russian accent of his homeland. Sol liked to listen to the man and try to parse out that smack of Israeli confidence from the years he had spent in Jerusalem after escaping the Soviet Union. "Vhy not?" he grunted. "Ve find out vhat's ronk mit your frent."

Sol was nearly tearful. Grinberg, though past retirement age, was the most astute neurosurgeon in Whitaker. He had honed his skills operating on eel brains in Novosibirsk, in Siberia, before the bureaucrats in Moscow recognized his prowess in teasing one strand of neural tissue from the next, and his patience to do it day after day for fifteen years. They brought him back to the capital in 1970 under a cloak of secrecy. His mission, ostensibly, was to operate on an "aneurysm" in the brain of Nikita

Khrushchev, the former Prime Minister. The long- retired head of state had tipped more than the occasional goblet of Dana's grandfather's vodka, and there was not much more than pudding left in Nikita's cerebrum when Grinberg drilled a hole to look inside. Khrushchev, though it was never made public, died on the operating table, as did Dr. Grinberg's star. He was ordered to pack his drills and scalpels and return to the outback and his eels.

But before pulling up stakes at the hospital, Grinberg relieved the Moscow People's Hospital Number One of a large portion of its supply of narcotics, which he used to barter with the captain of a Russian trawler for a lift to Israel. There, though touted as a master craftsman by scientists, and given a position in the Neurosciences Department at Jerusalem University's Ben Yehuda Hospital, he remained for years stalled as a junior surgeon, realizing he would go no farther because of his status as a foreigner. This surprised Grinberg, for the bulk of the citizens of Israel were immigrants, and he finally set off for the New World, which he often groused his parents should have done a century before. Before he left, a colleague whispered to him that the reason for his failure to reach the upper levels of the Israeli medical establishment was due to his abject incapacity to learn more than twenty-five words of Hebrew—over seventeen years.

Landing in New York in 1988, Grinberg aced the medical portion of the ECFMG, the astonishingly difficult examination foreign medical graduates were obliged to work their way through if they wished to practice as physicians in the U.S. Several universities contacted him and offered lucrative inducements to join their faculties, but none of the schools had noticed that Dr. Grinberg had horribly failed the English Language Skills portion. So, he moved to Whitaker to live with a distant cousin, laboring through several years of English tutoring while working as a lab technician at Whitaker General. Six years later, he squeaked through the language exam.

By the time he passed, on the fourth try, he was so old, he had to settle for a position as a staff surgeon at the Galena Hills Hospital. He often told his colleagues, though, that he was finally happy, for life there was slow and the odds were on his side, finally, that he would die in a bed, not in front of a firing squad.

At the Center Christmas party that year, one of the doctors at Grinberg's table, a man who had consumed far more than his share of eggnog, slurred, "Forte, I got a joke for ya. So, there's three men sitting in your waiting room. Jesus Christ walks in and approaches the first. 'My son, what is your ailment?'

"'Father, I have been blind since birth.'

"Jesus touches the man's eyes and mutters a prayer. The patient opens his eyes and wails, 'Oh, Father, oh, Father! I can see; I can see!'

"Jesus turns to the second man, 'And you, my son, what is your affliction?'

"'Father, I have been paralyzed since I was a small child. I cannot move my legs.'

"Jesus bends forward and touches the man's thighs. He mutters a different prayer, and the man jumps from the chair crying, 'Oh, Father, oh, Father! I can walk; I can walk!'

"Jesus walks to the third patient. 'My son, how can I help you?'

"The man snarls, 'Don't you touch me, I'm COLA.'"

There was a bit of laughter, and John turned to Dr. Grinberg. "So, Isak, what the hell are you doing here?"

"Hafing Christmas dinner vis my Gentile frents. Vat does it look like, John?"

"No, I mean what the hell are you doing in Whitaker, population fifty thousand? How come you're not at Harvard, or some damn thing?"

Dr. Grinberg thought for a moment and spoke quite seriously. "John, tell me. Are ze sick patients in Boston zo different, maybe more important zan ze sick patients in Whitaker? Tell me, if you can."

Sol breathed more easily as he made his way through the dust back to the Orthopedic Department. Kevin McAlister was in such torment, he did not look up when Sol entered the room. Forte had Roxanne put his patient in a wheelchair for his ride down the stairs, through the temporary doors, into the street, down one block, around the corner, and up the next block to the hospital wing.

CHAPTER THIRTEEN

It was Friday, and Sol was reassured that McAlister would be in the house for the weekend, in the hands of a master who would sort things out. He took a moment to think forward to the next few hours. There would be mandatory weekend meetings with administrators and lawyers, and he sat, feet up, devising excuses to absent himself. In truth, he planned to sleep through until Monday morning. Of course, the Board of Directors would inform his malpractice insurer of the potential for litigation over Mr. Sullivan's displeasure, and there would be reams of forms to complete. And then there were still diehard patients to see. He was more than two hours behind, and he rushed to the first room, snatching the chart from the rack without looking at the name. He would grovel and ask for mercy for having made that patient wait longer than he ever had made anyone wait in his life.

With head hung sat Ralph Tarkington. He was wearing the same shirt and drool-encrusted overalls as on the last visit and the first visit. Sol looked about for Ms. Famot, searching the various corners as if the woman was so petite, and the exam room so vast, she could be hidden in a niche or under the exam table.

"Mr. Tarkington, long time no see, my friend. Are you doing any better?"

Without looking up, he mumbled, "Don't know. You tell me, you're the doctor."

"Well, what brings you here today?"

"My lawyer told me to come. Says I need some paperwork."

Sol's face tightened, but he looked back at Tarkington and appreciated the shell of a spirit, one bereft of a past, a present, and most certainly, a future. Then the vision of Kevin McAlister, hunched in a wheelchair, stripped of breath, of dignity, and very likely a future as well, flashed across his mind. Forte jumped up, patted Mr. Tarkington on the shoulder, and smiled as he opened the door. "Let me call your attorney and find out how we can help you."

On the phone, El Haq asked Sol to review the notes of early 1985 and determine if Tarkington had a "demylorting" disease."

"I think that's de-my-el-en-ay-ting."

"Yes, and what is that?"

"It's a process in which the coating around the nerves, like insulation on a wire, gets screwed up, and the nerves touch, like bare electrical wires, and that causes short circuits, and things don't work right. I guess that could be a cause of bizarre behavior."

"Doctor," El Haq asked, sounding genuinely concerned, "how can you be sure he has this disease?"

"Well, I can't, but a neurologist can."

"I believe you just answered a crucial question." El Haq added, "You see, Dr. Forte, Mr. Tarkington never saw a neurologist after the first few months. Neuropsychologist? Yes. But a medical doctor specializing in demyelinating disease; that's not in the records, except in a couple of his independent medical exams. The only health care person who ever said his problem was a nerve disease was a nurse case manager for the employer. It's all in the records. Would you kindly look at the file and write a short statement that there really was no evidence of a demyelinating disease, except by the word of an untrained nurse? I'll need this by tomorrow."

"Mr. El Haq," Sol grunted, "we've been over this territory before—several times. I don't sit here waiting for your call so I can jump and do your bidding—for free."

"Doctor, I am very sorry, but as I have told you, if you want me to have you served with a subpoena to get your cooperation, I will be happy to do so. The court tells me when they are ready to deal with my motions. Please feel free to contact Judge Wheel and tell her of your displeasure with the system of justice in the United States. She's a delightful woman, loves to dispense fines, big ones, on the heads of those who don't treat her well, even doctors. I've explained in the past that it's a one-sided process. If you could simply review the nurse's letter, a Miss Calhoun, dated 28th March 1991. She says that my client sufferers from a demyelinating disease, and not one that was the result of grabbing an electric wire or a fall of a few feet …"

"That was the end of him," Sol muttered.

"Yes, very well, but that assistant attorney general used that statement in court, and the judge believed it. Nowhere did they ever follow up on the proof that he had this disease. And doctor, do *you* believe that Mr. Tarkington suffers from a demyelinating disease?"

"I don't think he does. I'm no expert, but I think those diseases are always progressive, and he hasn't changed in twenty years. If he had a demyelinating disease, it would have slowly worsened, and he'd be a vegetable by now."

"Doctor, all I need is a very short note to that effect. I am not trying to harm you. I have a job to do. Don't look at it as though you're doing my bidding. You must see it as helping your patient, and also staying in the good graces of Judge Wheel. You win all the way around."

Sol sighed into the phone but mumbled his concurrence. Roxanne, who had been listening, came into his office and sat down. "Why do you take that from him, Dr. F.?"

"You were listening? I didn't hear the heavy breathing. Because, Madame Mercy, right now, I'm trying to keep a low profile, trying to avoid opening yet another front in the war." He got out of his chair and fetched the thick pile of Tarkington's sepia records from the bottom drawer of his filing cabinet. In the section from the early-1990s, Sol came to a letter in which Debbie Calhoun, a registered nurse who worked for Argent as a case manager, proclaimed that Mr. Tarkington's infantile speech and behavior patterns, he read aloud, "'…while clearly present, are the sad result of a progressive degenerative neurologic disease, not of the insignificant slip and fall incident of the 2nd of February, 1989.'" Sol went on caustically. "She couldn't even get the date right—off by damn near a decade. Our Nurse Calhoun based her studied medical opinion on the fact that Mr. Tarkington had demonstrated occasional episodes of what she interpreted as hemiballism, a '…sure sign,' the woman wrote, 'that Mr. Tarkington is suffering from multiple sclerosis, or another, similar, not-yet-specified, demyelinating process.'"

Roxanne screwed up her face. "Okay, I give up, what's hemi-ballism? How could he have had kids?"

"It's not what you're grinning about. Sorry to take the air out of another tidbit for the rumor mill, but it's got nothing to do with the family jewels. It's when you're always flinging your arm or leg out wildly, and not on purpose. But that's appalling." He shook his head.

"What's appalling?"

"Look, an unwritten rule, and by now probably written-in-many-places rule, in medicine is that you *never* base an important diagnosis on a single symptom or lab test. You know that. What if old Tarkington was psychotically depressed, like me, and we know he was depressed after the accident, often happens after an electric shock, and he was hallucinating, swinging at imagined assailants? Doesn't mean he's got MS or hemiballism, or anything else.

"Then she lists a very slight protein abnormality in his spinal fluid. Just a tiny bit higher than *average*, but still within the normal standard range, and certainly nothing to write home about. Big deal. Between that and the hemiballism, according to lawyers at Argent, this nurse had made a brilliant diagnosis. Problem is, even if the spinal fluid protein level really was abnormal, which it wasn't, lab tests aren't perfect, far from it. What if the guy doing the analysis screwed up and contaminated the specimen? What if the lab accidentally switched Tarkington's paperwork or his blood with another patient's? Happens all the time. I had a doctor in medical school tell me that if a lab never admitted they lost a sample, he'd stop using them because he knew they were lying."

"I don't believe that happens. I think you're exaggerating."

"I told you about that fruitcake lab tech downstairs, right here in your beloved clinic, the one before you came on the scene, didn't I?"

"I donno know. You tell me a lotta stuff."

"I'm sure I told you. She was the one changing lab results because she was obsessed with Don Douglas, my pal over in Peds. She'd fudge numbers from the tests he ordered, made kids look sicker than they were, and then give the real result two weeks later to make it look like he cured them. Drove up his numbers, too. Kids coming back every three days for rechecks. That increased his stature with Anacota and the board of directors, to say nothing of raising his income and, it followed in her head, his fondness for her. Why can't you do that?"

Roxanne sucked in a deep breath, but Sol raised his palm, placing it nearly in her face. "What if our Mr. Tarkington ate something that raised the protein level a tiny bit, or one of his meds elevated it, or, maybe, that was just what his level was normally? And, best of all, sit back and relax young lady, what if the test itself was 'weak,' or even so primitive, that it hardly measured what it was supposed to?"

"If it doesn't measure what it's supposed to, why do you make me send patients to get poked and their blood taken?"

"It's a good question. It's not all tests. But some blood assays are actually *owned* by international medical conglomerates. They have a patent on the test or the machine that runs it, and they make handsome donations to politicians who exert influence over the FDA to keep the test running night and day, whether it works or not.

"No," Sol shook his head angrily, "Nurse Calhoun overstepped her boundaries at any number of junctures. She should have requested the test be repeated at least. It's not the first time I've seen an adjunct health care 'specialist' get up one rainy morning, all frustrated and emasculated, and flex the old payment muscle. You tell me how many times I've received a letter from a nurse case manager stating, 'Doctor, please respond to my letter with a full, objective substantiation of your diagnosis within seven days so that we may make a decision regarding the payment of the patient's outstanding bill.' And that's after we've already been waiting five months to get paid."

Though Sol was becoming more irked with the thought of his impotence in the face of the insurance companies that governed his life, his venom would have to wait. Roxanne stood and said softly, "I know how you feel, but they's a waitin' for ya out there in the trenches. Let's start with your old friend Mrs. Berry. You remember Edna and her boss, Crash Sullivan? Bet you do."

Mrs. Berry was still suffering from self-reported debilitating pain and swelling in her ankle. She had not returned to work, so Sol stood in front of her wheelchair and spoke bluntly. "Mrs.

Berry, you just can't stay out of work for months at a time without coming in here for me to take a look at you. COLA isn't a paid vacation. I have to see you every couple of weeks and decide if you're able-bodied to go back to work."

"Doctor," she huffed indignantly, "I can't do that job. I'm not as young as I was once, you know. I just don't have the strength to get up every few minutes and file papers and whatnot. My doctor says I'm very sick, and I have to rest."

"Mrs. Berry, I understand, and that's fine, but the rules say you have to come in here regularly to let me see how you're doing. And let me be frank. If you can't work because of the leukemia, I can't keep on signing time-loss authorizations for you. Maybe you should think about applying for Social Security. That's what it's for."

She stiffened, wagged her finger in his face, and spat crossly, "Doctor, you listen. I've worked my whole life. I'm not some *kid*, you know." She glared at Sol and brayed, "I *deserve* COLA."

Sol waited for the reasoning to bolster her argument, but Edna Berry had spoken, and she clasped her pocketbook tightly in her lap, fingers turning whiter as her scowl deepened.

"Well, Ma'am, let's take a look at your ankle and see how you're doing." She turned her face from Sol and snapped her leg up in a kick fit for the Rockettes. There was little, if any, swelling around the ankle. He asked her to push the ankle hard against his hand, and the leg went limp. He lifted her other leg, and the bad ankle tightened. When he touched it lightly, it went flaccid again. When he tried to put the ankle through a full range of motion, though, she fought back with surprising strength.

"You're hurting me, Doctor," she whined as she pulled her leg away forcefully.

Forte apologized feebly, stroked her ankle, and asked her in a surprised tone, "When I do this, on the left side of your foot, does your left shoulder hurt, Mrs. Berry?"

She thought for a moment and nodded as if in relief. "Why, yes, yes it does. Happened when I fell from that lousy chair. How did you know that?" As she relaxed, a satisfied calm came to her face, Sol pushed back subtly in his rolling chair a few inches. When he eyed her shoulder, it tightened defensively. While she was distracted by her shoulder pain, he moved her ankle through a full, smooth range of motion. There was not a peep.

"Well, Mrs. Berry," he smiled as he stood to roll her now-frozen left shoulder in circles, "Let me tell COLA that you're still my patient. Let's see how they want to proceed."

"Good. And be sure to tell them about the injury to my shoulder. It's their responsibility. They have to pay me for that, too."

"Not to worry, Mrs. Berry."

Roxanne grabbed him by the sleeve as he walked from the room. "Hospital's on the line. McAlister is writhing around on the floor screaming in pain. They want orders."

Sol took the phone. He could hear the groans and hollers in the background. The nurse stuttered breathlessly. "Your patient is screaming that he wants to die and that he…"

Sol cut her off, snapping an order for an injection, "Demerol, seventy-five milligrams IM, no, make it one-hundred, and fifty of Phenergan. And give it to him every two to three hours. Just keep him comfortable. Dr. Grinberg'll be over shortly."

"But, Doctor," she interrupted, "he's screaming that he broke his leg. He's on the floor and won't let anyone touch him."

Breath wheezed out of Sol's chest in foreboding. "I'll be right over." He left the center with a three-word order for Roxanne. "Figure it out."

CHAPTER FOURTEEN

Sol found McAlister on the hard tile floor of his hospital room, lying quietly, nearly somnolent, unable to lift his head from the ground. Half-a-dozen nurses stood in the hall outside the door, shoulder to shoulder, in a circle, facing outward like angry musk oxen.

Sol approached his patient slowly. "What happened, Kevin?"

Barely able to speak, he slurred, "My leg…exploded." He gathered up the material of his hospital gown, unabashedly exposing himself. In the middle of his thigh, protruding through what appeared to be a well-fed camel's hump, were several white hairs, but when Sol gently brushed his fingers over them, he realized the fibers were hard and sharp, like bone.

He turned to the nurses and barked at the oldest-looking, "Where are the x-rays?"

The woman grumbled, "You don't talk to *me* like that," then keeled around and bristled off to report the incident and, Sol eventually learned, to file a grievance with the Human Services Department. He looked at another of the older women, but a very young woman stepped forward and announced nervously, "I'm the charge nurse. They're just medical assistants, MAs."

The women stiffened and glared her. Sol focused on their name tags. While "RN" trailed the charge nurse's name, the others' were engraved with "MA" and one with "CNA", Certified Nursing Assistant.

"Well, Registered Nurse Johnson, do we have an x-ray cooking or not?"

"We ordered one, but they were busy on Two-West. They said they'd get here when they got here." As Sol's face tightened, she started to shake. "Doctor," she pleaded, "that's what the tech said. I can't make them do anything. They're Radiology. They hate us."

"No. She needs to come up here right now. This is a priority. Get her on the phone for me, please." It was minutes before the nurse handed Sol the phone, and more before he deciphered the x-ray tech's broken English, but it sounded as though she was on her way. He sat on the floor with Kevin, though when several more minutes passed, he jumped up and called the CEO's office, demanding action. He ordered another seventy-five milligrams of Demerol for his groaning patient, whose arms had begun to shudder. The charge nurse turned to get the medication, but Sol commanded, "No, you stay, Nurse. I need you here."

Minutes later, a tiny woman wheeled off the elevator outside McAlister's room. While weaving through the onlookers, she pivoted the motorized x-ray machine too quickly and lost control. The machine lurched forward, and the tech dug in the heels of her sneakers, but the one-ton contraption dragged her toward McAlister. The CNA, a large woman, shot forward and snapped the master switch off. The machine stopped short, and the tech flew over the handles. She doubled over, put both hands behind her to press on her hips, and began to cry. After a minute, she sucked in a deep breath and straightened her back. Grimacing, she carped, "Doctor, you will need to put the patient on his bed. I cannot bend over. I have injured my back."

Sol stood silently, his eyes fixed to a stain on the wall. As the heat in his face waned, he remarked indifferently, "I would have put him on his bed, but I just didn't want to disturb the poor man. He's resting so peacefully, don't you think? So, let's just take the x-ray so we can see what's wrong with him first and not kill him in the process."

The tech frowned and opened the film drawer. "Doctor, we are out of x-ray plates." Without another word, she pushed a few buttons, and the machine whirred into reverse toward the door, but Sol placed himself in front of it and demanded, "Leave it here. It takes too long to move the damn thing around."

She snipped, "I cannot carry the plates by myself," and did not wait for Sol to move out of the way before restarting the motor.

Some minutes later, a very dark-skinned man piloted the device into the room, stopping it smoothly with the x-ray cone aimed directly over the patient. McAlister, though, had already gone through the Demerol, his body so used to narcotic medication. He was flopping about in agony and screeching, "Let me fuckin' die, let me die!"

The new tech handed Forte a film cassette, and Sol placed it under McAlister's thigh, cautious not to move the limb a single millimeter. When the tech reversed out of the room, Sol fumed, "Where is the damn Demerol?" He looked directly at the nurse.

"Doctor, you told me not to leave."

"Then why didn't you tell someone else to get it?"

"I told you, they're just MAs—they're not allowed to open the narcotics drawer."

The x-ray man ran back up to the floor with the films. The break was obvious, but Sol gasped when he realized it was not a typical fracture of the thigh, the kind one saw after a two-story fall or a motorcycle accident. No, this was terribly different. There was a hint the bone near the fracture site had long-since suffered thinning, and instead of the sharp edges of a common break, the bone was moth-eaten, indistinct. This was disease-weakened bone, a pathological fracture, a femur that had shattered with just the patient's weight. Sol's hands trembled—it was cancer of the bone.

Though Kevin McAlister had left a trail of insupportable opiate consumption and obvious malingering in his wake, Dr. Forte shuddered coarsely as he grasped just how miserably he had failed to care for his patient's agony. Worse, the man would soon be dead for his negligence. His quaking grew as he conjured a string of fairytales to excuse himself for witnessing a man enduring the worst agony of all, cancer pain, particularly of the bone, and virtually ignoring it.

How could he have missed the red flags: the worsening pain, even when inactive; night pain that woke his patient from sleep; unexplained weight loss; and the lack of an obvious answer on the imaging studies? His audience would be the man's family, the administration, his colleagues, the State Medical Abuse Commission and, unquestionably, lawyers, jurors, and angry judges. How could he have missed it? He was numb with dread, though he couldn't tell if it was for his patient or for himself.

McAlister moaned, "I can't take the pain. Doc, do something." Forte stood straight, demanded his own hands stop quivering, and drew in a deep breath. "We've got work to do. A couple of people need to go down the ER and bring up a backboard." When no one budged, he pointed at two MAs and blurted, "You two, right now. Go. And Nurse Johnson, I want the Demerol, now!"

But the x-ray tech had, after delivering the film to Sol, run to the ER, grabbed a backboard, and sprinted back into McAlister's room just as Nurse Johnson was injecting Kevin. Sol patted the x-ray tech on the shoulder and muttered, "Good work, my friend. Thank you. Where are you from?"

The man nodded and spoke softly. "Sudan."

"So far away. So dangerous. You must be so glad to be here."

"No, sir, it is a beautiful country. You should go and be a doctor there. We need doctors who care."

Sol's chest clutched. "Okay, we're going to work together. Let's wait another two minutes, let the shot work, and then we're going to edge Mr. McAlister onto the backboard. Ladies," Sol nodded at two of the MAs, "when I give the word, roll him a quarter of an inch away from me, toward you. Let's see how far we can go. Ms. Johnson, you and I are going slide the board under him." Several of the larger nurses joined the x-ray tech and took places at the ends of the board. They lifted it onto the bed so smoothly, Kevin did not wake up. He was finally in the bed from which he would never leave.

Sol gave the team a thumbs up. "Look at that. The position of the leg hasn't changed an inch. This had to be one of the most distressing moments of our careers. Thank you all. You helped a sick patient today. Good work." The riled stares began to fade, and he helped one of the MAs start an IV and inject the first milligrams of morphine. Kevin dropped into a profound sleep, and the charge nurse covered him with a blanket. The African man lifted McAlister's head and placed a pillow under it. Sol left orders for morphine as needed, whatever dosage it took to keep his patient comfortable.

He went to the nursing station and called an oncologist from the center, mumbling, "Got a twenty-seven year-old, Caucasian male with an acute compound fracture of the left thigh. I can't tell if it's an osteosarcoma or a big met."

Miss Johnson overheard him, and when Sol dropped the phone numbly into its cradle, she asked, "Does that mean it's cancer?"

Sol nodded.

After seeing his last patient, Sol ran through a series of mystifying basement corridors, weaving his way back into the hospital building. His shivering peaked as he approached McAlister's room. It was nearly dark and just a faint streak of light from the shuttered blinds played on Kevin's face. His cheeks seemed more skeletal than they had in the office that morning. Sol's chest tightened uncomfortably, and he sensed nervous energy. As his eyes accustomed to the dark, he made out the silhouette of a woman sitting in the corner. He walked over and introduced himself.

An old lady rose slowly and asked with resignation, "Okay, what's he got, Doc?"

Sol thought for a moment, preparing to mouth the worst word in the English language, cancer, but he stopped short. Just as a sports announcer never screamed "touchdown" until the ref's hands, not the players', flew into the air, so, too, a doctor did not use the "C" word until the verdict was firm.

Ma'am, we don't have a firm diagnosis yet."

"Yeah, so what's he got?"

He whispered, "It's a broken bone."

Kevin McAlister's grandmother harrumphed, "I can see that. What the hell caused it?"

"Ma'am, we just don't know yet."

"Doctor," she asked directly, "the nurse told us Kevin's got a tumor in his bone, and that he's got cancer bad." The old woman paused, searching Sol's face for a sign. When he didn't answer, she went on, "Least she told us that's what you said."

Sol tensed angrily, wanting to fetch the nurse and have her take over the conversation, let her take the hit for saying one thing when no one on Earth knew what was true. But the bell had been rung, and in the interim, the family would go out of their minds with frustration and worry, not only over Kevin's illness, but also because the man in control would not even admit the truth they had already gathered, that there was no hope.

Sol stood with his jaw set tightly, waiting for a chance to leave the room and punish the nurse. But as the milliseconds ticked by under the old lady's stare, he reminded himself that a nurse wasn't responsible for anything she did shy of rape or euthanasia, and it now fell to him to backtrack a mile or two, and lie openly along the way.

"Ma'am, yes, he's got what we call a tumor, but we don't know what caused it. Could be a simple cyst in his bone. All of us have bone cysts. Some get large, and the bone breaks. First, we need to define the problem. No, first, we need to make Kevin comfortable. Then we need to do tests to be sure we understand exactly what's going on, like I said, define the problem. Please understand, we have not done that yet. And when we do have all the information, we are going to make a battle plan and fight whatever it is with a battalion of soldiers armed to the teeth. We're going about this step by step. I don't want any of us jumping to conclusions."

A man brooding in the far corner looked up. "Ain't you the one who didn't believe my brother that he was hurtin'? Didn't give him enough medicine, he said. Said you were gonna call the cops on 'im." The man rose and weaved about, the heavy spoor of alcohol heralding him many feet before he stopped inches from Sol's face. "Do you believe him now?" the man hissed, his fists tensed, the right cocked.

The grandmother took a step toward the men and spoke harshly. "Devin, go sit down. Let me handle this."

In the shadows, Sol had trouble making out the man's features, though when Devin turned to zigzag back to his chair, the meagre light played on his face, and Sol stepped back nearly breathless. He turned and stared at the bed. Kevin was still there; Sol was sure it was him. He turned back to the man facing him and blinked in disbelief.

The old lady spoke crossly. "I said sit down, Devin."

Very identical twins, Sol nodded to himself quietly, accepting the brother's bitterness. When Devin zigzagged and eventually found his chair, Sol went to the bedside. Kevin looked up and whispered groggily, "Hey, Doc, how you doin'?"

"You having any pain?"

"Nope. Feel great."

With that, Kevin's eyes drooped closed. Sol bowed slightly to the old lady and whispered, "I'll look in on Kevin in the morning. He's going to do fine here in the hospital. We have a specialist coming to see him. One of the best in the world."

"Yeah, right," rumbled from Devin's corner. There followed a snarled, "Grandma, you should sue that asshole."

As Sol took a step out of the room, the old lady called out, "Doctor, how long does he have?"

Sol sat with Dana that evening silently, just sipping wine. She was reticent to invade his reverie, but with the spirits warming her, she asked, "It's funny. I think you're suffering more than Kevin. This is *not* your fault. Who could have known the tumor was in his leg, not his back? How much did you spend on tests and referrals to other doctors?"

"Sweet Dana, that's not the point. I was the attending physician, and I missed the diagnosis. It's my lawsuit. I earned it the old-fashioned way. I screwed up."

Dana did not comment right away. She refilled both their glasses and waited until Sol had gone through half of his. "What worries you more; that Kevin has cancer, or that he may sue you?"

Sol took another long swallow and when the warmth spread evenly, he half-smiled. "You know, I kinda liked the guy. He was a royal pain in the ass, yeah, but for a good reason, it turns out. And I'll do anything I can to help him.

"What I hate the most is that I made a stupid mistake. All the years I prepared for this moment, and now some kid is going to die because I'm a failure. I feel like shit, fucking worthless.

"But there's also the other side of the coin. I begged him to get a bone scan. He decides he knows more about the evils of radiation than I do. ER docs also tried to get him to get the scan. So, on this side of the equation, I'm going to fry for a bizarre cancer in a bizarre guy who mostly brought it on himself with his bizarre smoking and drinking and drugging habits. Oh, and let's not forget that superior genetic profile. Why am *I* responsible for his mistakes and shitty protoplasm? And if it wasn't for grandma, I'd be in Bed B nursing a broken jaw. Who comes to the hospital loaded?"

Sol added bitterly, "This has been going on for generations in that family. I imagine we'll be meeting Mother McAlister over the next days. How much you wanna bet she's still having trouble with alcohol?" Sol raised his glass, laughed, and took a healthy swig. "And or drugs and a panoply of, shall we say, male partners? Bet you a quarter she's a piece of work."

Dana laughed sarcastically, "I thought you guys didn't judge your patients. Just so many Mahatma Gandhis selflessly giving of yourselves. Treat the ill, whatever the day brings."

"Like I said, I'll do anything in my power to treat him like a family member. If I need to clean up his vomit, I'll do it. And I care what happens to him, but I just don't want to be responsible for the actions of every squirrel that scratches his way into my cage.

"And just think about the Galena Hills Board of Directors. They're going to have my butt over this, too. Hospital's going to have to write off every penny of his care. Then the Center's going to be forced to pay back the money already collected for the MRIs, CAT scans, emergency room visits, and this test, and that test. Shit, the list goes on and on."

Dana screwed up her face in disbelief. "He's on COLA. They don't have deductibles, do they?"

"No, they don't. But the instant they hear he's got cancer, it's not their nickel anymore. COLA's not a welfare agency. Unless I can prove his cancer came from an industrial exposure, he's cooked, and so am I. Think of all my great friends at the Center who'll be calling me to ask why their salary is getting dinged to refund the money to COLA, and just because I begged them to take a look at him. And they didn't get it right, either.

"So, thanks to Solomon Forte, they have to deal with a patient who rips them off for drugs, and they're going to have to pay the state back for the privilege—with interest. Plus, don't forget the family. Can you imagine the venom they're going to be spitting when the Center bills them directly for a hundred thousand? That's an instant lawsuit by itself."

"Well, sweet boy, I'll bet you a dime no one has the nerve to say a word to you. Anyway, hospitals are covered by federal funds for this sort of thing."

"Yeah, but the doctors aren't. We're the center, not the hospital. So, I have to go my colleagues, hat in hand, and ask them to give back, with interest, the money COLA sent them, that by the way took six months to get there, and who knows if we got interest on it. In the next sentence, I have to beg them to increase their exposure and spend a few more months treating the guy for free, and get up close and personal with a family that's already pleased beyond words with the medical community, and a twin brother who's grumbling about lawsuits; yours truly at the top of the docket." Sol finished his wine and lay back on the couch, his head on Dana's lap.

She smiled down at him. "You're going to be just fine. You'll see. This, too, shall pass."

"You don't really believe I'm gonna dodge the bullet on this one, do you? It's a slam dunk for the prosecution."

"Solly," she murmured, "do you really believe that if you do right and get the job done to take care of this guy, you can get hurt? Superficially, maybe, but for real? That isn't the way the world works."

Sol laughed. "You sound like my sister. And you know what, the truth is, I am going to fry, and it's not because of his habits or his genes. It's because a man came to me asking for help, and I didn't. Period."

The next morning, Saturday, Sol got up early and drove back up to the hospital. Dana insisted she tag along. Sol sighed deeply before getting off the elevator outside Kevin's room. He knocked quietly. Kevin looked up and smiled. "Hey, Doc, how ya doin'?"

A thin, cute woman dressed in tight jeans and tight tee-shirt was sitting on the bed holding Kevin's hand. McAlister's mother had arrived from California. At first glance, she didn't appear much older than her twin sons, but as Sol looked into her eyes, he saw the careworn toll of the years, and he turned to Dana fleetingly as if to gloat, "I hate to be an I-told-you-so, but I told you so."

McAlister's mother stood slowly and walked toward Sol. He considered taking a step backward as the woman's hand started to rise, or raising his own to protect himself. The thought shot through his mind to turn to Dana again and reiterate his I-told-you-so glance, but there wasn't time, for Mrs. McAlister was extending her hand. It was warm and gentle. "You must be Dr. Forte. Kevin tells me it's been a rough ride, but that you really care about him."

Sol was about to answer, seeking to conjure an excuse for the months when his caring wasn't what it might have been, but Kevin looked up and whimpered, "Oh, shit!" A second later, he did.

The room filled with an awful odor, waves of putrid ether flowing from the bed to the far corners and out the door. Sol was surprised that, for the first instant, he, too, was repulsed by the stench, though a moment later, his olfactory memory hauled him back to his days as a resident, the endless hours of hospital duty in the bowels of the Bronx, and the never-ending parade of patients perpetually incontinent, usually of stool, but often of grotesque bodily excretions about which he had not learned in medical school. While those had been awful days, most of which had been consumed on the sharp verge of quitting, the brainwashing had apparently worked well, and now, in that sad hospital room, he suffered a peculiar guilt about having spurned that painful period of his life and the opportunity to have learned more medicine than he had.

The others in the room had no such nostalgia to buffer the scent of a dying man's feces, and brother Devin woke, gagged, and ran from the room. Grandma and the girlfriend were hot on his heels. Mom stood fast, her eyes clouding when she realized the portent of the accident, and Dana, with not a thread of association to the situation, did not bat a single, perfect eyelash. Though Sol was too embarrassed to look at her, she whispered from behind him, "Solly, I'll go get the nurse."

She needn't have bothered. The very young charge nurse, Miss Johnson, was already on her way, fresh sheets in hand. Sol rolled Kevin on his side, another trick of residency, so the nurse could rotate the soiled sheets off and wash the plastic pad. During the process, Kevin was silent, but the despair in his eyes was not lost on either the nurse or Sol.

She washed him gently with a warm, mild soap solution and put another soft pad under him. Kevin's face, which seemed to have hollowed even more deeply overnight, tightened as he whispered, "Hey, I'm sorry. I didn't mean it."

The nurse's eyes reddened. Sol's did as well.

Sol and Dana were about to leave when Dr. Grinberg limped in. Sol smiled in surprise and whispered, "Doctor Grinberg, you don't need to be here. I'm getting an oncology consult. You're off the hook, but thank you so much for the help yesterday."

"Vell, Dr. Forte, I told you I vould see your patient, and so I vill. So, vat is goink on vit ze patient zis mornink, undt who is zis lovely vuman?"

Dana's Mediterranean darkness blanched as Dr. Grinberg took her hand in a European gentleness. She bowed her head respectfully, and the old man asked. "You are Russian?"

"How did you know, sir?"

"How could I not know?" There was a momentary silence, but Grinberg looked up at Sol and shrugged, "Who else could be so beautiful?"

Sol delivered his report. "Mr. McAlister had spiked a fever of 103 overnight. He vomited several times, though he had eaten nothing, and the night staff said he had a ten-second grand mal seizure."

Grinberg shook his head. "No such sing, a seizure for only ten seconds. It vas a rigor, certainly." He turned to Dana. "A period of mad shaking due to ze fever."

Sol interrupted. "Dr. Grinberg, I'm sorry. I need to tell you your chances of being paid for your efforts are about halfway between nil and absolute zero."

Grinberg smiled. "You sink I am ze vun to suffer. Ve vill spend anozer twenty or sirty tousant to look for ze primary tumor. Bet you dollars to donuts ve vill nefer find it."

Sol smiled for the first time in several days and asked, "Where did you learn that?"

"I've been doctor for nearly fifty years. Some sings you yust know. Cancer, ze enemy, is vun."

"No, I mean the expression 'dollars to donuts'?"

"Oh vell, I love a nice sugar donut vunce in a vhile. Not every day, mind you."

"Apparently, you love them more than the dollars. Thank you. You just taught me something."

Dana and Sol returned to the hospital on Sunday. Kevin was so medicated, he did not open his eyes. Sol looked in the chart and saw that Dr. Grinberg had been by at 7 A.M., and left a note to order the panoply of imaging studies which he privately believed were a waste of time and money, for they would neither slow Kevin's demise, nor change the treatment. On the other hand, Sol acknowledged silently, these were tests no doctor in his right legal mind would fail to demand. It was just what one did. And if he was challenged, Grinberg could always argue that the patient, and the family, simply had the right to know.

Sol sat on Kevin's bed, and the young man opened his eyes. Sol spoke with him as well as he could, but Kevin was barely lucid. After a few moments, Sol patted him on the shoulder and said, loud enough for everyone to hear, "Each day that leg'll get better and better. You'll see. We'll have you back dancing in no time." Kevin, however, had fallen asleep.

Sol nodded to the family and started out of the room. Kevin's mother followed. In the hall, she asked, "Dr. Forte, could we talk just for a minute?"

Sol turned back and smiled. "Of course, for as long as you want. Let's go sit in the family room." Grandma followed and asked again how long it would be. He nodded to the comfortable chairs in the tiny room and offered coffee. They shook their heads nervously.

He locked their eyes and began. "Look, I'm going to be honest and direct with you. I don't know what kind of cancer Kevin has, no one does. And I don't think it's only spread to the bone in his leg. I may be wrong, and I hope I am, but it's probably in many organs. That's why Kevin's so weak. I'm sure we will offer him treatment with chemotherapy, and if he decides to take the treatments, he might get a little better for a while, but it won't be for long, and the chemo's no picnic. It's a hard road he's got to go. And all of us will be on the journey with Kevin." He paused and looked down. "I'm sorry."

"Doctor," his mom choked, "you say that you will *probably* treat him with chemotherapy. Why wouldn't you? Does it cost too much? Whatever it is, I'll pay for it. I'll take out a loan."

"No, no, ma'am. It's not the cost. It will never be the cost. The question is, do you want to put him through it?"

"Doctor, I want to save my son's life. Whatever it takes. I'll do anything."

Sol thought for a moment. He could explain that the end was going to be much, much sooner than later, and that the family simply had to accept that, for there was no reprieve. But he caught himself thinking back to the mini-course during Christmas vacation in his senior year of medical school, the one called simply and directly, *On Death and Dying.* He could still hear the words of the hospice nurse who taught the program. "At the end, all the medicine in the world isn't as powerful as the gift of hope. When you go to see your patient, gently open the curtains, and if it's winter, remind the patient that soon it'll be spring. Talk about the buds and flowers and rain and new baby birds that will be chirping in no time. If it's summer, remind your patient that soon it'll be winter, and there'll be fresh, pure white snow and holly and warm fires and butter cookies. You give a person reasons to live. It's more important, and more powerful, than all the medicine they'll be taking at the end. Please don't ever forget in the promising careers that lie ahead of you: always give hope."

So, Dr. Solomon Forte nervously changed course and embarked upon the art of medicine. "I promise to keep Kevin comfortable and clean and dry. He'll get every bit of medicine the President of the United States would get. His meals'll be the same swill every patient, every intern, every resident, and every doctor in this hospital gets." For an instant, the slightest smile came to both women. "If you want to sleep in a cot next to Kevin, so be it. I promise you will be accepted as part of our family here. And these aren't bad things."

Kevin's mother and grandmother nodded blankly as they wiped away tears. Sol left the floor cheerlessly for the administrative offices, to pay his long-delinquent hospital dues and resurrect his long-expired privileges. But it was Sunday, he realized, only after spraining his wrist trying to turn the doorknob of the office in the original wing of the building. He walked back up to the floor to get Dana.

She was sitting with Kevin's mother in the family room. She moved her head, surreptitiously sending Sol away with little more than a glance. "A girl thing," he whispered to himself, and he took a seat at the nurses' station to write in the chart until Dana came out holding the mom's arm. The two women hugged, and on the ride back to her condo, Dana wouldn't say what they had talked about.

CHAPTER FIFTEEN

Though it was Sunday, Sol asked Dana to drive with him past the front of the Center to show her the debris wrought by Mr. Sullivan's rage. He laughed as he described the mutilation, embellishing a bit, but as they turned the corner toward the main entrance, she gasped. The entire portico had been torn away. A front loader was driving in and out of the gaping hole, loads of dusty, broken, reinforced concrete overflowing its bucket, antennae of rebar pointing in myriad directions. They parked next to a bulldozer and walked to the job site, stopping to chat with the superintendent. Sol joked, "You always work on Sundays?"

"Not usually, but no problem. They're paying us double time. Doctors got dough." He turned away and shouted at the driver, laughing, "Hey, Joey, slow down."

Sol led Dana into the foyer. Much of what had been there three days before was gone, as if in a planned renovation. Milling about were a dozen construction workers pulling the elevator façade free. Sol crooked his neck to peer up the shaft toward the

Department of Orthopedics. The doors there were open, and he could see a tiny slice of the waiting room, desolate and nearly dark. He thought of Kevin McAlister, and how many times he had used that elevator, and the hours he had spent in that room waiting for the not so healing ministrations of Dr. Solomon Forte.

By Monday morning, less than twenty-four hours after he and Dana had toured the wreckage, a bank of temporary, automatic glass doors had been installed; the portico was enclosed; and one elevator was back in service. Sol hoped the relative normalcy of the physical plant would quell the spiritual unrest at the Center, but there was a note on his desk ordering him to Anacota's office. The CEO grumbled, "This is going to be big. We've decided to close the employee cafeteria and meet there."

The usual cast drifted in. Anacota, the CFO, several of the center's lawyers, and Dorsett, the Medical Director, seated themselves at a table in front, facing the neatly aligned folding chairs. A representative from the Commission on Labor Affairs walked in a few paces in front of a young woman dressed in a black jacket, black blouse, and tight black skirt. As Anacota made introductions, the woman interjected sharply, "AAG, *Assistant* Attorney General, not, *assistant.*"

As Sol looked up, expecting Anacota to begin, a second wave of officials swaggered in. Sol recognized the foreman from the work crew, who was followed by his boss, and trailing, a manager and a lawyer from the center's insurance carrier. Anacota stood and sucked in a deep breath to begin, but there was a loud knock on the doors opposite those everyone else had used, and an executive from Sullivan's auto insurance carrier and his lawyer whooshed in. Anacota stood and restarted the introductions dourly. He tightened at the next knock but pasted on a plastic smile as a representative of Sal's malpractice carrier tiptoed in.

Anacota called the meeting to order. A cell phone rang. The construction foreman interrupted to inform the gathering that his attorney was on the way, as well.

Anacota, a large, soft man, The Pillsbury Dough Boy as he was known throughout the Center, moved his beefy lips, reading from a script. "Thank you all for coming. We're here to establish an equitable solution to the matter of the costs of repair and lost income resulting from the destructive actions of one John Sullivan, employer of our patient, Mrs. Edna Berry. I must remind everyone present that the patient in question was, at the time of the incident, and still is, being treated by the Galena Hills Hospital and Medical Center on an accepted Commission on Labor Affairs claim for the injuries sustained in a motor vehicle accident." Sol began to raise his hand to note the correct mechanism of injury, but shook his head and remained quiet. "Now, just so we have some idea of where we stand presently, the total cost for repairs is estimated to be in the neighborhood of six-hundred-and-forty-seven thousand dollars. Lost income is predicted to be in excess of two-hundred-and-forty-thousand dollars."

The CFO nodded at the Center's chief attorney. He began abruptly. "There is also the very grave matter of loss of reputation for the Galena Hill Medical Hospital and Medical Center. There is no precedent for anything of this nature in our long history of service to this community and its injured workers. But there has been an obvious and permanent damage to our name, and we feel it more than appropriate to seek relief for that aspect of this unfortunate matter. Let me say that it is our sincere hope that we can settle this without having to litigate. My sense, looking about the room, is that we are all highly qualified professionals, and that we'll conclude this issue quickly and equitably so that we may go on serving tens of thousands of injured workers every year. It is an important part of our commitment to the community." He finished with a toothy smile aimed at the COLA representatives.

The Center's theory of responsibility for the disaster was crystallizing in Sol's mind. He wasn't particularly shocked when the attorney turned his gaze toward Sol and handed him a thick wad of papers. Sol recognized it as a copy of his chart notes regarding Edna Berry and John Sullivan.

The attorney went on. "Just to establish the basic facts, I'd like to ask Dr. Forte a few questions. First, is what I just handed you a true and complete copy of your notes regarding your patient, Ms. Berry?"

Sol shrugged. "I assume it is, but I haven't had the opportunity to study the document." Anacota shot Sol an acerbic stare, and Forte thumbed through the chart quickly. "Well, it certainly appears complete."

"Good." The attorney continued, listing several dates. He had Sol read portions of the notes regarding the informal meetings he had had with Mr. Sullivan. On the last entry, Sol added, "Oh, I remember this one very well. It's when the guy went ballistic. I thought he was going to punch me out. He knocked my nurse to the floor."

The attorney frowned. "I'd appreciate it if you would answer *only* by reading your notes verbatim. Thank you."

After thirty minutes, the attorney relinquished the floor, turning to the AAG, who began her cross-examination with fluttering eyes. She drew Sol's attention to the Physician's Initial Report, the document Sol had filled out the first time he'd seen Mrs. Berry. "Did you do any examination of the facts regarding Ms. Berry's purported injury the day you made legally binding statements on this official Commission on Labor Affairs document, in which you stated the patient had injured herself in the course of her usual duties, on a more probable than not basis?"

Sol answered simply with a, "Huh?"

The center attorney interrupted. "Please restate your question in a simple, not compound form, Miss. And Dr. Forte, please reply with a yes or no answer, not with colloquialisms. Thank you."

Question after question, objection after objection, until the principals tired of Sol and turned their attention to the bloated repair estimates. Sol looked at the clock on the cafeteria wall and tried to catch Anacota's eye to plead silently to be released to go to work, but the man was busy sniveling about the inestimable harm to the Center's reputation occasioned by the Department of Labor and Industry's archaic rules. Sol felt Roxanne's escalating wrath those many floors away. He considered his options. He had none, so he stood and excused himself as he had seen in the British movies, with a nod and a simple, "Good day."

Slack-jawed, the Center's attorney growled, "Doctor, we're not done with you!"

Sol grinned. "I have patients. I may be available after I've met my professional responsibilities."

On his way upstairs, Sol convinced himself that he had committed a victimless crime by deserting the meeting, though he accepted there would be a stiff sentence. Rounding the back-entrance hallway to Ortho, he expected Roxanne to be on the phone with the CEO, but her head was drooped, engrossed in filing her nails. A neat pile of dust had accumulated on the stack of notes awaiting his attention. He tried to sneak past her into his office, but without looking up or disturbing the rhythm of her filing, she called out loudly, "Good of you to show up. Let's start with Room Two. Guess who?"

"Well, it ain't Kevin McAlister. So maybe it's Lupe Sánchez."

"That's amazing. How did you know?"

"It is her? We haven't seen Lupe forever. I thought something bad happened."

"Well, you're not far off. There's good, and there's bad. Amazing, really."

"Tell me!"

"No way, boss. You have to see this with your own eyes."

"Tell me!"

"Dr. F., just go and see her!"

As Sol approached the door, Rosebac stuck his head out of his office. His stare bolted to Sol. Sol nodded a weak greeting and knocked on the exam room door. He opened the door very slowly, inching the handle forward, peering left and right. At first, all he saw was Lupe's young son, dressed neatly and sitting quietly, feet on the floor, hands obediently folded on his lap. Sol opened the door a few degrees farther. A woman, a dark-haired, dark-eyed, comely Hispanic woman, sat staring at Sol. She wore the slightest suggestive smile. If it was Lupe, where had she found the money for the transformation? He pushed the door halfway open very slowly, waiting for the other shoe to drop. The woman's blouse was crisp and white, though Sol fastened on her tight, low-slung jeans, and her bare midriff with a gold ring in her naval. He took a step into the room. If it was really Lupe, she was wearing a bit too much makeup, and the room hung too heavily with cheap perfume, and her hair had been too deeply colored with henna, but Sol's eyes couldn't help opening as wide as a full Mexican moon; Lupe Sánchez had been transmogrified.

He gathered himself and looked directly into her onyx eyes. Dismally, he recognized instantly it had all been a mirage. A corona of black-and-blue surrounded her left eye, the wound so deep, it could only be partially hidden by her heavy makeup.

Lupe read Sol's expression. It had only taken an instant for the doctor to uncover her humiliation. Her eyes dipped, but she smiled broadly when he took her hands in his. She clutched them tightly. Both glowing, they had made a mutual and silent pact to ignore the obvious.

She leaned forward and began to speak, but her son stood from his station and began rearranging her words. Lupe, not taking her eyes off of Sol, motioned with her hand, directing the child back to his seat. "Doctor, I so happy see you." With that declaration, she reached into her purse, pulled out a fifty-dollar bill, and thrust her hand forward to wave it in Sol's face. "*Mucho gracias*, my doctor. COLA, they send my money. Money for my sickness. Now, I pay for you so kind."

"*Señorita* Lupe," Sol smiled, holding back a laugh, "that's not the way it works, my dear. I can't take money from you. But that is so nice. You look great. I am very happy for you."

Lupe spoke to her son in rapid Spanish. He translated. "My mother, she say, you must take the money. This is money you gave her when we have no food. She must pay back money."

Sol thought for a moment, weighing the loss of face for Lupe if he refused the money. He looked away for a moment. When he turned back, her eyes had grown large, sexy, and a bit red. She pouted and leaned slightly forward, shaking the fifty again. He flushed, struck by her femininity, but pulled back a step and shook his head no. He said louder than he intended, "You are very beautiful, but I cannot take money from you."

Lupe stood abruptly and took a giant step. Her momentum carried her forward, the fifty-dollar bill flapping. At that instant, the air in Room Two became very still, as in the moments before a grand storm. Both Lupe and Sol sensed the change, but there wasn't time for thought as the door flew open violently, now setting the air inside whirling. Rosebac charged into the room, his head swinging left and right, searching.

The door struck Sol sharply in the back. He pitched frontward toward Lupe and tripped over his feet. She reached forward to shield herself but missed, and, in the nanosecond that preceded Lupe's crash, she shot her hand out farther, desperately grasping for purchase. She came up with a handful of Rosebac's crotch, and he fell forward. Lupe's blouse pulled up as she crashed on top of Sol, and Rosebac's arm wound up on her nearly bare chest.

Lupe giggled. Rosebac sputtered in outrage. Sol gasped, trying to breathe. The three were still on the floor when a full complement of nurses and receptionists, led by Roxanne, appeared at the door—speechless.

Rosebac flushed as he stood and gathered himself. Finally, he spat, "Dr. Forte, come with me," though his eyes were locked on Lupe's sheer bra and half-exposed left breast.

He grumbled, "Disgusting," as he as he picked his way through the cluster and bristled toward his office. When Sol followed him in, Rosebac slammed the door and barked, "Doctor, what is the meaning of this?" Before Sol could answer, Rosebac added, "I am suspending you immediately. Report to the CEO's office."

Sol countered loudly, "That's nonsense. She was just trying to return the fifty bucks I gave her when COLA cut her off."

"So, on top of everything else, you give young, sexy women with their tits hanging out money? What else did you pay her for? You seeing her on the side?" Rosebac's voice trailed off in arrogant disgust. "Breeding, or should I say, the lack of it?"

Though Sol had clearly heard Rosebac's final comment, he held his tongue, turning over in his mind the department chairman's uttered words, and how he could use them in the coming war.

"No, Doctor," Sol hissed. "I'm suspending *you*. Breaking into a room like a wild animal. I saw the way you were leering at her. I know about you. You were seeing her on the side and got jealous and acted out. Talking about a patient's breasts and referring to them as sexy, that's going to land you in a heap of trouble my friend. That shit don't go at the Galena Hills Hospital and Medical Center, not anymore."

"Forte, you're pushing me!"

"Why don't we ask Lupe what happened, who did what? See who she sides with. We'll get to the truth. No more of your games. I won't take it anymore. You were seeing her on the side, got jealous, lost it."

He marched four paces down the hall before Rosebac jumped out of his office and bellowed, "Forte!"

Sol stopped abruptly and keeled around. He was seething as he hissed, "And by the way, *Doctor*, I know all about your little assignations." He pointed at the man's wedding ring and blurted loud enough for the entire department to hear, "I've been waiting for a long time. We're gonna get all of this out on the table, the alcohol and the whores."

Rosebac froze. His complexion deepened to an apoplectic burgundy, and Sol waited for the charge. Of course, there would be a denial, for Sol had no evidence, not a shred, not even from the Center's rumor mill. But as he stared into Rosebac's eyes, there was a twitch, a rhythmic fluttering. His manicured surgeon's hands vibrated faintly.

Sol stopped the public assassination and started to his office, but pivoted abruptly, and turned back to Lupe's room. He brushed Rosebac's shoulder purposely as he passed, though there was not a wheeze of protest as Sol continued down the hallway. The hushed throng of nurses parted like the Red Sea as Sol approached. He knocked gently and plastered on his standard smile. Sol asked if she had been hurt, but without an answer, she jumped from her seat and waved the fifty near his face.

He promised to donate it to the Food Bank then ended the visit by asking if she had a phone at home. He promised to call with an interpreter to find out more about what was going on in her life. She pouted for a moment but left quietly when Sol withdrew from the room.

He stared out his window at the mountains, waiting for the call from Anacota. He considered just heading down to the CEO's office to grab the bull by the horns and take the offensive. Then again, there were Rosebac's eyes and his trembling hands, and that color that flooded into his face as he'd swallowed Sol's bluff. Sol declared vociferously to the wall, "Keep your mouth shut. You got him by the short hairs."

Sol's New York street sense implored him not to get involved with the authorities any more than he was already was, though his Catholicism goaded him to confess. Yet his loathing for Rosebac and the administration was so deep, it would be a pleasure, even worth a hunk of his own hide, to wedge the matter of Rosebac's sexually inappropriate, but meaningless, howling onto the Board's emergency meeting menu for that evening.

When the phone remained silent, Sol left his hutch, choosing to skate from room to room until noon, when he returned to his office to sit brooding behind a locked door. He tried to call Dana, but after he got her answering machine, he remembered she had flown out that morning on a trip to Portland, to hawk her medicinal wares. Her parting words: "Hey, Solly, try to stay out of dutch until I get back."

Sol was alone—nowhere to turn. Dana was gone; his sister was cloistered. There were no friends, no family members. All of the Fortes had abandoned him. He shook his head, thinking about the aunts, uncles, and even cousins, all angry with him, first because Papa named him Sol, and then because Sol chose to go to medical school at Albert Einstein, a traditionally Jewish university in the middle of New York City. Never mind that he was the first Forte to graduate from college, actually one of the first to get out of high school in four years. And, of course, there was the Jewish girl from Greece he'd almost married. "*Tu se battz*," the relatives snarled over Christmas dinner. "You are the crazy."

None of it made any sense to the extended, Sicilian Forte clan, a family that had nearly been murdered when they escaped the Mafia in the early twenties. Settling in New York City, they served in the working class, many toiling for pennies in Jewish-owned businesses. The inevitable friction between the two communities had lingered for decades, as had the bitterness.

Further inflaming the family was Michaela's choice of a convent in Boston, The Sisters of Ireland. It was the other ethnic group with which the family had had less than congenial relations over the decades; the Irish cops had made their living shaking down the Italian street vendors and gangs on the Lower East Side. Michaela's decision stabbed at the sensibilities of the clan elders, who, after the passing of Sol's parents, stopped including Sol and his sister in family affairs. Since the relatives were still squeezed into Little Italy, he couldn't avoid their snubs on the street, and when the chance came to leave the East Coast for a residency program very far away, he drove out of the City without looking back.

But when you escape, the first person to greet you at the other end is you, and his new home, though far more peaceful than the City, wasn't without its snags. He talked a little too fast, and some of the words he said didn't sound like English to the farmers and the loggers at the free clinics where he'd started out. He sat a bit longer, thinking of how far he'd come, remembering his second day in Whitaker, out running at dusk on an old, paved-over railroad track. Two young men hailed him, asking for directions. He stopped to answer, but when they approached within twenty feet, he sneered, "Stay where you are, or I'll kick your goddamn asses, and if you don't believe me, take another step and try it." The two looked at each other slack-jawed and moved off shaking their heads.

Sol had no choice, though he easily predicted Michaela's advice. The convent's emergency number was answered brusquely by a crotchety old woman who informed Sol that novices did not enjoy telephone privileges, and that Michaela could not come to the phone then, or ever. Sol considered hanging up, but he begged the woman to tell Michaela that he, her brother, a doctor, had called to let her know that he had just begun to do charity medical work for United Catholic Services, and wanted to know if the Sisters of Ireland needed any medical services.

His mood soured as he sat alone, feet on his desk, pondering his future at the Center and in medicine itself. So much roiled in his head, he could not remain focused, and began to doze off. He drifted into a dream in which he worked happily in a prison clinic, where everyone had more trouble than did he, where he felt aloof, but the harsh ring of his private phone jarred him awake.

"I have friends here, dear brother. We novices take care of each other. If we didn't, we couldn't survive. Just like doctors. It's no different."

After his sarcastic grunt, he wove the story of the past week. "You think I should take the offensive?"

"Big Brother, it's so simple. Have you done anything wrong?"

"What do you mean by wrong? Did I sin in my mind like Jimmy Carter?"

"What are you talking about?"

"I sinned in my mind by looking at the woman. But you know I wouldn't ever *do* anything about it. That would be absolutely nuts. No way in hell."

"Big Brother, mind your mouth. How many times do I have to remind you?"

"I confess."

"So, you didn't do anything wrong. I told you, we all have sinful thoughts, even Mother Superior. But what counts is if you act on them. And you didn't, and you wouldn't, and God forgives you if you learn a lesson in His name. So, go and tell them to mind their own darn business."

"Little Sister, what a foul mouth. Put Mother Superior on the line."

"Bet she'd love to talk to you. She'd have a stroke in ten seconds."

"Hey, you really think I'm in the clear?"

"You didn't do anything wrong, certainly not by the standards of the world out there." Michaela took a long breath. "Tell 'em to go jump in a lake. You've got God on your side, and me, too. You're home free."

Sol laughed, "You think I should go down and tell *my* Mother Superior what happened?"

"If you want to, go ahead, but what's the point? If your friend is intent on making trouble, you're not going to stop him. Sounds like he has an anger management problem. Even the people here don't crash into private rooms. It's hard to believe that a doctor would do that."

"It's true, though." Sol paused for a moment. He laughed, "In a way, thank goodness Lupe was there as a witness, of sorts. I should probably get an interpreter and call her and have her write down what she saw."

Michaela answered quickly. "Do you really want to do that?" Without pausing, she went on. "Don't call the patient. It'll be interpreted as you briefing her. The first question they're going to ask her: 'Did Dr. Forte ever call you at home? Did you discuss what happened in the office with Dr. Forte?' And she has to say, 'Yes,' 'cause if she lies, they'll find a million holes in her story, and the whole thing falls apart. Just forget the entire matter. And if you do hear anything about it, demand *they* get your patient there, and let them have an interpreter of their choice. If it's the truth, it always wins in the end."

"That's what I'm worried about—the end. That's a long time to wait."

"Be patient, Solly. For this, too, shall pass."

Sol asked, "How did a Forte get so smart?"

"You're the smart one, the family hope. I'm so proud of you, Solly. Uh oh, footsteps; gotta run." Her voice fell into a rapid whisper. "If I don't speak to you over the next two weeks, please forgive me, but it's our busy season, Christmas and all that. I love you, Big Brother."

Roxanne knocked just before one. She called through the door, "Let's head 'em up, move 'em out."

When Sol didn't answer, she slipped a note under the door; it was a copy of Kevin McAlister's bone scan report. "Multiple bony foci of Technetium 99 uptake compatible with widespread metastatic disease. Recommend clinical correlation." Translation: Kevin's cancer had spread to every corner of his body, particularly to his bones, where these most painful tumors would grow unchecked until the end.

PART TWO

CHAPTER SIXTEEN

David Rosebac, and many of the senior physicians at the Center, took a full three weeks off for the Christmas holidays. Rosebac always spent the time in Honolulu. He had stayed in the same hotel, same room, for nearly twenty years, and spent much of the month preceding the holiday preparing each meal and activity on a grand calendar that hung prominently in his office. Since Sol had not heard the name Lupe Sanchez since the incident, he assumed Rosebac had been too busy to take on the task of crushing his medical career before the end of 2000. It could wait. A delay was even better, for Sol would spend several weeks stewing in his juices, waiting for the incident to take on a life of its own. Rosebac knew him that well.

On the 3rd of January, 2001, Sol, went back to work, alone in Ortho aside from two physician's assistants. His schedule was three pages long, forty-eight patients to see before five. He sprinted from room to room until he could not longer postpone a visit to the men's room. Roxanne was at her desk. She caught Sol's eye and nodded nervously toward to his office. A man in a seedy jacket was standing just inside the doorway. He put his hand up to stop Sol. "Doctor, I'm sorry to ruin your day, but I got a subpoena here in your name. You need to sign on the dotted line."

Solomon Forte, M.D., nearly brought to his knees by the clutch of his solar plexus, scribbled his initials on the process server's clipboard, took the envelope and stared at it, mouth agape. He finally looked up to ask what it meant, but the process server pushed past Sol and was gone in a blur.

Roxanne stole into the office and craned her neck toward the document. He turned away and clenched his teeth in a futile effort to suppress the trembling of his jaw. He pulled free a single sheet, and when it stopped fluttering sufficiently to read, he tilted his head in confusion, for it was not in the usual format of a legal document. The only words that registered were in the letterhead: State Medical Abuse Commission. He wobbled into his seat, his stomach souring with each word.

The State Medical Abuse Commission requests you provide all documents in your possession regarding your patient, Kevin McAlister. We further request you provide a complete narrative report detailing the provision of any and all medications, including opioids, you ordered or provided the above captioned patient during his treatment.

Your failure to comply with this request, or your discussion with any patient or physician regarding this request, or any manipulation of the records requested, will constitute grounds for the immediate suspension of your license to practice medicine. It is recommended that you seek legal assistance from an attorney familiar with the regulations governing the provision of medical care by physicians in this state.

Sol searched the document, line by line, then word by word, for the name of the person who had made allegations about

Kevin McAlister's care. Why was the Commission concerned? What were the charges? There was no data, no contact person at SMAC, not even a telephone number for the agency, just a PO Box number in the state capital.

When a doctor received a subpoena, at least one that notified him that he was in the process of being sued, the policy established by the malpractice insurance industry was standard and well known to every practicing physician: Cancel the rest of the day's schedule and call the insurance company before you called your spouse. Sol asked himself, however, if those informal rules applied here, as it really wasn't the usual malpractice case, or was it? He was confused and scared and angry, and had not an inkling of what to do. He saw a couple of patients, but his shuddering peaked, and he darted back to his office, looked up the number for the Department of Health Affairs, and asked the receptionist to speak with someone from the State Medical Abuse Commission.

"Well, sir, there really isn't an office of SMAC. Not really. It's just a group of doctors and civilians and, I shouldn't forget, a nurse practitioner and a physician's assistant or two, who meet every three months, or is it six? I don't know. They meet to go over problem doctors who are in trouble. I mean, you can't really speak to *them*."

"Is there a leader, someone in charge?"

"Well, there's a committee chairman."

"And who might that be?"

She hesitated. "I'm sorry, I can't give out that information."

Sol barked, though his voice cracked, "That's nonsense. He or she is a public official. What is this, the Soviet Union? Look, I'm upset. I pay my state and county medical association dues every year. I'm entitled to know the name of SMAC's chairperson."

"Sir, we aren't the State Medical Association; that's a separate organization. We're the Office of Health. We're part of the official government. They're just civilians. Two different things."

"Ma'am, I don't care. I didn't do anything wrong, and I want to talk to the chairman."

While he was on hold for two minutes, he spent the time wiping the sweat from above his lip with the edge of his white coat. She came back on. "His name is Dr. Jergesson."

"What's his number?"

"Let me put you back on hold."

She came back several minutes later. "I'm not at liberty to divulge that information. Is there anything further?"

"What's his first name?"

The phone clicked to hold and a minute later he heard the grumble, "Jens."

"How do you spell that?"

Sol called information for Whitaker, but there was no Jens Jergesson, MD. He tried several of the nearby cities, then the more sparsely populated northern tier, until he found the man in a small town.

Sol rapped the buttons roughly. A recorded message droned that the number was no longer in service. He pushed the buttons again, even more feverishly, but got a dairy farm, though no one spoke English. On the third try, a bored receptionist answered, "Medical offices of Dr. Jergesson. How may I help you?"

Sol asked to speak to the doctor, and the receptionist asked if it was concerning a patient. "No. It's a personal matter."

"Well, doctor is with patients. I'll give him your number and have him call you when he gets a chance."

"No, ma'am. I demand to speak to him now. I am a licensed medical doctor." He was put on hold for nearly five minutes. More sweat dripped from his face. It was now shaded with an odor.

"This is Dr. Jergesson." There followed impatient, deep breathing."

Sol professed his absolute innocence and indignation. After another long pause and deeper breathing, the man huffed, "Doctor, let me give you a piece of advice—maybe two pieces.

First, you will be informed of the charges against you in due course, when it is appropriate for that to happen. Next, don't call this office again or call any of the members of SMAC. We are the judge and jury, so to speak, and you are tampering. This will not help your cause. Not one bit."

Sol started to reply but lost his train of thought. He finally stuttered, "I have rights, you know."

"Final piece of advice, Doctor. You have no rights. The State Medical Abuse Commission ain't a democracy. It's a quasi-governmental agency. We don't make rules. Legislators do that. We make policy, and we change it when we need to. Whatever it takes to get the job done. There is no due process. I suggest you get yourself a lawyer, preferably one who has come before us before, and do what he says. If you haven't done anything wrong, you don't have anything to worry about."

Sol was speechless, and Jergesson took the pause for a final statement. "Dr. Forte, was it? I will tell you this. There's a lot of patient grousing every year. Most we just listen to, talk to the doctor, gather the records, then play the game and inform the complainant that we don't feel anything untoward has occurred. It's the rare case that we act on."

The next step was to inform his medical malpractice insurance carrier, though he hadn't the slightest idea who that was. He called down to Administration. Anacota's secretary snipped, "Please wait." Minutes later she came back on to ask, "Dr. Forte, why do you want to know?"

Sol parried, "Who wants to know why I want to know?"

She snipped, "The CEO. I'm going to put you on hold."

The next voice was that of Hayes Anacota. "Dr. Forte, Margaret tells me you need to call our medical malpractice carrier. Is there a problem?"

Sol's Catholicism triggered a spillage of his guts. Anacota's side of the line went silent for a very long time after Sol was done. The CEO's lowered voice eventually hissed, "Do you mean to tell me you called the Chairman of the State Medical Abuse Commission? And pissed him off to boot?"

"Look, Hayes, they're telling me I did something terrible, but they won't tell me what, or who said it. And then the asshole says I don't have rights. That's bullshit. I pay my own malpractice premium. Comes out of my paycheck, and I want to know the number for the carrier so I can contact them and have them assign me a lawyer. I do have rights. This isn't Al-fucking-bania."

Sol heard Anacota breathe through his nose and respond tepidly. "Okay. Calm down. I'll get you a number. But let me ask, do you have any idea what's going on?"

"Nothing other than a patient who's dying of cancer. I figured you might. Rosebac talked to you before Christmas, didn't he?"

Anacota's interest was recaptured. "No, he didn't. About what?"

Sol snorted, "Suit scum," under his breath, not believing a word of Anacota's denial.

CEO Anacota had steered the Galena Hills Medical Center through the recent humiliations: the felony sexual offenses, the felony Medicare abuses, and the alcohol and drug scandals with which several of the Center's doctors had recently wrestled. He had wielded his five-foot-six, two-hundred-and-ten-pound mass like a mini-M-48 tank, threatening and cajoling, swearing and laughing, gifting and punishing, as he controlled the snippets of intelligence leaked to the *Whitaker Reporter Dispatch*. He had rewritten history as effectively as had the Soviet Politburo in its rehabilitation of Joseph Stalin.

Several of Hayes' less enthusiastic supporters had made known their contention that the deteriorating tenor of the Center's fabric had trickled down from the top. Others argued that, while he wasn't going to win the Nobel Prize for humanitarianism, Hayes Anacota was not a doctor—he was a businessman, and thus constrained by standards dissimilar to those demanded of the Center's physicians. Anyway, he had just opened six new satellite clinics to feed patients into the surgeons' practices. The eight knife-wielding doctors on the staff accounted for over seventy percent of the income garnered over the past ten years.

His plan to build clinics in all of the Whitaker's affluent neighborhoods, and beyond, generated such loads of cash, the physicians' retirement fund had burgeoned like bacteria in a warm Petri dish. When the financials for the past year were made public in late December, even the most vocal of the naysayers were grudgingly mollified, and they met with the Board of Directors over wine, in special session, to vote Anacota a Christmas present: a plump year-end bonus served over an enhanced five-year contract.

Anacota was silent for a long moment. "Dr. Forte," he finally said suspiciously, "I don't understand that. Let me be frank. Right before Christmas, right in front of the Board of Directors, Rosebac said that he had treated Sullivan several times over the years, and that the guy was a hopeless drunk. Sounded to me like he was on your side."

"That's a surprise," Sol muttered, "He seemed very angry with me before he left."

"Well," Anacota advised, "you leave him to me. This thing'll blow over. I just wish you'd be a little more generous with your time in helping us get COLA to pay for the damage to the building." He paused for effect then added guardedly, "Okay, here's the number for the malpractice insurer. Let me know what you learn."

But the malpractice insurance attorney didn't call back for several hours, and when he did, the reply was direct. "Dr. Forte, if you'll read your policy carefully, you will note that we do not cover individual doctors in matters of moral turpitude. I would posit that any subpoena from SMAC involves issues of that nature."

There was a long silence. The conversation had come to an end. "Well, I didn't do a goddamn thing that could be construed as immoral."

"That may be the case, and we'll look into it as a courtesy. In the interim, my professional advice is that you quickly hire private legal counsel."

"Where am I supposed to get money for that?"

The impatience in the man's voice was growing. "Doctor, you need to consult with an attorney, and I really have to go. Thank you very much." And Sol was alone again.

He sighed and propped his feet on the desk. The blood that had drained to his legs during the afternoon now rushed to his head. Instead of making it easier to think, or even seek asylum in a short nap, the sudden injection of fuel coursing through his brain served only to feed the plethora of impatiently waiting neurologic connections. A flood of disagreeable thoughts emerged from the sludge.

Solomon Forte did not have an attorney. He did not know one. He had never needed a lawyer in his whole life, aside from the college campus parking ticket. He thought back to how he'd contacted legal aid to ask them what to do, obtaining several opinions before agreeing with the bulk of jurisprudential wisdom that he pay the three bucks and forget the matter.

Perhaps that was what he'd do again. He wasn't getting rich at the Center; why shouldn't he avail himself of legal aid's services? Then he thought back to the level of expertise he had encountered in college with the committee of complimentary legal advice—two law school seniors and one second-year scholar.

Maybe he could ask Roxanne. She'd been in need of counsel on a regular basis. Sol had even had to bail her out of the county lock-up one Monday morning after a Saturday night scrap with her latest boyfriend. "Maybe I can ask him," Sol mumbled aloud, but with a moment's thought, he remembered that she'd lost her case and refused to pay the man's bill. He had sued her in Small Claims Court, and won.

His next thought was to call the State Bar Association, but when he got the lady at the referral service on the line, she gasped, "Good gravy, I've never heard of a case like that. Why don't you call your malpractice insurance company?"

He wracked his brain. When was the last time he'd even had contact with a lawyer besides the attorneys he'd helped with COLA cases? And even then, it'd been years, maybe three, since he'd had to sit through the deposition for a patient who'd been injured as a shelf-stocker at the Dairy Bargain. The woman's industrial claim was for a crushed foot. It had run been over by an overloaded shopping cart piloted by a seven-year-old, whose mother threatened to take legal action against the grocery chain because the employee had yelled at the child after the accident. The victim was adamant that she could never go back to shelving work, or for that matter, any work, even if she was given a stool and time to lie down during the day. But Sol had little to do with the attorney, for the patient was quickly ruled against in COLA Court and redirected to Social Security Disability Court. And, in any event, the lawyer lost there as well.

Through the clouds of denial, a name percolated into Sol's consciousness. "Nah," he snorted, "not on your life." A few seconds passed. "Well, maybe I can just ask him for a suggestion. Bet it'll probably cost me the price of a consultation." In less than a minute, though, he was speaking with Anwar El Haq.

"Doctor, this is a simple case. Any good general practice attorney can help you. Let me look into it for you. I'll do some calling around. Not to worry"

But Sol did agonize through the next few patients, unable to quell his growing anger and fear. It was only after he realized he was not paying attention, and had written a wrong prescription, that he accepted the wisdom of the insurance company's dictum that a doctor cease seeing patients immediately when a summons had been served.

By having continued healing souls that inauspicious afternoon, Dr. Forte had added a new snag to his inventory, Cassius Parmalee. Sol had come to care for Mr. Parmalee after the man passed out on the job at a local sawmill because of low blood sugar. During his fall, Mr. Parmalee had cut off his pinky on the thirty-six-inch ripper blade a month before. Sol was assigned to treat the man's slow-healing wounds after Rosebac's finger stump revision surgery had not gone smoothly. It soon fell to Sol to manage the man's insulin regimen as well, for the Center's diabetologist announced he was not an authorized COLA provider.

A simple insulin plan was easy, and Sol had designed it without effort, though the problem came when Parmalee's boss, in order to prevent further hypoglycemia, was making his employee eat a witnessed and recorded snack every hour on the hour. This regimen forced him to consume so many extra calories, he had gained twelve pounds since returning to work. As a result, Mr. Parmalee needed additional insulin to keep him from slipping into the opposite type of coma, a hyperglycemic, hyperosmolar state. But Sol had, in his inattention that sad afternoon, read the blood sugar numbers as 412 instead of 214, and so had written a prescription for too much insulin.

Sol noticed the error while dictating his note for Mr. Parmalee's chart and asked Roxanne to call him. She couldn't find him, so Sol had her call the local pharmacies. After the first five, she marched to Sol's door and grumbled, "No joy. That guy's more trouble than he's worth," adding as she shook her head, "I'll call his work and see if he went back to finish his shift."

She found him and tried to explain the change in insulin dosage had been a mistake, but there was so much wood-sawing racquet in the background, the man couldn't get it straight. She talked him into coming back in, but that only further deepened the boss's impatience, who commented snidely something to the effect that he now understood why the local business community had taken to parking their cars inside the Center.

Sol finally relented and told Roxanne he was going to take the rest of the day off, but he had to wait for Parmalee anyway, and by the time the man's boss released him to come back to the Center, the end of the afternoon had arrived. He called Dana's number, though he knew she was still out of town, and sat morosely at his desk, reading and rereading the summons.

Before he left for the evening, he checked his messages—nothing from El Haq.

CHAPTER SEVENTEEN

Despite Dr. Grinberg's efforts, the whereabouts of Kevin McAlister's primary tumor, as Isak had predicted, remained a mystery. The best the doctors who had taken an interest in the case could do was UPS a biopsy of the bony tumor in his leg back East, to Bethesda, Maryland, the National Cancer Institute. They, too, confessed ignorance, and their only suggestion was to treat the patient with a potent cocktail of noxious medicinal poisons—perhaps one might work.

The oncologist met with Drs. Grinberg and Forte, advising that Kevin's therapy would be a shotgun approach to a cancer of unknown origin: a little of this, a little of that, and if all it gave him was a few more weeks, it was, they stressed, perhaps, better than nothing. Kevin McAlister was clearly too weak for surgical exploration to find the original tumor. Even if the surgeons searched with a scope, the patient would likely not survive the anesthesia. And if the tumor was located, he certainly wouldn't make it through an extensive procedure to remove it.

The final sorrow for Kevin McAlister was that even if he did survive the long and dangerous surgery, the main tumor had already spread so widely, according to the bone scan, the primary mass was no longer the primary problem. It was now just a minor player, for the cancer was on an autopilot setting that couldn't be switched off. All of the new little tumors were, like the original mass, sending out their own cells to create fresh colonies, exponentially increasing swarms of uncontrollable nomadic cells that settled briefly, sometimes only for hours, before showering Kevin's circulation with a vanguard of new, and more rapidly dividing, cancer cells.

In just a couple of weeks, Kevin McAlister had lost forty more pounds, essentially all of his bodily reserves, and much of the nourishment provided by the hospital was quickly co-opted, stolen, by the swiftly growing tumors, speeding his demise. He was now the skeletal remains of a heavy construction worker whose legs had once whirled like mighty tornadoes. So weak from the disease that consumed him, he lie unmoving all day, every day. Soon, with no pad of fat or muscle left to protect him, sores were ground open on the bony areas of his hips and legs that touched the bed. The best the nurses could do was turn him every few minutes.

As the soul ebbed out of Kevin McAlister's wracked skeleton, his family's anger softened into a profound sadness. Even Devin sat quietly during Sol's daily visits, occasionally grunting, "Hey, Doc."

Day by day, the yellow cast of Kevin's jaundiced skin deepened as the tumors invaded and squeezed off tiny passages in his liver. The yellow-green bile produced by the liver was a noxious fluid that normally drained from that organ via those passages directly into the small intestine. From there it was carried out of the body mixed with the stool, and was in fact, what gave it its dark color. In Kevin's case, with the liver choked off, the bile had nowhere to go except back into the blood stream, and when that was full, it squeezed out into the skin and whites of the eyes, turning them an alarming yellow. When it leaked into the urine, his water became a very dark brown. By now, Kevin's stool was white, and his urine black.

Soon the liver, the body's chemical jack-of-all-trades, would be totally closed off, blocked by ever enlarging tumors. Then, it would not be just obstructed bile backing up; all the poisons the liver normally detoxified would be denied exit from the body. They would retrogress, just like the bile, back into the circulation. From there, the contaminated blood would make its way, albeit sluggishly, to every corner of the body, including, and especially, the brain. That would spell the end of Kevin's ability to think. Finally, gratefully, the toxic flux would render him unconscious until his passing.

On a morning several days after New Year's, Sol arrived very early to check on his patient. Kevin looked up and recognized Sol in the darkened room. He sucked in a feeble breath and whispered almost inaudibly, "Doc, that nurse last night, whoa, did you catch her rack?"

Sol hadn't, but he smiled, squeezed Kevin's skeletal shoulder, and laughed, "Why do you think I spend all night here, my man?" With those words, Kevin McAlister's face relaxed ever so slightly. He smiled, stared at the ceiling, and slipped before Sol's eyes into a coma from which he would not surface.

Two weeks had passed since Sol had been served with his subpoena to appear before the SMAC. It had taken several days for El Haq to get back to him. He called Sol in the middle of clinic hours and began with a history of the Commission, a litany about which Sol tried to hint he wasn't terribly interested. Nevertheless, El Haq explained after Forte's yawn, "Doctor, it is always best to know one's enemy thoroughly."

Sol's stomach tensed, and he countered nervously, "I didn't know that we were already foes. I haven't done anything wrong."

"Oh, Doctor, you are very much at war, whether you've done a thing or not." El Haq went on to explain that the Commission had been founded to address a growing number of complaints from patients and doctors alike. Over the years, the commission had adjudicated tens of thousands of claims by patients, pharmacists, and other, usually anonymous, physicians, over a list of wrongdoings to include, El Haq read from a document, '…unprofessional conduct, acts of lying, corruption, incompetence, immorality, sexual misbehavior, use of unprofessional language, professional dishonesty, medical carelessness, or any act in which a patient is harmed.' Need I continue, Doctor?"

Though Sol made it clear he'd heard enough, El Haq went on to describe the composition of the Commission: of the seventeen members appointed by the state governor, two-thirds were physicians, fifteen percent physician assistants, and ten percent nurse practitioners. There were always two members of the lay public. At least twelve members of the Commission had to be present before the panel was empowered to act as judge and jury in regard to a doctor's future. A sub-panel of two physicians, a physician's assistant, a nurse practitioner, and one member of the public, would decide which cases merited adjudication by the full tribunal.

Sol bridled, "You mean to tell me I'm going to be judged by a physician's assistant and a man who has no medical training? That's not right."

"That is correct, Doctor. It isn't right, but you must understand that you are not dealing with torn tendons and broken bones. You live, here in your country, in a mire of political correctness. Everything is backwards. He, oh, excuse me, or she, who shrieks the loudest is often heard first and foremost. These are the facts of life, Doctor. This is what you must plan to battle. And please do remember, you are certainly not the first person to be faced with this challenge."

El Haq could hear Sol suck in a deep breath to squabble, so he went on quickly. "There will be an attorney for the Commission's side, and therefore, it is in your vital interest to be represented by a professional."

Sol balked, "Why do I need a lawyer? Why can't I just tell my side of the story, whatever that side is? I'll tell the truth, explain my actions, and they'll see that I've done nothing wrong."

"Doctor, you know what they say about a man who represents himself in court."

"No."

"That's a man who's got an incompetent for an attorney, and a fool for a client. Don't forget, the Commission is going to present their case to the panel using the testimony of witnesses. They have a lot of money. They can even hire expert doctors from anywhere they can find them. They'll fly them in, put them up in four-star hotels, and make sure they sleep well the night before the proceedings, though you will not. Then, they'll pay them upwards of five and six hundred dollars an hour to decimate you."

Sol asked, "Well, who pays for my experts and the attorney?"

"Why, you do," El Haq laughed sarcastically.

"But," Sol huffed indignantly, "what if I'm innocent of all charges. What then? Why should I have to pay?"

"Doctor, this is the way of the world. If you get off, like most people do, I think it's eighty-six percent or thereabouts of the complaints that get to the Commission don't even come to a hearing, you just thank your God, and don't do again whatever it was that they said you did, but couldn't prove."

Sol was quiet, and El Haq continued. "Doctor, you have to make a decision about who you want to represent you. I will simply tell you that I am available."

Sol spoke obsequiously. "What do you suggest, Mr. El Haq?"

"I have to leave that up to you."

Sol asked, "What's the worst they can do to me if I don't respond? Can they put me in jail?"

"No, the Commission doesn't have that power. They can't even fine you, but they can recoup costs. But that isn't important. They can suspend or revoke your license to practice medicine, or include a penalty that you discontinue a segment of your practice. For instance, they can set practice limitations so that you can't do therapeutic injections, or write prescriptions for pain medications. Or they can decree that you are not allowed to minister to women or children. They can demand you do remedial training or even attend chemical abuse programs, whatever they want. It all depends on what you did...what they say you did, and what they can prove on a probably basis."

"So they can't fine me?"

"No, not directly, but they can have you pay expenses. And if they find you guilty, you can bet the prosecuting attorney is going to take a look at the case. Then it can become a criminal matter. Two different agencies, you see."

"That's double jeopardy!" Sol snapped.

"No, Doctor, two different systems. In the first, you don't have any real rights. Oh, on paper you do, but not really. In truth, there is no due process at the Medical Abuse Commission. They base their Findings of Fact, Conclusions of Law, and Final Order, that's what they call their verdict, on the 'standard of care' in that community.

Sol interjected angrily, "And who decides that? Where is it written? I want to see the book."

"It's not written down. It's whatever they think it is; whatever they say it is on the night they make their decision about your life. As I said, you need an attorney. Let me know."

CHAPTER EIGHTEEN

The call came that night at 3 A.M., from a nursing assistant at the hospital. "Dr. Forte, your patient has expired."

Sol rubbed his eyes and asked, "Which patient?"

"Your Mr. McAlister. We need you to come in and pronounce him. Family's getting squirrelly."

Sol ran into the shower, shaved in seconds, and left for Whitaker, speeding along the nearly empty highway in a sad trance, incapable of holding a single thought in his head for more than an instant. He flew past a State Police car, not bothering to look down at his speedometer.

Kevin's mother was sitting on the bed holding her son's yellowed, skeletal, frozen hand. Occasionally, she stroked the hollow face. Grandma was in her seat in the corner, silently rocking back and forth, staring out into space. Devin, however, reeking of alcohol, sat in a chair punching his fist into his palm, slowly, matching the rhythm of his mother's stroking and his grandmother's rocking.

Only McAlister's mother spoke. "Doctor, what happens to Kevin now?"

Sol said softly. "I'm so sorry." He paused and thought for a moment. "Well, I will sign the legal papers, and you call the funeral home. They'll come and care for Kevin."

She hesitated. "We don't have a funeral home. We thought he'd pull through. And how are we going to afford a funeral?" With that, she fell forward, sobbing.

Sol handed her a box of tissues and stood over her until she quieted. He walked slowly to the nursing station, got a stethoscope, warmed it in tepid water from the sink, excused himself to Kevin's mother, and placed the bell on his patient's chest. He listened for a full minute, and hearing nothing, nodded, took a deep breath, and whispered again, "I'm so sorry."

Though he knew he shouldn't have, he was so driven to say something positive, he added, "I'll contact COLA and see what they do in cases like this. There may be a death benefit to help defray the cost of burial."

"Thank you, Doctor. Anything you can do." Her voice was gentle.

Though Kevin's mother had soothed Sol's guilt with her tone, he had now dumped the obligation back on his shoulders. He didn't tell the family that it was going to be nearly impossible to convince COLA to accept the claim in the first place, now that it was so clearly evident Kevin's fall at work had had nothing to do with his extended work-up and hospital stay.

The best the estate was going to do was find a greenhorn attorney so starving for a case that he'd represent them, and perhaps put off the inevitable financial reckoning for a few months. Maybe there would be some money from the car accident, but not enough to cover a funeral. And no matter how hungry the lawyer, it was certain he wasn't going to work for a commission of a third of the state's scanty death benefit, a grant the Commission on Labor Affairs wasn't going to disperse anyway. It would have to be cash on the barrelhead for any attorney in this case, upfront, an hourly rate, and no matter how reasonable the counselor, it would be far beyond the family's means.

Sol asked himself what was to be the outcome of the state's inevitable lawsuit against the family to recoup the time-loss pay Kevin had been granted on Sol's insistence, a draining of public funds that went on for over a year. Then there was the Center's bill to consider, and the Hospital's. Could COLA demand recompense? Was there even a slim chance the Center and Hospital would forgive the debt? He was in no position to demand anything from either branch. He twitched nervously, wondering if the Center could sue *him* for the balance. His head hung sadly as he conceded that in one fell swoop, the Galena Hills Medical Center and Medical Center could force his resignation and dun Mrs. McAlister to recoup their loss.

For a man who had had but a parking ticket in his first 38 years, the turn of legal events over the past weeks left him as deeply depressed as if his entire life had been a series of extended visits to Juvenile Hall, the county lockup, and finally, the big house. He phoned Dana, who was back from her business trip.

She greeted him at the door. "Defendant Forte, welcome to Romanov Prison. It is hopeless to attempt escape." They talked for hours. Dana cringed with the growing frustration and anger she was hearing from this gentle man who had never before raised his voice in her presence. They shared a glass of iced vodka, sipping, rather than drinking, though after an hour, the alcohol asserted itself, and Sol slid slowly into a maudlin humor. Dana put her arms around him, and in her warmth, he let his eyes redden.

They sat together, motionless, for a nearly an hour, drifting in and out of sleep. Each time Sol came to, he held her more tightly. He could sense the world going away, his heart calming, and he allowed himself to fall into a deep slumber.

BANG! Sol's pager squawked so vociferously, his arm swung out and knocked the glass of spirits off the end table. The telephone number that appeared in the little beeper window was unpleasantly familiar, the emergency room at the Hospital. Sol showed the pager to Dana and snarled, "I know, I know, it's God. He wants to talk to me about refilling Kevin McAlister's pain med prescription up there."

Dana tightened her lips and rebuked, "Solly!"

He rolled over and called the ER, forcing a smile as he spoke to a physician's assistant who informed him that Mr. Tarkington had presented, via the aide car, shaking wildly. The PA had taken it upon himself to treat Tarkington with a slug of intravenous Dilantin and, as predicted, the patient had immediately stopped quaking, and was shortly back to baseline, babbling in infantile speech patterns.

The PA droned apathetically, "Dr. Forte, your patient is postictal. What do you want the admission orders to say?"

"Well," Sol spoke, still smiling unhappily, "I think we've proven in the past that he doesn't have a seizure disorder. It's an atypical anxiety reaction. It's all in the chart."

"Doctor Forte, I've never heard of that kind of anxiety reaction. It looked like a seizure to me."

Sol wanted very badly to ask just how many grand mal seizures the young assistant had witnessed, but the vodka had not sufficiently disengaged his frontal lobe, and he bit his tongue. "Well, give him five Valiums, two milligrams only, and send him home. He'll be fine. Tell him to come see me at eight."

⇌ ⇋

Sol went in to the office early the next morning. He retrieved the pile of still-disheveled documents that made up Tarkington's chart and sat reading intently, to keep from thinking about the State Medical Abuse Commission. While searching for a single shred of evidence that Tarkington had ever suffered a true seizure, he came upon the next chapter in the saga, the hiring of yet another lawyer. He couldn't put the chart down.

After Mr. Tarkington had been diagnosed with a disease of his nerve coatings by Nurse Calhoun, the caseworker for Argent at the Commission on Labor Affairs summarily closed the claim. The argument was that unless the patient could prove that the electrical shock and fall from the cherry picker had led to the demyelinating condition, the Commission had no further responsibility. They reminded Mr. Tarkington that he was lucky the Commission wasn't suing to be reimbursed for a claim that now had been proven groundless.

In his conciliatory letter to COLA, Lippard retreated from his earlier position questioning the capacity of a nurse to make sophisticated analyses. He was well aware, even in those nascent days of political correctness, that the sniff of a depreciatory comment about Nurse Calhoun's diagnostic acumen would trump the facts. Everything spoken or written about the case would be used against him in front of the state adjudicators or his medical malpractice insurer, both of whom had perked their ears as evidence of wrongdoing committed by Lippard began to accumulate.

Sol had, long before, asked around about Lippard and discovered the old general practitioner had lost his license, as Judy Famot related, for an inventory of lukewarm misdemeanors. The most egregious was a charge of drinking on the job. This was after he was accused of having AOB, alcohol on his breath, while tending to a patient. He did not deny before the Commission that he had had, on a Saturday night at a party, one drink while he was fourth ER back-up physician. In his long career, he testified, he had never heard of the *third* back-up being summoned to the emergency room. The judges were not moved by his explanation that the second and third back-ups had refused to come in because they had been at the same party.

But there was also the sexual harassment claim filed against him by the mother of a patient who was using the lady's room in his office. Lippard burst in, hurrying to grab a second or two for himself before darting off to see the next patient. He was so upset to encounter the woman squatting on the toilet seat, he barked that she should have locked the door. She broke into tears and complained to the disciplinary committee that the hasp was broken, or maybe it had been too hard to use for a seventy-eight year-old, she couldn't remember which, but no matter, she proposed the device had been disabled purposely to allow the wretched doctor to commit his voyeuristic act.

The final straw was when Lippard hugged a gay man in the hallway outside an exam room, a patient who had just been diagnosed with AIDS. That, in itself, was only mildly suspicious. The actionable offense took place when he put his hand on his MA's shoulder as he stood above the assistant and asked him to set up a referral with the HIV staff at Whitaker General. The MA packed up and left the office mumbling homophobic epithets, his next stop, the ER, where he demanded shots against AIDS. How Lippard escaped a civil suit was beyond Sol, but those were different times.

With Lippard gone and the case closed, the family enlisted the services of a new attorney, Felix Mao, a distant relative of the Chinese Chairman. The lawyer picked through the records meticulously and discovered a previously ignored piece of evidence. In the original ER report, on the day of the industrial accident, there was a scrawled remark that Mr. Tarkington had complained of "unspecified back pain" after being tossed out of the cherry picker. Dr. Lippard had also made mention of it several times in his chart notes, but they were barely legible, and it was cited only in passing, for that complaint had been shelved in the frenzy over the loss of vision and the behavioral changes.

Mr. Mao sent Tarkington to a local chiropractor for an evaluation of the neck. That practitioner took a host of x-rays, which revealed a pattern of arthritis consistent with trauma, rather than aging. He ordered a CT scan of the spine, the state of the art test in those days before MRIs. That imaging study demonstrated probable nerve compression in the neck due to what appeared to be a prior traumatic injury, which, Mao argued, accounted for both the patient's spinal pain and the aching that radiated into his arms, pain that Ms. Calhoun had interpreted as a sure sign of a demyelinating disease. There was now ample evidence to discount demyelinization as the cause of his spinal and arm pain. That forced the Commission to reopen the claim, and back it lumbered to square one.

Next, Mao contended it made more sense than not that anyone who had been dumped to the pavement from an elevated platform would suffer neck trauma. Working on an hourly basis, he fought long and hard, though quite slowly, to have the neck arthritis included in the claim. He argued that Tarkington had never seen a doctor for spinal pain prior to the industrial injury, and that the pattern of arthritis had now been proven, with state-of-the-art imaging, to be consistent with trauma, and that the only trauma he had suffered was the fall. Mao wore COLA down to the point that they accepted the neck injury as part of the original damage.

Finally, Mao sent Tarkington to a newly arrived neurosurgeon, one just out of training, who invited Mao out on a rented yacht to talk about Tarkington and, perhaps, a word or two about future referrals. In no time, Ralph was slated for a multi-level neck fusion surgery. The hungry doctor prodded so convincingly that Tarkington would wind up paralyzed if he didn't undergo the expensive, complicated procedure, and that the claims manager would be personally culpable if the procedure was denied, she agreed without protest. She also had no choice but to reinstate Tarkington's time loss payments, adding a few dollars as Mao argued Tarkington was suddenly the sole supporter of a grandchild, presumably, but never demonstrated to be, Judy's illegitimate issue. It was at this point that Mr. Mao called the family in for a serious meeting and persuaded the family to switch from an hourly fee to contingency, arguing that with surgery and the possibility of complications, the case was going to last for a very long time. Thus, it was in their interest to switch payment plans.

Mr. Tarkington, however, missed the first surgical date, alleging a cold, and the second because his granddaughter had to have her shots for daycare, and the third because he didn't have anyone to take care of him at home beside the little girl, who had gotten sick after her inoculations. By this time, the new surgeon had abruptly given up his practice in Whitaker and returned to the East Coast, where he took interim work selling Isuzu Troopers. Mao was unable to find another doctor willing to tackle the delicate surgery, with its overwhelming chances of a poor outcome, to say nothing of the inexorably ponderous legal and bureaucratic jumble both before and after the procedure. Mao was forced to steer the family off the surgical route. Tarkington went on receiving time loss payments, one-third of which went into Mr. Mao's account every fortnight.

Several years passed during which Ralph Tarkington had, apparently, dipped below the Commission's radar, for the medical notes were exceptionally sparse over that period. Occasionally, he would present to the doctor who had taken over Lippard's practice and complain bitterly of neck, arm, lower back, and leg pain. He was described by the new physician as demonstrating infantile speech and behavior patterns, and being facially expressionless, basically because his neck was so flexed forward the doctor couldn't really see the man's features unless he got on the floor and examined Tarkington by looking up. Eventually, that doctor made the discovery that Mr. Tarkington had a habit of drooling, and duly recorded that observation in his typed chart notes.

That was an unfortunate comment, for it caught the vigilant eye of Nurse Laytonia Bliss, who had taken over for Nurse Calhoun as the custodian of Argent's medical coffers. Nurse Bliss forthwith diagnosed Parkinson's disease, basing her studied opinion on the absence of facial expression the patient had demonstrated for many years, and, of course, the drooling. She traveled on her own time to Mr. Tarkington's neighborhood and poked around until a neighbor mentioned Ralph had a brother with Parkinson's.

Armed with that familial evidence, and the fact that, in her interpretation of the medical literature, Parkinson's was not associated with accidental electric shock, she made the instant recommendation that Mr. Tarkington's COLA claim be closed immediately. She submitted that his Parkinson's was simply a hereditary degenerative condition, one for which neither Argent Public Utilities nor the Commission on Labor Affairs held any pecuniary responsibility.

She recommended, as well, that he be required to repay every penny of the funds the Commission had already dispensed, aside from the bill for the first visit to the emergency room. She sent her report to her supervisor, and a "cc" to the corporate CEO, who nominated her for the employee of the month. She graciously accepted her award, a three-day paid vacation to Durango, Mexico, and returned refreshed, her investigative appetite sharpened. On her first day back, she demanded all of

Mr. Tarkington's previous medical records, including those from the Navy.

The family protested but lost, for the claims manager happily wrote to them quoting chapter and verse of the state legal code, which declared that once you filed a COLA claim, your right to medical privacy was waived. In those records, she discovered, serendipitously, that Tarkington's father had also developed Parkinson's at a young age. That single fact served as the death knell for the case, and Nurse Bliss proudly accepted the award for employee of the month once again.

At that juncture, though, Mr. Mao became incensed. He snatched the case out of the State Industrial Court system and into the mainstream legal path, to Dunton County Superior Court, though the matter skidded to a stop after a private meeting with Argent's in-house legal staff. Mao called Ms. Famot at dinner time and begged out of the case, explaining that Argent was prepared to drag the matter on for years, and he didn't feel it was ethical to continue taking a third of the payments that were about to stop.

Mr. Mao met with the family a final time, explaining that the law was on Argent's side, for a worker had only seven years after the day of the injury to reopen a claim. Though Mao's interpretation of the law, they would later learn, was flawed, the tired family conceded. Out of money again, they did as their attorney urged, but refused to pay a penny in recompense to Argent, simply accepting the lien that was filed against Tarkington's meager estate, intending to worry about what that meant another day.

⊶ ⊷

And that was where the case foundered for several more years, until Attorney Anwar El Haq opened an office in town. He patrolled Whitaker's pharmacies, hospital parking lots, waiting rooms, and cafeterias, trolling for citizens who limped or with appendages in plaster and slings.

Mr. El Haq first encountered Judy Famot in a Drugs for Less, where she was wobbling badly after spraining her knee while skiing for the first time. He approached her in the anti-inflammatory aisle, asking obsequiously which of the myriad products was most powerful for his own painful leg. It was abeam the Motrin and Aleve that he learned the tale of her father's industrial injury.

One thing led to another, a business card was offered, and a formal meeting with the family was arranged for the next morning, Mr. El Haq having discovered an unusual opening in his schedule. He explained that he had had a court appearance scheduled for 9 A.M. in another case, but when the other side realized he had the goods on them, they settled quickly, and for a handsome sum. "These matters often settle when I finally place before them the facts," he assured, fluttering his eyes.

At that first meeting, El Haq enlisted the family's help in gathering the records, though Judy explained many were no longer available, lost in the fog of battle. He sent threatening letters to Argent demanding their archives but received no reply. Finally, he filed a summons and complaint against Argent in Dunton County Superior Court. The judge, though, was the granddaughter of a crusty businessman who had, just months before the trial, made a substantial contribution to the governor's war chest. Days later, his granddaughter was appointed to the bench by the state's chief executive. What El Haq did not know was that the old man also owned the land upon which Argent was planning to construct a new power station.

The young judge made a series of opening warnings. She peered directly at El Haq and snarled, "I will tolerate no slander or defamation in my courtroom."

El Haq bristled to his feet. "Your Honor, excuse me, but defamation does not pertain in certain instances when a statement is considered privileged. For example, when a witness testifies at trial and makes a statement that is both false and injurious, the witness will be immune to a lawsuit for defamation because the act of testifying at trial is privileged."

"Mr. El Haj, you do not need to teach me the law in my courtroom and in *my* country. I find you in contempt. You can write a check to the court for one hundred dollars before we proceed."

El Haq pulled a checkbook from his briefcase, scrawled a few arrogant lines, walked up to the bailiff like a bandy rooster, and dropped the check on his desk. The court officer handed the check to the judge, who scrutinized it and growled, "Okay, Mr. El Haj, why are we here today?"

He asked if he might approach the bench; the judge nodded and accepted the brief. She thumbed through the papers and glared at him. "You have attached an addendum to this motion, one Argent has not had an opportunity to answer."

The company lawyers steamed, "Your Honor, this attached motion has caught us by surprise, and it is such convoluted legal posturing, we can't possibly address it today. Mr. El Haj has wasted our morning. This needs to be remedied."

She agreed. "You're wasting the court's time! What's wrong with you?"

When El Haq squeaked, "Your honor, it is a very minor mistake, and…"

She fined him an additional one thousand dollars for wasting Argent's time, which he would have to pay before the case could go forward. She ended the session by sneering down at El Haq, "I don't know where you learned law, sir, but in America, there are rules, and we follow them."

Even Argent's attorneys were embarrassed by the nascent judge's behavior, and in the spirit of reconciliation, offered to forego their portion of the penalty, but only on the grounds that the case be dropped and the Tarkington family file no further legal papers. El Haq promised to get back to them before the close of business.

He met with the family an hour later and announced that things had gone according to plan, that he had found a crack in the opposing attorneys' case, and they were beginning to talk compromise. But, on the other hand, the case had become more legally involved than he had expected, and there were further fees with which to be reckoned before it could go forward. Ms. Famot agreed to the new financial arrangement, and El Haq, ignoring the Argent attorneys' demand for a decision by the close of business, flew along the highway into downtown Whitaker, back to the courthouse, and into the law library, where he corralled a few students and appealed for help. He put on his best foreign accent and claimed to be a new immigrant studying for the bar, under the gun to submit documents for a moot court appearance involving a wayward judge and an injured worker. The kids looked up the court rules for him and helped phrase the appeal.

El Haq ran up the stairs to superior court, where he double-checked his paperwork with a clerk. Satisfied, he demanded a meeting with the chief judge, explained the proceedings earlier that day, and respectfully requested a new judge. His Honor hemmed and hawed until El Haq sighed and grunted under his breath, "Maybe I'll just, well, there's always the Anti-Defamation League…"

The judge ordered El Haq out of his office, but an hour later, a call came from Clerk of Court Regina Slam, who changed the venue of the next hearing to Courtroom Two, on a different floor, in a different wing of the courthouse.

El Haq began his legal argument by citing a little used regulation, one explained to him by the students he had consulted at the law library. A COLA claim could be reopened if it had been less than seven years, not since the day of the original injury, but from the day the injured worker received the notice of claim closure in the mail, a fine point Mr. Mao had failed to appreciate. Since Tarkington was well within that time frame, El Haq prevailed, a date for formal trial was set, and the family continued paying his fee for the mountain of motions both sides belched in endless succession.

That was as far as Sol got in the tale of Ralph Tarkington, having been ripped from the dialogue by Roxanne's, "Are you out of your mind? Chop chop, Dr. F."

As Sol raised his hand to knock on his first patient's door, Roxanne stopped him. There was a call from CEO Anacota. "The pleasure of your company is requested in my office five minutes ago, and, no, I won't discuss the subject over the phone."

A man in a dark, pinstriped, Brooks Brother's suit was sitting on the couch across from Anacota's desk. He didn't bother to rise when Sol put out his hand, though he did shake it limply. Anacota nodded at the man and spoke to Sol. "He's a colleague of one of the Center's attorneys."

By the time Sol realized this meant the stranger was a lawyer, the man had already mentioned that he had been a lay member at SMAC. "I know the ropes, Doctor. I've defended many a wayward physician." Sol sucked in an affronted breath, but the man cut him off. "I am available to represent you. I want you to know I have handled far more complicated legal matters in the past than your minor brush with the state. You're too young to remember the Lippard affair." Anacota snorted.

Sol queried if he could be required to pay for even a small percentage of the legal bills. The lawyer clucked, "Dr. Forte, you are responsible for the entire amount unless you have a world-class umbrella policy in your homeowner's account."

"I don't own a home."

Well, sir," the lawyer continued, "It can't be on the Center's nickel, or on your malpractice insurance, because neither entity is responsible for moral or unprofessional transgressions."

When Sol's jaw dropped, he looked over at Anacota, who smiled unctuously and added, "It's in your contract. I'm sure you went over that document thoroughly before you signed it. It's all there."

Sol implored, "I didn't do anything immoral or unprofessional!"

As Sol shuffled back into the Department of Orthopedics, the greasy subpoena server materialized, this time out of Rosebac's office, to shove an envelope under his nose. Sol snatched it and signed with a slap of the pen, rumbling, "Fuck me," as he passed Roxanne on the way to his office.

She followed him in. "I have a right to know what's going on in this department. I'm just as important as anyone."

He handed her the envelope. She ripped at it then let go a deflated sigh when it turned out to be only a subpoena commanding that Solomon Forte, M.D., present himself before the Honorable Bentley B. Ballbrine, in Dunton County Superior Court. He was to testify in the matter of Tarkington v. Argent.

He groaned, "When?"

"This Monday afternoon."

"That's three days!"

"Don't yell at *me*. It also says you are to bring every document in your possession."

"Let me see that." And, indeed, the subpoena commanded Sol have at hand every record, every x-ray, and every note of every conversation he had ever had concerning the parties involved in the litigation. Failure to produce said documents would result in a fine and imprisonment.

He grinned. "Since you're such an important member of this department, you are directed to have every scrap of that stuff on my desk by 8 A.M., Monday. If you fail, you will be condemned to the State Correctional Facility for seventeen to twenty-five, where you will share a cell with Dr. Rosebac—*and* his daughter. Thank you. And have a wonderful weekend." He bounced past her to see his first patient.

CHAPTER NINETEEN

Sol arrived at the county courthouse over an hour early to insure his heap of documents made it through security. The carton was searched, and Sol was directed to the one working elevator, but the deputies turned him away as there was a prisoner on board. He schlepped the carton up the three flights to Courtroom Two and dropped onto a worn bench at the end of the long, dim hallway. To his left and right were massive double doors leading into courtrooms.

Before he left his office, Sol had placed a ream of unfinished Commission on Labor Affairs paperwork on top of Tarkington's records. He pulled his COLA forms free and began to work, but scrunched his nose at the odor pervading the halls, a disturbing spoor of impersonal bureaucratic power comingled with the scent of the unwashed, petty criminals who lined the halls waiting their turn before a judge. That culled from within him a groundswell of trepidation over the time he would soon squander, the irretrievable minutes, precious hours, and whole days soon to be frittered with him sitting nervously on hard pews of discolored mahogany, restlessly suspending his life, waiting to be interrogated and judged in the case of the State Medical Abuse Commission v. Solomon Forte. Gone forever would be those irreplaceable breaths of his life; his spirit would be paid out, vaporized in a haze of tension and sadness. He apprehended defeat before the battle had begun.

Pale, detached ladies shuffled past him, coming and going, hauling thick files from one room to another, and soon the same folders back again. Sol smirked that is was like watching the Nazis beat prisoners to fill holes with rocks and then turn around and batter the next shift into removing them. He smiled at one of the women as she passed, recognizing her as a patient from the Center. She stared straight through him in practiced arrogance. As she'd bristled into a courtroom, nose trained on the ceiling, he nodded to himself, recalling her from after-hours clinic. Yes, it was Dorothy Love. He had treated her for a sexually transmitted infection. She'd begged him not to report the disease to the Dunton County Health Department, sobbing it would end her thirty-year marriage. He had taken a chance and coded the diagnosis as a urinary tract infection.

"Hey, where's the love?" he called out in a mocking, New York-accented undertone after the door closed sharply behind her.

He stared down at his pile of work, ready to tackle the first sheet, but a couple of defendants destined for Courtroom Four stopped next to Sol. The boy, his greasy hat set backward on greasier, stringy hair, dropped onto the bench. Sol straightened himself but stole a glimpse at the sallow, pockmarked face and wispy attempt at a mustache. Sol was nauseated by the fog of stale cigarettes and pot wafting from the kid's ratty clothing. His girlfriend, maybe fourteen, bent forward in front of the boy to cuddle his head. She wore a halter-top without a bra, and Sol averted his eyes.

The girl shifted her gaze from her boyfriend to Sol several times, drawing the boy's attention to the man in the suit. He turned to Sol and asked, "Hey, man, you Mr. Sylvester, my lawyer?"

"Huh?" Sol answered, puzzled. "Oh, no. I'm here for a case over there, in Two."

"You a lawyer, man?"

"No, just a doctor."

"You in trouble or somethin'?"

Sol's gut clenched, and he hesitated. He could feel his face redden. "Nope, just a witness in a trial."

When Sol's stomach ceased trembling, he stood and mumbled, "Well, have a good day." Outside Courtroom Six, he found an open seat between several other offenders, and studiously kept his eyes down as he picked through the COLA papers, choosing the easy forms to complete first. He wrote in great concentration, hoping no one else would query his legal status. There was, however, quite a bit of rustling to his left, and he shot a quick glance at the woman seated there. She was in her forties, also enshrouded in a patina of rank tobacco smoke. Her boyfriend was probably sixty, but with hair and clothing much like that of Sol's young acquaintance down the hall. As Sol started to return his attention to the neglected work papers, his eyes brushed the man's greasy jeans, and he couldn't help notice the woman's hand slowly, rhythmically, rubbing his escalating crotch under a ream of papers the man held in his lap.

Sol was up again, settling back outside Courtroom Two, the skinny kid and his barely pubescent girlfriend gone, inside Four, pleading their excuses. On the bench to his left now sat a middle-aged, neatly dressed couple. They held hands nervously as the wife mumbled, "When that lawyer comes, Honey, you tell him you don't know nothin' about Ralph and them electrician jobs. You tell 'em."

Sol delved back into his work, though within thirty seconds, he felt a prickly sensation, and became aware of the presence of a dark figure hovering over him. As his eyes lifted, he saw a short, swarthy face smiling down. "Dr. Forte, I presume."

The man next to Sol startled, popped off the bench, and grunted, "You El Hatch?" Before El Haq could answer, the man blurted, "My wife, Helen here, and me, want you to know we don't know nothin' about Ralph and them electrician jobs."

The swarthy man patted him on the shoulder, nearly pushing him back onto the bench before nodding reassuringly, "Of course not. Don't worry. Everything's going to be fine. Don't worry. I'll take care of everything. You just answer the questions, yes or no, just like we practiced on the phone."

Sol laughed to himself that in all this time, he had never set eyes on the man, yet he could have described him perfectly to a forensic artist. Sol stood and shook hands, though there was no vigor in El Haq's moist grip. The lawyer quickly averted his gaze from Sol and looked guardedly up and down the hallway.

"Please come with me so we can talk." El Haq spoke authoritatively, suddenly firming his grasp. He led Sol by the hand out of the corridor, down the stairs, and into the law library. He bid, "Dr. Forte, you must sit," then disappeared into the stacks. Sol heard him speaking on his cell phone and tried to get back to his paperwork, but El Haq was sitting across from him before he could find where he had left off.

Sol remarked to himself on the English cut of El Haq's rumpled, shiny suit. Somehow, the man's apparel matched his face and demeanor. Removing a yellow legal pad from a cheap briefcase, El Haq whispered to Sol, "Well, Doctor, this is an important case we have together. Let's talk about what you need to say to make sure we win."

Sol raised his palms toward the attorney. "Whoa. Mr. El Haq, you know I have to answer truthfully. I mean, I can't have you tell me what to say, not specifically, at least."

"Of course not, Doctor. My point is that when the other side asks you certain questions, they'll try to trick you into saying things that you don't want to. I know these people. They are as dishonest as can be. Their only mission is to make money for their uncaring employer, no matter who gets hurt. Now, for instance, they are going to ask you to look at documents that claim Mr. Tarkington made a few dollars doing wood carvings while he was on COLA time loss. What would you say to that?"

"I don't know. Did he do that?" Sol asked, his face tensing.

"He did some very light carpentry around the home. He couldn't just lie in bed and feel sorry for himself. Don't you think he had a right to do something, to stimulate his mind? Just because a man is on time loss payments doesn't mean he has to be sitting in a chair with his arms tied behind his back. Does it?"

"Mr. El Haq, this is getting a little dicey. You're telling me that Ralph Tarkington, who sits in my office and drools on himself, was making a living, 'stimulating his mind,' while he was on time-loss? As far as I know, that's against the law. Am I wrong?"

"Doctor, you are neither right nor wrong. He wasn't getting rich. He was simply cutting a bit of wood, perhaps drilling a hole with a little portable drill for the neighbors. He wasn't up on a ladder painting houses. He wasn't coming near making up the difference between what he used to make at Argent before the electrocution and high velocity fall…"

"That was the end of him…"

"Yes…and the unlivable pittance that COLA gave him each week. Mr. Tarkington had a family to support, which he did honestly before the accident. Your father was a union man. You tell me if that is illegal."

Sol flinched. "Okay, I'll bite. How did you know my father was a union man. Who told you that?"

El Haq pushed back from the table subtly. "Please, Doctor, you seem upset. I am an attorney. I am paid to be thorough. You have nothing to hide, nor do I. In this case, actually, I think you mentioned it to Ms. Famot. She thinks highly of you, you know."

El Haq stopped abruptly and watched Sol's eyes. Forte's gaze shifted away from El Haq's, and he thought very briefly that maybe there was an opening, the slightest crack in her armor, that she had used El Haq to send him a signal. His gut clenched, and he wondered if he was going to allow himself the mistake of acting on the stirrings inside him.

Sol nodded. "Well, I guess that is your job. What else do you just happen to know?"

"I know that you have labored very diligently for your patients, and that they appreciate it. That is why I chose you. I've told you this before. I have the sense you're not one of these arrogant doctors who have been groomed for the profession since childhood." El Haq's jaw tightened as he went on. "The best private schools, the best universities, mommy and daddy paying for fancy cars and private housing during medical school. Most of them didn't grow up the son of a working man like you did—*and* I did. You know the despair of the streets in Brooklyn, just like I know them in Alexandria and Cairo. You see, Doctor, we are more alike than you knew."

"Ah, that's where you're wrong, Mr. El Haq."

El Haq stiffened and sucked in the slightest gasp. Sol wasn't sure if he had rattled the man. "Oh, please correct me. I am interested in the truth...the facts, please."

"Well, sir," Sol smiled, "it was Manhattan, not Brooklyn."

Again, El Haq's gasp was faint, but Sol knew it was real. "Of course," El Haq smiled weakly, relieved. "Manhattan. Now Doctor, may I say that it would not be politic to correct your own attorney in the courtroom setting. We must be very careful."

"Mr. El Haq, I was just kidding..."

El Haq interrupted before Sol could go on. "I'm sure you understand that might confuse a jury. These are not sophisticated people. They might not see the humor in it. If you make jokes, the judge may hold you in contempt of court. You wouldn't want that. I have a lot of experience with these juries. These are work-ing people: truck drivers and janitors. Limited education."

"Yeah, just cement truck drivers," Sol smirked.

"Yes, exactly. Or *halal* butchers like my father. So, we must be cautious." El Haq folded his hands in his lap.

"You're so right," Sol nodded. "We must be careful. I'm really impressed with the amount of research you've done for this case. No surprises for *you* in court. Well, you know, if Mr. Tarkington made a few carvings while sitting in a chair and drooling, and someone wanted to give him a few bucks to help out the family and preserve his dignity, who am I to grouse about that?"

"Doctor, thank you for your humanity." With that, El Haq stood and nodded his head toward the courtroom. "I must go in there and get started. I will come out and call you when we are ready for your testimony. It won't be long."

But after an hour, Sol stood and searched the hall for signs to the men's room; it had to be close, he assured himself. Why make people walk far if they had to be near the courtroom? He traveled down the hall past the man whose girlfriend had had her hand on his crotch. The old man was leaning back against the bench, relaxed, bleary-eyed, and Sol smirked to himself thinking of El Haq's warning about "contempt of court." At the far end of the hall, the young man with the stringy hair and barely-pubescent girlfriend had found the only open seats. Their legs were shaking, hands wringing, awaiting to be re-called into Four to learn their sentences. The kid looked up as Sol walked by and whispered to his girl, though loud enough for Sol to hear, "Hey, that's that doctor. Wonder what the judge gave 'im."

Sol kept walking until he found the lavatory two hallways deeper into the courthouse. By the time he wound his way back to the courtroom, the boy with stringy hair was gone, but the old man outside Courtroom Six was still smiling, eyes peacefully closed. The other couple who, "…don't know nothin' 'bout Ralph and them electrical…" were gone, and Sol peeked inside the courtroom. The man was on the stand, another attorney in front of him, firing questions.

Sol also noticed Judy Famot sitting next to her father at the plaintiff's table. Her blond hair was perfect, makeup subtle, her snowy white blouse ironed crisply. She must have felt him staring at her, for she turned and faced him. An extra button of the blouse was open, but the lapels were held slightly touching by a gold necklace. She locked Sol's eyes and smiled gently.

He started to walk in, but El Haq turned and waved him out roughly, and Sol exited, taking a seat back on the mahogany bench, where he sat for another hour, until El Haq came through the doors and shook his head sadly. "Doctor, where were you? I had to call the other witness. These judges, they don't like to wait around wasting time. Where were you?"

"Well, I was in the men's room for three minutes, and I've been here for two hours since. What's going on?"

"Doctor, I *had* to call the other witness. I'm sorry, but we're not going to have time to use you today. It's too late to start with a new witness. We'll have to do it tomorrow morning."

Sol's face, already red, deepened to purple. El Haq took a step back as Sol snarled, "I've got patients tomorrow morning. This is bullshit, my friend."

"Doctor, you have to calm down. That attitude won't help our client. The judge won't put up with it. Now, please wait here for a moment. Let me see what we can do."

Sol nodded angrily, but having believed he was going to get his way, sat quietly and waited. Several minutes later, Judy Famot came out of the courtroom and approached him; the first thing Sol noticed was that the gold necklace was now over the lapels, which were inches apart. He rose. Judy extended her hand in an arc.

She smiled warmly. "Doctor, I'm so sorry. Mr. El Haq told me what happened. He's upset. You're our star witness. We can't lose you after all my father's been through. There must be something *I* can do to help. Please tell me."

"Well, Ms. Famot…"

"I thought you were going to call me Judy."

"Well, I gotta tell you, I'm pretty hot right now. I came early, and El Haq knew I was waiting. I went to the men's room for a second, and now that costs me another day of my life?" Sol calmed and added, "I'm sorry, it's not your fault. Here I am taking it out on you. I am sorry. I just have to get over to my office and make some changes in my schedule for tomorrow morning."

Judy sighed and stepped an inch closer to Sol. "No, I'm really sorry. I wish I could make it up to you."

"It's okay. I'll live," Sol replied, feeling the color in his face lift from irate to flushed.

Judy leaned an inch closer. "Doctor," she spoke softly, "Can I ask a big favor? I don't have my car here. If you're going back to the Center, can I bum a ride to the bus station? It's a block away from your office. Mr. El Haq drove me here, but he wants to stay and work with my father for a while. I need to get out of here. The place is, well, it's greasy."

Sol thought for a short moment, "Of course. No problem."

"I just want to get out of this building as soon as I can. Yuk." She took his hand and squeezed it. "Just let me say goodbye to my father. I'll only be a second."

Judy Famot gazed at Sol, dashed into the courtroom, and was back out in an instant. They walked to the parking lot under the building. Sol opened her door and closed it gently after Judy had slowly pulled her legs inside. "You really are a gentleman, aren't you? I thought all the men like you were long gone."

Sol didn't answer—he couldn't speak. He turned on the radio and managed to squeak, "Rock okay?"

She touched his hand gently and asked, "Maybe something slow. I'm just so keyed up."

They drove out into the late afternoon. It was already dark and rainy, the water on the windows shutting out the other traffic. Judy's body leaned a bit toward Sol's, her head back, eyes nearly closed. Her coat was open, and he stole a glance at her blouse, shaking his head. They did not speak for the next minutes, both silenced by the classical music Sol had found.

When they turned onto the street where the Whitaker Municipal Bus Station sat, Sol turned to her. "It's raining. I'm not putting you out there. I'll drive you home."

She leaned forward and shook her head very subtly. "Oh, no. I can't do that to you. We've put you through too much already."

"Nah," Sol spoke softly, "No way. You're not standing out there in the rain for an hour, or for two minutes, either. Just tell me how to get to there. It's no problem."

She gave him directions quickly, and he nodded that he knew the neighborhood. He whispered, "You just put your head back again and rest. Everything's going to be fine. You'll see."

Sol drove slowly though the teeming rain, quietly thinking to himself how much he had wanted to be near her, and how the strange, very unpleasant legal machinations of the day might grant his fantasy. As more quiet minutes passed, Sol's chest tightened with expectation, but also fear. Judy sighed almost inaudibly, and he looked at her, head back, almost in a trance, her thin, flawless face relaxed. She opened her eyes and smiled at him, letting her left-hand slide slowly toward Sol's. When she finally touched him, he flinched slightly, and she started to pull away, but he took his hand and covered hers gently. He left it there despite the tremor.

It was three more miles to her house, and he reckoned that at thirty miles per hour, that meant only six minutes before the feelings gripping his insides would be over. He sat through one green light then drove on at twenty-five, trying, futilely, to calculate the number of additional seconds that would buy. As they turned onto her street, she took his hand in both of hers and brushed it against her lips. He slowed to fifteen until a car appeared down the block behind them.

At her front path, he put the car in park but left the motor running, the measured tones of Bach's *Symphonia* and the warmth of the heater mesmerizing them both. Now *he* leaned back, quivering, uneasily, aware of what was going to happen if he didn't walk her to her door and leave, and very quickly. Both had closed their eyes—neither noticed their shadows moving as the car behind them passed.

She sighed softly. "You're a sweet man, Dr. Forte. You've been so good to my father…and me. I don't want you to leave. I'm sorry. I shouldn't have said that, but I couldn't help it. From that first day in your office…" She leaned further back and brought his hand to her lips again. "Please don't leave me. Come in. No one will know. Please."

Sol got out of the car. It was pouring. He took an umbrella from the back seat and held it over her as they walked to her front door. She embraced his arm tightly. Under the porch lights, she let her coat open and nodded down toward her breasts; Sol had to steady himself. As hard as he tried not to give in, he simply didn't care what the cost might be some indistinct, vague day in the future.

Judy whispered, "They hurt. I need to get out of this bra. Oh, my God. What are you doing to me?" She opened the door, pulled him in, and brushed her lips against his. She undid the rest of the buttons of her sheer blouse. She took his hand and held it against her left breast but abruptly turned away to run upstairs. "I'll be back in a sec. There's beer and wine in the refrigerator."

Sol was now shaking as hard as when he had gotten the subpoena from SMAC. He knew that what he was about to do would come back to thrash him. There was no escape from that truth; nor, however, was there any escape from the out-of-control freight train with its drugged fool for an engineer. Maybe the alcohol would calm him, and he started toward the refrigerator, weaving as he walked, his shaking now turbulent. The shivering deepened, and he never remembered breathing so hard when not having lifted a finger. In the darkened house, he could not be sure if he was in the midst of a very pleasant dream, or on the fringes of a nightmare.

And then, out of the darkness of the kitchen, there appeared a blurry apparition. Sol recognized it at once as the uncompromising countenance of Chairman Jens Jergesson, M.D., from the Medical Abuse Commission's web site. Sol gasped, and though the specter floating in front of his eyes vaporized in a heartbeat, he understood immediately that it had done its job. The Commission was on duty around the clock. Snatched from his reverie, Sol heard the shower turn off and Judy's stirrings upstairs. He was light-headed, and considered drinking the entire contents of the bottle of cheap wine he had found in the fridge, but instead, put it back and quietly made his way to the door. He turned toward the inside of the house for a moment, sighed sadly, and left, closing the door softly. He ran to the car through the rain, remembering as he jumped in that he had forgotten his umbrella on the porch. He didn't go back.

El Haq called late that evening. "Doctor, I am so sorry for what happened today in court. I know how upset you are, but we must move forward. We cannot trip on what's behind us. Now, tomorrow morning, we will start with you at nine sharp. The judge is aware of what happened today, and he will allow you to testify first."

"'Allow me;' big of him, eh what? Okay, I'll be there, but I've been thinking about something. What did that man, your witness this afternoon, mean by, 'I didn't know nothin' about Ralph and them wires, or whatever it was?' You told me about the wood-working, but wires? What was that all about?"

"Oh, Doctor, I'm sorry, I can't discuss what another witness has said on the stand. I would never do that. It's unethical."

"Okay, Mr. El Haq, I sure wouldn't want to be part of any-thing disreputable. No, sir. But I hope they don't hit me with any surprises tomorrow morning. Do you foresee any, sir?"

El Haq paused then sputtered, "Doctor, I am expecting their side to cross examine you. Naturally, they will be tough. There is a lot of money at stake here…"

"Oh, I forgot, all that money. And, am I still being over-remu-nerated at ten dollars per day? By the way, where do I pick up my ten bucks for today?"

"Doctor, is that important?"

"I don't know. You like working for free?"

"No, of course I don't. But to be frank, I don't think they'll pay you for today. You didn't *do* anything. You can ask if you'd like. Most likely a waste of time. The law is the law. I didn't make these rules. It is sad that the legal system doesn't recognize how valuable your time is. But that is the constitution. You can fight it, but to be honest, you can't win."

Sol was standing outside Courtroom Ten at eight-fifty-eight the next morning. He was hiding at the very end of the hallway, wait-ing until Judy and her father come out of the elevator and turned toward their courtroom. El Haq was several minutes late, and the judge was apparently even later, for Sol peeked in and saw Judy and Tarkington sitting quietly next to El Haq, the bench and the jury box quite empty.

Sol was called at a quarter to ten and took the stand, his eyes averted from Judy's and from the jury. He was sworn in staring straight ahead, concentrating on the sparsely occupied spectators' section. El Haq began the questioning by asking Sol to recount his educational and professional work experience.

As he mentioned his work as a physician at the Galena Hills Hospital and Medical Center, one of the jurors muttered, "Ah ha," and Sol turned toward him. The man, with snowy white hair and beard, in his mid-sixties, was dressed in a pair of dungaree overalls. He nodded pleasantly in greeting, and Sol nodded back with a smile. Sol recognized him as a gentleman who had rolled off the side of a hill in a heavy construction vehicle. He had bounced around inside the cage and sustained a fracture of both his pelvis and femur. The employer fought to deny the claim because the worker had not used his seat harness, a violation for which the man was terminated while he was still a patient in the ICU. Sol had fought for the man and won. He was sure it was him.

He also remembered the patient mentioning in passing that getting old was hell, particularly in the plumbing department, for his urinary stream had become increasingly, weak to the point that he was up eight and nine times a night to relieve himself. Sol, unable to ignore his formative years in family practice, had worked the man up, and, discovering very early prostate cancer, sent him to a local urologist. The surgery had apparently cured him, and when the man came back to Dr. Forte to close his industrial claim, Sol wangled a substantial settlement from the state for the broken bones. The patient was so thankful for the COLA compensation, and for the referral to a surgeon who didn't make him impotent from the prostate operation, he brought several cases of Coors beer to the Orthopedic Department.

Sol felt quite relieved to see a friendly face on the jury, but Argent's legal team snarled in unison. The lead attorney was on his feet before the man's smile had faded. He demanded a side bar. When El Haq and the entire team of defense lawyers were done, the judge turned to Sol and growled that he was to leave the courtroom and wait outside until further notice.

When El Haq emerged, he was shaking his head. "Doctor, the trial has been continued. You are not allowed to know a juror. Are you not aware of that?"

"Well, pardon me. I didn't choose the jury. The guy was my patient. I've treated what, over twenty-five thousand sick and wounded in this city? Law of chance: someone I've seen as a patient is going to be in the grocery store when I'm buying my Wheaties, or in the post office when I'm mailing my demand to the court for the ten bucks."

"Doctor, as soon as you saw that juror and recognized him, you should have turned to the judge and said something to that effect. Now, we have to stop the trial."

"How many hours is that going to take?"

El Haq sighed, "I don't know. The alternate juror just stood up and said she wasn't feeling well because of all the turmoil, so we'll have to wait until she calms down, or we'll start all over again. I imagine it will be several days. I'll let you know."

"Days? I have to come back again?"

"Doctor, I've told you, I don't make the rules."

The courtroom door opened and Judy started to emerge. Sol was already pink in the face, but now his color deepened into a mortified scarlet that even El Haq noticed. She quickly turned back into the room, but not before Sol could taste her anger. He sighed, and his shoulders dropped. El Haq asked hurriedly, "Doctor, is there something wrong? Are you ill?"

"Nah, I'm just fine. So, you'll call me?"

El Haq nodded and was already turning to reenter the courtroom when he added over his shoulder, "I'll see if I can speed things up.

Sol returned to the Center and sat quietly, with little to do for the next few hours as Roxanne had hurriedly canceled his patients for the morning. Though he tried to ignore the unanswered letter from SMAC, the shadow it cast would not fade, and he reached into his desk drawer. He read and reread it, wincing that *he* was soon to be the center of a legal tornado with no storm cellar in sight. He chided himself to get started on a defense plan, find an attorney, and study the world's literature on what he had been accused of doing, whatever it was. He also needed to learn as much as he could about the Commission.

On the other hand, he had slept poorly the night before, apprehensive about facing Judy in the morning at the courthouse, and he grinned sickly, muttering to himself, "Why do now what you can put off until tomorrow?" He spent most of the next hour checking his e-mail and browsing the Internet.

He plugged in the name of the attorney he had met in Anacota's office. No university affiliation was listed, and the note under "Law School" documented only that he had been apprenticed to a superior court judge in Whitaker. "Law degree out of a Cracker Jacks box," Sol muttered, "not even been to law school? And he couldn't get off his fat ass to shake my hand? If my pop ever saw that, he'd have grabbed the jerk by the neck and pulled him out of his seat."

Sol reconsidered his options: It was either El Haq or face the Commission and its attorneys uncovered, bare, nude. "The devil you know is better than the one you don't," he whispered, recalling his mother's phrase when the family wanted to move from their apartment because the super was so inattentive to their plumbing needs.

CHAPTER TWENTY

El Haq phoned Sol late in the afternoon three days after the trial of Ralph Tarkington had been continued. The ill alternate juror had returned the very next day, but another juror had gone to the judge in tears to admit that her son had been treated by Dr. Forte, and she had to be replaced by the final alternate. Traditionally, there was no court on Fridays. On Monday morning, long after Sol had taken his seat outside Courtroom Two, jurors number six, seven, and eight called within minutes of each other complaining they had been disabled by the flu, but promised to show up the next morning.

Before Sol was sent home, El Haq warned, "The jurors are not in a pleasant state, and they want to get this case over with." He told Sol that he must appear the next morning at nine sharp. "It is better if you are on time tomorrow. We don't want to antagonize the jurors anymore."

"What, they're angry at *me*?" Sol snapped.

"Well, Doctor, they seem to have gotten to know you without having seen you very much, haven't they? First it was your mysterious disappearance, then the little misunderstanding that cost them extra days away from work and their families…"

Sol interrupted, "Yeah, but they get their ten bucks a day, don't they? What are they bellyaching about?"

"Doctor, we've been over this ground many times before. Right now, we must keep our attention on the ball. Our client's future is at stake. I hope we can let go of some of our anger for a short time."

Sol nodded in resigned compliance. "Okay, but on another note, we're running out of time in answering that letter to the Commission. We're down to sixteen days."

"Doctor, I've been so busy with this trial. Day and night, you know. We will attend to your matter before the deadline. Do not give it a second thought. Those deadlines don't have to be satisfied to the minute, you know. We'll just tell them we were gathering papers or something. Like I said, Doctor, please, let us keep our concentration on this case. We'll get to your problem in no time."

Sol was on the mahogany bench before eight-thirty the next morning. He had remained in his car until he saw Judy and her father enter the courthouse, then waited until they went through the metal detector and security. He scowled as he watched her smile seductively at the young guard who slowly played the wand over the front of her jacket, and more slowly a second time.

At nine-twenty-five, he was escorted into Courtroom Two. He was sworn in again. The judge admonished him to look directly at the jury and speak without hesitation if he recognized any of the unhappy faces staring back at him. He fixed his gaze on each citizen in order and pledged he had never laid eyes on a single one. The judge squinted down at him. "I certainly hope not."

El Haq was first, stumbling slightly on an electric cord as he left his table to stand in front of the jurors. To start his direct examination, he queried Sol about his entire educational history, all nineteen years of formal schooling. He established that Dr. Forte had graduated near the top of his class at every one of the fine universities he had attended before coming to the Galena Hills Hospital and Medical Center. El Haq questioned Sol on his treatment of Ralph Tarkington. It was easy. Every one of El Haq's questions was drawn from Sol's chart notes, and El Haq simply had him read the record verbatim. They established that Mr. Tarkington had, indeed, been in an awful industrial accident. El Haq took two drawn-out steps closer to the jury box, glancing slyly to see if Argent's lawyers were paying attention.

He whispered a question. "Doctor, might this awful, debilitating industrial accident have been avoided if Argent had installed automatic fail-safe power cut off breakers on the so-called," he made quote signs with his fingers and burped, "'dead wires' that ruined this unprotected employee's life?"

The heads of the legal team snapped up in unison. The lead Argent attorney jumped to his feet. Almost shouting, he objected that the question was compound, confusing, leading, and that, "…Dr. Forte is not an electrical engineer, and he has no educational or professional basis for making that determination."

Before the judge could rule, though, El Haq spouted, "That is not the case at all, Your Honor. We have established that Dr. Forte has a college degree in physics. Further…"

The judge interrupted and muttered, "Sustained, let's move on."

El Haq withdrew his question and went on to ask Sol to confirm that it was almost impossible for a man of limited intelligence to pull the wool over the eyes of dozens of Whitaker's most prominent physicians and psychologists for over twenty years.

Argent's attorney was on his feet again. His objection was upheld on the basis that Dr. Forte had never met or spoken with any of Mr. Tarkington's previous physicians. "Why, Your Honor, the witness wasn't even a doctor when these physicians treated the claimant. He was barely into his teenage years. He, therefore, has no grounds to testify regarding their competence."

El Haq was trembling. "Why," he squeaked, "the only so-called health care workers who challenged the veracity of Mr. Tarkington's claim were *former* nurses who were paid directly by Argent Public Utilities for the sole purpose of nullifying everything that had happened to the claimant after the terrible accident. Isn't that true, Doctor Forte?"

"Objection. He's testifying for his witness, Your Honor."

There were myriad additional objections by Argent's lead counsel before the judge allowed Sol to read the portions of the patient's record in which the Argent nurse case managers pronounced medical conclusions that dozens of board certified medical doctors had missed. El Haq asked directly, "Dr. Forte, are nurses trained to make medical diagnoses, particularly of complicated diseases?"

Sol started to answer, but Argent's lead counsel was on his feet. "Foundation, Your Honor. Dr. Forte does not know what those nurses were trained to do. He never went to nursing school. He never met the health care providers in question, and as far as our records indicate, there is no evidence that their credentials were included in the chart notes that he reviewed. He knows nothing of their capacity to make simple medical diagnoses."

El Haq spread his hands and arms toward the judge and shrugged. "So, Your Honor, doctors and nurses have been working together for centuries, each doing what they do, nurses nursing the ill, doctors prescribing medicines, doing procedures, making diagnoses, but the two professions exist in parallel universes, simply going along day by day, with no idea what the other has been trained and licensed to do? Please, let's be honest and direct here. The system could not work if there weren't intimate knowledge of the respective, and may I stress, very different roles. Counsel's argument makes no sense, Your Honor."

The judge agreed with El Haq and permitted Sol to opine on the propriety of the diagnoses the case managers had proffered; he even allowed the comment Sol made at the end of his assessment: "Well, if these nursing diagnoses had been credible, I would imagine *some* doctor along the way, *somebody* over the years, would have taken the time and effort to prove or disprove them. I think the nurses made a good try, but their thinking was not terribly sophisticated, medically, that is."

The objections flew like the blowing snow outside the courtroom windows. Sol took the maelstrom to look out at the weather. He smiled, happy and comfortable with the notion of driving home in the winter storm, actually looking forward to it, practiced in the art of wild-weather maneuvering from his years in the Northeast. The jurors, however, were beginning to rustle about in their seats. Though the snow had been falling for just an hour, the jurors were staring at the judge and then out the window, back and forth, waiting for him to release them before the roads became impassable.

The judge finally turned toward the windows. He shook his head as if making a difficult legal decision, banged his gavel nervously, called a recess, left the bench, and conferred with the chief judge, who ruled that if the weather went on for another thirty minutes, court would have to be adjourned for the day.

The flurries thickened into a snow shower before the judge was reseated and the jury brought back in. He dismissed them immediately, warning them not to discuss the matter at trial with anyone. He pointed his finger sternly at Sol, wagging while he cautioned him not to see any of the jurors, their family or friends, or anyone else associated with the trial during the balance of the proceedings. He banged his gavel twice.

Sol started toward the door, but the bailiff jumped in front of him and warned him not to take another step until the judge and jury had vanished. As the parties dispersed, El Haq promised to call Sol later in the day.

Sol raced back at the Center to see if any of his cancelled appointments had not gotten the word and come in anyway. With the snow falling in earnest, however, Roxanne had long since departed, and most of the offices were closed. Sol, though he tried to conjure excuses, grunted and took out the phone book, searching for defense attorneys with experience in matters of professional moral turpitude. That was the phrase El Haq had used. But all the offices were closed due to the weather, so he drove home slowly, got into bed, and read *Queen's Bench Five*, his father's favorite book.

Sol was outside Courtroom Two the next morning at eight-fifty-five, just behind Judy Famot and her father. He made no effort to avoid them. He nodded to himself how time was the mind's best salve, and how each day he was less and less anxious about being near her. He hoped time would work its magic and someday cleanse his mind of her and of all his other petty dilemmas. He laughed sardonically, for he knew there would be plenty of new headaches to take their place.

He was called as the first witness, reminded that he was still under oath, and that he would remain so until the court was done with him. El Haq began the questioning, repeating the ground they had been over the day before. Yes, Sol was a board-certified physician; yes, he had gone to a fine, American medical school; and no, he had never had a medical *malpractice* suit lodged against him. El Haq emphasized the word malpractice, for he was surreptitiously reminding Sol to distinguish medical negligence from the simple summons for moral turpitude generated by the State Medical Abuse Commission.

El Haq had Sol again read from Tarkington's chart, but this time only the entries that described the industrial accident, the immediate aftermath, and the report of the eye doctor a few days after the injury, the one who claimed to have found no evidence that Mr. Tarkington had been injured. When El Haq asked Sol to reread the part of the record from the emergency room less than an hour after the accident, the sentences that described singed eyebrows and the redness of Tarkington's burned facial skin, the opposing attorney jumped out of his seat and crowed, "Objection. This doctor wasn't in the emergency room to confirm the nurse's note. And, anyway, all nurses are capable of doing medically is change bed pans, according to Dr. Forte."

The judge, however, allowed Sol to continue demonstrating the contradictions in the chart, and El Haq led him through the years of notes, and again emphasized the quite varied diagnoses proffered by the nurse case managers. El Haq debunked all of the medical opinions skillfully, culling from the records contradiction after contradiction. Sol nodded to himself, pleased that this lawyer was creating the foundation of an argument that clearly demonstrated the poor treatment Tarkington, a humble, hard-working, military veteran, had suffered at the hands of the heartless Argent Corporation. Even Sol was beginning to see pieces of the Tarkington puzzle fall into place. He was proud to be on the stand defending the man, and he sat up straighter.

Late in the afternoon, though, El Haq took his seat and the lead attorney for Argent Corporation began his cross-examination. It wasn't until just after the attorney walked up to Sol's witness chair and said, "Good afternoon, Dr. Forte," that Sol was faced with a series of questions that took him by surprise. As he paused to measure an answer, the door at the rear of the courtroom opened, and Dana slipped in quietly. She took a seat in the last row, smiled, and puckered her lips subtly. Sol smiled back.

The lawyer wasn't amused and turned to shoot Dana a haughty, yet cross, look. "Doctor, please, your full attention, if you don't mind. First, sir, would you describe for the jury your medical training after attending so prestigious a medical school?"

"Do you mean my residency?"

"Yes. What medical specialty was your residency training in, Dr. Forte?"

"Family medicine."

"So, Doctor, you have no training in orthopedic surgery. Is that correct?"

"I have years of training in orthopedics, but I'm not an orthopedic *surgeon*, if that's what you mean."

"Doctor Forte," the attorney interrupted, "please be so kind as to answer *only* the questions I ask."

"Okay."

"So, you're not a trained orthopedic surgeon at all? Is that correct?"

"Yes, but…"

"Your honor, may I respectfully request that you remind the witness that he is to answer only what I ask, not what he feels like saying?"

The judge did so, and the lawyer went on. "So, Dr. Forte, you were taught how to treat basic illness in your residency. That's what a so-called general practitioner really does."

Sol chafed, sucking in an angry breath to fight back. "We are not general practitioners. We are family physicians. We are trained in depth in many specialties."

"Doctor, may I ask, how many years was your residency?"

"Three years."

"Three years. I see. And how long is, say, a real orthopedic surgeon's residency?"

"At least five years. Usually seven, often more."

"And, how long is, say, an eye doctor's residency?"

"At least five years. Maybe seven, often more."

"And a simple one: a radiologist's, the doctors who all they do all day long is read x-rays?"

"At least five years. Sometimes seven."

"So, are you telling this jury that you have, in three short years of residency, the skills to do what it takes a minimum of fifteen years of training to do for everybody else?"

"Not at all. We take care of the vast majority of medical problems." Sol hesitated but was surprised that the lawyer didn't nip his answer in the bud, so he went on. "It's really quite easy to explain. We handle over nineteen out of twenty patients who come to our offices. The one out of twenty-or-so patients we don't feel comfortable treating, we refer to the sub-specialists. The complex issues are referred out."

"So, Doctor, Mr. Tarkington's injuries were simple."

"Well, no, but…"

This time, the lawyer glanced up at the judge, and Sol stopped. The attorney stole a peek at the jury, rolling his eyes in apology for the waste of their time. The lawyer sighed again. "Doctor, have you had any formal, sanctioned training in the field of orthopedics."

"Well…"

"Any training in which you were awarded a certificate of competency that is recognized by the American Board of Orthopedic Surgeons?"

"I've had many courses…"

"Yes or no, Doctor."

"No."

El Haq was on his feet with an objection. "Your honor, counsel is badgering the witne…"

The judge answered before El Haq finished his statement. "No, he is not. He is trying to establish the qualifications of the witness to make statements regarding traumatic injuries. Sit down, Mr. El Haq."

Though El Haq had made the objection to interrupt the lawyer's timing, it had backfired, and the attorney was now dancing forward like Muhammad Ali, unstoppable, preparing the crowd for the thrill of an early knockout. "Doctor, let's not waste any more of the jury's time. I'm going to cut right to the chase. I want to know two or three things with a yes or no answer. Number one: You have never been a defendant in a lawsuit, so you testified earlier today, but have you ever been called before the State Medical Abuse Commission?"

"Objection, your honor. No foundation, and no relevance whatsoever. It is a fishing expedition. No, it is an outrage."

"Mr. El Haq, I believe defense counsel is seeking to establish the credibility and competence of your witness. But, Counsel, please do lay the foundation for your question."

"Doctor, are you familiar with the State Medical Abuse Commission?"

"Yes."

"What service does the State Medical Abuse Commission…? Strike that. What is the task of the State Medical Abuse Commission?"

Sol thought for several seconds before answering. "I believe their job is to adjudicate complaints about doctors."

The lawyer half-turned to the jury and nodded. "That is correct. Now, does the Commission have the authority to take the medical license of a doctor they find to have broken the rules?"

"I think they do, but I know very little about the Commission."

"Are you aware of the process they use to determine if a doctor has broken the covenant?"

"I don't know what you mean by covenant."

"You *know* what I mean. Doctors who break the rules about how to treat patients." The lawyer was genuinely angry, and Sol sensed it.

"I believe that is what they do for a living."

"Is it a living, Doctor, or are these all volunteer doctors and members of the community?"

"I don't know the makeup of the Board. And I believe they are remunerated for their services, but I don't know how much. I think it's…No, I'm not sure."

The lawyer's face relaxed. "Doctor Forte, you said the word Board. Why?"

"That's what it is called, or what it used to be called, I think. I know very little about that aspect of the medical community."

"Was it the Medical Excellence Board before the name had to be changed to something more in keeping with the public's outcry for control of unruly, dishonest doctors?"

"I believe so."

"But that's what they do—discipline wayward doctors."

El Haq jumped up. "Objection. Is there a question in there? Counsel is testifying for the witness."

"Withdrawn," the lawyer harrumphed and verily ran, with a poorly hidden grin, to a stack of papers from which he pulled a typewritten sheet. He lifted it high above his head and waved it toward the jury box. "Now, Doctor, and I remind you, yet again, that you are under oath, have you ever received a letter from what was then called the Medical Excellence Board, and is now called the State Medical Abuse Commission, asking you to justify your care regarding a patient?"

Witness Dr. Solomon Forte drew a deep breath, fixed his eyes on the letter, and believed he recognized the seal of the Commission. He started to explain, but the lawyer's eyes shot up toward the bench. Sol's shoulders drooped. "A letter, yes."

The lawyer nodded to the jury and relaxed. "*Thaaank* you. Now Doctor, let's just sum up where we've been. We've established that you are not an orthopedic surgeon, and that you have not had any formal orthopedic training as part of a sanctioned orthopedic residency. Is that correct? And I'd appreciate a yes or no answer."

Sol's face tightened angrily. "Yes."

"We've also established that you have received a letter from the Medical Disciplinary Commission asking you to provide them with information regarding your treatment of a patient. Is that correct?"

"Yes."

"Let's move on. Now, are you aware of any income Mr. Tarkington generated during the period from the date of his so-called industrial injury to the present moment?"

"Yes. He has been on time-loss, getting a small sum from the state for having been injured." Sol was going to leave it at that, but he saw the glint in the attorney's eye, and he went on. "I have also been informed by Mr. El Haq that Mr. Tarkington created some wood carvings. As I understand it, he did some whittling for his neighbors, maybe ten years ago. I don't know how much he made, but what's he supposed to do, just sit in a chair and drool for the rest of his life?"

There was an embarrassed gasp from the jury, and the judge struck his gavel down twice. Sol shot a quick glance toward Judy, who looked away, but Tarkington grimaced and tightened his lips. The attorney again half-faced the jury and shook his head before turning toward the judge and asking, "Your Honor, we would like to present Exhibit 13A at this time, if we may."

The judge allowed the request, and the lawyer turned to his assistants and called out, twisting his index finger high in the air, as if an emperor hastening the execution of a rebellious serf. "Bring in the video recorder and the televisions."

Several of the lesser attorneys shuffled toward the back of the courtroom and dragged electronic equipment to the bar. With practiced hands, they plugged wires into wires, and wires into black boxes. When they were done, the number two man nodded toward the lead lawyer, who reached deep into his tooled leather briefcase and drew out a VHS tape. He lifted it into the air with a flourish before opening the box with great theater to establish no sleight of hand was afoot. He smiled at the jury as the tape was inserted into the recorder. The assistant attorney rotated the larger of the two televisions toward the jury and asked fawningly if everyone had a good view of the screen. He rolled the second set nominally in front of Sol, but turned it just enough to give the judge a better view, making So lean forward and turn his head uncomfortably to view the screen. The assistant stood at attention. When the nod came from the lead, the assistant did not hide his broad grin as he pushed the play button. The lead attorney took a melodramatic step backward toward the jury box.

There were several seconds of fuzz, and the attorney glared at his assistant. Suddenly, though, a banner across the screen:

RECONNAISSANCE OF RALPH TARKINGTON
CLAIM NUMBER TRD-980-556
15 MARCH 2001

Fuzz again and then colors and shapes and muffled sounds. The picture was in front of a simple clapboard house, one that was vaguely familiar to Sol, but he could not place it.

The attorney spoke. "Let's just stop the tape here. Doctor, do you recognize this house?"

"I'm not sure I do."

"Well, let me help you. This is Mr. Ralph Tarkington's house. Now do you recognize it?"

Thankfully the lights had been lowered by one of the lesser lawyers, and neither the jury, Dana, nor even the lawyer could see the crimson rise in Sol's face. "Yes, I do now."

There was a long theatrical pause, and just as the attorney took a gleeful deep breath to continue, the doors from the judge's chambers sprang open, and a chubby lady walked directly up to His Honor and whispered in his ear. The judge shook his head angrily and banged his gavel twice. "Ladies and Gentlemen, apparently, the City of Whitaker has experienced the rupture of a gas main adjacent to the courthouse. I've been assured there is no danger to the public, but in the interest of safety, we are going to adjourn for the day. Bailiff, please accompany the jury into their chambers and assist them in an orderly evacuation of the building. Members of the jury, please remember that you are not to discuss this trial with anyone, including other jurors. For the rest of you, please exit the courtroom via the main doors and proceed as directed by the authorities posted in the hallway. I trust we will re-adjourn in the morning. Thank you. Court dismissed." And with the annoyed crash of the gavel, Sol and the other petty players flowed out into the hallway.

There was, however, no one posted in the corridor to tell them what to do, and Sol quickly slipped out thorough the abandoned security checkpoint with Dana in tow, stepping into the frigid, gray, Whitaker morning. Dana left to do some work, and Sol promised to call her. He drove to Center, but it had also been evacuated, and he escaped the city back to his tiny apartment.

Sol left messages on El Haq's answering machine. There was no response. Had El Haq known about the reconnaissance tape? Where was the other attorney going with the fact that Sol recognized Tarkington's house? Had Sol been followed that night? No, he reassured himself, it was impossible. He was just a small player. But, then again, what did they know?

When he called Dana's that evening, he studiously avoided talking about the case, citing the judge's admonition, but she circuitously asked how he recognized the Tarkingtons' house. "You remember. I dropped off a letter at his place way at the beginning of this fiasco. It was so early in the morning, before dawn, and I didn't recognize it, but really, Sweet Pea, I'm not going to talk about this anymore. If they're following me, they're probably bugging my place, and maybe yours. Could be tapping our phones. This whole thing sucks, and you know what, it would probably be best if you didn't come to court when I'm on the stand. It makes it hard for me to concentrate."

Dana was silent, and Sol apologized. "It's not that I don't want to see you, it's just that this'll be over tomorrow and, really, it's tough if you're there. You know what I'm thinking about when I see you. You want me to stand up to look at a piece of evidence and be embarrassed?" He laughed at his declaration, but Dana was remained silent. "Hey, I'll talk to you tomorrow. I miss you."

"Uh huh," she grunted, and the phone went dead.

Sol did not sleep well, wondering what would happen when the gavel fell in the morning. He was there at 8:30; the judge rushed in at 9:10, and Sol waited on the bench for nearly an hour while the judge entertained motions.

After a few pleasantries and a recap of the previous day's testimony, in which the lead attorney reminded the jury that Dr. Forte was at best a general practitioner, and one who had run afoul of the state authorities, he pushed the button to start the tape. The front of the Tarkington's home appeared on the screen. "Doctor, have you ever been there?"

El Haq was on his feet. "Asked and answered, Your Honor."

"Overruled. Answer the question, Doctor."

"Yes."

"Who else lives there?"

"I think Mr. Tarkington and his daughter, Ms. Famot. I don't know who else does."

"Ah, Ms. Famot, Mr. Tarkington's daughter. Is she here in the courtroom today?"

El Haq was now vibrating in his chair. He stood and bellowed, "Your Honor, many doctors go to their patients' homes. This line of questioning is inflammatory and out of order."

The judge looked down. "Where are you going with this, counsel?"

The lead attorney smiled arrogantly. "Your Honor, bear with me for one minute. You will see it's all very, very appropriate—or perhaps not."

The judge nodded, "Go ahead, but you are limited to one minute."

The lead asked Sol again, "Is Ms. Famot present in the courtroom today?"

"Yes."

"Please point to her."

Sol did so.

"Doctor, were you ever inside the house owned by Mr. Tarkington with Ms. Famot?"

"Yes."

"When was that, Doctor?"

"Recently."

"How recently? This week?"

"Yes."

"Was there anyone else in the house, the house owned by Mr. Tarkington, at that time?"

"I don't have any idea. I was only there for a minute."

"Not very long, Doctor?"

"Yes, I said, for a minute, probably less."

"Only for a minute, Dr. Forte? The lawyer's voice raised an octave as he demanded, "You spent a romantic evening with Ms. Famot, didn't you, sir?"

The gavel stifled the gasps, and the judge grumbled, "Order," but the sound of pencil on paper in the jury box was like wind from the mountains.

For a split second, Sol's face loosened. "Absolutely not!"

Sol heard stirrings in the jury box again and then gasps, though he was loathe to look over for fear the jurors had not believed his vociferous denial and were dissecting his humiliation.

The jurors were indeed flustered, but not based on the salacious testimony. It was because Juror Number 5 had fallen forward and was clutching his chest. A middle-aged woman next to the man jumped from her chair and climbed over her neighbor, shrieking, "Oh, my God, oh, my God!" She spilled over the front of the jury box onto the marble floor, landing on her back, legs aimed toward the tooled ceiling. Her print dress came to rest around her waist.

Sol's first thought was how strange it was that some women chose not to wear panties, though his eyes fixed a moment later on the man, who had now completed his collapse and lay crumpled between several empty jurors' chairs. Sol was quite aware that it was not his place to react to an emergency in the courtroom; that the judge was responsible and in control, trained to handle every exigency, and that any move on Sol's part would be rewarded with a thump from the bailiff's baton.

When the judge finally banged his gavel, Sol relaxed and waited patiently for the command to action, the mobilization of professional forces to manage any challenge to the meting out of justice. The only sound, though, was a shouted, "Order in this courtroom!"

Sol flew out of his witness cage to the front of the jury box. He turned to the judge. The bailiff had taken a defensive posture next to his boss, baton raised, shuddering menacingly. Sol barked, "Are you going to do something or not?"

The judge was apoplectic and shrieked, "Order, I said order in this court!"

The bailiff took a threatening step toward Sol, who shook his head and growled, "Well, if neither of you is going to do something, I will."

The two officials froze, and Sol hurdled over the jury box railing and threw mahogany chairs until he had room to maneuver. As one of the soaring chairs landed with a crash onto the floor in front of Argent's attorneys' table, a leg snapped off and flew toward the panel of lawyers, just missing the lead's head. Sol stretched the victim out on the floor, opened his collar and belt, put his ear next to the old man's open mouth, and listened intently for breath. There was none.

The next step was to feel for cardiac activity. He was frightened, but not surprised, when none of the usual spots pulsed. Sol reckoned he had witnessed a heart attack, and that directed him onto a very specific treatment path. With only seconds left, Sol pulled the man's tie free and ripped open his shirt. "Call 911!" he snarled to the retreating judge and bailiff, who were making for chambers. The jurist's face was as bloodless as the dying man's on the floor, and Sol wasn't sure the order had registered.

"One, two, three," Sol counted aloud then brought the side of his fist to punch the old juror's thorax a fraction to the left of center. This was Sol's first cardiac thump, a technique he'd only read about, and one to be drawn upon only when the cardiac arrest had *just* happened, *and* been witnessed by the person planning to do the resuscitation.

Sol put his ear to the man's chest. No pulse. He punched harder. The jurors gasped, and two of the men stepped forward to stop Sol's brutality, but Sol raised his palm as he placed his ear back to the man's heart. There was a weak, uneven beat, though it became regular, and he lifted his thumb toward the approaching men.

Though the heart had started working, it made little difference, for there were no respirations. Sol dropped his head and began mouth-to-mouth resuscitation. After a series of breaths, he brought his ear back to the man's chest. A weak heartbeat, but still no inhalations. More mouth-to-mouth. No breath. More mouth-to-mouth, weak beat but no breath. More mouth-to-mouth, deeper this time, perhaps too forceful, he worried, but recognizing there was little to lose, he pressed on. With the deepened pressure of Sol's respirations, the old man vomited up the coffee and Danish the City of Whitaker had provided an hour before.

Now, Sol was faced with the possibility that some of the food would find its way into the man's trachea, blocking off the air he was trying to get into his patient's lungs. "Clean out the mouth with your finger," Sol roared to himself, but one of the one of the jurors stepped forward.

Sol was familiar with vomit from his residency, but that was not the case for several of the jurors, who ran from the courtroom gagging. Sol went on delivering mouth-to-mouth, though that begot only another episode of vomiting without any spontaneous respirations. It was becoming apparent the old man would not be resuscitated, and Sol fretted that his failure had taken place in front of a jury of his peers. He made the decision to puff one more breath into the man's mouth.

He leaned back, for just a second, to reevaluate the situation and stretch his shoulders. He growled aloud, "I don't quit, damnit," and returned his lips to those of a creature whose precarious acquaintance would soon change his life. Even with the doctor's deepest breath, though, there was only silence in the old man's chest. Sol sighed, obliged to accept there was nothing left to do.

He puckered his lips and started back down, probably by reflex, but halfway to the man's lips, he detected the slightest pinking of the indigo face, then the most trivial twitching of the muscles around his mouth. Sol was frozen. There began the most subtle batting of ancient eyelashes until the eyes, themselves, opened—bloodshot, terrified. The spectators gasped in unison.

The old man whispered, "What the hell am I doing down here? What's going on?"

Several of the jurors fell backward a few steps, slack-jawed, lightheaded; some wept; three began to clap. Then two more joined the ovation; soon, there were five, and finally, the several jurors who had fled dashed back to applaud the resurrection. The old man started to clap himself and tried to get up, but Sol gently held him down and spoke softly. "Sir, that heart of yours did a little flip flop...gave you fits there for a minute. It's okay now, but you just lay here and rest for a second. Court's adjourned anyway. Just lay back and we'll keep you warm and comfortable." Sol placed his suit jacket over the man's bare chest, and one of the women draped her shawl over his legs.

Sol held the old man's wrist and monitored his pulse. The patient took his other hand and held Sol's tightly. "Okay." he mumbled then smiled, "Hey, you're the doctor on the stand, aren't you?"

"So they tell me," Sol half-laughed and looked around. "Where the hell are the medics? Did anyone call them?"

The bailiff, who was watching from the door of the judge's chambers wide-eyed, yelled, "I'll go check," and disappeared inside.

The patient looked up and whispered, "You know, Doc, I don't feel so good. All hot and sweaty. Am I going to be okay?"

"Ah, you're fine, sir—just a blip on the old radar scope. No problem. You just hang on for a minute. Everything's gonna be okay."

Sol squeezed his hand and reassured, over and over, that he'd soon be out dancing. In minutes, there was a commotion at the rear of the courtroom, and Sol looked up as the medics rolled a gurney toward the jury box. They listened to Sol's report, took notes, started oxygen, and had the man chew an aspirin. They placed an IV, attached myriad monitoring devices, and when all the thin green lines on the scopes were stabilized, lifted him onto the stretcher. Through it all, the man held tightly to Sol's hand.

As they wheeled him out, the judge reentered from his chambers, and the bailiff called in a tremulous voice, "All rise for the Honorable Bentley B. Ballbrine."

The judge sat and ordered, "Take your seats."

But before the judge could utter another syllable, the lead attorney jumped up and sputtered, "Your Honor, I call for a mistrial. This jury is…is…is tainted by Dr. Forte's actions."

Sol, shaking as if a coiled wire ready to spring, gathered a deep breath to holler, but an old woman juror with blue hair piped in his stead, "What the hell are you blabbering about? What was he supposed to do, just sit there…drooling like the rest of you and that pansy judge" Her colleagues started laughing nervously; a few called out, "Yeah, you're right." She lifted her nose in the air and went on. "There's nothin' wrong with this jury. I didn't sit here and waste a week of my life to be told by some chitchattin' lawyer that…"

The gavel pounded harshly. "There will be order in my courtroom. Madame, you are a juror, not a judge. Sit down and be quiet, or I will hold you in contempt."

The jurors, all eleven of them, laughed derisively in unison. The gavel pounded harder. His Honor barked, "Counsel, approach."

After a brief meeting, the judge decreed that the jury had been defiled. He turned to them. "This case is clearly a mistrial and is hereby adjourned. The jury is dismissed."

The judge leapt from his seat and strode toward chambers, but stopped and glared when the blue-haired lady laughed, "We don't even get a thank you for our service?" The judge's lips tightened, and the bailiff took a step toward the woman. The jurors tightened their circle around her, and the judge ducked through the door into chambers.

Sol took the opportunity to look at Judy, and this time she held his eyes for a moment but soon looked down. Mr. Tarkington turned away.

El Haq started to approach the witness stand, though Sol rushed past him toward the rear of the courtroom. Dana was pale, but smiling. She took his hand and held it close to her. "My hero."

Sol mumbled, "Very funny," and shook his head.

"No," Dana insisted, "you *are* my hero, and everybody else's too. Let's get out of here. The place gives me the creeps."

They drove together to the hospital to check on the old man. Sol waited for the other shoe to fall, but Dana made no comment about his testimony and his liaison with Judy. Unable to contain himself, he asked her, "Hey, when did you get there? Did you hear the part right before the old man keeled over?"

Dana shook her head. "Nah, only the part where you chewed the judge's butt and then saved a man's life."

The old juror was still in the emergency room, sedated with morphine for his chest pain, but he recognized Sol and murmured, "Doc, they told me what you did. Thank you, sir."

Sol picked the man's chart off the gurney, searched for his name, and smiled reassuringly, "Like I said, Mr. Fluellen, just a blip on the old radar scope. You're gonna be fine."

The man looked up weakly. "Doc, and I don't mean to be a wise guy, but you're too young to know what it was like on Guadalcanal; probably never heard of it."

Sol put his hand on the man's bare shoulder. "Of course, I've heard of it, sir. My dad was a Marine at the Choson Reservoir. All he ever talked about was you heroes in World War Two. It's what kept him going when he was in combat in Korea."

"See, Doc, I thought I was gonna get it there. I was the sergeant. They could see my rank. All that enemy firing at the leaders. Everybody got it that day—well, almost everybody did. I always wondered why not me. Today, I figured it out. That insurance company was trying to screw the worker. They always do. I wasn't gonna let 'em. I was gettin' so mad. And look what it got me. I guess I can't do it all on my own like in the old days, huh? You just do what you have to do to defend that poor jerk."

"I will, Mr. Fluellen."

Sol patted him on the shoulder and left the room. He was not surprised that Dana was standing at the door waiting for him. She took his arm and smiled. "What'd I tell ya?"

CHAPTER TWENTY-ONE

Sol arrived early the next morning, having convinced himself the Lord had orchestrated his good work, and in reward, He would magically resuscitate Sol's medical career, as Sol had the life of old Mr. Fluellen. But his schedule was lightly peppered—five new patients, most of whom were grouped around a short lunch hour. In essence, he had been dealt another day without patients, through which he would sit and stew in his juices. He used the time to search the Whitaker Yellow Pages for a real lawyer. This time, he started at the end of the one-hundred-and-ten pages of attorneys and came across a name that appealed to him, a long, WASPish patronymic, dripping with a respectable, "The Third" tailing off across the page. He dialed, a sour taste in his mouth, and an even sicker feeling in his gut, for he was about to expose himself, yet again, to a perfect stranger. While the phone rang, the bitterness in his heart deepened, and just as a receptionist's voice answered, "Legal office," he dropped the receiver into the cradle, leaned back, and trembled.

Finally, he tried to page through a medical journal about pulmonary edema, but the pooling of body fluids in the lungs did not hold his attention, and the automatic stress shut-off mechanism that had sustained him through medical school and residency fired. His eyelids drooped, and his head bobbed; Dr. Solomon Forte fell asleep at his desk, escaping into his usual refuge, comfortably seizing the deferment from a life that daily seemed to hurtle further out of control. He dreamed about a petite woman with a perfect body but a face he could not make out. Even in his dream, he suffered guilt, for he knew it was Judy Famot he could not erase from his mind.

He remained pleasantly anesthetized, drooling on his desk for perhaps three or four minutes, until Roxanne blared from the door, "Your pal El Haq is on the phone. Says it's important." Sol yawned and stretched as if he'd been gone for hours. Roxanne shook her head. "And I'm sorry to wake you."

El Haq came right to the point. "Well, Doctor, that was an impressive display of healing yesterday. Unfortunately, we are going to have to do the whole trial over again. The judge will have to find an opening in his schedule, a new jury will have to be chosen, and it could take months."

"Well, at least we'll have time to plan our answers now that we know some of their questions. And by the way, I can assure you that nothing happened when I was in Ms. Famot's house… nothing at all."

El Haq answered cautiously. "Well, I am relieved to hear that. It would not help our client if something did happen. I'm sure you understand how a jury might see that."

"Well, nothing happened, so you can relax."

"Good. Now, Doctor, I do want to meet with you to discuss your problem with the State Medical Abuse Commission. I might have some time tomorrow."

Sol paused and quickly thought through the possibilities he'd considered. "Well, sir, I'm, ah, not going to be available tomorrow. Full schedule. I've been gone so long, I can't put these patients off another minute. I'm sure you understand."

El Haq grumbled, "You know that answer is due in just a few days. You don't want to make them mad before the investigator even starts the fact finding."

"I thought you said there was plenty of time. We could just ask for a postponement."

"Doctor, you *can*, but I'm sure we can get the work done in five or six hours. I have the time tomorrow. I suggest that if you have the materials together, you do what they ask of you. Don't forget, they're in the driver's seat."

Sol hesitated again. "By the way, what is your hourly rate, Mr. El Haq?"

Though Sol expected El Haq to assure him that this one was going to be on the house, El Haq huffed in delay for a moment. "Well, we can go over that tomorrow if you like. I'm sure you'll find my fees to be competitive with those of the better attorneys in Whitaker, so you have no worry in that regard."

Sol ended the conversation with the explanation that he simply couldn't cancel his patients yet again, and that he would get back to El Haq in a day or so.

"Well, Doctor, that's very courageous."

CHAPTER TWENTY-TWO

Sol's absence had angered his patients. Their appointments had been cancelled at the last minute, and in several cases, after they arrived at the Center. A few of them groused so boisterously, they were injected into Dr. Rosebac's panel for the day. That infuriated the man for whom Punctuality, Habit, and Order were the holiest of the holy in the pantheon of gods he worshipped.

On ordinary days, Rosebac stuck to his schedule regardless of the challenges, and he became testy when his timetable did not please him. The receptionists lived in fear of making scheduling blunders, for even if it was the Center's error, if two patients showed up at the same time, Rosebac sent one of them packing, refusing to squeeze the second patient in when he had an extra moment.

That day, when the six minutes he allotted for each of Sol's overflow patients came to an end, so had their appointments, even if it meant standing and walking out of a room while the patient was in mid-sentence. And David Rosebac didn't leave it at that. He left the room to march down the hall in a rage, cussing aloud that he wasn't responsible for Forte's blunders. Then he'd attack Georgia, his own medical assistant, who ruffled down the hall to take it out on Roxanne, who detested keeping anything inside, for she had read in the *Inquirer* that is wasn't healthy to let things fester. With that proscription in mind, Roxanne would hound the young physician's assistant whose obsessive-compulsive disease was so profound, he was taking four-times the regular dose of Prozac. Despite the medication, he spent much of the day washing his hands and did not have time away from the sink to bully anyone. The MAs and the PA gathered in conference outside the break room, exchanged apologies, then marched over to Anacota's office to file a grievance. The CEO inscribed a note in Sol's personnel folder.

There was a certain beauty in the symmetry of Sol's life, his sister, Michaela, laughed that night when she called him and sat through the saga of his brush with the jurisdictive organism and the fallout at the Center. "Solly, it's the same around here: the mud flies up, and it flies back down again, somehow gathers energy, and up it goes again, like the Lord's beautiful cycle of the seasons. Nobody's immune. Remember what Papa used to say? 'If it isn't one thing, it's the other.'"

Sol laughed. "That was Uncle Anthony, not Pop. I think you've been studying too hard. Memory's all used up." Sol thought for a moment before going on. The smile left his face quickly. He sat silently, wondering if he should tell her about being charged with a misdemeanor before the State Medical Abuse Commission. He worried this story would shock Michaela, and anger her, for she knew Sol wasn't capable of harming a patient, or even of breaking the rules. And it would also hurt her, and she would have to seek refuge in confession, spill her guts to Mother Superior, a woman who did not know he existed, or care. In the end, Michaela would be instructed to pray to God that her brother be forgiven his sins. Sol's indignation peaked. "What sins? Bullshit!" Then, in his foreboding, he snapped aloud, "I didn't do a goddamn thing!"

Michaela gasped. "Sol, what is going on? You can't talk that way to me or anyone else. What is wrong with you?"

Sol had gotten what he really wanted, an excuse to bare his soul. He recounted the saga of Kevin McAlister, and how he had tried so hard to treat him, but not cross the line. "I couldn't cure his back pain. Nobody could. It's well known there's such a thing as chronic pain syndrome. The best doctors in the world pay lip service to the 'team approach for *managing* pain,' but they can't cure it, and nine times out of ten, they can't manage it either. What was I supposed to do? Just let him suffer? I had to give him something. Michaela, when nothing else worked, when all the great medical minds threw up their hands in frustration and started calling the patient names, what was I supposed to do? I was acting responsibly. The only thing I had was pain medicine. It hasn't changed in a thousand years. Nothing's changed!"

Michaela was confused. "Solly, I don't understand. God gave us all this technology at our fingertips, and the best we can do is just cover up the pain?"

Sol laughed. "Of all people to take the state's side. We don't understand a damn thing about..."

"Solly!"

"Sorry. I was going to say 'pain' before I was so rudely interrupted. We know nothing of God's design. I sent this guy to the best doctors around. All they could do was huff and puff about this trapped nerve and that misaligned spinal motion segment, and spinal pathways, and pain receptors, and the damn..."

"Solly!"

"Sorry, thalamus. No one was able to do a thing about it, and very few people cared to. As far as everyone was concerned, including me, and that's what really hurts, was that the guy was a COLA drug-seeker. MRIs, cortisone shots into the spinal cord, and tens and tens of thousands of dollars later, it all came down to me making an executive decision to let him suffer or keep him comfortable. Could've done that for all of ten bucks a week, and I could've done it with a better attitude. Or, I could have stayed out of trouble, protected my own bee-hind, and cut him off cold turkey. He would have wound up dying under someone else's care. You be the judge. No, I take that back, I'm sick of judges."

"Well, Solly, unfortunately, no fortunately, I'm not the judge. You know who is. So, like I've said so many times, it's out of your hands. If you didn't do anything wrong, and I know you didn't, it's all going to be okay. You'll see. Works every time."

"Well, it sure doesn't feel that way right about now. But anyway, Sister Michaela, you really are the best. How long?"

"One hundred and twenty-three days and, let's see, fourteen hours and twenty-five minutes. You want the seconds?"

"Have you heard anything about where you're going next?"

"Yep, Whitaker."

"You're kidding!"

"Yep, I'm kidding. I'll go where the Lord sends me, and when I earn it, it'll be Whitaker, and not a day sooner. It's the way of the world."

Sol laughed. "You and your faith. What a gift."

"You've got it, too, Dr. Forte. Look at what you've accomplished. Look at what you give people. Your life is perfect. You have everything you need to be the happiest man on Earth. You just don't realize it…yet. You will. And by the way, how's Dana?"

"Great, I guess. I think she's, ya know, thinking this is getting serious."

"Solly, from what you've described, she's perfect."

"Yeah, but I'm not."

"Yes, you are."

"If you only knew. But I love you, my sister the Sister."

Sol placed the phone down and started for the fridge, for the frosty beer he had put off for several hours, but sat back down and picked up the receiver again. He never did get his beer that night, but he did share a Vodka Collins with Dana.

CHAPTER TWENTY-THREE

At work the next morning, Sol spent the hours between the six or seven patients on his schedule pouring over Kevin McAlister's chart. He added the number of Vicodin and Percocet he and, he growled to himself, Chief of Medicine Roxanne, had prescribed over the year he'd been involved in Kevin's care. His chest squeezed—seven hundred and seventy-six pills. But when he divided the number by 365, it came to just over two pills per day, quite reasonable for someone suffering from end-stage cancer. In fact, it was gross undertreatment.

He went to the SMAC website, typed in "regulation of narcotic medication," and was presented with page after page of papers published by the Commission and the State Department of Health Affairs. He scanned uncomfortably through the summary of threats and warnings, then through the case histories of mighty, but fallen, healers who had overprescribed. He read on, his mouth souring with each report, until coming to a paragraph buried deep within the Commission's writings that made him sit up and nearly scream, "Well there it is! Seek and thee shall find, brother."

Roxanne was in his office before the sound of his happiness stopped reverberating in the halls. "Dr. F., are you okay?"

"I'm just fine, Roxy Pie. Look at this. The Department of Health Affairs and the State Medical Abuse Commission have been saying for years that health care professionals were under-treating cancer pain, and that no doctor should fear retribution from SMAC for addressing the agony of dying patients. I win. They lose. Hot dog."

"I'm glad you're happy. It's about time. Now, go ahead and savor it for fifteen seconds."

"And then?"

"Then there's a nice lady here to see you."

"Thank God, a paying patient."

"Not so fast, Abernathy, she's not a patient, and she's not paying. Just someone who wants to talk to you about her husband; that you did something to him, and she's sobbing, and…"

"I did something to her husband, and she's crying? Great."

"I'm not sure. I didn't understand her. Like I said, she was bawling. She's in Room Two."

There was no chart outside the door, and Roxanne hadn't caught the woman's name. He gathered himself, knocked on the door, and opened it gently. A gray-haired, elderly woman sat on the exam room table, dabbing her eyes with a tissue. Sol was perplexed. "Ma'am, I'm Dr. Forte. I don't think I know you, but how may I help?"

She took a deep breath and whispered, "Well, you did that to my husband, and I just came here to…"

"Well, first, ma'am, let's get you off that horribly uncomfortable table and into the horribly uncomfortable chair." A tiny smile opened as he helped her down. "Now, what did I do, ma'am?"

"Why, you saved my husband's life. Don't you remember?" Sol waited for more, but she went back to wiping her eyes.

"Ma'am, I'm sorry. I don't understand. May I ask your name?"

"Martha."

"Martha, ma'am?"

"Martha Fluellen."

It was familiar. He pressed his concentration. Fluellen? And then it coalesced from the mist of emotion—Mr. Fluellen, the juror, the World War Two Marine, Guadalcanal, sole survivor, and the cardiac arrest in court. "How is…?" His heart sank as Mrs. Fluellen's tears began to swirl off her sagging cheeks in torrents. "He didn't make it, did he?"

Between sobs, she spoke weakly. "We were friends since before the War, since elementary school in Whitaker. Almost seventy-five years, married sixty-four. I never held another man's hand. We breathed for each other. What am I going to do? I'm so alone. What-am-I-going-to-do?"

Sol helped her off the table into the chair. "Can I get you a cup of tea, Mrs. Fluellen?"

She nodded, and Sol left the room to ask Roxanne for two cups. When he returned, they sat together silently for a while. Sol held her hand. They sipped the sweetened tea, and she calmed.

A few minutes later, Roxanne knocked softly and actually waited for Sol to say, "Come in," before she opened the door. A tall, handsome, well-dressed man in his fifties came into the room. Sol was confused, for he seemed sure it was Mr. Fluellen, though he thought back and realized he'd never seen the man standing.

The man nodded to Sol, put his arms around Mrs. Fluellen, and whispered, "Everything's going to be all right, Mom, I promise." He turned to Sol. "Are you Dr. Forte, sir?"

"I am."

"I'm Eugene Fluellen. Our family wants to thank you for what you did in court. I heard you were amazing and that no one else raised a finger to help my dad, not the judge, even the bailiff. That's a crime. What were they thinking?"

Sol stood and took his hand in both of his. "Nice to meet you, sir. Well, maybe nicer under other circumstances. You know, I think people aren't trained to act in an emergency. It probably never happened before. I'm sure it wasn't on purpose. Anyway, I feel graced to have met your dad, even for such a short time. World War II, an all. He and I talked about it: Marines, Guadalcanal, that's a big deal, Mr. Fluellen. Your pop was a hero. Eighty-something years old and still looking out for the little guy."

"Yeah, he was a great parent. The best. So's my mom." He put his arms around her and kissed her cheek again. "Let's go, Mom. I'll spring for lunch."

Her face brightened. "Oh, my son the lawyer," she smiled. "You're on, Mr. Money Bags."

Sol shook his head. "You're an attorney? What kind of law do you practice?"

"General law. Been in practice around here for nearly thirty-five years. I have an office in Whitaker."

"You taking any new clients?"

"Of course. I'm always interested in the twists and turns of life. And I'm also an entrepreneur. Do you have someone in mind?"

It happened so quickly, Sol was tongue-tied, and he floundered through a disjointed discussion of his dilemma, trying to hide the specifics from Mrs. Fluellen.

"Doctor, this is an interesting problem." He paused sheepishly. "I'm sorry, Doctor, I don't mean interesting in a glib sense. No, not at all. Actually, I did some work a few years ago for a colleague, a trial lawyer, who was called before the county legal ethics committee. And please don't tell me that's an oxymoron. Look, if you want to come in, I'll be glad to sit down and talk with you, see what we can do, at least get you pointed in the right direction. Yes, I'd be happy to. How much time do you have before they want an answer?"

"Six days, ah, I think I'm down to five now."

"That's no problem. I'll give 'em a call and get an extension. Everybody does it. Also, I can make nice-nice to the investigator and start a dialogue. Squeeze some information out of them. It's a game, I'm afraid. Always better to get the first shot in; gives you a psychological advantage. Works, you know."

They shook hands warmly, and Sol hugged Mrs. Fluellen. She had begun to weep again, and Sol handed her another tissue. "Here," he laughed, handing her the box, "there's a ton more where these came from. Compliments of the Galena Hills Hospital, and let's not forget, Medical Center."

Sol went to his office and leaned back in his chair, his heart lighter than it had been in months.

Gene Fluellen called Sol later that day and explained that he had had a cancellation toward the end of the afternoon. He invited Sol to come in. Sol laughed to himself, "Seek and thee shall find…Knock and the door will be opened unto you."

CHAPTER TWENTY-FOUR

Fluellen's office was in one of the tonier professional complexes in downtown Whitaker, and Sol's hand shook as he prepaid the fifteen-dollar parking fee for the first hour. He choked when he looked at the directory and saw "Forty-Third Floor—Suite 4336" next to Fluellen's name. When he got off the elevator, he nearly swallowed his heart, imagining the bulk of his savings about to vanish, as he followed the suite numbers to the right toward the side of the building that faced the snow-capped mountains. Several of the pieces of Chinese art in the waiting area were encased in glass—blue Ming Dynasty pottery and a pair of bronze Chun Dynasty stallions. Sol did not have time to admire the craftsmanship, or the vista, for Eugene Fluellen greeted him almost immediately and guided Sol into his corner office.

Outside the window, on the ledge, sat a female Peregrine falcon. Fluellen remarked that the species was endangered, and that he was not permitted to open his window, or even approach the glass. The Feds had been up there several times cautioning him that, as an endangered species, the birds were wards of the Federal Government, and, in essence, possessed the privileges of eminent domain. Eugene Fluellen, Attorney at Law, would be "… watched like a hawk," the federal agent had warned with a sour laugh.

With Gene Fluellen shaking his head, the male Peregrine, fulfilling his courtship requisites, returned to the nest, beak gnawing on a still-thrashing ferret. His mate-to-be devoured the offering in seconds then deposited the remains, including the tiny leather collar and nametag, in the heap of other diminutive bones. She began bustling, and the male took flight, dipping and turning spectacularly, until he landed again on the ledge, and the pair bowed up and down to each other, vocalizing so loudly, Sol could hear them through the double-paned glass. Fluellen remarked, "They have it better than we do."

The two men talked for hours about Sol's time as a kid in New York City, their fathers' military service, and about the senior Forte's thirty-years as a concrete truck driver. They chatted about Sol's mother, her harrowing trip from Sicily, about Sol's sister in the convent, about his exceptional standing in medical school, about his past patients, and about his dreams for practice. They went over Sol's finances, including his $70,000 outstanding student loan.

Fluellen asked, "You mean to tell me you aren't burned out? Sounds like you've already squeezed in a full career. This must make you really mad."

Sol thought for a moment. "You sound like a decent man, Mr. Fluellen. I'll be honest with you. Yeah, I'm mad. I guess a man's not allowed to say that anymore, huh? Hostility isn't politically correct, is it? Maybe I should be sent to an anger management school or something."

Fluellen smiled acceptingly and added, "Sounds like you have grounds to be pissed."

Sol went on. "Well, it's bullshit, pardon me. I don't feel as though I deserve it." He sat quietly before continuing. "Then again, to tell you the truth, I'm more scared than mad. I don't know what I'd do if I couldn't be a doctor. And what's worse, what's my family going to think, that I really did something to break the Ten Commandments or the Golden Rule? My mom and my pop, neither of them'll be able to handle it. They'll know. This just ain't right."

Gene Fluellen spoke quietly. "No, it isn't, my friend. Tell you what we're going to do. After you called, I got a hold of another colleague, a lawyer, a good one, who's also a doctor. He can't take the case right now, but he offered to meet with us, if you'd like. Trustworthy guy; he's not all that impressed with some of the Commission's tactics—thinks they're unconstitutional and draconian." Fluellen noted the color drain from Sol's face and laughed. "Hey, it's not a problem. Don't stress out about it. But you have to know your enemy—*then* you can decapitate the son of a bitch."

It was nearly nine when they finished. The falcons were quietly nestled on the ledge, and Sol helped Fluellen clean up the sandwich wrappers from the dinner they had ordered in. Sol asked, "Mr. Fluellen, a little proverbial housekeeping, if you don't mind. We should discuss your fee, don't you think? I would like to write a check for this evening now, just to keep things kosher."

"Nah, this one's on me. Part of the price of doing business. Everything'll work out for the best. Things have a way of doing that. I've been at this for a long, long time. You'll see. It'll be fun."

"Fun?"

"Yeah, I love it when I can be an I-told-you-so."

⟨⟩

Two days later, Sol met again with Gene and his friend, Michael John Matsukawa, MD and LLD. Sol shook Matsukawa's hand and thanked him for his interest but grumbled, "Then again, I shouldn't have to be asking your help, or Mr. Fluellen's, for that matter." Sol stared out the window for a few seconds. When he turned back to his hosts, he griped, "You know, there are laws and rules, and there damn well ought to be. But I didn't break any of them. I'm getting screwed."

Matsukawa smiled gently. "Dr. Forte, Sol, if I may…"

"Of course."

"Please take a seat and listen closely. My friend, let me tell you something about how I got into this business, or, should I say these businesses? I'm a fourth-generation Japanese. My family's been here since the mastodons. My great-grandfathers worked on the Transcontinental Railway. The next generations of ancestors farmed in California for nearly a century. Some of them bought stores and businesses; a bunch held local office; a couple even served at state level. But all of a sudden, along comes World War II, as if my family was responsible for Pearl Harbor, and my parents, my older brother and sister, and most of my aunts and uncles, find themselves interred. They lost a hundred years of work, my family did. My father never got back his electrical contracting business, or the land that was appropriated, or the furniture and the dishes and the books and the photos that were looted in the name of patriotism. Never saw 'em again. So, Dr. Forte, I know all about getting screwed.

"My family made me go to medical school so I'd have a trade that I could pack along with me, one that I could put in my head, safe inside my brain, that would work anywhere in the world. They didn't trust America after what they suffered. They still don't, and neither do I. That's why I went to law school—to fight the bastards and get back some of what is owed my family.

"You may be getting screwed, Sol, but that's too damn bad about you. Excuse me. You have a fight on your hands, and you better start digging trenches and priming the cannons. And Gene and I are your heavy artillery. Questions?"

Sol sagged in his chair a bit and finally answered. "Nope, I was out of line. I apologize. Where do we start?"

Matsukawa nodded pleasantly and smiled. "Glad we got that straightened out."

Gene Fluellen added, "Sol, we need to know every single detail of your care of Kevin McAlister. If you did something inappropriate, wrote the wrong prescription, we have to know. Your ego needs to be left outside on the ledge next to those damn birds. We have to trust each other. From what Mike tells me, the Commission'll find every note you wrote, every phone call and every comment you made. They'll call your relatives, your colleagues from medical school, and especially the nurses and physician's assistants you work with right now, and they'll start the conversation with something like, 'This is Joe Blow from the **State Medical Abuse Commission**.' They'll say it just like that, loud, bold, like they're FBI or CIA, and they'll manipulate your doctor friends into believing that they had better cooperate, or they might find themselves a practitioner of interest to the Commission. These people take themselves very seriously; they have prosecutorial complexes like St. Paul. It's who they are. They can't help themselves."

Matsukawa laughed. "Gene, who says St. Paul was a prosecutor?"

"Mick Jagger."

"Jagger?"

"That's right, *You'll Never Make a Saint Out of Me*. Any more questions?"

"I forgot. Gene's a rock aficionado. Used to also be a Hell's Angel. Seriously, he was an outlaw biker. See, Doc, this is where Gene gets his legal precedents…not from law books or the Bible, but from errant rock stars. That's going to help you a whole lot in court. Sure you want to stick with him?"

With Sol's shoulders finally slackening, Matsukawa went on. "Okay, let's get serious here. Sol, first the Commission will appoint an investigator. These guys aren't doctors or voting members. They do the legwork for the state. They'll start researching the complaint, no matter how baseless the accusations…"

Sol interrupted, "You mean even if there isn't anything to the complaint, even if it's pure bullshit, a full investigation gets started and everybody finds out about it?"

"I'm afraid that's about the size of it," Matsukawa nodded. "I mean, people have a right, and really a duty, to turn in bad doctors. And there are some, maybe not that many, but a number out there practicing who shouldn't be. Happens in every walk of life, except the law. Just the way it is. Surely you've seen your share?"

"I've seen some."

"Like I said, it isn't many. Look at it this way. Over the past four years, there were nearly thirty-two thousand doctors registered in this state. How many doctor-patient interactions is that? Do the math: fifty to a hundred patients a week per doctor, times fifty weeks, times thirty-two thousand, times four years…it's astronomical: maybe a hundred million! These are unbelievable numbers, and yet there were only around five thousand complaints filed over those years, of which, I think, less than five hundred came to some sort of disciplinary action. That's not bad, and to be honest, probably not enough. Right?"

Sol nodded. "Yeah, you're definitely right."

"So, someone has to look into each complaint before it can be thrown out. I mean, how else could you do it?"

Sol sighed. "I guess so, though it doesn't feel real good even being one of five thousand. See, even if you're exonerated, it's too late. The word's out—you're damaged goods. The appearance of impropriety is worse than the impropriety. Even if you're innocent and they don't punish you, people'll just say that the Commission goes easy on doctors because the judges are doctors, and…"

Matsukawa interrupted. "No, I'm not sure that's completely true. 'People,' as you say, I'm afraid, have the wrong idea. Maybe doctors stuck together in days of yore, but right now, the Commission is made up of some pretty tough-nut physicians and a bunch of activist civilians. They're looking for scalps. There was this article in one of the local papers, I think the *Whitaker Reporter Dispatch*, back in '92, that doctors were getting away with murder, literally. I'll see if I can't dig it out of my files. Anyway, since then, the Commission's been loaded with angry people, especially the non-docs. They're digging deep for trouble. Makes 'em feel important and righteous."

Sol countered, "Well, *you* know that, but I don't think the votin' public does. I don't want my name dragged all over the county. Like I said, I haven't done anything to deserve it."

The two attorneys glanced at each other, and Fluellen spoke. "Sol, you gotta get over it, my friend. That attitude ain't gonna win you any votes on the Commission. These guys want to see contrition. Like I said before, you have to leave your ego on the other side of the threshold.

"Now, on the other hand, you *can* take a get-tough approach, as long as you understand that you're going to piss them off. I mean, if you have the facts on your side, hit 'em as hard as you want. They certainly deserve the scrutiny, but I'm not sure it's worth it from the standpoint of what's best for Solomon Forte. Once the thing's over, it's over, and you might want to make that happen as fast as you can. People forget about things like this *very* quickly; most of us are too consumed with ourselves to spend much time worrying about anybody else.

"Now, that's just my advice. I won't drop you as a client if you want to take a tough stand; just be sure it's the hard road you want to hoe if we start fighting from the kickoff. Some things are worth fighting for, others are best left to disappear on their own. Your call."

"You're right. I know that. That's me emoting, just my New York sense of never take any crap from anybody. I'll be different in front of these guys. You'll see."

Matsukawa and Fluellen again shot looks at each other.

Sol's schedule began to pick up, though there were still large gaps. He spent the time composing his reply to the Commission. Fluellen had already contacted the investigator and obtained a stay, though he had not been able to squeeze any information out of the woman, especially in regard to who had filed the complaint. Nonetheless, Sol went forward, spicing his reply liberally with the expression "cancer pain", and quoting the State Medical Abuse Commission's own statement that doctors had nothing to fear if they addressed the suffering of terminally ill patients. He finished the document with a statement over which he mulled for several days. "I believe I treated Mr. McAlister with full consideration given to the standards of care and, moreover, I did so with a devotion identical to the one I would extend to you or a member of your family. I addressed my patient's pain in a responsible and professional manner. He would have suffered terribly during his last months without my care."

Sol faxed the final draft to Fluellen and sat back, comforted that it would all be over very soon, just a blip on the radarscope as he often told his patients, though he remembered that's what he had advised old Mr. Fluellen. He put his feet up on his desk and fell off to sleep.

CHAPTER TWENTY-FIVE

Sol's life mellowed at the Center; fewer nurses and staff whispered after walking past. Rosebac started grunting, "Good morning." Sol sat at his desk during lunch reading *People Magazine,* focusing on the legal problems of the rich and famous. He smiled about how minor his headaches really were. Maybe Michaela was right. Soon, it would be back to life as usual, and perhaps he would have learned something from all of this, a life's lesson, like how to choose his patients a bit more carefully. It was all just part of the sinus curve of life, up and down, up and down.

He rested comfortably until Roxanne crowed from the hall, plucking him from his reverie. There was a long-distance call for Sol, and he picked up the receiver with the requisite smile, though, this time, it was less of a sham than usual. A man's voice on the other end introduced himself as a case manager in Arizona's Department of Administration, Risk Management Division.

"Who, what, sir?"

"Dr. Forte," the churlish voice noted, "I think you call that Commission on Labor Affairs up there." Before Sol could answer, the man went on, "Are you familiar with a Lupe Sánchez?"

Sol hesitated, took a deep breath, and smiled spuriously. "Yep, I sure am. What's she doing down there? I just saw her."

"She *was* working in Yuma, but she's filed an industrial claim stating that she hurts on the left side of her body, and that it all began in your state. She asserts she re-injured herself here in a fall from a tree where she was picking fruit. She had this curled up little business card with your name and number in big letters. Said you'd tell us how badly she was injured up there—something about a fall in a kitchen. We're just trying to decide whose nickel this should be on, yours or ours. What can you tell me?"

Sol went over Lupe's history then sputtered, "Well, wait. If she was well enough to get hired, she must have recovered from her injuries here. So, I have nothing to do with it, right? That makes sense, doesn't it?"

"Not entirely. You see, Doctor, migrant workers are hired on a daily basis in Arizona. I'm sure no one questioned her about any previous injuries..."

Sol interrupted, "Well, someone should have. Not my problem if the due diligence thing didn't get done."

"She was a warm body willing to work for less than minimum wage. What else counts?"

Sol laughed. "Let me ask you a question: how long was Lupe on the payroll before she took her little tumble?"

"Who knows? Could have been one hour, one day, three weeks at the outside. Who keeps records? These are illegals; they're paid by the day. No one has contracts, and whether you like it or not, no one cares down here. Just the way it is."

"Well, if you get the paperwork done to make it all legal, which does count *up here*, I'll forward the records to you. Hope you have a few weeks with nothing else to do but read chart notes. Three volumes, if I remember correctly. Over a thousand pages."

With the conversation concluded, Sol rubbed his eyes unhappily, summoned Roxanne, and asked for Lupe's chart. He skimmed the documents, discovering it had actually been quite some time since he'd last seen her. It was the day she had presented in a see-though blouse, the day had she repaid Sol's fifty dollars, the day Rosebac had summarily suspended him and, he smiled, the day he had turned around and summarily suspended Rosebac.

He shuffled through the rest of Volume Three, coming to the last entry, one from the Commission on Labor Affairs. They had approved, on Sol's recommendation, that Lupe Sánchez be availed of the state's retraining services. She had chosen to study flower arranging, and Sol noticed in the records that he had read through the twelve-page job description, approved it, and sent a copy to Lupe's last known address. He had not heard from her since.

He called Whitaker General and asked if she had been admitted recently, but she had not. He called the other psych hospital. They hadn't seen her since the day she had tried to jump off the balcony outside Sol's office.

As far as Sol knew, Lupe had not recovered from her injuries, and supposed, as far as the state was concerned, he was still her doctor of record, the "attending physician," as COLA labeled him. As such, he'd remain in that role until her claim was closed locally, which, if she was residing elsewhere and complaining of a worsening of her pain, was going to take some time and manipulation. On the other hand, the Lupe Sánchez matter was going to simmer on the back burner for a while, until the claims manager in Arizona got the paperwork together to legally obtain the massive records. Sol placed her sixteen pounds of records on the top of his file cabinet, there being no room in the bottom drawer, the one already stuffed with Ralph Tarkington's twenty-some pounds.

He went back to his magazine and a warm cup of tea. Lupe's case would vanish. This, too, shall come to pass, he smiled and nodded. He was about to take a sip of tea when a knock stopped him. He did not turn toward the door as he mumbled, "Roxy, just gimme a minute, please."

Soundlessly, an envelope came to rest an inch from his nose. Sol stared, bewildered that the bureaucrat in Arizona could have, or would have, acted with such alacrity. The document was, though, marked with the stamp of the Dunton County Superior Court. Without looking up, he picked a pen off his desk, reached over his shoulder, scribbled a curlicue near the signature box, tore open the envelope, and had it read and digested it before subpoena man was able to turn on his heels. Sol was testify at the criminal trial of The People v. John Sullivan.

"Not to worry," Anacota, reassured eight minutes later. He had gotten word that the district attorney's office was considering dropping the criminal charges against Sullivan for endangerment, malicious destruction, and assault with a motor vehicle, because he was very drunk at the time, and the best she thought she could do was slap him with a DUI. He'd plead out on that as a first offence.

The DA had squealed to Anacota, "He's a pillar of the community, a self-made old man with a serious and understandable grudge against a clinic full of rich, uncaring doctors. The worst that's going to happen is that he might be forced to sit through a driving responsibility class for three nights." Sol understood that with a single signature, the DA could croak, "Justice has been served," but more importantly, she would have corralled a prominent, affluent voter, a vocal citizen, one sure to be a strong advocate in the city's watering holes around election time.

In an hour, the subpoena man was back. He caught Sol in the men's room. This summons ordered Sol to testify in the Center's civil suit against Sullivan. As Sol examined the document, he was stunned to read he was being called as a witness by the defense, to testify on behalf of Sullivan. His eyes dropped to the bottom of the document for the defense lawyer's name—Anwar El Haq, Attorney at Law.

Sol walked back down to Anacota's office. The CEO had just been handed a copy of the subpoena. He was laughing. Sol grumbled, "Hayes, isn't that like double jeopardy, or conflict of interest? The guy's already used me as a witness in another case."

"Nah," Anacota snorted. "No such thing. You have no contractual connection with him, do you?"

"I don't know. He was going to be my lawyer in the SMAC thing. He still thinks he is."

"Did you hire him? I mean formally? Is there a written or even a verbal contract?"

"Well, no."

"Are you going to use him?"

"No way."

"Then you're on the hook, not off it. And anyway, no matter who you testify for, the answers are going to be the same, right? Doesn't make any difference, if you catch my drift."

Sol walked back to his office slowly, shaken at how fast a relatively good day had gone so terribly sour, especially because, as in most of life's phenomena, and certainly in medicine, things happened in threes. Sitting on his desk was yet another subpoena, one that had appeared out of the ether. This was surely a record for one day in the life of a non-surgeon. It was the top page of a thick fax from Lupe's new claims manager in Arizona. Sol was commanded to forward all of Ms. Sánchez's medical and administrative records, along with a complete narrative report covering Lupe's case from soup to nuts.

Sol searched, but there was no note regarding remuneration for Sol or the Center for time spent, aside from a flat, twenty-five-dollar copying fee. Postage was not covered. Attached was a copy of the Arizona State legal code regarding the worker compensation responsibilities of physicians in cooperating states.

The CEO's phone was busy, and Sol crawled back down to Anacota's office to ask if he needed to comply. Anacota shrugged, "Get yourself a lawyer and find out. How 'bout El Haq? Nah, gimme the thing."

Sol handed the document to Anacota, who scribbled in a corner:

We will be happy to comply with your request when we are in possession of a check for $175 for copying fees, and $375 to cover the one-hour of dictation required for the narrative report you desire.

With best wishes,
Hayes A. Anacota
CEO
The Galena Hills Hospital and Medical Center

Sol took the document back to the Orthopedic Department and faxed it, smiling into the machine as the paper was drawn within. He wondered if the assistant attorney general at the Arizona Department of Administration, Risk Management Division, had smirked as he faxed a note an hour later upon which he'd scratched, "Our two states share fee schedules when exchanging legal documents. As a courtesy, though, I have authorized the case manager to pay eight cents a copy for records and five dollars per full typewritten page for your narrative report. Please send the requested documents to avoid contempt charges."

Sol nodded to himself that this was the time to employ one of Rosebac's ten commandments—ignore it. He placed the day's correspondence regarding Lupe back on the pile of her records. He called Roxanne and asked for Edna Berry's chart, where he had saved all of his notes regarding John Sullivan.

Perusing the chart, he realized he had again not seen Edna in quite some months and wondered how she was faring. He considered calling her and asking, but acknowledged that she was probably seeing a different doctor, for he had not received any correspondence from COLA demanding updates on her work status. The last he remembered, she was still receiving time-loss. Maybe he would phone the daughter, and he wrote her number on a slip of paper, promising himself he'd call before the end of the day, or maybe tomorrow.

He dug through Edna's chart for the pages regarding her employer, John Sullivan, and the record Sol had made of his threatening visits to the Center. He considered the incident where Sullivan had become enraged, and he rehearsed his testimony. The crazed man had attacked Roxanne, slipped, and cracked his skull on the x-ray room floor, then bled profusely over the office. Surely, a jury would agree that behavior was inappropriate, no matter how unjustly the defendant felt he had been treated.

CHAPTER TWENTY-SIX

Roxanne sat at her desk yawning, carelessly slicing open the myriad daily letters from the Commission on Labor Affairs. Each was a brusque communication enjoining Sol to answer questions or provide documents regarding one patient or another. She was nearly comatose until her eyes brushed a document halfway down the pile. She jumped out of her seat and ran to Sol's office. Kevin McAlister's case manager was requesting a narrative report describing how the claimant's cancer was related to the fall at work for which the claim was originally filed. She wrote that in the absence of objective data linking his cancer to the fall, the Commission could not consider paying any of the hospital or doctor bills associated with his illness. That meant every penny of the $485,000, from the birth of the claim until the final hospital charge for preparing the body, would have to be repaid.

The manager justified her position by enclosing pages and pages of the state code. She ended the letter by insisting upon a reply within two weeks. She warned that if Dr. Forte failed to answer by that deadline, it would be legally recorded that he was in agreement with the Commission on Labor Affairs' position that the state was not responsible for a single dollar of the claim.

Sol had known the letter demanding recompense would come someday, and unlike most things COLA, this time there was a very clear deadline. He reread the laws, especially the endless sections about the penalties afforded those who didn't comply with the reporting requirements. There was no choice; he would have to explain his actions over the past year if he wanted to remain a COLA provider, and even if he chose to never again treat an injured worker, the law said he still had to justify his treatment of those he had treated. The civil penalties were brutal.

He knew a call to the claims manager would be a colossal waste of time—thirty minutes on hold before the computer voice terminated the dropped call. He would call back, leave a message, and wait days for a reply. And all she would do was insist he pose his question, or state his position, in a written document. Every sentence manufactured for that document would have to be perfectly crafted to avoid the charge of insurance fraud.

His first thought was to argue that the back pain and the cancer were two different problems that simply happened to occur simultaneously. All he had done was continue to treat the worsening back pain, the accepted industrial injury, and when the patient was finally admitted to the hospital, it was for the back pain and not the cancer. It just so happened the cancer was discovered serendipitously, but was never the primary reason for the admission. And, the cancer complicated and aggravated the underlying back pain, for as any claims manager worth her salt knew, lying in bed after a back injury was the worst thing one could do. Movement cured back pain, not rest. He would argue that the cancer had, indeed, made the patient bedridden, but his back pain, a separate issue to be sure, could not improve if he remained supine. So, it was quite reasonable and necessary for Sol to carry on treating his patient for the spinal injury. And he was still treating the back pain toward the end when Kevin had passed away of complications from another malady.

That reasoning, however, opened another can of worms, and he shook his head dolefully. I'm saying the Commission on Labor Affairs must separate the back pain from the cancer pain and allow me to argue that Kevin had a COLA reason to be in the hospital. Then I have to argue that the hundreds-of-thousands of dollars spent on the tests were ordered to find the source of his back pain. But if I argue that these were two different medical problems, and put that in an official written document, and it gets back to SMAC, as it surely will, the Commission will turn around and charge that I used ongoing narcotic pain medication to treat back pain, your primal no-no according to COLA's SOP. That'll mutilate my argument that I was treating cancer pain all along.

He brightened a bit. Yeah, but what if I say the fall at work "lit up" the underlying condition of cancer, just like attorneys pled in court that their plaintiffs complained of neck pain only after a car accident, your basic whiplash lawsuit, because the accident "lit up" latent arthritis. Yes, the arthritis had been there before the accident—no lawyer could argue that it developed in the hour between the crash and the first x-ray at the emergency room. But before the collision, it just wasn't causing any symptoms, and the arthritis would have remained "silent" for who knows how long, perhaps forever, had there never been a crash? "But for accident..." attorneys for the plaintiff argued, and usually won.

He turned the problem over and over in his mind, like a chicken roasting on the rotisserie, creating ever more self-contradicting, legal-sounding hogwash. Were it not for the fall at work, he postured at his desk, gaining confidence, there would never have been the stress of a low back injury in Kevin's life, and it was *that* stress that weakened his patient's immune system, allowing the cancer to run roughshod through his body. If Kevin had not injured himself at work, perhaps his cancer would have festered indolently, silently, as do many malignancies, often for years and years, maybe forever. Who could have said just when the cancer would have gone wild were it not for the fall? "Yes," Sol snapped aloud, "The fall accelerated Kevin's demise for, through well-known, stress-related hormonal pathways, it allowed the cancer to grow, and Q.E.D., COLA has to pay for the back pain *and* the cancer treatments."

Even better, he could argue in his letter that *if* Sunset Aviation, Kevin's employer, was so interested in protecting itself from a worker's preexisting medical condition, they should have had all prospective employees undergo a physical examination to avoid just such complications. Had such a thorough assessment been done, Kevin's cancer might have been exposed, and there would have been no offer of employment. Hundreds-of-thousands of dollars could have been saved, and if it had been discovered earlier, perhaps it could have been cured.

Sol got a cup of tea and returned to his desk. He reminded himself, on the other hand, that COLA would contend the employer had to offer the job to the worker *before* they ordered a pre-employment physical. Unless what was found on the physical prevented the applicant from carrying out the demands of the job at the time it was offered—which the cancer wouldn't have because no doctor on a basic physical exam would have ever found the tumor that no one found even after it killed the patient—the employer had no legal basis not to offer the job. That was one of the principles of the Americans with Disabilities Act. Sol smirked at the stupidity of the law but asked himself: "What if it was me, and the Galena Hills Hospital and Medical Center refused to hire me because my pop had suffered a premature heart attack, and someday in the murky future, I might succumb as well, through no fault of my own? Does that mean I'm unemployable?"

In any event, there were still nearly two weeks before he had to submit a reply, and he stood to place the papers on the middle pile of burgeoning, three-dimensional charts that had spilled out of his file cabinet onto the floor near the window. Roxanne, however, appeared at the door before he even got all the way out of his seat. "Phone, Doc. It's Kevin McAlister's mom. She's crying. Wants to talk to you."

Kevin's mother had also just opened her copy of the order regarding the nearly half-million dollars the state claimed she owed. Sol spoke flourishing soothingly. "I just got the letter, too. I've been thinking about it. Now, not to worry, ma'am. These things have a way of working out. Let's do this. First, I'm going to write a nice letter. But why don't you go out and find a good attorney? We'll go at this from several directions, and we can all work together and get this thing settled. I've got some ideas."

Mrs. McAlister was silent for a moment but gathered herself and spoke firmly. "Dr. Forte, where am I going to get the money to hire a lawyer? This is not one of those cases where they take a third of the money if they win. There is no money. I called to ask if you would write a letter to COLA and request they do something. I'm already two thousand dollars in debt for Kevin's burial. How can I pay half-a-million dollars?" She began to sob uncontrollably. "And Kevin's gone. How could you let this happen? He shouldn't have died!" With each sentence, her voice blared more shrilly, until she sucked in a huge breath and shrieked deafeningly, "You let him die for so long!"

Sol's head buzzed. As the seconds ticked by waiting for the phone to slam, he could taste his own bitterness, a year's worth, years and years worth, swelling in his heart. Soon, he became conscious only of red and white bursts flashing in front of his eyes, and he could feel his body tightening, about to snap. Words started to form in his mouth, and he fought to hold them back.

He came so close to shouting, *"Look lady, I'm not responsible for your son's smoking and his drug abuse, and the crappy diet you gave him as a kid, and the way he lived in a filthy room, if you can call that living. And I'm sure as hell not responsible for all the shit that went wrong with your pregnancy because, look at you, you were probably smashed and high on cocaine the whole time, if you even knew you were pregnant because you got laid by so many guys so often, you probably thought you couldn't get pregnant any more, and even if you did, you'd just go out and get another one of the million abortions that I've paid for with my taxes. So, lady, Kevin McAlister's cancer was your problem, not mine. And so are his bills—they're yours, not mine."*

The words remained inside his head, though a few got far enough to burn the back of tongue. Then Sol remembered having spit that same argument at Dana a long time before, and he knew that in the real world, he *was* responsible for Kevin's demise. Young people didn't just up and die. The doctor had had a good year to save him. Solomon Forte should have done something.

He also knew that she knew that the only way for her to raise the funds was to file a medical malpractice lawsuit against him. Even El Haq could get a jury to ignore the argument that the claim was only filed to allow her to buffer the awful financial burden of her son's death. And perhaps, that is exactly why it should be filed. She would be even more sympathetic if all of her settlement went to paying bills incurred by the incompetent doctor.

And when it was all over, win or lose, the lawyer who took her case would have to take her part in the fight against COLA to get the bill eradicated. If that attorney refused, she'd find another, somewhere, who would sue the first one for malpractice and abandonment.

Sol shook his head sadly, allowing Kevin's mother to calm a bit. He answered slowly. "Mrs. McAlister, I have already been thinking about how to approach COLA. If we appeal to them on a personal basis, we might just be able to convince them to cover the expenses. Here's my plan. Instead of just writing a letter, I think it would be better if I drove down there myself and just sat with the claims manager and made an argument that Kevin's passing was hastened by the industrial injury. We'll find some way to connect the fall at work and Kevin's canc…illness."

She interjected, "You need to take care of this. Tell the lady there that I ain't got any money. Maybe she got kids. Make her understand. I don't care how you do it. I just can't pay this. You gotta get this done right away."

"Mrs. McAlister, I'll tell her all those things, and you're going to have trust that I will do my best to help you, but I can't promise anything. I'll take the time off and make the trip within a few days and call you with a report. Right now, it's the best I can do."

She mumbled, "Okay, but if it doesn't work, I just don't know what I'll do."

Sol phoned the case manager, Michelle Herman, and made an appointment to drive to Olympia, declaring he had discovered additional information regarding Kevin's injury, facts that clearly impacted the case. The manager was polite, but he could tell this was not the usual way in which business was conducted at the Commission on Labor Affairs. He fretted that he might have already blown the appeal, that it was now clear he was begging. If the manager went to her superiors with the "Strange Case of the Overly Concerned Doctor," they would look into the matter, dig through Sol's past, discover the SMAC investigation, if they were not already aware of it, and puzzle out his modus operandi. Either way he cut it, Solomon Forte was going to lose.

He thought of the case manager's flat, business-like voice and cringed at the thought of spending ten minutes face to face with an angry, bureaucratic, dragon lady. Nonetheless, he had few options, as he had already committed himself to Kevin's mother and the case manager, and he instructed Roxanne to cancel his appointments for Thursday, two days hence. He downloaded a map of the government buildings in the capital and called Dana, basically imploring her to come with him and serve as a buffer. She had already scheduled a trip to detail her meds out in Seattle, but she giggled, and he could hear her smiling into the phone, "You know, Solly, I wouldn't miss watching you charm the pants of this lady for the world. How 'bout I drive?"

⇥ ⇤

The first patient of the afternoon was Mr. Porcher, the black man who had fractured his arm on the job months before. Sol had been seeing him every three weeks, guiding him through a period where the bone had refused to heal, and then through months of physical therapy, where Sol did nothing medical for his patient, though dutifully filled out forms for the Commission on Labor Affairs to ensure the man's time-loss payments remained authorized.

Porcher had not been able to return to his job as a brick layer for the construction company that had been forced to hire him. They required all hands be capable of full, unrestricted duty before being allowed back after an injury. That demand had two prongs: the first was to protect the corporation from liability for further injury if Porcher wasn't able to get around a dangerous job site safely. It was also to set the stage for firing the man if it became clear that he was not capable of carrying out his complete responsibilities within a reasonable time after his injury.

The law did not require that the employer hold a job open forever. And even if a worker came back fairly quickly, he was tainted, far more likely to reinjure himself. He was also usually a disruptive influence, disgruntled about the way he had been treated by both the company and the Commission on Labor Affairs while on time loss. It seemed to Sol that once a worker was off the job for more than a few days, and particularly after he'd been gone for three or four weeks, the chances of going back to that job, at that company, and living happily ever after, were diminishingly small. It was smarter for the worker to start searching for new employment before he was fit to return.

In Porcher's case, his arm remained weak, the bone far too fragile for carrying hod, and Sol informed COLA over and over that the worker might never again be able to manage the heavy demands of construction. He recommended a retraining program, to be paid for by COLA, the next to the last stop when all medical treatment had failed to bring a patient back to pre-injury status. Though Sol had not yet heard COLA's decision, he reckoned that if they had seen fit to approve Lupe Sánchez's educational plan, Porcher was a no brainer.

Aaron Porcher, despite Sol's best administrative efforts, was in a foul temper that visit. "Doc, how the hell am I supposed to feed my kids on the shit money COLA gives me? When is this arm gonna git better?"

"Mr. Porcher, we've been over this ground before. Sometimes bones don't heal the way we want them to." Sol thrust his mildly deformed right hand forward, as he had many times for Porcher's benefit. "I've shown you my own wrist. Broke it. Some asshole pushed a bunch of us off a subway platform. It's never been the same. That's just the dings and cracks of life, my friend. We don't cure everything."

"Yeah, but you sit all day long. Don't do nothin' but move your gums. I'm a workin' man. I got a family. You need to do somethin'."

Sol took a deep breath. "Mr. Porcher, I am doing something. Do you know how many letters I've written for you, trying to get COLA to approve a retraining program?" Sol was beginning to raise his voice. "Please don't blame me if the system is totally fucked up. It's not my problem."

"Damn well is your problem. You the one gettin' paid to fix me."

"Mr. Porcher, you know what, you're too damn angry for me to help. We all have shit going on in our lives. Maybe you need to find another doctor to handle your claim. I got nothing else to offer you except to stick with you while the process goes on."

Sol sprang up and started for the door. Porcher hissed, "Just 'cause I'm black, you people gonna treat me like shit. Don't you dis me, honkey bitch! You ain't getting' away with this shit no more. You hear me?"

Sol was through the door and on the phone to security before Porcher was out of his seat. The man marched out of the room and saw Sol on the phone. That made him even madder, and he started down the hall toward Sol with fists clinched. Roxanne watched for a moment but jumped off her stool and placed herself in front of the charging bull, like a blocking fullback, but just as Porcher reached her desk, he stopped as quickly as he had started and let his shoulders droop. His fists relaxed and his eyes reddened as he spoke softly to Sol. "Doc, I'm sorry, man, I'm just in deep trouble with my life, man. I didn't mean nothin' by what I said."

There were tears rolling off Porcher's cheeks. Though the man's head hung dolefully, he extended his hand. Sol thought for a moment and put the phone down gently, though he allowed himself to glare at Porcher before nodding and taking the trembling man's hand.

"Doc, I'm truly sorry. You're the only one who's done anything to help me. It's just the stress, man. My family. I don't know how long I can hold on."

Sol guided Porcher back into the exam room, where they talked for half-an-hour. Before adjourning, Sol promised to continue working on the request for retraining. "My friend," Sol ended the conversation standing at the open door, "listen closely. There's a reason for everything the Lord does. I don't know what it is, and you don't either—nobody does. Someday, it'll all be clear why this is happening. Now, you have the opportunity to make it through the bad times in a good humor, or you can get into a lot of extra fuckin' trouble waiting for the next shoe to fall. Your choice, my man.

"I want you to come back in a week with a pad of paper all filled in." Porcher's eyes rose as if he were facing an idiot. "You need to make a list of the jobs you want more than anything else in the world for the rest of your life. Put down everything you want to do. Don't worry that you think they're impossible. Get it all on paper, every single job, except for one."

"What's that, Doc?"

"Don't you put down, 'I wanna be a doctor.'"

"No way, man."

"Good. And get your wife to help you. Find something that you like and that pays. Find things she likes, jobs that she can be proud to say you're doing. When you come back, we'll go over it and send it off to COLA. Then I'll have something concrete to show them. Concrete, ha ha, you get it? You're a stonemason."

Porcher's eyes rolled, and he grumbled, "You mean *was*," but stood and took Sol's hand again. "Doc, I'm sorry, man. Hope you understand. Thanks." He patted Sol on the shoulder awkwardly.

More bewildered than Sol had ever seen her, Roxanne sat at her nursing station and watched as Porcher walked away from the exam room. She shook her head and asked Sol, "How does that make you feel?"

"How does what make me feel?"

"To be probably the first white man he ever really touched."

"What are you, my shrink? Dr. Von Roxanne. Very good, if you must know. But now, I need to get a hold of his claims manager and do something."

"Well," Roxanne smiled sarcastically, "she's in the same unit in the COLA office as Kevin McAlister's claims manager. Kill two birds with one stone, how 'bout?"

Roxanne arranged a second appointment for two days hence. Porcher's claims manager was not that surprised he had called. "Yes, we've heard that you're coming down. I don't know what we can do face to face that we can't do in written correspondence, but you have a right, as the attending physician, to discuss his case with me. I have to warn you, I'm very busy. I won't have a long time to spend."

CHAPTER TWENTY-SEVEN

That night, Sol met with his attorneys. He fretted silently about paying two hourly fees, but thought back to his own words to Porcher earlier in the day, that there was a reason for everything, that nothing in life was by chance. He closed his eyes, and the first image that came to him was Alfred E. Newman. Sol snickered, "What, me worry?"

He went over the argument he proposed to pitch at the Commission on Labor Affairs, about demonstrating, with fresh new research, that the elevated levels of stress Kevin suffered as a result of the fall at work, through a complicated, but demonstrable hormonal labyrinth, lowered his immune system's ability to fight the cancer, hastening, probably by years, his demise. It was the same argument researchers proposed to explain why so many highly stressed, unhappy women developed breast cancer prematurely.

They nodded as if impressed with the logic, and Matsukawa smiled. "There's a germ of plausibility in there, Sol. We'll make a trial lawyer out of you yet."

Fluellen liked the argument, too, but warned that the cost of the claim was so extreme, a lot of high-placed bureaucratic necks were going to be on the chopping block for not having stopped the financial hemorrhaging much earlier in the process. He went on to warn Sol that it was going to be nearly impossible to get anyone to listen to him, regardless of his facts. "But, do it the way we do it. Find out everything you can about the claims manager and her supervisor, and how to get to the Commissioner, his email, the church he goes to. Find out just how high this thing's gone. When you're fully armed, then you can move out into enemy territory."

Matsukawa added, "And don't tell them any more than the bare bones of your medical argument. Make it sound like it's well known, a provable physiologic process that you are going to introduce at trial, because that's where this whole thing is headed. But don't say it like that. No threats, at least not direct. It's got to be so subtle, she won't be able to tell what you're implying. And for God's sake, don't plead for the family's well-being. Don't even mention them. You're presenting pure, objective science.

Fluellen jumped back in. "And don't give them anything in writing. Don't offer references to scholarly papers. As long as your discussions down there aren't recorded, you're safe. You can always come up with a different argument later and claim that's what you said in the first place. Now, on the other hand, *you* take notes about what she says. That way, if there was ever an argument about what transpired, you'll have the greater credibility."

"Maybe I should record the conversation."

"Nah, don't do that," Fluellen shook his head. "If you do it in the open, she'll freak, and all you'll get is the party line. And if you do it covertly, well, it's against the law in this state to record a conversation without the other person knowing you're doing it. You'll never be able to use it in court, and you might get fried. You gotta be careful."

Matsukawa interjected, "Try this. Play dumb. Ask her to list the things you need to do to be in compliance with COLA's regulations regarding payment of a claim. Be the retarded Bronx boy; take a scrap of paper out of your pocket. Maybe look through several pockets before you just happen to come across an old envelope. Borrow a pen if you have to. Pretend to jot a few of her instructions on the back. That way, she probably won't bother to take notes herself. How could she take out a fancy pad when you're scribbling on the back of an old envelope you just happened to find in a pocket? No way. It'd be too embarrassing. And, anyway, you've got her pen! But be sure you make cryptic notes about everything she says. Get names. In court, if it comes to that, she'll turn red if she sees the old envelope, and she'll tell the truth if she hears her own statements thrown back at her. These people are too scared to lie under oath, and why should she, anyway? Commit perjury for the Commission on Labor Affairs? I don't think so."

Fluellen smiled, "You're a wily one, Michael." He turned to Sol. The corners of his mouth turned down. "He's got a point, Doctor. You're fighting on two fronts, but they're not mutually exclusive. You need to cover your ass on both of them. Done right, with lots of documentation to back you up, this thing is going to work out just fine. Now, on the letter to SMAC, I think you're on the right track with the treating-cancer-pain argument. If you can tie the two together, the commissioners'll fold. Those guys are scared of the public, and if we can sell this as a doctor going the extra mile to help a sick patient and getting hammered for it, they'll bristle around for a while, but let the matter drop in a matter of weeks."

Sol nodded but added, "My only fear is that they're going to ask me, 'When did you discover Mr. McAlister had cancer?' And when I tell them, they're going to say my *intention* was not to treat his cancer pain, but to give him drugs just to get him out of my office. And to be honest, a couple of times, yep; I did just that, added a few pills to the prescription, like every doctor who ever practiced real medicine."

"Okay, Doctor Forte, that's fine," Matsukawa warned, "but you don't need to tell us *everything*."

On Thursday morning, Dana drove. They listened to Simon and Garfunkel's *Concert in the Park*, and Sol laughed when they sang about one of Paul Simon's old girlfriends who called herself a human trampoline; everyone she met, everything she did, boomeranged on her. "I know how she feels," Sol laughed sourly.

They sat in the Mustang in front of Building G-333 silently and listened to the music a third round until it was time to go in. They debated whether Dana should accompany him, just to settle any question about his motivation for meeting with the women. Sol suggested they introduce themselves as husband and wife. Dana blushed and squeezed his hand.

Sol laughed and added, "Well, maybe you shouldn't come in…patient confidentiality and that sort of thing. A man can't be too careful these days." They finally decided that he could start the conversation by alluding to the fact that Dana was there in the coffee shop, waiting for him, so he didn't want to take too much of their time.

Kevin McAlister's claims manager sat at a desk between two fabric partitions. Sol knocked obsequiously on one of the dividers, and she looked up, startled at first that anyone would bother to announce themselves with anything other than a boisterous, "Hey, Michelle, I need…" But she replaced her surprise quickly with a warm smile. "Oh, you must be Dr. Forte. Please come in."

Sol gulped, "Good morning, Ms. Herman." Though he had expected standard governmental fare, Michelle Herman actually wore make-up, and an elegant black suit that set off her gleaming blond hair and hazel eyes. His glance shot toward her left hand. She fetched a chair from another cubicle and brought coffee. Sol was nearly paralyzed, and his hand trembled as he fought to rip open the pack of sugar.

Absentmindedly, he touched his pocket, the one in which the crumpled envelope sat poised, and then searched her desk for pens—half-a-dozen. As she thanked him for coming all the way there to settle the McAlister case, she pulled a yellow legal pad from a desk drawer, crossed her legs, and put the pad on her lap. He couldn't help but notice the tiny red and blue flower tattooed on the inside of her left ankle.

Sol made his case. McAlister's immune system had been damaged irreparably by the fall at work. The stress of that injury had hastened the unbridled growth of the cancer that had long been present, no argument, but held in check by his young-man's immune system.

She pulled her head back skeptically. He blurted, "Really. Stress, like from a serious physical injury, leads to depression, which raises interleukin levels, and that promotes inflammation, and that undermines the immune system. It's a vicious cycle. Then there's the release of excess amounts of cortisol, and that blunts the immune system's ability to fight infections *and* cancer. This is all quite well known in research circles. I can send you the articles."

"I don't doubt you for a moment, Doctor. I'm sure there are excellent studies to back up your claim, but…look at this." She smiled sadly and pulled a ream of documents from her desk, struggling even while using both hands.

Sol shook his head. "Mr. McAlister's chart. I know it well."

"Nope, not his chart," she spoke in a soft voice, "just his bills; all $486,565.36 of them."

Sol looked at her curiously. "I thought it was only four hundred and eighty thousand. Where'd the other six thousand come from? Oh, I forgot, sales tax."

She started to answer then looked into his eyes. Sensing the twinkle, she pretended to hit him. She plopped the files down in front of him. "I know what you doctors think, that we're all here to screw the worker, and if you appeal to us, we'll be able to make everything just go away. Little exceptions, yes, like allowing ten pain pills, or even approving one more MRI on a patient who's already had six. But with the big disbursements, that's not how it works. I'm afraid, when one patient spends a fair portion of our entire yearly budget, the blame takes on a life of its own. We do serve the injured worker. That's what we're commissioned to do. But we also have a responsibility to protect you, the taxpayer.

"I haven't been here that long, maybe two years, just part-time, while I'm working on my PhD in public health, but I have to tell you, this case is a record for me by about a factor of ten; the boss says it is for him, too, by a factor of three, and he's been here twelve. Half-a-million dollars. Lotta money, even for the government. All of a sudden, the state legislature's suddenly aware of one Kevin McAlister, and they want answers."

"Do you know who?"

"*All* of them. But that's still not the hard part. We can bamboozle them if it is in the interest of the worker, *and* it's legal, but Mr. McAlister's employer is livid. He has an argument. I know you won't believe this, but it's not up to me, or COLA for that matter, to erase these bills. Even if we did, the employer can turn around and sue us all the way to the United States Supreme Court if he has the cash, or the outrage, to go that far. From his standpoint, it'd probably be cheaper to take it all the way to the top than allow us to pay. His rates are going to skyrocket, no matter what happens, but if we *do* pay, it might put him out of business. I have to ask you, Doctor, is that just?"

Sol could not answer, and he thought for a moment before asking softly, "What do you think I should do, ma'am?"

"I'll be honest. It's not the employer's fault—any of this, even the fall, if you really look at what happened, though we had to accept that part of the claim simply because he did it on the job. But don't you agree the whole claim is unjustified?"

"In fact, I do, but my job is to protect the patient no matter what, until the patient proves he isn't worthy of my efforts. And that means he has to lie, or cheat, or get violent, or something along those lines, before I stop fighting for him. Anyway, I'll get off my high horse. You were going to say, and I need to hear?"

"I was going to suggest that maybe you can meet with the various doctors and hospital administrators who submitted these bills and ask them, in the name of decency, to unburden Kevin's family. That's my suggestion. I'll copy this whole sickening pile and send it up to you. I hope you understand that our hands are tied."

Sol nodded and stood. "You're not at all what I expected. You're a good person. Kevin was lucky to have you as his claims manager. Thank you, Ms. Herman."

"And you're a good doctor. Everyone here knows your name."

Sol laughed, "Oh, God."

"You always take the patient's side. Like you said, that's your job. Doesn't make ours any easier, but that's just too bad, isn't it? Hope you won't stop." They shook hands, and she started to walk him toward the cubicle where Mr. Porcher's claims manager sat waiting. Before Ms. Herman turned away, she whispered and giggled, "Good luck with your next meeting."

Porcher's claims manager, more of what he'd imagined, snapped a yellow legal pad from her desk and wrote continuously without looking up. She agreed to review the file, but added she wasn't hopeful COLA would approve retraining for a worker who would soon be healed, and already possessed skills. Sol answered, "Lupe Sánchez had a skill, too, and her retraining was approved."

The woman answered caustically, "I'm not responsible for what everyone else around here does. I have my rules to follow. Now, Doctor, if you don't have anything further, I'm very busy."

She did not rise when Sol left and guided himself out. As he walked past Kevin's manager's cubicle, he considered one more good-by, but she was crouched over her desk, and he walked past.

CHAPTER TWENTY-EIGHT

Sol spent several days drafting a letter to the CEOs of the dozen institutions that had filed claims with the Commission on Labor Affairs for care rendered to the late Kevin McAlister. He wrote personal notes to each of the countless doctors at the Center who had billed COLA on their own. He asked Anacota for the Center to cover the expense of the postage and transcription services, but the CEO demurred, offering with a plastic grin, "No, it'll look much better if you make the personal commitment on his behalf. Don't you think?"

Sol was going to answer that he had already taken a day away from the office over the matter, and that he had already foregone all of his payment for seeing McAlister over the past year, but he looked into Anacota's eyes. "How 'bout I just hand deliver the one addressed to you? Wouldn't that be a nice touch? Save thirty-seven cents, too."

"Be nicer if I just got it in my in-basket, like all the rest of the day's business. I can't be playing favorites with the Center's finances. The doctors, my bosses, all one-hundred-and-eighty-seven of them, would have my head."

⇥⇤

In between patients that morning, Sol received a call from Gene Fluellen. The State Medical Abuse Commission investigator had received Sol's letter of explanation and, while she was sympathetic, felt that an inquiry was warranted. She was going to get her examination started immediately and wanted Sol to be aware that she was going to be poking around.

Sol told Fluellen, "Fine, let's get this over with. The sooner the better. I got nothing to hide."

But Fluellen cautioned, "Doctor, we just went to unofficial stage two. Mike tells me we've got three or four months to go if things just stop here. The wheels of justice turn very slowly, particularly when there's no justice involved. I'm afraid you have no right to a speedy trial with these caring physicians. They're not covered by the rules of decency. I'm sorry, but you already know that. Look, I'm going to need a list of all the places you've lived in the past fifteen years and your entire work history with names, dates, addresses, and telephone numbers."

Sol snapped back, "Gene, I don't have that stuff. I'm busy. I'm a doctor, remember? And where I lived before I was a doctor has nothing to do with whether I treated a patient's pain appropriately. I have some claim to my privacy, don't I?"

"Nope."

"Why not let them get the information? That's what they're getting my tax dollars for, isn't it?"

"Doc, we're trying to cooperate, remember. Let's not piss them off at the beginning. Looks like it may turn into a long fight, more than ten rounds. Pretend it's like the heavyweight championship.

Take each round one at a time, and do your best in each one. So, put down what you can remember. Give it your best shot."

Sol grumbled, "This isn't justice, damnit. I didn't do anything wrong. Can't you auger that into their heads?"

"We've been over and over this. We're gonna play the game and walk out on top. You're gonna get cut and bruised along the way, but that doesn't mean you've lost the fight. Just keep going. My brother was a Navy Seal. He says when the students were about to quit, when they couldn't go on, the instructors would scream at them to put a leg out in front of them and take another step; they did, and then they took the next, and the one after that."

Three days after Sol turned in his life history, he got a midnight call. It was his sister. She was whispering loudly. "Solly, I don't have much time. I snuck into Mother Superior's office. I got a call today from a lady who said she was representing the State Medical Abuse Commission. She was real pushy. She wanted to know if you had ever used illegal drugs or sold them. I don't know if I did right, but I told her, oh, Solly, I hope this is okay, I told her to go to Hades. And then I hung up—hard. Did I do wrong?"

Sol laughed. "No, man, you did great. Good for you." Sol started to ask how many days and hours were left, but the phone clicked softly.

Sol started receiving calls from people he hadn't heard from in ten years, since college, fraternity brothers that he loved and some he didn't, and even team members from wrestling and track. At first, he did his best to explain the situation, pledging his innocence, but soon he just answered their questions with a tooth-gritted declaration, "It's bureaucratic bullshit. Tell 'em to go straight to hell."

CHAPTER TWENTY-NINE

By late March, many months after he had first received the subpoena from SMAC, a host of doctors, a handful of nurses, and one maintenance man at the Galena Hills Center had stopped Sol in the hallway to tell him the investigator had contacted them. All swore they had answered her demanding questions with dismissals of the possibility that Dr. Solomon Forte had ever been involved in drugs, or that he had made inappropriate use of his Drug Enforcement Agency license to prescribe narcotics. Sol was heartened by the unexpected support from his colleagues, both on the grounds that with their input, his SMAC problems would soon be over, but also because he had not been aware that so many people cared a damn for him.

He called his attorney to learn if he'd heard anything, grousing that it had been nearly four months since the investigator had made her first call, but Fluellen reminded him that he was dealing with little people whose only power lay in their ability to keep the fires burning under a victim's feet. "I know what this is doing to you, Doctor. There's always a gnawing in your stomach.

I think you guys call that the solar plexus. When you get up in the morning, there's always that little irritation inside. There's never a moment when you don't feel it hanging over your head. Am I right?"

Sol slurred, "Why, you're just making me feel great. I really appreciate it. Yeah, you're right."

"Well, what I'm trying to do is to tell you how predictable these feelings are. We all get them in life. It's part of the ride. I've been thinking about you a lot. The worst part's over, the bit you were most upset about. So, everyone knows. Is that what makes you worry all day?"

"Nah, the people who know me, they're pissed off that there could be something as feudal as the Commission. They know who I am, and they know very well who those people are. Most of my friends told me to hire someone to dig up the dirt on those bastards, that they're the ones who are usually the guiltiest, the ones who set themselves up as the judges, the holier than thou crowd, the Bible thumpers. I don't worry about my friends. The others, to tell you the truth, yeah, it pisses me off a little that there are fruitcakes out there that get their kicks out of harming people, but it's not so bad anymore, 'cause I decided they can kiss my ass. Each day that gets better.

"You know, in medical school and residency, they take great pains to beat the individuality out of you. Everybody's taught to act the same, aloof, arrogant, cocksure. If you show weakness, they swoop down on you like those falcons on your ledge grab a kid's pet gerbil. Since I got into medicine, I never felt all that sure about what I was doing. Always second-guessing myself. That wasn't tolerated, not for a second. But now that I'm in practice, I see the ones who appear so confident, they make as many mistakes as the next guy. What's worse, they don't even grasp they've harmed anyone. They're screwing people's lives, charging money for it, and when the treatment doesn't go well, to add insult to injury, they huff and puff about the patient's life choices, essentially blame the patient when the treatment doesn't work. And then the final declaration, 'Sorry, nothing further I can do for you. You need to go out and find a good primary care doctor.'

"This whole thing's a good lesson. I learned to bluster on the street in New York when I was kid, not in medical school. It turns me off to use it, but I'm starting to get tired of turning the other cheek. The people giving me crap are going to start getting it back with both barrels. Watch me now."

Fluellen laughed. "Good. Sounds like you've gotten your head into a better place. So, let me ask, what *is* it that's bothering you? I can tell there's still something eating at you."

"You know, now I think I'm worried about what they're going to do to me. I never hurt a patient in my life. But apparently, they have a God-given right to decide whether I practice anymore. And this investigator, I haven't even heard from her, but she's done a life study on me. Why can't she just sit down with me and discuss what happened?"

Fluellen spoke softly. "First of all, it's highly unlikely, *highly* unlikely, that you'll lose your license. It's unlikely, even in the worst-case scenario, that you'll have to do any more than promise not to write narcotic prescriptions for COLA patients after the first or second visit."

Sol grumbled, "But that's all I have to offer in a lot of cases. Take care of a patient's pain, because we sure don't do very much curing, us healers. Even better, think about this, Gene: If I ignore a patient's pain, I'll get sued for malpractice for neglecting their suffering, and that'll get me dragged before the Commission."

"Again, I don't know what they'll decide, but what I just suggested is not a particularly harsh penalty. They might examine every fiftieth chart note you write for a year—so big deal. In regard to meeting the investigator, let me give you a piece of advice. You don't want to meet her: short, chubby, cropped hair, lots of wrinkles, like she's been angry her whole life, which she apparently has. Kind of waddles, head swinging back and forth, making sure everyone knows she's watching, that she's the one with authority to kick people around. She found the right line of work. We need to get past her to the doctors who review her work and makes recommendations to the panel. So, my friend, let her have her way, and for that matter, let them all have their way. Remember, I think it was Mike who told you, these people have to have their butts kissed, or they're not fulfilled. That's how their world swings. Been that way for all of time. Let's just get through it. Okay?"

"Okay. But…"

"But what?"

"But nothing. I'm on board with the plan. Thanks."

At that moment, Roxanne came into the office and put a note in front of Sol. "El Haq. Says it's important."

CHAPTER THIRTY

Two days later, Ralph Tarkington's retrial recommenced in Courtroom Two. Though Judge Ballbrine claimed to have fought to get the case rescheduled promptly, it had taken several months. Then there was the week to empanel a new jury. El Haq growled to Sol that there had been several possible jurors excused, for they allowed that a Dr. Forte, "...or some foreigner-sounding name like that," had treated them or their families. With each dismissal, the judge had shaken his head more vituperatively, threatening El Haq with sanctions if things didn't move ahead more quickly. When El Haq countered it was Argent's lawyers who were dragging their feet, he was fined fifty dollars for contempt. El Haq's final admonishment to Sol before he entered the courtroom was, "Doctor, please, if you see anyone you recognize, anyone at all, you must stand up and inform the court immediately. Let's not have any trouble this time."

But when Sol was eventually called to the stand, the judge barely acknowledged him. Though Sol thought one or two of the jurors looked familiar, he muttered to himself, "So, anyone who has a common face, I'm supposed to jump up and point at them? Make this idiocy drag on another day? No way." He kept his speculation to himself.

The lead attorney laid out the same case he had at the first trial. He reached deeply into his briefcase and pulled out the videotape, held it above his head, and waited magisterially as his lessers connected wires and turned video screens at angels that made Sol twist his neck uncomfortably. With the push of a button, there, before his eyes, appeared the image of Tarkington's house.

The lead grimaced. "Do you recognize this house, Doctor?

Though Sol had rehearsed his answer to the question for a fortnight, his throat closed in fright, and he hesitated guiltily. "Yes, I do," he finally replied.

Sol was rigid, waiting for the next stab, but El Haq shot up to protest. "Your Honor, I object. Doctors make house calls every day. The good ones like Dr. Forte do, at least. We all know what counsel is trying to do; he's trying to taint the jury."

"Mr. El Haq, counsel simply asked a probative question. If I may say, *you're* tainting the jury. Please sit down. Objection overruled."

The attorney went on. "Were you ever in the house?"
"Yes."
"Was there anyone in there with you?"
"Yes."
"And who was that, Dr. Forte?"
"Ms. Famot."
"Well, Doctor, let's backtrack a bit," the lead attorney smiled. Was anyone in the house with you *and* Ms. Famot?" When Sol hesitated even longer this time than in the first trial, the lawyer went back to his table and dug deep into his briefcase. He slowly and deliberately extracted a manila envelope from the depths of the tooled leather satchel and waved it menacingly toward the witness stand. Slowly, he undid the string and finally pulled what appeared to be glossy photographs from within, but slid

them back inside quickly. He held the envelope tightly as he re-approached Sol. "Was there anyone else in the house while you were there?"

"I have no idea."

It was at this point that Sol glanced over at the jury to see if any of the old men were clutching their chests. None were. They clutched only pens to scribble notes as fast as they could.

"Let me ask you, Doctor," the lawyer asked deadpan, "Did you kiss Ms. Famot's hand in that house that night?" He waved the thick envelope menacingly.

"Yes."

The requisite gasps from the jury box and gallery had a lesser bite this time, but Sol watched the jury closely, hoping that would cull a coronary victim or two. They, however, just stared back at him.

"Did she kiss your hand?" the attorney snapped.

"Yes, but…"

"Your Honor."

"Answer only the question you are being asked, Doctor."

"Did you kiss her on the face?" The attorney wagged the envelope with the pictures in front of him."

Sol looked to the back of the gallery. Though he hadn't heretofore noticed, Dana had slipped in after the lights had dimmed for the video. He saw her face, and his shoulders drooped. "Just a peck on the cheek in greeting. There was nothing sexual about it. I left bef…"

The judge growled, "Doctor!"

Sol sighed, "Yes, sir."

"Now, Doctor," the attorney blathered, "thank you. Please turn your attention back to the video display."

The screen came alive with movement and the patchy appearance of evergreens and a spotless, azure, cloudless, Whitaker summer sky. The Tarkingtons' garage door opened a few inches at the bottom, an out-of-focus form in blue bib overalls pushed the door up energetically, then raised his arms far above his head to stop the rocking. The figure went back inside the garage, climbed into a brand-new Ford 350, and backed it out into the driveway. The form got out of the truck, strode jauntily to a spigot at the side of the house, uncoiled a water hose, and within a minute was briskly washing the vehicle. He climbed on the chromed running boards, reached over the top, stretched easily, and scrubbed the truck's roof. The only thing he didn't do was drool.

"Please stop the surveillance video," crowed the attorney. He shook his head sadly and approached the jury. "Doctor, do you recognize the person in this surveillance video?"

"It is a fuzzy picture. The person appears to be dressed in a manner similar to that in which I have seen Mr. Tarkington in the past, if that's what you want me to say."

"I don't want you to say anything that isn't true. We are here to establish facts. Is that Mr. Ralph Tarkington? Yes or no?"

El Haq was on his feet. "Your Honor, I object. That image could be a man that looks like my client, and they might have dressed him in that outfit to mislead the witness, and the jury as well. That is a well-known trick insurance companies use to mislead jurors."

The lead attorney was apoplectic. "I beg your pardon, sir!"

"Your Honor," El Haq ground on, "in the matter of United Alder v. Glick, that was exactly the tactic employed by the defense, and it was proven later that it was a staged, phony surveillance video filmed at the worker's home when he was on vacation. As a matter of fact…"

The lead attorney was on his feet spewing saliva many feet to his front as he countered, "This is an outrage. I will not stand being accused of fraud by this, this…"

The judge intervened before the attorney, who was no longer acting, uttered the magic word and disgorged a racial epithet that would have summarily ended his legal career. His Honor slammed the gavel. "The case which counsel cited is real. It did happen. The jury is instructed to ignore the fact that dishonesty happened elsewhere, for there is no indication at all that that is the case here. Counselor, please move on with your surveillance video, and just make sure we learn in short order, and on a more probable than not basis, just whom we are observing. Can you do that?"

The lead attorney jumped forward. "Watch me, Your Honor. And, question withdrawn. We've wasted enough of the jury's time with ill-founded objections. Please forward the surveillance video to Marker Three. Let's get down to brass tacks."

In this scene, the man on the screen was on the roof of the Tarkington home ripping and flinging slabs of composite shingle to the ground. The camera was at a different angle, and much, much closer, as if it was in the house next door. In fact, it was— the filming had been done through the neighbor's kitchen window. Tarkington's friends, concerned that Ralph, the purported victim of a tragic industrial injury and disabled to the point that he was forced to live on disability, was physically overextending himself. One of them had telephoned the Commission on Labor Affairs asking if something might be done to corral Mr. Tarkington's need to be active before he hurt himself. COLA hired an investigator to create a surveillance video. Via a disgruntled employee at COLA, the tape fell into the hands of Argent's legal team.

"What about now, Doctor? Is that Mr. Tarkington?"

"It looks like him, but I was not there to examine that person, and I cannot say it is without a doubt."

"Okay, Doctor, fair enough. Let's go on. Maybe you'll recognize your patient in this segment. Mr. Hilton, please move the tape forward to Marker Six."

Here, a man who appeared very similar to Ralph Tarkington, though quite handsome and dressed in a starched, open-collar, button-down shirt, and a pair of pressed beige slacks, was seen strolling through a garden at the back of a suburban house.

At his side was a young couple glowing like newlyweds, holding hands, listening intently to the man who appeared to be showing them around the yard. The man spoke for a moment or two, took them into the two-car garage, gesticulated happily, then walked them back to the house. The tape stopped for a moment, and when it resumed, the three subjects left the house through the front door. The man in the starched shirt placed what appeared to be a key in a lock-box around the door handle.

"Doctor, do you recognize the real estate *salesman* in the surveillance video? Do you see the mole on his left cheek?"

"Yes."

"How about the little scar over the right eyebrow? Do you see that, Doctor?"

Sol was quietly furious. "Yes, I believe I do."

"Who is that, Doctor?"

"It appears to be my patient, Mr. Tarkington."

El Haq objected strenuously. Again, he culled the argument that the face of the man in the video was too indistinct for a witness to positively identify, and that the scars and moles could easily have been created by Hollywood makeup artists hired by Argent, to whom money was no object.

The judge rubbed his temples and stretched his neck. "Mr. El Haq, they say everyone in the world has a double, but let's be honest here and stop wasting time. Objection overruled."

The lawyer nodded to his assistants, and the next piece of video began again at the Tarkington home—this time, Judy Famot was pulling the pickup out of the garage. Ralph Tarkington, back in his drool-encrusted overalls, strode briskly from the house. Judy got out of the truck, and her father jumped into the driver's seat.

The attorney charged up to the witness stand. "Is that Mr. Tarkington and his daughter, Ms. Famot, Doctor, or have we created a double for his *daughter* as well?"

Sol mumbled, "Sure looks like them."

The clip went on, an uninterrupted diary of an automobile excursion, the camera rolling from a chase car, starting at the Tarkington home. It recorded every traffic light Ralph ran and every stop sign he ignored. On the screen, what appeared to be the same Ford 350 the investigator had been following whip-turned into the parking lot of a McDonald's, nearly striking a bicyclist, who shot his middle finger up toward the driver. Tarkington laughed and yelled at the cyclist. It was easy to read his lips forming the words, "Fuck you, asshole."

Tarkington jumped from the truck, ran inside, bought a bag of food, and strode out jamming fries into his mouth. He and Judy traded seats before speeding from the parking lot.

The automobile portion of the tape ended when they arrived at the Galena Hills Hospital and Medical Center parking lot and settled in a disabled spot. The camera followed as they walked, Tarkington in a stooped near-crawl, making his way painfully through the battered front doors of the Center. It was the day after Mr. Sullivan's crash, and though the pictures of Tarkington waiting for the service elevator were distorted, the sound wasn't, and it was the first time Sol had ever heard the true voice of Ralph Tarkington. The camera followed the pair into Sol's waiting room, where Tarkington's gait deteriorated further, and the drool began to flow in torrents.

That section of the film ended when Roxanne came out of the hallway to call Tarkington into an exam room. In the background, there was Dr. Solomon Forte standing at the receptionist's desk writing a prescription for another patient. It was plain to see, and hear, Sol greet Mr. Tarkington respectfully. The old man barely nodded then grunted in recognition.

"Doctor," the lawyer asked gently, "let's cut to the chase. Is there any reasonable doubt in your mind that the man in the video is Mr. Ralph Tarkington?"

A pink-faced Solomon Forte mumbled, "No, there is not."

"At the beginning of the day of filming, does Mr. Tarkington appear to be the disabled victim of a horrid accident?"

"The man in the video appears pretty chipper."

"Doctor, I thought we had established that was, in fact, Mr. Tarkington. Is that Ralph Tarkington, Doctor?"

"Yes, it appears on the film to be him."

"Okay, now, please turn to your chart note for Mr. Tarkington that very day. Please read the portion regarding his work status."

Sol was deflated, numb, and unsure of what to think or say. He hesitated, but the lead attorney spit acidly, "Please read your notes, Doctor!"

Sol took a deep breath, though read with a soft voice. "It says, and I quote, 'Mr. Tarkington remains unable to perform even the most sedentary of duties. He is permanently and totally disabled as a result of the previously captioned industrial injury, and should be pensioned after his previously withheld time loss compensation is reinstated for the period during which it was unjustly withheld.'"

"Thank you." For the first time since the trial began, the lawyer's face softened, and Sol relaxed a bit. He went on, "Doctor, I know you are a caring physician, but even the best of us get duped sometimes. I'm afraid not every one of us is a saint. Some," he turned his stare to Tarkington, "are cheaters and thieves. I'm sorry you have to go through…"

El Haq exploded out of his seat. "Your Honor, I object in the most strenuous terms. Counsel has degraded these proceedings to a name-calling match."

"Counsel," the judge directed, "Mr. El Haq has a point. Please confine your comments to verifiable facts. Continue, please."

"Withdrawn. Doctor, I do have one more subject to go over with you." Sol rolled his eyes in unhappy expectation. The lawyer spoke quietly. "For completeness sake, let's dot the i's and cross the t's. Mr. Hilton, please forward to Marker Ten. He turned to the jury and slipped on a very solemn mask. "Before we start this last section, may I warn you that what you are about to see may shake your sensibilities. I am sorry, but we must, and we will complete the record."

The final chapter began with the mirror image of the trip to the Galena Hills Center. A defeated Tarkington pulled himself painfully into the passenger seat of the F-350. His daughter drove out of the Center parking lot, but they changed seats at the Whitaker Mall. As Ralph and Judy passed around the rear of the vehicle, they laughingly traded the beers they had been drinking, and Ralph stopped, placed his hand on Judy's backside, gave it a pinch, and finally a rotating massage. This squeezed the breath out of several of the jurors. The judge snorted, "Oh!"

Sol's body deadened.

As the video progressed, Tarkington chuckled and kissed Judy on the lips. He put his hand on her left breast and rubbed for a moment, then pinched. She did not protest. In fact, she laughed and rubbed his crotch. He ran into the store and, in seconds, flew out with a case of beer under one arm and a bottle of cheap red wine in the other hand.

Back inside the truck, they embraced and made out for a few minutes. In the last few frames, Judy's head disappeared. The tension in the courtroom was peaking when the lead attorney said in a sad voice, "Lights please."

But before the glow of the fluorescent tubes refilled the courtroom, Ms. Famot had roughly pushed her seat back and was through the doors at the rear of the courtroom, steaming out into the hallway. Without missing a beat, though, the lead attorney asked, "So, Doctor, were you aware that Ms. Famot was really Ralph Tarkington's live-in girlfriend, in fact, his common-law wife. Do you know how many years they've been together?"

Sol could not hide his smirk. "No, sir, but I bet you're just throbbing inside waiting for the chance to tell me."

The judge banged his gavel. Sol's grin broadened.

The attorney tried, but could not hide his smile. He turned to Judge Ballbrine and mumbled, "I have no further questions for this witness." He strode quickly to his seat and hid his face in the briefcase, pretending to search for papers.

The judge was as flushed as Sol, the jury, and even the gaggle of Argent's lawyers, who were also making the effort to maintain the decorum of superior court. He turned to El Haq, shaking his head. "Redirect."

El Haq mouthed a few words seeking to establish that Dr. Forte could not be sure that Argent hadn't hired look-alike actors to stage the entire tape. El Haq was dripping with sweat in the cold courtroom. He paused, drew in a grand lungful of air, then played it out, hissing at Sol, jabbing his finger at the witness. "Dr. Forte, can you swear beyond a reasonable doubt that the persons in the video are who defense counsel claims them to be, or that the man you have been seeing in your office during the past many months was really Ralph Tarkington? Is it possible your so-called patient is actually a plant created by the evil minds of Argent Public Utilities?" He nearly fell into his seat sucking in his next breath.

The lead attorney rose. "Objection, Your Honor. He's badgering his own witness. And, the level of proof in this case, that Mr. Tarkington defrauded Argent Public Utilities and the Commission on Labor Affairs on a more probable than not basis, has been easily demonstrated. In fact, Your Honor, if this was a criminal trial, I believe we have, beyond a reasonable doubt, surpassed that higher standard."

"Mr. El Haq, if you have nothing of substance, please conclude your redirect."

El Haq bristled to his seat. "I have nothing further for this," he paused and pouted, "witness."

There was no re-cross, and Sol was excused. He wobbled toward the rear of the courtroom and searched the back rows with his eyes, but Dana Romanov was gone. There was no one to take his arm. He looked for her in the hallway. It was filled with dozens of the usual players, but no Dana. He shook his head and smiled weakly, whispering to himself, "I guess that's the beauty of life, isn't it? You get up in the morning, but you never know what's going to be dumped on your head that day. You can't tell me the soap opera ain't worth the price of admission. Good work, Forte."

CHAPTER THIRTY-ONE

Sol did not hear from Dana. He called several times, but the phone went unanswered. He groused that he hadn't promised her anything, and anyway, he hadn't done a darn thing, really. "I'm not married," he yapped to the wall, but with each justification, the discomfort in his chest built, and he again warned himself not to care so much.

It didn't work. He drove from his apartment to her condo at 2 A.M. She finally answered the door after he pleaded, and a neighbor stuck her head into the hallway and glared at Sol. Dana nodded toward the couch, and Sol spilled his guts about the night he'd given Judy a ride home.

"I thought I could trust you. You are only the second man I have ever been with. Now, are you glad I told you?"

"I'm flattered. It's hard to believe. You're so beautiful, I thought a million guys would have been chasing after you."

She didn't answer but sat down, put her arms around him, and then her head on his chest. She began to weep very quietly. They held each other for an hour. He kissed the top of her head and drove home but called back at four. "Now, it's for sure; I don't think I'm gonna ever be able to get you off my mind."

⊨⊣ ⊣⊨

Roxanne popped into Sol's office jabbering but stopped short and stared at his eyes. "You okay, Dr. F?" You look like you haven't slept in days."

Sol nodded, "Been studying medical books all night for the past week."

"Yeah, right. Hey, that El Haq guy called an hour ago. First time I ever heard him raise his voice."

"To you?"

"Well, sort of. He just, like he was just upset. He didn't really yell at *me*, I don't think. But a couple of times he was almost screaming about 'how could this happen?' or something. He kept on saying, 'I have to speak doctor, I have to speak doctor!' It was all of a sudden like he couldn't talk English right anymore."

Sol thought for a moment. He gnashed his teeth and hissed, "Screw 'em. He's caused me enough trouble for a lifetime. Whatever it is, tell him I'm not available. Maybe he'll finally get the message and leave me the hell alone."

Roxanne screwed up her face. "I don't know, Dr. F., that's not like you. Are you sure you want me to sass the guy? And like I feel like there really was something bad going on."

"Roxalita, this is the new and improved Solomon Forte. No one's going to take advantage of me anymore, not Anacota, Rosebac, women, or El Haq. He made a fool out of me in court, and what's worse, it took him a lot of my days to do it. And then the son of a bitch wanted to charge me for legal work. Kiss my ass! No, Roxanne, this is the modern, Twenty-First Century Solly Forte. Tell him to go 'f' himself. No, don't, I'll tell 'em myself."

Sol's anger grew before Roxanne's eyes, and he lunged for the phone, but Roxanne jumped faster, snatched it out of his hand, and jammed it back into the cradle. She was breathing as hard as if she had run the hundred-meter dash, and Sol, astounded, exclaimed, "What's wrong with you, girl?"

"Dr. Forte, I just don't want you to do something you'll be sorry for. You shouldn't talk to anyone that way, not to anyone, even that guy. It's not right, not while you're on the job. You're not out on the street. Please don't. Just let me handle it."

"I'm tired of taking shit from all these people, Roxanne. I'm done with it," he nearly shrieked.

"I don't blame you Dr. F., but you need to calm down. You're beginning to sound like Mad Dog Sullivan." She patted him on the shoulder. "Can I trust you?"

After she left the room, Sol sat shaking, unable to contain his outrage. He jumped out of his seat and slammed the door so hard, the windows in his office bowed. He fell back into his chair, his heart sprinting, his solar plexus locked in as crushing a knot as he'd ever felt, more smothering than at the end of his mother's life, more painfully choking than the night his pop died. His foot pulsed up and down with such wrath in the resentment of his powerlessness, the concrete floor vibrated his desk, making the steady red light on Line 3 shimmer. He thought about picking it up and demanding Roxanne turn the line over to him, but the LED went out a second later, and he put his head in his arms on the desk and allowed the bitterness to calm until his heart rate dropped to double its normal rhythm. He wiped the tears from his cheeks.

After a few more minutes of reflection, he called Dana's cell phone. She was in a meeting but could sense that Sol's tension, and she whispered, "Hold on a minute." He heard her in the background excusing herself, asserting a family crisis.

Sol told her that he had almost picked up the phone and taken out a year's worth of rage on El Haq, and how Roxanne had saved him, but that he was hanging on by the thinnest thread, that he was not sure he could contain his anger much longer. "I need to see you. You're the only solid thing left in my life."

She mumbled, "Thank God for Roxanne."

Sol asked, "Are you still there? Are you too mad to talk to me? I need to see you. I'm sorry for everything."

"I'll be done here in an hour. Can you get out of the Center? Tell them it's a family emergency. That seems to work."

"I suppose I can."

"Good. Let's go to dinner. You'll feel better if we talk. I promise. You just remember this: a lot of people love you, Solly. It'll all be over soon, like, what is it you always say? Oh yeah, 'And this too shall come to pass.'"

Sol smiled, "It was Michaela."

"You'll see."

They met at Althea's. Dana was right; seeing her and listening to her tales of mindless competition and pettiness at her drug company salved his choler. After a fast pint of very dark, very savory ale, he smiled at her. He took her hand across the table and squeezed it gently. "You're a good kid, Dana Romanov. Thanks."

He stared into her eyes and was about to blurt the question he had begun to believe he would never utter to any woman. It was too soon, but he was so near her, the heat, the wounds she had soothed through the painful months. And the sparkling, cobalt eyes. "So beautiful, so classy, so smart," he mumbled to himself, but loud enough. He took a nervous breath and stared into her eyes, she back into his. He touched her hand gently.

"Dana, like I said, I think I, I guess I've fallen for you. I was wondering if…"

The shrill ring of his cell phone startled him so, he nearly knocked over his chowder. As he fumbled for the phone, he dropped it. By the time he'd retrieved it, the call had been forwarded to the answering service. He waited impatiently for the call from the page operator.

"Doctor Forte, A Mr. El Haq called you. He said it was an emergency."

"Yeah, I know. He was electrocuted, and he's in the hospital with a seizure," Sol sniped.

"No," she answered tremulously. "He's in jail and needs to talk to you. He sounded very upset. He said they would only allow him two phone calls, and he used the first one up calling here. Doctor, he was crying."

Sol asked unsteadily, "Did he tell you why? What did he want me to do?" Dana reached across the table and took Sol's hand. He bent forward and kissed it before whispering, "Hold on, Dana. This is unbelievable."

The page operator added, "Mr. El Haq is going to wait fifteen minutes and try your number again. If he doesn't get through, he wants you to find him a criminal lawyer. He said something about homicide. I'm sorry, Doctor, that's all I could understand."

Sol told her his phone was in his hand, and was waiting for El Haq's call, but that if they didn't connect, to please find out where he was and assure him he would find someone to help. Starting to explain to Dana what he knew, he got through the first three words when his phone rang again, and since far less than fifteen minutes had passed, Sol raised his index finger to push the end button so he wouldn't be on the line when El Haq called, but he took a chance and answered.

It was El Haq. He was breathing so unevenly, Sol had difficulty understanding him and thought that perhaps the man had been drinking. "Doctor…try to call you…today. I, I…needed… help. I…but then you were…could no come to phone…"

Sol was barely able to decipher El Haq's rambling, not because the man was intoxicated, but because he was sobbing. "Mr. El Haq, what is it? What has happened?"

"Oh, Doctor, crazy woman…oh, that Judy Famot…she…she come to office. *Al hum de le la.* She was maddened. A devil… she spit on me, on my face, for losing trial. Then she took out gun, small one, I don't know what you call, and she point to me…at head. I grab for gun, but I fall back, and I close eyes pray to Allah before I die. *Al hum de le la.* My eye close, but I see explosion. A light like sun, and scream, maybe from me. I thought I am dead, in hell, but it was devil who is dead. She dead. On ground. I call you. You only smart good one, only man to trust."

Sol was voiceless. His eyes reddened. His mind darted back to the call he had refused to take from El Haq earlier that day. His heart sank, and Dana reached over to touch him. "What is it?"

Sol's eyes were closed. "Dana, hang on just a minute. Mr. El Haq, where are you right now? Please speak slowly. I have to understand every word, sir."

"I am remanded in county jail. I don't know what to do. It is hell. Please help me. These are your people. You understand them. You have to help me!"

"Mr. El Haq, listen to me, sir. Everything is going to be okay. We have to calm down for a minute. I know this sounds crazy, but do you have an attorney?"

"No. I have no one. That is why I am call you. They refuse to listen, the police. They take passport, and they call FBI and INS. I have to be in court in morning. Doctor, they say to arraign me tonight, but I tell them I am American citizen and must to speak to lawyer first. The DA, she say, said I was crazed murderer and blot on the attorneys."

"Slow down, Mr. El Haq!"

"She tell judge that I had been plan to run Egypt, so judge, he make special not to give bail. I had to defend myself, even though I know that is irrational."

"That *is* irrational. You must know a hundred lawyers right here in Whitaker…don't you?"

El Haq's breathing slackened. "Doctor, thank you for talking to me. Just give me minute." While he gathered himself, Sol shook his head toward Dana and raised his eyes to the heavens. He mouthed, "You *won't* believe this."

El Haq sighed and went on. "Thank you, Doctor, I am feeling better. I will be honest. The lawyers of Whitaker don't like me. I have always taken cases they refuse and have made mockery of their arrogance. They hate me. I do my job, and they curse me. I don't go to their meetings, and don't pay to sit in country club after work each night and drink their alcohol. I have no friends here. *Al hum de le la.*"

Sol spoke. "Mr. El Haq, let me be very direct, sir. I'm sorry to ask, but do you have the means to pay for a top-notch lawyer?"

El Haq was silent for a long period, and Sol thought they might have been cut off, but he finally acknowledged in a very low voice, "I am financially well."

"Good," Sol breathed in relief, "Let me give a friend of mine a call. If he can't represent you, he'll find someone who can. He's excellent." Sol began to reassure El Haq again that everything was going to be fine, but he heard a gruff voice in the background informing the prisoner that his time was up. Without so much as a good by, there was a sharp click, and El Haq was gone.

Sol explained briefly what he could of the story to Dana, excused himself, and went to stand outside the restaurant and call Gene Fluellen. He told the attorney that he had a friend, a lawyer, who was in big trouble, but that he had the means to pay for representation.

Fluellen remarked, "Never a dull moment, huh? No problem, I've been up there in superior court more times than I want to remember. I'll be there at 8 A.M., at the county lockup. Let's see if I can get in to interview my new client, a lawyer no less, homicide, what next? I have to warn you, sometimes the, ah, 'authorities,' like to play little games with us, so it may not be possible to interview him at the lockup. But if he calls back, tell him that no matter what, I'll be there in court before his arraignment, and we can talk then."

Sol called back and left a message for El Haq, though the woman on the other end groused, "This ain't a answering service."

Dana and Sol arrived outside Courtroom Two precisely at 8 A.M. Sol grinned and commented, "Déjà vu, ain't it? Let's see if I can stay out of trouble this time." Dana's face tightened, and she gave him a death look but took his hand, squeezed gently, and finally smiled. Sol added gravely, "Even a baboon can learn." He pointed to himself with both index fingers.

Moments later, Fluellen arrived. As he passed through security, Sol noticed him immediately, struck at how unbent he held himself, how in control he appeared as he strode the stairs toward them. He took Dana's hand first, and then Sol's. "You're smiling," Fluellen said. "You haven't seen the papers, have you?" They shook their heads, and Fluellen opened the copy of the *Whitaker Reporter Dispatch* folded under his arm. "It appears the district attorney here is doing a lot of talking before she engages her brain."

Sol took the paper. He and Dana read the front page.

WOMAN MURDERED IN WHITAKER LAWYER OFFICE
Foreign Attorney Charged by Dunton County DA with Murder of Client

Anwar El Haq, who practices law in Whitaker, has been charged in the brutal murder of Judy Famot, the niece of one of his clients. The shooting took place in El Haq's Whitaker office yesterday at noon. El Haq was held without bond, deemed a flight risk by Mary Outbroad, the Dunton County District Attorney.

El Haq is an Egyptian national whose family, according to District Attorney Outbroad, has purported ties to a radical Islamic organization in Cairo, specifically the Muslim Brotherhood. He has been in the United States for seven years, and though he has passed the Washington State Bar, has yet to be granted U.S. citizenship.

According to Outbroad, the victim, Judy Famot, came to El Haq's office at around noon yesterday to confront the lawyer, who had badly mishandled an industrial claim her uncle, Ralph Tarkington, had filed in County Superior Court. Apparently, again according to Ms. Outbroad, El Haq fired a single shot into Ms. Famot's body. She died in his office.

El Haq is scheduled for arraignment this morning in Whitaker.

"Wow," Sol let out. "They've convicted him in the press already, haven't they?"

Fluellen nodded and proposed, "Let's go in. I had a chance to talk to him for a second. My gut is that he's innocent, but his name's in the toilet. This is ugly. I'm pissed. Maybe you can calm him down. He really respects you."

El Haq's case was the first called. He was brought into the courtroom in manacles. It was clear he had not slept, had not washed, and was in an orange jumpsuit several sizes too large. Sol gasped and took Dana's hand. "Look," he muttered, "there's splatters of dried black something still on his face. Oh, my God."

The presiding judge to whom El Haq's case had been assigned was The Honorable Bentley B. Ballbrine, the jurist who had presided over the Tarkington matter. Though the judge had been on the civil court side during the Tarkington trial, he had just, that morning, started his rotation on the criminal bench. When he came face to face with El Haq, his expression soured as if confronted by an apparition. Sol murmured in Dana's ear, "I bet you this case has been rigged. Do you remember the way that judge humiliated El Haq during the Tarkington trial? This time, I'm not going to stand for it."

Sol jumped up and made his way briskly to the defendant's table. He whispered to Fluellen, "That's the same judge that was on the Tarkington case. Isn't that grounds for the guy to recuse himself?"

Gene whispered back, "Let's wait and see. We have one challenge to use. I mean, we can demand the first judge be removed from the case, but you can only do that once, and we don't know yet what this one's got up his sleeve. Let's give it a minute."

The charges were read by the bailiff, and El Haq pled not guilty, though his voice was so tremulous and weak, the judge snapped at him to speak up or be held in contempt.

DA Outbroad stood. "Your Honor, we are asking that the refusal to grant bail in this case be continued. This is not rocket science. The man is clearly guilty of a heinous, brutal homicide, Your Honor. He isn't even an American citizen…"

Fluellen snapped, "Objection! Mr. El Haq is, indeed, a naturalized citizen of the United States. Just another fact Ms. Outbroad has missed."

"Overruled. His naturalization does not preclude escape to his country of origin."

Ms. Outbroad continued, "Your Honor, his grown children, who I might add still reside in the Middle East, have ties to Islamic extremists, and he is a disgrace to the legal profession. It would seem to be a very open and closed decision."

Fluellen stood. "Your Honor, the only disgrace here is that this man has been condemned in the local press, based solely on the word of the DA. It hasn't even been eighteen hours from the time of the incident, and Ms. Outbroad already has him convicted of murder, and his children guilty of international terrorism. This is wrong, sir. The only way this could have been leaked to the press is through the DA's office. That is the disgrace."

The judge countered, "The public has a right to know about the status of murderers in their midst."

"He is not a murderer, Your Honor, until a jury says so."

"You are correct, Mr. Fluellen. Bail is set at two million dollars. All passports held by the defendant are to be surrendered to the district attorney's office." The gavel slammed, and the judge was off the bench making for chambers as fast as if a juror had suffered a heart attack.

El Haq was led away by a deputy sheriff. He turned to Sol, tears on his cheeks, his eyes besieging.

Dana held Sol's arm while he spoke with Gene. They left court together, and Dana rode with Sol to the Center. As she was getting out of the car, she scrunched her eyes and queried with a grin, "You were going to say something to me at the pizza place. Do you remember?"

Sol's chest clutched. "Dana, like I said, I've fallen for you. I tried not to, but…"

"Oh, that's so romantic."

"Because I don't think a classy dame like you would be interested in spending the rest of her life with a cement truck driver's son. There, I said it." He turned away, his eyes reddening.

She pulled him around toward her. "Solomon Forte, you are the most beautiful man I ever met. I don't care where you come from, and, by the way, where you come from is so much better than any guy I've ever dated."

"Dana, I'm sorry. There's just too much now. I'm sorry."

She nodded. "Whatever you want, Sol, but what I just said is from my heart. I love you."

CHAPTER THIRTY-TWO

E l Haq called Sol several times a day. He spoke of destroying himself, and Sol contacted the jail nurse, who put him on suicide watch. Sol visited every night. El Haq asked him over and over when it would be all over.

Sol laughed, "Mr. El Haq, you know as well as I do, it will never be over. None of us will ever escape this life in one piece. My father used to say, 'Kids, if it isn't one thing, it's the other. Or, maybe it was my uncle. What are you going to do when this is done? Sue the bastards? I hope you do."

"No, Doctor, I will go home. It is enough. I know you think my country is a social and political cesspool, but I wish you could see Cairo. If you could go to Alexandria. It was the greatest library on the Earth until the fire. The government is one thing, but the common people are kind. It is not what you have heard in the news."

━━+ +━━

Several days later, Sol took a call as he was preparing to see his first patient. It was from Fluellen, and he held his breath. The judge's clerk had called and ordered Fluellen appear in court within the hour. It was time to set a trial date and rethink bail.

Sol left the Center, calling out to Roxanne as he sped down the hall. "Cancel the next hour." She gasped, and he popped, "Just take care of it."

The judge blathered about the consideration he had given to the matter of the People v Anwar El Haq. He reiterated several times how every servant of the public had the sacred responsibility to live by the highest standards of moral liability. He took a deep breath, and Sol shook, waiting for a terrible pronouncement, but at that very instant, a plump young woman with unwashed hair rushed into the courtroom. She pushed through the swinging gate at the bar without so much as a glance at the bench. She skidded to a stop by DA Outbroad and whispered loudly.

The judge shook his head in disbelief. "And who are you, young lady?"

The woman stood bolt upright. "I'm Jackie, sir; I'm the new Assistant DA. I have to talk to the District Attorney. It's very important."

"Very important. I see. Well, just go right ahead and stop the proceedings, *Jackie*. We'll all wait here patiently until you're done, won't we?"

Outbroad smiled sourly, "Your Honor. If we could have a minute? I'm sure this is quite important."

"Why, by all means, take two or three, Ms. Outbroad. We have nothing better to do than sit on our thumbs while the girls chitchat."

They left the courtroom, and in less than five minutes, two police officers in uniform, and four men in civilian clothing, entered, trailing the DA and her assistant. Outbroad asked for a sidebar.

Fluellen shrugged, muttering, "This is the first time I've ever heard of a sidebar before the case has started but," he now griped under his breath, "after all this *is* Dunton Superior Court." He, too, approached the bench but stood outside the circle of the DA, her assistant, and the six men. The judge wrote furiously as the men spoke. The conference went on and on, and after ten minutes, the air peppered with arms and hands gesturing hotly, mostly Ms. Outboard's, Fluellen turned to El Haq, smiled, nodded, and winked reassuringly.

Judge Ballbrine directed, "Mr. El Haq, please rise. Apparently, the police and the county coroner worked on this matter last night. I have been assured that Ms. Famot's death was a self-inflicted injury. Dr. Svenson, here," one of the besuited men nodded at El Haq, "the distinguished Dunton County Coroner, and these homicide detectives have agreed that it would have been essentially impossible for the deceased to have had an assailant put a thirty-eight neatly in her mouth from across the desk, which is nearly five feet wide. If the accused had pulled the trigger, he would have had spatter marks on the trigger hand, which he did not and the deceased did. Also, retrograde expulsion of blood and tissue from the entry wound was found in a concentrated pattern on the deceased's hand, but in a wide dispersal on Mr. El Haq's suit jacket. Apparently, Mr. El Haq, you were at some distance from the deceased at the time of the fatal gunshot. Is that correct, detectives and Dr. Svenson?"

They all responded, "Yes, Your Honor"

"Ms. Outbroad, do you have any reason to hold Mr. El Haq?"

"Your Honor," she whined, fluttering her eyes, "I have not had the time to study this brand new, unconfirmed evidence, and further..."

The judge interrupted, "Mr. El Haq, the Court clears you of the charges of Second Degree Murder in the death of Judith Famot. The court apologizes for any inconvenience you have experienced. This matter is hereby closed."

As the judge raised his gavel, the DA jumped in. "Your Honor, the criminal portion of this matter may be closed, but that does not mean there will not be an investigation regarding the defendant's actions leading up to this suicide."

"He is not a defendant, madam, but regardless, I am sure that you will leave no stone unturned in the pursuit of justice to reinstate his status as such. It will not, however, be in *my* courtroom." He slammed the gavel. "Case dismissed, and without prejudice."

Gene Fluellen sidled up to the DA as she was leaving the courtroom. "Ms. Outbroad, let me assure you, if I sense a single word of retribution from you for having had to shelve this case because you pulled the trigger too fast, I'll have you kneeling before the bar association so fast, you'll wish you had perished in law school."

"Are you threatening me, sir?"

"Oh, by no means. I am promising you—promising from the bottom of my heart." He turned to El Haq and pointed. "You put this man through hell. You accused him of murder, made him spend a week in the county lock-up, bunking with the scum of the Earth, and what's worse, you and you alone made sure that his name would be dragged through the muck just to satisfy your racial prejudices and your ambitions. If he'd been a white lawyer from around here, you'd have done your damnedest to keep it quiet, and made sure he'd persuade his colleagues to back you in the next election. There would have been an investigation before you ever mentioned his name. I know all about you." He smiled gently but caustically. "You be careful, now."

She hooted again, "Are you threatening me?"

Fluellen keeled away from her, strode over to El Haq, took his arm firmly, and guided him out of the courtroom. "I apologize for her. She's a bum, but you already know that. Look, Anwar, I've got clients to see downtown. I need to dash, but we'll be in touch if you'd like representation until the rest of this matter is

cleared up. I also want you to start thinking about a slander action against the local rag, false arrest against the cops, and a bar
association complaint against Ms. Outbroad. Teach them all a
little humility."

El Haq shook his hand warmly then turned to Sol and hugged
him. Though El Haq's body hung with an unsavory spoor of the
week he had endured in jail, most particularly of stale urine,
Sol hugged him back comfortably. Fluellen saluted jauntily and
raced for the exit.

Sol invited El Haq to join him for breakfast. "Dana, do you
have time?"

She smiled warmly at El Haq. "I wouldn't leave you and Mr. El
Haq for all the world."

They sat and drank tea at the Denny's under the interstate. The
three could barely hear each other amidst the rumble and groan
of the traffic rushing in and out of the city, but they pulled close
together, and for the first time in several weeks, Sol allowed himself to relax.

El Haq proffered a vivid account of the tragedy, trembling as
he described Judy Famot bursting into his office, weaving about
as if drunk. "But I think it was drugs, Doctor—her eyes, the
points so tiny. She stood on the other side of my desk and put the
gun toward my head. 'Argent paid you and that doctor,' I think
she was talking about you, Doctor, 'to throw the case.' I prayed,
Doctor, I prayed to Allah.

"I told her that I did nothing but try to win her case, but she
spit at me, saying that I sold to the company for money. I told her
that was not true. I told her I had done my best for her father,
that I never knew about all the other things, but she screamed

like a devil and pulled on the back of the gun. I prayed and prayed, *Al hum de le la*, and I saw her fingers turn white pulling on the gun parts. I put my hand across the desk to take the gun, but she was too far away. I don't know. She was squeezing, and then she stood up very straight. She pointed the gun across the desk near my face.

"She said, 'I'm going to blow your head out the…window, nigg…' She used a curse. Then she vomited and squeezed. I closed my eyes. Tight. Tight, and I thanked Allah for my good life he had given me. *Al hum de le la.* The explosion was so loud, I was choking. I thought I was finally dead, because there was only darkness and buzzing. You know, I was relaxed, and not feeling anything. I was not unhappy to be done. And there was no pain, so I cried out to thank Allah for that gift. *Al hum de le la.* I opened my eyes to gaze on my reward, but that devil was still there; now, she was on the floor, and I was still in my room. I thanked Allah for that. *Al hum de le la.*

"Then I tried to call you, but your Roxanne told me you were out. I called the police, and they came to take her away. When they started asking questions, I was so nervous, I had trouble speaking English, and they became very mad at me. One of them shoved me, and the others screamed at him, and then they were yelling at everybody to get out of the room. Then the DA came, and she told them to put me in handcuffs behind my back. Then she raised her hand to slap me, but one of the policemen stopped her, and she told them to take me out of her sight to the police car. All the people in the neighborhood, all the lawyers with their offices on that street, they all watched.

"In the police station, they threw me into a little green room…"

"Sounds like on TV," Dana shook her head.

El Haq shook his head. "I don't know. I have never watched TV, and I have never been thrown in prison before."

Sol corrected. "That wasn't really prison, Mr. El Haq. The cops had to do their jobs. It was a mistake, but it was over quickly, thank God."

"No, Doctor, it wasn't over quickly, but I thank Allah, no matter. *Al hum de le la.* I had to go to the court for a bail hearing. The judge refused to let me go. I was very much imprisoned."

"Then the animals in the cell, I am very sorry to say this in front of you Madame, but they made their water on my face. They thought it was very funny. One big one with pimples said, 'Piss on the Chinaman,' and they all did."

Sol paused, thought, and asked, "Are you sure you wouldn't like a drop of rum in your coffee, Mr. El Haq. It'll relax you. I'll be glad to drive you home."

"I would never do such a thing, Doctor. Alcohol, never in my life, not a single drop. *Al hum de le la.* Oh, this is a week of hell for me." He moaned in Arabic, the only word of which Sol recognized was, "*Allah.*"

"I'm sorry, Mr. El Haq, I didn't mean to offend you. We Americans, you know, we turn to booze whenever the going gets rough. I'm sorry."

Dana reached across the table and took El Haq's hand. She asked, "Can we order you something to eat?"

El Haq nodded to Dana and replied, "Thank you," but he averted his gaze from her. Sol thought to himself how foreign was the realm from which this man had emigrated. He wondered how it was possible for someone so different to land on these shores, learn the language better than most Americans, examine the culture sufficiently to argue our law in our courts, in rural-suburban Whitaker, and still not imbibe in the temptations of our culture. Perhaps it was his understanding of money and how to make it in America that appeased the rest of his human needs. Perhaps the ability to thrive and be a man on his own terms had salved his loneliness.

El Haq asked forgiveness from Dana before going on with his story. "This is terrible, Ms. Romanov, what I saw in my office before they took me away."

She nodded and patted the top of his hand. "Please, Mr. El Haq, we're all adults here. My family is from Russia. You can't shock me. I want to know what happened. Maybe, if we understand it, we can help you make sense of it, but from what Solly has already told me, and from what I've seen of her and her pal or husband or lover…"

El Haq winced at the expression. "Allah knows I have never done such things to know about, as you said, that word…lover."

Dana paused. "Well, Mr. El Haq, let's face it, we weren't dealing with terribly ethical human beings. They were nuts. It happens. It's part of life. It's not your fault. Please tell us what you saw. We'll figure out something."

El Haq went on. "On the floor, oh, this is so wretched, her head was gone and there was blood dripping on the walls, and even on the ceiling, everywhere. There was her brain all about my law books and my diplomas. Everything is ruined. *Al hum de le la*. All my years of work. I can never touch those books again. They have been defiled. She has made them profane with her insanity.

Sol asked, "Do you have family here in Whitaker? Friends?"

"You are my only friend in Whitaker. *Al hum de le la*. I have no family here."

"Where is your family? Surely, you have a wife, a man as handsome as you," Dana asked.

El Haq blushed. "You are very kind." His eyes reddened. "I did have a wife. She died in a plane accident many years ago. My children remain in Cairo. They refuse to leave Egypt to come here. I have asked many times. If they were here, you would see what good children they are, and they would see that there are many good Americans."

Sol was surprised. "I'm sorry to hear about your wife, but why won't your children come here?"

"You see, Doctor, and I hope you will not be angry at me for saying this, because I know you love your country, but my wife was in the Jordanian Airline plane that was shot down by the American Navy. *Al hum de le la*. This was many years ago. You don't remember, I'm sure. It was all a mistake, the Navy said, and I understand that life brings these things upon us, and I have forgiven it, but my children are still very angry. It is better they stay away from this country. *Al hum de le la*."

Sol nodded. "Yes, Mr. El Haq, I do remember that. It was a tragedy. Political tensions were high in the Middle East. We screwed up royally. Were you at least compensated for your loss?"

El Haq stiffened. "Yes, Doctor, but what does that matter?" He paused for a few seconds, and his face hardened. "Yes, compensated. They gave me $15,000. You see, my wife was just a housewife. She had not been to college, so what was losing her," and he made quote marks with his fingers, "worth?" *Al hum de le la*. That was what the American Navy negotiator asked the judge. And that Egyptian judge, he was a pig, not a man, deep in the pocket of the American government. He just said to me when I hollered my protest in his courtroom, 'In a civilized society, we make reparations in the form of money. You are a so-called lawyer. Don't you know that?'

"I had no answer for him. I still have no answer." El Haq rose, and though his head was hung, he came over to Sol and hugged him. "Thank you, Doctor. It is God's will that this is happening, *Al hum de le la*, but I am very happy to have you as a friend. I am sorry for what happened at the trial. It was my job to represent Tarkington, to make the facts favor him. Now I am ashamed in front of Allah for all the things I failed to see, because I did not look hard enough. But I promise, *Al hum de le la*, I did not know any of the things those people had done to humiliate you.

I would never have let them do that to you if I had known. I hope you believe me."

After breakfast, Sol took El Haq to the Center, where they called a company that cleaned up after crimes and accidents. He drove El Haq back to his office, but the police barriers were still there, and El Haq was too shaken to drive, so Sol drove to El Haq's home in the hills just outside Whitaker. The house was small but tasteful, and the neighborhood quite exclusive. He thanked Sol again. "You are my only friend."

PART THREE

CHAPTER THIRTY-THREE

Eugene Fluellen telephoned Sol in mid-April. His tone was somber. A physician-member of the State Medical Abuse Commission had reviewed the matter of Dr. Forte's prescribing practices and deemed them incompatible with the standard of care to which local physicians were held. As such, he recommended the case go forward and be judged by a panel of the full commission. Fluellen apologized for not having been able to forestall the leap to the next level, but reminded Sol, "And this, too, shall come to pass."

Sol was ordered to appear with counsel, if he so chose, for his first hearing at the North Stadium Hotel on September 6th, 2001. He grumbled to Fluellen, "That's four-and-a-half-months until the trial. Why should it take so long to get this over with?"

Fluellen added, "And two or three months after that before they give you their decision."

"That's inhuman," Sol snapped.

"It is indeed, my friend, but there is nothing we can do. They don't meet during the summer months…"

"Why not?"

"I don't know, maybe they're drugged by the sunlight—disoriented by doing something other than reading sordid tales of colleagues run astray. Then there's no one to be better than. Puts 'em in a foul mood.

"Seriously, if we try to squeeze it in beforehand, they'll just get pissed off because you cost them a little more work. Anyway, this is one of the most powerful tools they have to keep you doctors in line. Everyone'll know how they torture anybody who falls into their clutches, so all your colleagues'll want to keep their noses clean. It's a very effective system, just like the IRS when they pick on the little guy. I'm sure you can see their logic.

"In the meantime, we need to come up with some solid arguments about the appropriate treatment of pain, whether it was cancer or chronic, or even, God forbid, COLA lower back pain. By the time this is all done, you're going to be the local expert on the subject. Think of it as a mini board exam."

Two days later, as Sol arrived in his office after lunch, the process server popped out of the employees' breakroom to hand Sol a subpoena to appear in Dunton County Superior Court. This time, he was to testify against John Sullivan in the matter of the man's single-handed destruction of an entire wing of the Galena Hills Hospital and Medical Center. The case was scheduled to begin on the 1st of June, so Sol phoned the DA, but she superciliously told Sol she couldn't tell him what time or even the day he might be called. "That's up to the judge. They're in total control, and aren't you the one who was involved in that El Haq affair?"

Sol laughed and answered, "Yep, that's me. You know, we gotta stop meeting like this."

She huffed, "And just what do you mean by that comment, Doctor?"

Sol gave brief thought to hurling back a smart answer but grunted, "See ya in court."

It wasn't a day later that Sol came out of a room to see Roxy coming out of the lady's room and subpoena man hovering over her desk. Sol would provide testimony at the Dunton County Courthouse for the inquest regarding the demise of Judy Famot. He phoned the DA's office to set a time to testify, but again, she couldn't or wouldn't tell him when or even where. He muttered, "We really have to stop meeting like this," but this time, as she drew a breath to lambaste him, he pulled the phone away from his ear, waited until the last of the screeching sounds leapt from the earpiece, then hung up very gently.

He dialed El Haq, with whom he had not spoken in some time, but the garbled message, recorded in hesitant, disheartened tones, said that he was on a special project, and would not be back in his office for two more months. Sol thought back to their last conversation, and remembered El Haq making open references about how unhappy he was away from his children, and the poorly cloaked allusions as to how difficult he found it to suffer a society so taken by materialism and the demon alcohol. Sol was sure El Haq had gone back to Egypt, and he knew in his heart the man would not return for the inquest, if ever.

Sol was surprised to feel a bit empty and cringed at the thought that perhaps he missed El Haq and the turmoil that had seemed to cloak him. Even the acrimony of their early relationship had taught him about the realities of the legal system that underpinned the freedoms Sol so cherished in America, and he snickered at how both of them had postured and threatened so truculently, how he had thought he'd suffer legal consequences if he crossed El Haq, and how El Haq had likely believed the same.

He realized the dearth power either of them really wielded, muttering, "A doctor and a lawyer, top of the food chain, and neither one of us can get a clerk in a county courthouse to pay the twenty bucks she owes me."

Sol was still vexed that, by his accounting, the court owed him for two more of the three days he had squandered perched outside Courtroom Two. When Clerk of Court Regina Slam sent a check in the mail for ten dollars, El Haq had immediately, and zealously, sent a blistering letter demanding the additional twenty. He had even proclaimed to Sol that he'd take them to court if they didn't pay.

Sol also pondered El Haq's reflection that he, Sol, had been the only friend he had made in America. And all that time, Sol thought the man despised him. Why, he asked himself, is there such disjunction between how we view the world and how the world views us? El Haq was the last man on the face of this blue island of extraordinary potential, this asteroid floating in the unfathomable reaches of space, the last man upon which Sol ever thought he'd have the slightest positive influence. But it was a lesson that was to be burned deeply into his heart. Each day, he pondered, we bumble through our lives, rarely thinking about, and surely never truly understanding, the impact our poorly fashioned comments, our gestures, even our lives, have on the souls we touch. El Haq was an enigma, but Sol did, indeed, miss him.

That night, he met Dana at the pizza shop near her condo. She had been out of town raining boxes of free medication on doctors' offices from New Orleans to Atlanta in a final push before another new antidepressant was scheduled to be released. She spoke slowly and quietly, "You know, Solly, I plug away at this job, and I think I've got thick skin, but in the thirty offices I called on, two, just two of the doctors, stopped to say hello and thank me for the samples, and those two spent the time coming on to me."

"You have to be kidding. Coming on to Dana Romanov?"

"No, wiseacre, I tried to get them to look me in the eyes, but it's like they had a ptosis of the eyeballs, and they were locked on my chest, just like yours are now."

"I can't help it. No man could help."

"And it's why Guilliani hired me, but it doesn't get you past the receptionist. Theramar is a good drug, but they don't know how to use it effectively. All they want is the samples. When I pop through the door, they sound the alarm, like three beeps on the intercom, and the docs dive into rooms. Never saw guys so eager to see patients.

"In the old days, when we brought them a gourmet lunch, they cut off clinic hours at eleven-forty-five. They even stayed to chat after one. The old timers at Guilliani said that when we were giving out the junkets to Scotland, these guys would take off a full morning to schmooze with the reps.

"Yesterday, I forgot my umbrella, and when I started back through the door, I heard one of the docs telling the receptionist, 'Next time a drug rep comes in, tell him to leave the samples in the waiting room. I don't want those people in the back. That's our office policy. We don't talk to reps. They used to make it worth our while—waste of time now. You don't even get a decent lunch out of 'em anymore.'" Dana shrugged her shoulders. "What, did I forget to brush my teeth or something?"

Sol smiled and took her hand. "I couldn't do it, kiddo. I'd be marching back there, arrogant bastards, right in their face. Maybe I'd get into two offices before hospital security tossed me out onto the street."

"That's what I feel like doing, too, sometimes, but it's a better job than working at the Galena Hills Medical Center. They pay me well, I'm in control of most of my day, no one's breathing down my neck. You, on the other hand, have that Rosebac and, what's his name, Anaconda the Snake, watching you through a microscope day and night. You keep plugging away, patient after patient, roller skating from one unhappy soul to the next. Nah, I've got it pretty good. I just don't know how *you* do it."

"I think about you. That helps." She held his hand as he filled her in on the latest demands for his presence in various courts of law, and his growing relationship with the DA. "Poor baby," she smiled. "It's so hard being you."

"It is. And I don't like being me alone."

Dana looked at him and screwed up her face. "Are you okay? You're red as a beet. You're shaking. You catch something from one of your patients? Maybe from the DA?"

He *was* shaking, and he could feel the heat in his face. He drew in a gulp of air but was distracted with the fumbling of his left hand as it dug deep in his pants pocket. It took him so long to pull out the tiny, antique jewelry case, he had to take another breath. He handed the box to her and spluttered, "Sister Michaela won't be needing this. Anyway, she wants you to have it."

Dana's hands trembled more intensely than had Sol's as she struggled to slide the clasp on the old-fashioned box. The diamond was tiny, the setting quite simple. Her eyes started to tear.

Sol took her hand over the pepperoni and black olive pizza. He stammered, "Dana Romanov, you are the best there is. I don't think I can live without you. Please let this seal my promise to you that I'll clean up my act. I swear, no more courts or…"

"Solly," she interrupted, "What are you saying?"

"Dana, will you marry me, a cement truck driver's son?"

"Shush. *You* are the best there is. I can't wait to spend the rest of my days with you."

They finished their beers, took the pizza with them, and left. At the exit off the interstate, a bearded man, no more than thirty, stood bent forward like Tarkington and poked a hand-lettered sign toward their windshield.

VIETNAM VET—HOMELESS—HUNGRY

Sol pulled over and handed him the box of nearly untouched pizza. The man grabbed it and hummed, "God bless you," but when he opened it, he yelled to them, "Hey, I don't like them goddamn black olives."

Dana turned and watched him while they waited for the light to change. "Solly, he put the box on the ground, and he's picking off the olives and tossing them into the street. Now, he's wiping his hands on his pants."

By the end of that week, DA Outbroad spewed another subpoena with Sol's name engraved at the top. It was, though, delivered by a different greasy man, his teeth even yellower than Sol's pal. Sol asked, "Where's the usual guy."

"Oh, you mean Jimmy?"

"Yeah, Jimmy."

"He's doin' a nickel up at the state joint."

"What!"

"Yeah. I don't mean to be talkin' outta school or nothin', but he had a habit of ducking into offices where he was serving papers. Riffled a purse too many. Sad. He was a good guy. Devoted to his profession."

Sol was to present himself as a witness at Courtroom Two on Monday at 9 A.M., Monday morning. He arrived at his appointed station, but the courtroom was dark. He went to the Clerk of Court's office and knocked on the wooden partition that sealed Mrs. Slam's domain from the balance of the world. She slid the barricade aside and peered suspiciously into his eyes. He asked, "What happened to the case in Courtroom Two? I'm supposed to testify at nine."

"Oh, the Sullivan case. Yeah, he had a heart attack a couple of days ago. DA's dropping the case, figures he been punished enough."

Sol drew in a deep breath, hesitated, but gave in, and cracked, "You think she could have told me before I cancelled my patients for the morning? And that guy deserves the electric chair."

"Excuse me, sir," the clerk held her palms up toward Sol's face and blustered, "if you have a problem with the DA, you take it up with her. I have nothing to do with that office."

"Do I at least get my ten bucks for showing up? And how about my twenty bucks that you owe me?"

"Are you the one who made such a fuss over ten dollars? You can take that up with her, too." And the heavy wooden partition slid shut with a clunk.

Though he was relieved about not having to be humiliated publicly over his part in the Sullivan matter, there was still the El Haq—Famot affair, and, of course, his appearance before SMAC. With the morning unscheduled, he plodded along the interstate to the medical school library, intent on copying five or six basic articles on the subject of pain and how to treat it. He availed himself of the librarian, who laughed heartily and declared that there were hundreds of books, and literally tens of thousands of scholarly journal articles, on the subject, and in a dozen or so languages. When Sol asked for the bottom line on the subject, the three seminal papers, she turned toward the packed shelves and waved her hand grandly, scolding, "There is no such thing as effortless research, Doctor."

Sol chose two books, thin ones, and copied three journal articles, but when he went to the desk to check them out, he was challenged for his university I.D. "Hey, wait a minute, I'm a medical doctor, duly licensed in this state," he objected, "and this is a state supported institution."

Despite his protests, the checkout man pulled a worn copy of library regulations from his hip pocket and opened to the requisite precept. Sol would have to pay $150 to be granted borrowing privileges for the year, no quarter or half-time plans were available. "And please be aware, it takes a week to process the paperwork." Sol left quietly with his copied journal articles. Back at the Center, he planned to read for the half-hour left of his morning but realized the articles were basically pages of references to other articles and books. He tossed them in the trash.

Sol got on the internet and plugged in "chronic pain." He laughed to himself. The librarian had been way off the mark. There were one-million-eighty-thousand references, and the first ones, the sites not peddling the colored oil of exotic ostrich-like fowl, the venom of bees and reptiles, or magnets, were official-sounding websites that required user names and passwords. When he gave in and applied for one of these, the first question on the screen was how he wanted to pay for the privilege, Visa or MasterCard. He logged off and told Roxanne he was ready to start seeing patients.

She answered from the hallway, "It's about time. We're already two behind already."

The first patient of the afternoon was Edna Berry, who still hadn't gone back to work. Sol hadn't seen her in some time, and had filled out paperwork from the Commission on Labor Affairs every thirty days saying as much, offering that he had no knowledge of her present status and, as far as he was concerned, unless COLA had evidence that she was being seen by another physician, the claim could be closed without an award of cash for partial permanent impairment.

That last sentence drew the case manager's attention. He closed the claim summarily and sent notification to Ms. Berry. That caught her eye, for she presented to Sol's office the very next morning and was, according to Roxanne's note, in quite a huff that Dr. Forte had not demanded a large settlement from the state. He pasted on a smile and knocked twice.

Edna Berry hadn't given much thought to a wig and was as bald as the moon and as yellow and sallow as Kevin McAlister near the end. She couldn't have weighed eighty pounds. Her scowl, however, was as unyielding as the first time he saw her. "Ms. Berry, it's been a long time. How are you getting on?"

"Like shit."

Sol smiled reassuringly, "Well, you know, the chemo is bad at first, but it's worth the temporary inconvenience. I mean if it cures you…"

"It isn't curing me, so let's get that straight. Now, why did you say that I can go back to work? I can't walk. I'm so tired, I can't hardly get out of bed. That broken bone took a lot out of me. Stressed me so much, the leukemia went wild; took over my body."

Sol thought hard about where she could have learned that bit of medical posturing, though informed her directly that she suffered from a couple of problems, two very separate conditions, and that he was sorry, but the Commission on Labor Affairs wasn't responsible for the leukemia or its symptoms.

While she was devising a retort, he sought to convince himself the two were very different cases. He toyed with the argument that it was the leukemia and her drinking that had thinned her bones to the thickness of the shell of a robin's egg, and for a moment, he was proud of himself for not being hobbled by someone else's tragedy. Perhaps, he was finally becoming sufficiently professional to refuse to bear the cosmos on his shoulders. You can't cure the world, he assured himself. But Mrs. Berry began to weep pitifully, and he castigated himself for his callousness.

"At least, those COLA people owe me some money for the ankle. It'll never be the same. It's John, isn't it?"

"Ma'am?"

"John Sullivan, isn't it. He doesn't want to pay, does he?"

"Ms. Berry, were you aware that John Sullivan had a heart attack this weekend? He was supposed to be in court because he destroyed Center property, but they called off the case because he's so sick."

"Oh, my God," she howled. "Why didn't anyone tell me? Oh, my God!" She stood and began pacing the room with barely a limp.

Sol shrugged. "Ms. Berry, I don't mean to be rude, but I thought you didn't care all that much for Mr. Sullivan."

"Oh, my God, is he okay?" she moaned, tears rolling from her yellowed eyes.

"I'm sorry, ma'am, I just don't know."

"Didn't you care enough to ask?"

"Ms. Berry, I think it might be best if you come back when you're feeling a little less angry. All of this has been a shock to your body. You need to get some rest. Don't worry about the COLA thing. We'll get it straightened out. I'll send them a nice letter explaining that you were too ill to come in, and we'll get the claim reopened. I'll tell them it's my fault. No sweat. Everything's going to be just fine. You'll see."

He patted her on the back, was shocked at the meatlessness of her skeleton, and asked Roxanne to help Mrs. Berry to the waiting room while he called a cab for her. "I don't have money for a cab," she protested feebly over her shoulder.

Sol replied quietly, "Not to worry, ma'am, I'll pay for it."

The last words he ever heard from Edna Berry were, "I suppose I'll have to pay it back?"

⟞✦ ✦⟝

The next patient was a muscular young woman who complained of lower back pain. She sat stiffly on the exam table, her face dripping with silent pain, her legs bobbing a bit, and Sol stopped to wait for them to spin up into a whirl. She related that she had recently become an ambulance assistant, and asserted that lifting stretchers was killing her back. But she also listed on her intake form that she was a competitive weightlifter, and she looked the part in her skin-tight, sleeveless top and cycling shorts. When Sol queried about the difference between pumping iron aggressively and hefting the sick and mutilated into ambulances, she took umbrage and announced, "My boss don't like me."

He mumbled to himself, "They never do," and then aloud, "Why?"

"I can lift more than him any day."

"I'm sure you can. But how does that fit into the big picture?"

"Don't you see? If I can lift more than him, it makes him look like a dickwad. So, he sticks me with all the four-hundred pounders, and lemme tell ya, we get a lot of 'em."

Sol, deflated from his profitless morning and the dismal reunion with Mrs. Berry, fathomed that he was just seconds away from generating yet another ungratified patient. He nodded reassuringly and asked, "Ma'am, have you had any other COLA claims?"

"One or two."

"Were they for your back?"

"Yes."

"Tell me about them, if you don't mind."

"What do they have to do with what's going on now?"

"I really want to help you, so it's very important for me to understand your total medical picture."

"Oh, okay. It was when I was working at the gym. I was teaching lifting, showin' the weak jerks how to do snatches. Terrible pain. I told the boss, but I was kinda like a temp, kinda getting paid under the table. So, they didn't give me insurance, and they couldn't put me on COLA."

"How did you get on COLA then?"

"A guy at the gym told me to get a job at McDonalds or somewhere. Then I could claim it on COLA. Sure enough," she winked, "it still hurt when I lifted a box of frozen fries on my first day. So, that's how."

"The boss's name McAlister?"

"What?"

"Same thing this time?"

"You got it."

"Well, ma'am, I'm sure you know the rules. If you had a specific moment where you were lifting a patient, then we can file a COLA claim. Was there one instant where you felt your back go out at work?"

"At the gym, there was."

"How 'bout at work as an ambulance assistant?"

"No, but you try lifting some of those people."

"I'm sure you're right, but here's my problem. If I file this as an industrial injury claim, I'm liable for a $50,000 fine. It's called insurance fraud. So, we're stuck. Do you see my predicament?"

"So, you want me to say that there was a certain patient that caused me to hurt my back. If those are the rules, fine. Okay, there was this fat guy having a heart attack that my boss made me lift. I told him I didn't want to, twice, but he made me do it all the same. And all of a sudden, I couldn't move, and my legs tingled, and I'm having trouble peeing. That good enough?"

"Well, you know your stuff, don't you? But that's fraud, my dear. Look, just put it on your regular medical insurance."

"I don't have any yet. Only been there a week. And I don't have the money."

"Well, our accounts department will work out something with you. We always do."

"What the hell. I'll just go to another doctor. Give him my business, now that I know what to say."

As she stood to leave, Sol asked, "Ma'am, let me ask you one more quick question. While this man was laying there on the stretcher waiting to go to the hospital, you know, the fat guy with the heart attack, is that when you refused to pick him up, twice?"

"Yep. You try lifting some of these people."

"Was he awake, I mean, could he hear what you were saying?"

"Yeah, I guess so. I mean, I didn't look at him. Too disgusting."

As she walked past Sol through the door, he spoke quietly. "Ma'am, when your back gets better, you might want to give another line of work a try," and when she was out of earshot, he turned to Roxanne and laughed, "Two for two." He rubbed his hands together excitedly. "Okay, who's next?"

"Call for you. Lupe Sánchez's case manager in Arizona."

"Go ahead and take a message."

"He says it's important." She rolled her eyes.

"You still look like Rosebac's daughter. And no matter what I said before in front of him, that ain't a good thing. I bet Lupe's filed a third claim, this time in Tijuana, and the *Federales* want copies of her chart. I'll take it in my office."

Sol grabbed the phone and said heartily, "Good afternoon. And how are the industrially-challenged fairing in the great Southwest?"

The case manager was silent for a moment. "Doctor, I have called to inform you that Lupe Sánchez is deceased. She was murdered. The police think it was her husband."

Sol's mocking smile faded. His first rational thought trundled around the legal ramifications of his role in her case. He pictured the man in the rumpled sports jacket and yellow, cigarette-stained teeth, delivering the subpoena, and the arguments the Center would cull to avoid paying for his trip to Arizona to testify.

The next was the image of Lupe the final time she had come to the office, her expectant, seductive smile as she pulled out the fifty dollars to repay him. She had become, basically overnight, a comely woman with new clothes, makeup, and the will to start a fresh life. He flogged himself for a moment then stammered, "Is there anything I can do? I actually liked her. She got a rotten deal in life."

"No, Doctor. We've taken care of everything. Thanks to your letters and complete chart notes, we accepted her claim in our jurisdiction, and we're going to pay for her burial. By the way, her son, I think it's Carlos, he kept on using your name, 'Dr. *Fortune.*' He said he wanted you to know you were his mother's best doctor."

"Do you know who's taking care of him?"

"I have it in the records. I can fax it to you later this afternoon."

Sol asked Roxanne to keep an eye out for the message from Arizona. He told her of Lupe's demise. She shook her head sadly. "Dr. F., I don't mean to be rude or nothin', but we got more dead COLA patients than anyone in history."

"It's only because we *got* more COLA patients than anyone in history."

When the fax arrived, Sol called the number listed and found Lupe's sister, who had driven from Mexico and was preparing to take Carlos home. She had run into trouble, as the boy had been born just north of the border. Sol got the number of the Mexican immigration officials involved and made a call, all the time hoping no one in the Center's administrative offices kept tabs on the doctors' telephone habits.

He spoke with a woman at the border who listened politely, and Sol prepared for the fruitlessness of the coming conversation, but the woman thought for a moment and offered to help. Sol was so relieved, he sang in Spanish, "*No es problema? Es mui bien. Mucho gracias Seniorita.*"

She answered in accentless English. "Sir, that's fine. Give me your number, and I'll keep you informed of the boy's status."

Sol wrote a check for five hundred dollars in Carlos's name and sent it next-day delivery to Lupe's sister. He called her back and told her to look for the money, but she said she wouldn't accept it. "Doctor, you've done enough. My family thanks you." She started to weep, and, unable to speak, Sol gently put the phone down.

CHAPTER THIRTY-FOUR

Over the spring months, though Dana tried tenderly to discuss plans for their wedding. Sol kept grousing that he couldn't put his heart into the rest of his life until his problems with SMAC were resolved.

She asked him to meet her at the pizza place one rainy June evening. Dana took his hand. "Sweetheart, I love you very much. I don't give a damn about your Medical Behavior Committee, and you are not going to from this day forward. Period. You don't answer to them, or even to me, or anyone else on this Earth. You are accountable to a sovereign so much more perfect than Rosebac and Anaconda and all the rest of us. I want to marry you so I can tell you that every day, forever. A priest or rabbi, it doesn't matter, but we are both slaves of the way we were raised. It won't be complete until we take vows to cherish each other for all of time."

They married in front of a Justice of the Peace on July 17th.

CHAPTER THIRTY-FIVE

At the Center, his schedule waned, and several insurance companies put him on a watch list, requiring letters from his colleagues to keep him, at best, on temporary status. When he asked Fluellen how Blue Cross could have found out about his troubles, the attorney was very direct. "SMAC publishes their information on the web. The insurance companies check it once a month. It's just SOP."

A few days later, Fluellen called. "Got a notice from S.M.A.C. You are to appear on Thursday, the 6th of September, at 7:30 P.M. Can you make it?"

"Do I have a choice?"

"What do you think?"

"I'll have my secretary check my bursting social calendar. Will you be there?"

"We will."

"Is that the royal we?"

"No, Mike Matsukawa wants to come, too. Show of force, safety in numbers. How's the study of chronic pain coming? You must be the best on the block by now."?

Sol sighed, "Gene, every time I sit down to read, I get so angry, I start pacing the room. When I finally do try and study something, it goes in one ear and out the other. Nothing sticks. Maybe it's age, but it's not working."

"Well, Doc, better drink some super glue. Maybe pour it in your ears. That's, let's see, about six weeks to go. Sounds like a lot of time, but from what I've been able to dig up, there's a whole bunch to learn. Remember, this isn't a jury of average citizens; it's your peers, for real this time, colleagues, a bunch of doctors who know a lot about the subject, or will by the time you're sitting there in front of them. You need to know more than they do."

With his spotty patient schedule, Sol consolidated his appointments to the mornings and spent afternoons at the medical library. What surprised him was the burgeoning interest in the neuroscience of chronic pain, and the growing number of research studies that debunked the old rub that the syndrome was a pseudo-disease. Sol and most of his colleagues had been taught that the symptoms were simply the manifestation of obnoxious personalities, mental defects, greed, and that the bulk of these people were simply drug seekers. That was what he had believed drove patients to complain bitterly and unremittingly about their pain, and do nothing but beg for narcotics. And there *were* a lot of drug seekers out there, no question, but there were also those in misery from chronic pain syndrome. For these people, it was as if all the other elements of being human, their children, their careers, their homes, and even their self-respect, played second or third fiddle to their obsession with the pain. They howled when test after test failed to prove their suffering, and even louder when doctors refused to give them enough narcotics to make their lives tolerable. It seemed indistinguishable from a meth or heroin addiction.

The sad result was that many practitioners had trouble accepting these patients as worthy of their full attention. They appeared to the world as nothing more than garden variety drug addicts. Sooner or later, they became pariahs, to their families, to their friends, and, eventually, to their doctors. No one wanted to be around them, and this only embittered the patient and deepened the disease.

But as he read further, he began to see that their behavior actually had a basis in scientific fact, and he sheepishly wondered how many times he had rolled his eyes at the histrionics of some of his stars, at the incessant references to their pain. He thought back to a patient who'd injured his back on the job. After the disease was well entrenched, Sol tried to make light conversation. "Hey, you must be out of your mind proud of your son. What is it, two weeks before graduation from law school?"

"Yeah, but the pain's really killin' me, and you're not doing a damn thing for it."

During the weeks of study, he chided himself for having paid only lip service to the studies dribbling out of neurology centers that chronic pain was as real as a broken femur. Though he had spit back to lawyers, insurance company investigators, and to the Commission on Labor Affairs claims managers what he'd gleaned from skimming the research, he had never really taken the time to understand that, for those suffering with chronic pain syndrome, pain *was* the disease. In normal organisms, pain was a *symptom* of disease, a signal that something was amiss, a warning that a malady was gnawing away at them, or that they had injured themselves and had better protect the wound at once.

But in chronic pain syndrome, nerve pathways that had originally carried noxious feelings, that is, pain from an injured or sick organ to the brain, were now disconnected from the originally damaged body part, and were acting without provocation. The nerves were sending pain signals, capriciously, on their own, but to the patient, it truly felt as if the long-healed body part was still being traumatized. Yet there was no longer anything for a doctor to see, feel, or listen to, for it was the microscopic nerves themselves that had taken on a life of their own. There was no test or x-ray that could be done on the living patient that showed these worker bee nerves making the patient hurt. The tail was wagging the dog, and no one could prove it.

Recently, though, researchers had begun studying cadaver nerves with the electron microscope. They discovered that, in chronic pain patients, the nerve fibers, the wires themselves, had transformed, not only in shape, but internal structure as well. He read that even the chemical composition of these microscopic nerves had been altered, changes that allowed them to jump into the driver's seat and decide when to make the patient suffer. Sol had trouble believing what he was learning. It simply flew in the face of his long-held beliefs.

But delving deeper, Sol came across example after example of fractures of the lower back, the ankle, or the shoulder that had long since "healed," that is, the skin and bones appeared totally regenerated on x-ray, yet the patient's perceived pain was as bad, if not worse, than on the day of the injury. Without cadavers, or electron microscopes in local clinics, it wasn't until autopsy that true diagnoses were made. He was beginning to see answers for why so many of his patients never got better, no matter what he or his partners did.

The rub was convincing the hard-boiled, cocksure examiners COLA kept in their stable, a herd of self-selected adjudicators who had been born without the gene that allowed for opinions other than their own. And even if they all suddenly became disciples of Mother Theresa, the truth was that new medical information was incorporated into everyday clinical practice slower than COLA patients returned to work.

He read that there were also psychological elements in the development of chronic pain, for it occurred far more frequently in the poorly educated, and in workers who felt no element of control in their lives, before or after the injury. That spilled over into the workplace, where employees who did not get along with their bosses or co-workers were far more likely to develop chronic pain syndrome.

But the bottom line was that, regardless of the psychological elements that *helped* create the problem, once the nerves had physically changed, it no longer mattered who loved or who hated the patient. The pain was now as real as if they had been placed on the rack. Maybe it wasn't their fault, after all. Maybe it really was a true, observable disease, one that he and most of his colleagues simply did not yet realize existed, much like AIDS in the early 1980s. His guilt expanded. These patients had deserved better treatment.

After two weeks of study, he went to the Medical College Book Store and purchased, *The Classification of Chronic Pain*, the Bible of pain syndromes. He hardly scowled when the clerk debited his MasterCard for $275.

He created a notebook bristling with tabs and indexes, a compilation of his work, then crafted several pages of scripted testimony that he smiled would dazzle the Commission members. They couldn't know about the newest research, even those who were obsessively up-to-date. He felt prepared and excited. He would teach them a thing or two.

He bought a new white shirt and a deep blue and burgundy tie, a duplicate of the one he saw the Duke of Edinburgh wearing in a documentary; his new shoes were burnished to a fare-thee-well. By late August, he phoned Eugene Fluellen and announced he was ready. They met several times and polished his presentation. Michael Matsukawa was so impressed, he made a copy of Sol's notebook so he could better treat his own patients.

CHAPTER THIRTY-SIX

On the 6th of September, 2001, Dr. Solomon Forte appeared before the Medical Disciplinary Commission. Soaked to the bone from the rain, he nonetheless held his head high and patiently waited to be offered the chance to testify, to develop his thesis of chronic pain and its treatment.

Just as the Commission members settled in, Dana quietly entered the back of the room. She had been on a sales trip to Fargo, North Dakota, and though she had not been scheduled to fly back to Whitaker until the next afternoon, she had combined several calls, and sailed home secretly on the commuter shuttle. Sol turned and saw her blow him a secret kiss. Seconds later, Sister Michaela knocked quietly two times on the hearing room door and entered obsequiously. Though it was the first time they had met, the two women embraced and sat together holding hands.

After the introductions, and the heated posturing, just as Commission Chairman Jergesson was about to turn the floor over to the commissioners to take their turns interrogating Sol, a woman with an unhappy scowl grunted an interruption from the far left. "Doctor, if I may. I am a lay member of the Commission; that is, I am not a doctor. But I have to tell you, I was recently divorced. It was a very trying time. My former husband was a very disturbed man. I was under a great deal of stress; I fell down the stairs and severely twisted my ankle. I had pain, lots of it, yet *I* didn't take any medication at all. Why is it necessary for you doctors to throw pills at everything that walks into your office?"

Fluellen stretched his arm across Sol's chest to hold him back, but when Sol calmed, Gene allowed him to answer. "Madame, I do not believe we are here to reorganize the practice of medicine. I would add, however, that it is difficult for you, as a lay member of this commission, to appreciate what a physician is faced with when a patient presents in real pain. We are talking about authentic, scientifically measurable pain."

The woman nearly flew out of her seat, spitting, "Are you saying my pain wasn't real?"

"Not at all. But it wasn't *cancer* pain, ma'am. Respectfully, you can't have any idea what that's like."

"It hurt plenty whether it was *cancer* or not."

Chairman Jens Jergesson interrupted. "Ms. Baer, we need to stay on task here. The matter before us is not what defines pain, but if Dr. Forte followed accepted prescribing patterns. Do you have anything further?"

"Yes, I do. The question is, sir, who sets these so-called prescribing patterns? It seems to me, doctors are setting the standards, when this is really a larger societal issue, one that must be defined by the community."

The rubor was intensifying in Jens' face. "Madame, we have been over this argument every time the Commission has met for the past eighteen months. The Governor has weighed in on the matter, the Secretary of Health Affairs has weighed in on the matter, and they both agree this is not the forum for that discussion. You know their feelings."

"I wasn't appointed to this Commission," she hummed, jaw set, "to reflect anyone's opinions but my own."

"Fine, let's give some of the other members a chance to query the defendant, and then, and I promise, we'll get back to you."

Fluellen was on his feet. "Sir, Dr. Forte is *not* a *defendant*. You are not a duly, constitutionally appointed judge, and we need to move forward here. You are trying my patience."

Jergesson's facial ruddiness deepened. Sol smiled to himself that this drenched Whitaker evening was becoming more of a nightmare for the Commission members than for him. He turned to Fluellen and gave his attorney's leg an appreciative little tap under the table. Fluellen's eyes flicked almost imperceptibly. While the bickering simmered, Sol turned and grinned reassuringly at the two loves of his life, both of whom sat far back in the ballroom, still holding hands. He saw in their faces slight, furtive smiles.

Jergesson acknowledged a man at the far right who introduced himself as a psychiatrist from a small city in the western part of the state. "Dr. Forte, I think the question here is not if you treated a man with cancer pain, but if you over-prescribed a simple COLA lower back pain."

Sol, fortified by his supporters, both of them, answered resolutely, "My patient wasn't a scholar, but he was a decent human being, a good kid from California who injured himself doing manual labor. He was not a 'COLA lower back pain.'"

"Point well taken. My question is, though, what did you know about this patient, and when did you know it?"

Fluellen shot to his feet. "This is not the Watergate Hearings, and you're not Senator Howard Baker. 'What did the President know, and when did he know it?' Dr. Forte is not Nixon; this is a caring doctor dragged before this committee, basically because of the tenets of political correctness."

The psychiatrist was not placated. "Regardless of your historical prowess, Counselor, I'm afraid that the question remains: was your client treating what he *believed* was simply COLA lower back pain, or was he treating cancer pain?"

Sol put up his hand to intervene, but Fluellen muttered, "Solly, this one's mine." Sol nodded his deferment. Fluellen went on forcefully. "Doctor, let me simplify the question. Did Dr. Forte treat a man in pain? Yes or no?"

The psychiatrist muttered, "I don't know, I never met the patient, but I must inform you that it is my understanding that in this forum, *we* ask the questions, and *you* answer them."

"Well, the answer to my question is, yes, he did. Dr. Forte used his clinical judgment, and also his willingness to see the patient repeatedly, dozens of times in fact, despite all the hassles that entailed, particularly with this particular patient, to determine that the man was truly suffering debilitating pain. As it turns out, Dr. Forte's instincts were one hundred percent correct. So, the question is not what he knew and when he knew it, but what was the quality of life he assisted this man in achieving during his final months of life on this sad planet?"

Another commissioner raised her hand. "I'm Lisa Oberfelder, a pediatrician. Dr. Forte, I have to tell you that I'm quite impressed with your sense of caring and decency. Just by looking at you, and reading your exceptionally thorough chart notes, it is clear. This panel would be well advised to view your devotion to medicine as a model, not as a platform to express archaic notions of health care. I do have one problem. In keeping with the line of reasoning of my psychiatric colleague, if you didn't know the man was suffering from a neoplasm, you were bound by the regulations of the Commission on Labor Affairs. Yes?"

Sol thought for a moment and answered. "Ma'am, I am a law-abiding physician and citizen, not a loose cannon. There are indeed rules by which the Commission on Labor Affairs controls the use of narcotics in patients under their jurisdiction. I follow them. In this case, there was no ongoing provision of narcotic medication. The rules say no *ongoing* provision of opioids. I refilled his prescription when there was an obvious worsening of his condition. While one might argue that worsening is not the typical path one sees in the care of lower back pain patients, it is in cancer. Viewing the situation through the retrospectoscope, or were I a better doctor, perhaps the most perceptive physician in the region, I would have diagnosed a carcinoma and sent him off to the oncologist."

Another member intervened. "I have a question in that regard."

Jergesson spoke. "Please introduce yourself, Jack."

"Sorry, I got too involved in the process. I'm Arthur John Bruston, orthopedic surgeon from the state capital. My question, Dr. Forte, has two parts. First, if this man was in," he stopped for a moment and made quote marks with his index fingers, "'so much pain,' it should have been obvious that he was a chronic pain patient, and should have been sent off to the pain clinic, not treated with narcotics. Why wasn't he sent to a state-licensed pain treatment facility?"

"Excuse me, sir," Sol answered in somewhat miffed tones, "he was. It's in the records. Did you not see it there? I can point out twenty or thirty typewritten pages regarding his sojourn in one of the most touted pain clinics in Whitaker. You want me to find the pain clinic notes for you?"

"No, no, that's fine. There's hundreds of pages of documents here. I'm sure I read it. Well, in that case, why did you continue to treat him with pain medication if he'd been to a treatment center?"

"Because he was still in pain, and now we know why. All the relaxation techniques, the yoga, the self-hypnosis, and TENS units in the world that he got from the pain clinic weren't going to address his suffering. He was dying of cancer, Doctor. And it's not a treatment center. That's for patients with addictions. He wasn't addicted to anything. Patients dying of cancer who are in intractable pain don't get addicted to narcotics. Everybody, well, every doctor, *should* know that by now. Addiction is a whole other disease. There's *no* connection between the use of opioid analgesic medications and the development of addiction in a man dying of cancer.

"I would hope everyone sitting here tonight knows that addiction is the preoccupation with the obtaining of narcotic medications. Addiction is loss of control over the use of narcotic medications; addiction is associated with adverse consequences, like the loss of your job or family based on the use of the medication."

The orthopedist was on his feet. "Are you trying to tell me that you don't have to keep upping the dose to get the same effect?"

"Of course I'm not saying that. But what you're referring to is *tolerance*, and yes, even in dying cancer patients, there is tolerance, and so what? They're dying, for God's sake." Sol stole a sneaky glance at the nun. She flashed the subtlest smile.

Several of the Commission members nodded in approval, and the orthopedist noticed, though it only fortified him. Stridently, he continued. "Dr. Forte, I have another concern. Please tell the Commission why it took so long for you to diagnose cancer."

"We, I mean the doctors who took care of him at the end of his life, never did discover the location of the primary tumor. We never even discovered the type of tumor. With all due respect, sir, the ways of soft tissue neoplasms are very different than the problems faced by an orthopedic surgeon. You can *see* on a hundred tests what's wrong before you operate. I, and those I enlisted to help me, one of whom was an internist with oncology training, did the best we could.

"And, by the way, if you read the notes, you'll find ample evidence that Mr. McAlister had seen myriad doctors over that year, including a board certified orthopedic surgeon who, I might add, didn't find anything either, but commented, as I'm sure you noted in your thorough evaluation of the record, that he had the impression the patient was malingering."

The surgeon went on. "You're telling me with all you spent on diagnostic tests, you couldn't find a primary tumor?"

Sol answered politely. "Sometimes, we can't see tissues that are behaving badly. They don't announce themselves with cracks and shattered bits of calcified bone like you guys detect on x-rays. You often can't even see tumors on an MRI. It's not like a torn anterior cruciate ligament, the ACL. And be honest, Doctor, how many times has it appeared an ACL was pristine on the MRI, and your patient doesn't get better, so you finally go in and scope the knee and find the ACL is damaged beyond repair? The MRI is not perfect in its ability to diagnose. Maybe ninety-five percent correct, and that's very good, but it's not a hundred percent. Think about it. If your practice sends thirty or forty patients a week for MRIs, that's one or two patients a week who you're giving the wrong information to…maybe even operate on them for no rational medical purpose. That's forty or fifty patients a year; fifteen hundred people in a thirty-year career. Multiply that by how many doctors are practicing ortho locally—tens of thousands of badly misdiagnosed patients. Our tests are not perfect, and neither are we."

The surgeon snapped, "Maybe in your practice, Doctor."

Sol growled, "So, you're saying before this Commission that you never had a crummy looking ACL on MRI, and you scoped the knee and found it was really quite normal?"

The surgeon answered sharply, "Like I said, maybe in your practice it happens that way, but not in mine."

There were several sarcastic grunts from both sides of the Chairman, and Dr. Jorgenson intervened. "Ladies and gentlemen, we're getting off track. This hearing is not about the state of medical diagnostics. We have to move on."

Sol smiled at the opening he had waited for. "Dr. Jergesson, may I make some observations regarding the treatment of chronic pain? They will be directly applicable to my case. I believe when the Commission hears this, you will better understand the reasoning I used to treat Mr. McAlister. I think you will be pleasantly surprised and intrigued by the information."

"By all means."

"Thank you. And may I respectfully ask, since this is my posterior in the proverbial frying pan, that the commissioners allow me to complete my discussion before intervening with other questions or comments? It's sort of a 'let-the-man-talk-then-hang-'em' request I'm making."

He looked up and down the line and saw several nods, and a couple of smiles, so he went on. "Chronic pain: think of it as a telephone which is designed to bring information to our ears, occasionally painful things we may not want to hear, but it brings that information, and it does so efficiently. In chronic pain syndrome, it's as if the telephone's wires get crossed, the phone gets a mind of its own, and every time you pick up the receiver, whether it's good news, or even no news at all, all you get is the same recording, bad news. The other problem with the chronic pain scenario is that the phone's ringing all the time, day and night, and it's delivering shocking news, yet it seems to be coming from historically reliable sources, whether it's true or not.

"So, what do most of us do? We get sick of it and refuse to answer the phone. That's fine in the real world; it may even work. But in the world of chronic pain, you can't stop answering, whether you want to or not. So, you get sick of it and become grumpy at first, and then angry, and then enraged. But you are powerless to stop it, and like the prisoners in the concentration camps, you become abjectly depressed, and then obsessed with the pain because it just won't stop. It's like the water torture. Drops of water don't hurt, not until they don't stop, and then it's unbearable.

"Most of the medications we have at present to treat chronic pain, the antidepressants and membrane stabilizers, they help only marginally. But if you combine them *judiciously* with narcotic medication, it allows you to address that patient's quality of life, and that's what this is all about, I hope. I mean, that's why we're sitting here tonight, isn't it? I hope when all is said and done, this hearing is about quality of life for our patients.

"Now, to finish my comments on chronic pain, let me inform you that recent, excellent research demonstrates that certain tissues, like the discs in the lower back, are not normally endowed with pain nerves. If the disc is injured, ruptured, that is, if it 'slips' out of place because of trauma, like lifting too heavy a basket of laundry, it's very painful. We all know that. Everybody knows that. But the reason it is painful is because the piece of disc that slips out of place pushes on structures that *do* have nerves, i.e., pain receptors. Now, this next bit is going to be very controversial, but the latest research shows that discs do repair to some degree. I am quite aware that that statement flies in the face of what we've always been taught, that discs never heal, but, in fact, they do; and when they do, the new blood vessels that grow into the damaged tissue to bring about the healing carry along with them new nerves that were never intended to be there. So, a tissue like a lower back disc that was never meant to feel pain because it is so constantly stressed absorbing the shock of walking and even, or I should say especially, sitting, now has brand new nerves coursing through it that don't belong there. That's not a good thing for a structure under such everyday stress. Add to that the notion that these nerves, because now they're under constant stimulation, may transfigure into the capricious ones we talked about a minute ago. They keep on firing and sending the brain pain messages. This is a no-win situation for the patient, and for the provider, and for society."

An elderly man sitting next to Jergesson's immediate left smiled at Sol and raised his hand. "Doctor, I'm Ezra Paul, retired OB from right here in Whitaker. In my line of work, I didn't see much in the way of orthopedic chronic pain, but I saw my fill of nonspecific pelvic pain. I imagine each of us has our own cross to bear when it comes to chronic pain. When I was trained, in prehistoric times, we were always taught that chronic pain was a psychiatric disease, one to be treated with psychoactive medications like antidepressants, not narcotics. So, my question is, if you believed you were dealing with chronic pain before you discovered the diagnosis of cancer, why didn't you use these other medications?"

"Dr. Paul, I used a host of non-narcotic medication, none of which addressed his pain. It's all in the chart, sir. I used anti-inflammatories, anti-depressants, and membrane stabilizers. Nothing worked, sir. They just made him sicker. Sir, I have to repeat, yet again, that *nothing worked*! It seldom does in these patients."

Sol turned to the Commission at large and said resolutely, "The bottom line here is that I did what I had to do to care for my patient. I would do it again. And then over again."

Sol stopped abruptly and placed his hands in his lap. Another commissioner spoke. "I'm sure you had your patient's interest at heart, but I'm afraid that does not allow the individual practitioner to interpret the law on his or her own. You acknowledge that you were aware that COLA did not permit the use of ongoing narcotic pain medication to treat the chronically ill. Is that correct?"

"Yes, but, as I said earlier, my patient, Kevin McAlister, was not totally, i.e., textbook, chronically ill. His situation ebbed and flowed."

"It wasn't just chronic pain syndrome?"

"There was some element of that disease that I was faced with treating, and alone, I might add. But he was suffering from cancer pain, and that complicated the issue to the point that his basic problem wasn't diagnosable."

The orthopedic surgeon snapped, "Yeah, in your practice."

Sol waited until the commissioners stopped shaking their heads and went on. "My patient was in pain, and I relieved it without harming him. I hope every one of us would have and will do the same."

The questions continued. "But, sir, you broke the law. Maybe not a civil law, but the laws of the Commission on Labor Affairs, which you tacitly agreed to uphold by signing their provider agreement. It's like saying, 'I'll use heroin or marijuana on a patient if *I* feel it is in the best interest of the person.' Where's the difference?"

"The difference is I did not use *illegal* drugs. I used standard medications that are used to treat COLA patients every day of the week. I believed that I was treating a complicated, ongoing process, one in which there were additional episodes in which the patient reinjured his back, such as an intervening motor vehicle accident. It's all in the records."

"Well, sir, I think you're talking out of both sides of your mouth, and to be frank, I remain concerned."

Jergesson stretched and addressed the gathering. "We've been at this for some time. We still have two more cases to review this evening. If anyone has anything further, please make your comments brief and to the point."

Only Ms. Baer, the lay Commissioner, spoke. "I want it on the record that I find it an outrage the way in which doctors are jamming pills down our throats like so many French ducks to harvest pâté." She took another deep breath but stopped short.

"All very interesting," a proctologist mumbled from the far reaches of the right. "I still don't buy it."

Sol shook his head sadly. "Well, the bottom line here is, yet again, that I did what I had to do to care for my patient. I have nothing further to say."

Jens Jergesson jumped at the chance to end the trial. "So entered on the record. Dr. Forte, thank you for your participation. It was a lively exchange of information. I'm sure all of the members of the Commission will consider your statements very carefully before we come to a consensus. We will deliver that decision to you as soon as possible. We will certainly attempt to do so before the new year."

Sol rushed to the back of the room and hugged Dana and Michaela together. "What a surprise. I love you two so much. I'm blessed."

Dana whispered, "You are, and you should be. You deserve it." She said louder, "You were great. You knocked 'em dead."

Gene Fluellen joined them, as did Mike Matsukawa, who had been in the spectators' seats taking notes. Several of the commissioners walked by on their way to a break, and there were polite nods on both sides. When Sol's entourage left, they passed a poker-faced array of the condemned waiting on chairs outside the Ballroom. Sol wanted to address them and extend his condolences, but he nodded politely and, when out of earshot, exhaled loudly.

They settled into a booth at Denny's. Michaela explained that she had flown in for the hearing but had to leave again in two days for New York. She had been posted to Korea to attend to the growing Christian movement there. "I can't wait to do the things I learned in the convent. Soon, I'll actually be carrying out the Lord's work."

Sol was concerned. "You already are. How did you get Korea?"

"I asked for it."

"Even after what Papa told us about that place?"

"Solly, that's why I begged for it. For Papa's sake, in his honor. Usually sisters get to Asia after five or six years' work at home. Mother Superior liked the idea. Her brother died in Korea during the war. Who would have guessed? Anyway, I will be in God's hands. I'm always in God's hands. So are you, and you, wonderful Dana. Thank you so much. I'll never forget what you did for me. The two of you are perfect for each other. Thank you again, Dana." She hugged her."

Sol looked askance at both of them. "Okay, Miss Dana, what did you do? Let's have it."

"Why, nothing. What are you talking about?"

Michaela took Dana's hand. "Solly, she paid for my trip out here. I'll never forget it. You done good, my brother. And you know what?"

"What?"

"I convinced the archdiocese to let me travel east instead of west, so I will get a day in Jerusalem. I can't wait. I'll go to the Wailing Wall and thank Solomon Schlamowitz's ancestors for putting him on Earth to save Papa."

"So, when does all of this begin? And I don't like you going to Israel. Ain't safe."

"Don't worry, I'll still be in the States for a while. First, I have to stop in New York for a couple of days to get all the paperwork done. Visas and shots, and…"

"And?"

"And I convinced them to let me have one hour for myself next Tuesday afternoon. Do you think it's enough time to look up some of our relatives in Manhattan?"

"Michaela, my beautiful sister, it isn't enough time, and why would you want to?"

"Solly, when they see me in my nun's dress, they will realize how wrong they have been."

"And if they don't, the pig heads?"

"They will be acting that way in front of God. Their mistake. But anyway, I'm sure you're right. I know there won't be enough time. I just thought, you know, before I leave."

"Maybe all three of us will go and see the family when you come home on vacation."

"Solly, we don't go on vacation. I probably won't be back for twenty years. It's the way of our mission."

Dana interrupted. "Solly, I want to go to New York with Michaela. We can get to know each other. It'll be so much fun."

CHAPTER THIRTY-SEVEN

Sister Michaela Forte was prescient in her intuition that she would not have the opportunity to see her family. The office of the Korean official empowered to grant foreign nationals long-term work permits was located on the 92nd Floor of Tower Two of the World Trade Center. Michaela's interview was set for 9 A.M., September 11th, 2001.

It took two days for the archdiocese to determine that Sister Michaela had perished in the catastrophe, and another day to find Sol to tell him. Though he had frantically tried to call Dana, her phone went right to voice mail. He took a leave of absence from the Center, could not get a ticket on a train, and drove to New York. It took him three days and three stops for speeding, and three cops who let him go when they heard the story and escorted him, lights and sirens blasting, to the state boarder.

He came upon a group of thirty nuns who had gone through seminary with Michaela. They'd camped out in vigil as the wrecked bodies were brought forth from hell. Sol also lost two cousins that day: a fireman and a police officer.

Not a trace of Dana was ever found.

CHAPTER THIRTY-EIGHT

He returned to the Center in mid-October. By this point, the people of Whitaker were just beginning to talk again. A few even smiled. He sat at the Mall, in the food court, watching the young girls with their midriffs exposed, and the sullen teenaged boys with pants hanging below their butts, the tips of their long, phallic belts dangling near the floor. He watched as they poured over the magazines near the south doors. Curious, he finally stood and walked slowly to the newsstand to scrutinize the reading material on which they were spending their parents' money. He thumbed through the vacant Hollywood weeklies and the smut the kids were buying as fast as they could pull dollar bills from their jeans. His anger deepened.

At the Center, he was left to himself. Rosebac nodded good mornings, and Roxanne modulated her cackling. For several weeks, Anacota urged Sol maintain a light schedule. He obliged, though he missed the hubbub of a busy practice, and by early November, he opened his schedule again to anyone who felt they needed to see a doctor.

It began as a normal morning, but Roxanne came to Sol at ten, pale and barely able to speak. "Dr. F., you are not going to believe this one. Room One—take a deep, deep breath." She shook her head and walked away.

Roxanne had not put a chart in the door, and Sol was flying blind when he knocked, forcing a trace of a smile. He rolled the door slowly forward, his eyes shooting left and right before he took more than a half step into the room. The patient was dressed in clean slacks and a button-down shirt. A pale and sweaty Ralph Tarkington coughed hollowly several times as Sol entered the exam room.

"Mr. Tarkington, what brings you here, sir?"

"I'm sick."

"I certainly know that. But what specifically, sir?"

"I got this cough, and I'm so weak I can't hardly get out of bed, and…"

Sol interrupted him. "I know, and it's all because of the electrocution."

"Dr. Forte, I'm coming to you for help because I don't know any other doctors. I got cash, and I'll pay my bill, whatever it is."

"I'm not interested in your money, sir. I will examine you and give you my best advice. But I have to be honest…"

"You don't need to tell me, Doctor, I'm hurting enough inside, and I've hurt enough people as it is. I'm sorry for what happened. It's all my doing, and if you want me to leave, I will."

Dr. Solomon Forte examined Ralph Tarkington and ordered an x-ray of his chest. There was scarring in his lungs, perhaps, maybe likely, from the electrical shock of decades before, but there was also a flaming pneumonia. So, Sol admitted him to the hospital and, rather than loading a specialist with his dirty laundry, cared for the man himself over the next week.

Late at night, when Sol was rounding on his hospitalized patients, exercising his newly obtained privileges, he'd walk the halls, gathering the nerve to confront Tarkington, to ask the countless questions that still tortured him, but in the end, he grit his teeth and just passed by the man's room. When Tarkington was discharged days later, he turned to Sol and tried to hand him a fistful of fifties. Sol shook his head no and walked away.

EPILOGUE

Just after Christmas, which he spent with aunts and uncles in Little Italy, Sol visited the Embassy of the Republic of Sudan. He had read of the most recent famine raging across that star-crossed patch of desert. He applied for a long-term work permit, though was told it could take nearly a year to have it approved. The Sudanese Consul thought for a moment and smiled back. "There is always the fast track. But, of course, it is expensive, like all good things in life." Sol slipped the man six one-hundred dollar bills, and had the document before the close of business.

Armed with the visa, he took a cab the next morning to the Madison Avenue offices of Please Help the Children. He waited five hours for an interview. The next day, a secretary called and offered him the position of lead physician in a crumbling refugee camp in Darfur Province.

Sol telephoned the Galena Hills Hospital and Medical Center and gave notice, though he agreed to return for a few weeks to smooth the transition. On the last day of his employment, Sol screwed up his courage and went to Rosebac. "You were the one, weren't you?"

The man blustered, "I don't know what you're talking about," but his eyes blinked rapidly, and he flushed so deeply, Sol turned and left the clinic for the last time.

Sol sent a letter to Anwar El Haq, who had not returned from Egypt, and never would. Anwar was so excited to hear from him, he called the very evening he got the note and invited Sol to his ancient home in the alleys of Cairo. "If you come, I will never let you leave. You can be a doctor here. You are so smart, you will learn Arabic in a week. It's easy."

Sol stopped there on his trip to Sudan, arriving at El Haq's home in late May. While El Haq's sons were standoffish, their wives were not, and after two days, the women cajoled their husbands into joining the family for dinner. The young men sat politely, but silently, those moments more awkward than meeting Kevin McAlister's family. Sol was the first American they had ever met, and the anger in their eyes cut him more deeply than Rosebac's sullenness. After ten minutes of the family sitting through a dozen of Sol's dreadful jokes, one of the sons, the eldest, could no longer stifle his laughter. The others followed. Over the next three hours, the men fired question after question at Sol about life in the United States.

Sol told them of the tragedy his wife and sister had suffered, and the family fell into a cloud of melancholy, sitting with eyes welded to the floor. "Doctor, I hope you do not think all Muslims are like this," the eldest man stammered. "We hate your government for murdering our mother, but we do not hate you; the people who did this to your family, we spit on those devils."

Roxanne left the Center shortly after Sol departed for Africa. She opened a bar, and soon a second. A check to care for the kids in Darfur soon followed.

Sol received a letter from Eugene Fluellen. The State Medical Abuse Commission had met with him to discuss the case. They were concerned that Sol was absent. The orthopedist remarked, "If he thinks a bunch of natives are more important than his career, so be it."

Jergesson warily accepted Fluellen's presence as adequate, though the Commission chose not pass final judgment in Sol's absence. The case would remain open until he returned.

Ralph Tarkington was convicted of insurance fraud in county superior court. His attorney argued that he had become deranged by both his service in Viet Nam and the electrocution that had been the end of him. District Attorney Mary Outbroad sent her underlings into the field to do some digging. They discovered that Mr. Tarkington had never been in the military.

Fluellen wrote to Sol. "That concerned the jury, but his attorney played the explosion card to the hilt, and the jerk was sentenced to thirty-days at the same county lock-up our Mr. El Haq spent his sad week. Are you sitting down, Doctor? Judge released him on the second night. Something about suffering a grand mal seizure!

Consistent with the inscrutability of COLA's inner workings, Kevin McAlister's medical bills were swallowed by the beast that capriciously tortured some of the state's wounded workers and inexplicably allowed others to go scot-free for years at a time. The demand for recompense never materialized.

Devin McAlister got roaring drunk and drove to the Center. He pushed his way into Anacota's office and swore he was going to sue everyone there, then sprinted out, cursing, wagging his middle finger high above his head. Before he reached the next block, he smashed his pickup head-on into a truck that was coming to the Center to deliver concrete for the new front entrance. The brain damage was so extensive, he was made a ward of the state.

Robert Porcher, the man who had broken his arm so badly that he couldn't return to work as a stonemason, had done exactly as Sol had urged. Months after his injury, he took out a sheet of paper and put down all the things he wished of life, and what kind of work he dreamed of doing. At the top of the list, after caring for his kids, was to work with animals. He loved them more than people, more than helicopters, and far more than hauling bricks. He gladly accepted the Commission on Labor Affairs' offer to retrain him as a veterinary assistant, a request made by and fought for by Rosebac, who had been forced to take over his care when Sol left. Two years later, he was hired by the Whitaker Zoo. When Sol last heard, he was in charge of the large cats.

John Sullivan's business failed, and he declared bankruptcy. The Center recovered not a single dollar from the civil suit they'd easily won against him. In fact, they squandered more than two-hundred-thousand in legal bills, and nearly one million to repair the building.

As Sullivan lay dying in the Galena Hills Hospital of cirrhosis, the nurses wrote on the chart that he spent the hours smiling and sometimes breaking out in fits of uncontrolled laughter. When they asked why he was so happy, he chortled, "I owe you bastards a million dollars, and I'm dying on your nickel."

OTHER TITLES BY
WILLIAM S. GOULD, MD

AT YONAH MOUNTAIN

B rand new Second Lieutenant J.W. Weathersby is on orders to depart for a combat tour in Viet Nam. At a West Point wedding, though, he commits a very public faux pas and is thrust as punishment into a class of 160 select young officers who sweat and freeze through months of brutal training at the United States Army Ranger School. J.W. joins an African American PhD candidate and a Rose Bud Sioux Harvard graduate, the three pushed together to trudge the mountains, forests, and deserts as Ranger buddies. As half the class is weeded out, they share their disparate lives and dreams. J.W. struggles to be cut from the program, and at the same time fights desperately to remain. At Yonah Mountain is a coming of age adventure, an examination of race relations in the military, and an authentic tale of Army Ranger training.

CAPTAIN IRON MUSTACHE

Captain Iron Mustache takes place in 1968 and 1969. United States Army lieutenant, J.W. Weathersby, just out of Ranger School, volunteers for duty in Viet Nam. It is not long before he changes from naïve youngster to hardened soldier. Something about rural Viet Nam, though, captivates him, and he convinces his commanding officer to allow him to live as the sole American in a remote rice-farming hamlet. His mission is to win the hearts and the minds of the peasants. J.W. forms a deep friendship with the village chief, and falls in love with the schoolteacher, Miss Lin. During a mid-night battle, Miss Lin is arrested and tortured as a communist agent. At the same time, the chief is critically wounded, and disappears after being flown out of the village by an American medevac helicopter. J.W. and the chief's wife spend the last month of his tour driving the deadly roads of Viet Nam searching hospital after hospital for the man. Nearly half a century later, J.W. and his wife return to Viet Nam in a surreal effort to find the chief. He also wants to see Miss Lin, but the Vietnamese government is suspicious of his motives, and the days of his sojourn are fraught with struggle and frustration until a simple act of kindness changes his life.

IN BLACK GRANITE

In Black Granite is set in the decade after J.W. Weathersby returns from the war in Viet Nam. He eventually accepts the assessment of family, friends, and medical school deans that he will never become a doctor. He drifts without focus until the miracle of his first child's birth rekindles the craving to study medicine. This is a narrative of his dogged struggle to beat the overwhelming odds against a man in his mid-thirties gaining admission to an American college of medicine. In Black Granite scrutinizes the ruthless battle for places in medical school, and how the psyches of the chosen are sieved as they are herded through the decade as students and residents. The strain of endless days and nights away from family, of sleepless months, and of pervasive arrogance, distort the souls of even the strongest. Some find the path more treacherous than surviving a war.

A HEART WIND FROM THE DESERT

D r. Solomon Forte has lost everything. There is little left but to offer himself to the wretched in war-torn Sudan. Arriving in the desert, heart brimming with hope, it does not take long to recognize that the social and political beliefs that have spawned the war and famine are the very forces that prevent him from carrying out his dream of caring for the dispossessed. At first, despite the warnings of the tiny European medical team left at the refugee camp in Darfur Province, he fights back with typical, strident, American resolve to save the entire population of refugees. The obstacles of central African life, however, soon draw the spirit from him, and he turns his efforts to preserving the lives of his Western companions. He falls deeply for a gorgeous, but outwardly hardened, British nurse. When she disappears from camp, he spends what strength is left searching for her. A Heart Wind from the Desert examines the need in all of us to accomplish something meaningful in the tiny fragment of time we are allotted, and the impossible hurdles faced when trying to change the way people have thought and behaved for the millennia. It is a tale of beautiful, warm children, but also of the stark life in the sub-Saharan Sahel.

RAPHAEL'S BLANKET

Raphael Blumenkopf is born clandestinely at the Bergen Belsen Nazi death camp on the 14th of April, 1945. His birth is an unprecedented miracle, as is the liberation of the camp by British forces that very afternoon. He has only his mother and a few surviving villagers from their home in Checzonovska, Poland. While the majority of the refugees leave Central Europe for Israel and the West, his band travels across Russia to China. A relative has promised jobs in Shang Hai's old Jewish settlement. The journey is fraught with threats from starving Russians, barbaric border guards, and destitute Chinese peasants. Just as the lives of the immigrants begin to normalize in China, the victory of Mao Zedung's communist army forces them to flee, this time to Hanoi. Five years later, the communist movement in North Viet Nam topples the French government, and the Jews run again. They settle in Saigon until the unrest there compels them to emigrate to America. Raphael's years in the U.S. are colored indelibly by the poison that follows him from the Holocaust, and he formulates a plan to extract revenge from a Federal judge with ties to the Nazis. Who could have envisaged the price he'd pay?

LINCOLN FRIDAY

Lincoln Friday is born into nothing, an obscure, dirt farmer's son, destined to live dominated by the jagged edges of two wars. His early years are an endless series of losses, yet he struggles back after each blow, and slowly, a strongbox of dreams emerges from the fog of his hopelessness.

The harshest test of Lincoln's life, though, comes when the effects of his exposure to Agent Orange devastate both his and his daughter's lives. While the Fridays fight back passionately, the courts, Congress, and the VA turn their backs on them.

In the end, his deeds were neither profound nor dazzling, but he left his mark on disparate people in disparate lands. The world he touched chafed less for his quiet dignity.

.